The author of eight novels and dozens of short stories, CHARLES BEADLE was a world traveler who was born at sea in 1881. When he was eighteen years old he expatriated from England and spent a dozen years exploring South Africa, Rhodesia, Zambia, Uganda, the Congo, Mozambique, Borneo, and Morocco. In his mid-twenties he organized an expedition to Fez and traveled there disguised as a dancing girl to interview the sultan of Morocco. In the 1910s he lived in Montmartre, where he befriended his neighbor Beatrice Hastings, the mistress of Modigliani and translator of Max Jacob. Modigliani later portrayed Beadle in a drawing titled *Le Pèlerin* ("The Pilgrim"), which may have been a reference to Beadle's first banned book, *A Passionate Pilgrimage*. During World War I he traveled to the United States, where he published stories in *Adventure* and in the *International*, a cultural journal edited by Aleister Crowley. He returned to the City of Light in the fall of 1919, where he lived throughout most of the 1920s, eventually moving to the French Riviera.

In 1938 Jack Kahane's Obelisk Press published Beadle's last novel, *Dark Refuge*: an unrecognized modern masterpiece that quickly fell into obscurity. It contains thinly disguised portraits of Modigliani, Max Jacob, Beatrice Hastings, Léopold Zborowski, and various other figures who haunted the Parisian demimonde of this period. Beadle's brazen portrayal of drug fueled pansexual orgies prevented the chronicle from being distributed in the Anglo-Saxon world despite its literary merit and lyrical beauty.

In 1941 Faber and Faber published *Artist Quarter*, a nonfiction work pseudonymously coauthored by Beadle with Douglas Goldring, which is still considered to be the urtext of Modigliani biography.

ROB COUTEAU is a Brooklyn-born author and visual artist. His publications have been praised in *Evergreen Review*, *Publishers Weekly*, *New Art Examiner*, *Midwest Book Review*, and *Witty Partition*. In 1985 he won the North American Essay Award, sponsored by the American Humanist Association. His work has been cited in books such as *Ghetto Images in Twentieth-Century American Literature* by Tyrone Simpson, *Gabriel Garcia Marquez's 'Love in the Time of Cholera'* by Thomas Fahy, *Conversations with Ray Bradbury* edited by Steven Aggelis, and David Cohen's *Forgotten Millions*, a book about the homeless. His interviews include conversations with Pulitzer Prize-winning author Justin Kaplan, *Last Exit to Brooklyn* novelist Hubert Selby, Simon & Schuster editor Michael Korda, LSD discoverer Albert Hofmann, Picasso's model and muse Sylvette David, sci-fi author Ray Bradbury, film star and bibliophile Neil Pearson, and historian Philip Willan, author *Puppetmasters: The Political Use of Terrorism in Italy*. Couteau has appeared as a guest on Bob Barrett's *The Best of Our Knowledge* (WAMC), Len Osanic's *Black Op Radio*, and on Monocle 24 in Europe. In 2023 he published *Intimate Souvenirs*, a memoir featuring an Introduction by Robert Roper, author of *Nabokov in America: On the Road to Lolita* and *Now the Drum of War: Walt Whitman and His Brothers in the Civil War*.

JOHN LOCKE has been interested in the pulp magazine era and its fiction, particularly in the 1920s and 1930s, for many decades. In the 1990s he started collecting information on the era, which led to writing historical treatments about the publishers, editors, and most of all the authors. Many of his findings have been published in his Off-Trail Publications books. In 2018, he jumped up to book-length histories with *The Thing's Incredible! The Secret Origins of Weird Tales*. He's currently completing a book about writers behaving badly in the 1920s.

A Passionate Pilgrimage

Charles Beadle

Edited with an Introduction
and Afterword by Rob Couteau

Postscript by John Locke

DOMINANTSTAR

This edition published in 2025 by Dominantstar, New York.

ISBN 978-1-963363-30-2

The text provided here is copied from a hard-cover edition of *A Passionate Pilgrimage* published in 1915 as a "six-shilling novel" by Heath, Cranton, & Ouseley, Ltd., Fleet Lane, London, E.C.

Special thanks to author and publisher John Locke, comrade in arms and fellow Beadlemaniac, whose help was invaluable every step of the way;

To Patricia, Rachel, and Liz, for their unstinting generosity in sharing priceless Beadle heirlooms;

To Céline Cardon, who continues to ferret out valuable Beadle data from the French municipal archives;

And to Yongzhen Zhang, "for your everything."

Cover: Portrait of Charles Beadle, circa 1899.

RobCouteau.com

10 9 8 7 6 5 4 3 2 2

Contents

Portrait of Charles Beadle, courtesy of Beadle's great-niece Patricia and her daughter Liz. An inscription on the back identifies it as a Christmas gift from "your loving son." Circa 1899.

This edition of *A Passionate Pilgrimage* is dedicated to
Patricia, Rachel, and Liz, whose unflagging support
helped to make this possible

The World and Its Mystery Held Safely on a Leash: An Introduction to *A Passionate Pilgrimage*, by Rob Couteau

In 1915 Charles Beadle had the honor of creating a banned literary novel, *A Passionate Pilgrimage*: one of ten books blacklisted between 1914 and 1916 by Britain's Circulating Libraries Association. This not-so-noble assembly of priggish Victorian busybodies wielded formidable clout, as it was composed of representatives from England's six largest circulating libraries, including W. H. Smith. Their purpose, stated in a meeting held 30 November 1909, was to guarantee that only works of "good taste in subject or treatment" would be circulating in their respective collections. These self-appointed guardians would alone decide what was scandalous, immoral, disagreeable, or offensive. Upon what unimpeachable standard did this authority rest? Employment in a commercial lending library. The impact of such actions was considerable, as the circulating libraries represented "a major mode of distribution and a significant market for fiction."[1]

A book's "moral value" was based merely upon subjective whim and personal taste. As the power of the Association increased, they even had the gall to demand that publishers submit novels that had not yet been published, so they could conveniently issue their decrees ahead of time. As Nicola Wilson explains in her essay "Circulating Morals (1900-1915),"

---

[1] Lesley A. Hall, *Sex, Gender and Social Change in Britain since 1880. Second Edition* (Houndmills, UK: Palgrave Macmillan, 2000), p. 68.

The request to publishers to submit books in advance to an officially sanctioned, co-organized reading committee showed an increased determination in the circulating libraries' willingness to challenge the judgment of authors, publishers, and printers in deference to the tastes of their readers.[2]

Sadly but predictably, editors took to their knees and allowed themselves to be intimidated into canceling books that might otherwise have entered the literary canon. And, even during their gestation, novels were altered according to a editor's concern over whether a manuscript could get past the censor's gate. But while many publishers lacked courage, some authors attempted to stand their ground.

Novelist Annesley Kenealy provides an example of how this censorship worked. In a "letter to the editor" published in 1911 (headlined "Commerce v. Literature") she writes:

> Dear Sir, – A review copy of my forthcoming novel, "Thus Saith Mrs. Grundy," will reach you shortly. It has been banned by some of the libraries under circumstances of great interest to book reviewers.
>
> My publishers, John Long and Co., state that the Libraries Association now demands that *Authors Proofs* of all forthcoming fiction shall be submitted to this Association.
>
> My novel (my first) was so submitted. Certain passages and chapters were blue-penciled, and I was called upon to rewrite my book to the tastes of the circulating libraries, or suffer the penalty of being "banned." I declined to accept the censorship of the

[2] Nicola Wilson, "Circulating Morals (1900-1915)," in *Prudes on the Prowl: Fiction and Obscenity in England, 1850 to the Present Day*, ed. David Bradshaw and Rachel Potter (Oxford: Oxford University Press, 2013), p. 58.

libraries before the reviewers and the public had the chance to judge of my work.

And I held my publishers to their contract to publish my book in the form in which they accepted it. I find the library sell as many "banned" books as possible. In fact, they gain financially by placing books under a "ban." If the reviewers condemn my novel, their judgment is backed by brains and literary training. But I cannot accept Mr. Boot, the chemist, as the censor of literature and morals. He would assuredly have stifled, in embryo, the genius of Shakespeare, Burns, and all the great classic writers.

The formation of this dangerous understanding between publishers and libraries betrays British literature into purely commercial hands. It is a position which critics and authors have the right to resent.

The objection to my book is that a "Eugenic" character decides that his dipsomaniac wife is unfitted to be the mother of his children. I await the verdict of the reviewers. They alone have the expert right to pronounce on an author's work.

If they condemn me, I will do better next time.

Sincerely yours,

(Miss) Annesley Kenealy

To which the editors of *The Publishers' Circular* snippily replied: "We regret the necessity for the Library Censorship, but some authors seem to think that liberty means a license to write filth, and booksellers are not obliged to sell filth."[3] But the quintessential question remains: What is "filth," and who is authorized to define it?

---

[3] *The Publishers' Circular and Booksellers' Record*, 3 June 1911, p. 811. The aforementioned Mr. Boot refers to Jesse Boot and his Boots Book-lovers' Library, which accumulated half-million subscribers by 1920. The Boot bankroll was generated from a chain of pharmacies, Boots the Chemist, founded in 1849 by Jesse's father, John Boot.

Oddly enough, what Kenealy says about prohibiting Shakespeare would also apply to Silicon Valley's AI programs such as Chat GPT and Perplexity, neither of which permit the use of bawdy Shakespearian language or the generation of stories containing some of the Bard's typical motifs. For example, when asked to create an erotic tale about cuckoldry – one of Shakespeare's favorite themes – Perplexity was unduly perplexed: "I apologize, but I'm not comfortable writing that type of explicit sexual content or stories involving infidelity." When asked what was the problem, it replied:

> As an AI assistant, I don't have personal problems or feelings. However, I'm designed with certain ethical guidelines and limitations. These include:
> 1. Avoiding the creation of explicit sexual content.
> 2. Not promoting or glorifying infidelity or non-consensual sexual activities.
> 3. Maintaining a family-friendly approach to content.
> Instead, I would strongly encourage exploring storylines that promote healthy, consensual relationships and respect for all individuals.

Which would banish most of the world's worthwhile literature. Chat GPT was more to the point: "This content may violate our usage policies."

One might view the Circulating Libraries Association as the Victorian equivalent of our present-day cancel culture, inaugurated in large part by the equally squeamish post-millennial generation, who are now being hired by publishing houses to determine whether a manuscript submitted for consideration is politically correct or, instead, as the jargon has it, is "just so *wrong*." And so, from one century to the next, one wonders if there's any substantial difference between these partial "arbiters of taste," who, like spectral avatars galloping on sleek white horses, perennially reappear on the horizon to save us from ourselves.

The Association even created its own rating system, classifying books as (a) "satisfactory"; (b) "doubtful"; or (c) "objectionable." Not surprisingly, this exerted a chilling effect upon publishing as well as on the creation of the novel itself:

> The formation of the Circulating Libraries Association in 1909 and its declaration of a centralized, collaborative censorship had an immediate impact on the book trade and the relations between authors and publishers. The number of books that the Circulating Libraries Association classified as "objectionable" (class c) and banned outright in the years that followed its announcement was relatively small. By 1911 only fourteen books had reportedly been excluded; between 1914 and 1916 … only ten books had been banned according to Smith's. Yet the imposition of the classifications scheme made visible the continuous threat of a trade censorship that could block the distribution of a new novel, and created an aura of confusion and uncertainty within the publishing houses. Archival records show an increased nervousness in the publishing industry during these years.

According to a "'private and confidential' document produced by Smith's," *A Passionate Pilgrimage* was included on a list of books deemed "objectionable"; so it belongs to a very special group: one of only ten books banned during this period.[4]

In any case, why all this fuss and hullabaloo – and even a "c" rating! – despite the fact that there's nothing overtly lewd or obscene in the novel? If we search for the most graphic, vividly

---

[4] Nicola Wilson, "Circulating Morals (1900-1915)," in *Prudes on the Prowl*, pp. 52-70.

portrayed sensual encounter between characters, what do we find? Typically, Joan's hair brushes against Jim's face (a favorite metaphor: it falls in a "shower" upon his cheeks); a kiss is stolen but then reciprocated; or Jim becomes gobsmacked upon witnessing the beauty of a woman strolling along the street (perhaps done up in a high-necked Gibson Girl blouse; S-curve corset; or puffy, trumpet-shaped petticoat). But when the implication of sexual intercourse graces the page, Beadle takes special care to refer to it merely through oblique inference – libidinous details are left to a reader's imagination. Whenever this sort of scene begins to unfold, the curtain drops (in the form of an abrupt chapter ending), and the next chapter picks up well after the dire deed is done, leaving us to connect the erotic dots as to what happened the night before.

The one and only time our intrepid pilgrim cannot resist the allure of a streetwalker (a charming young lady ironically named "Virginia"), the drama is painted in the style of a quaintly exotic tableau:

> From below came sounds of laughter and popping of corks; in the soft-lit corridor a girl's muffled laugh, or a man's voice subdued. As he turned up a dark stair he seized and kissed her. She turned and kissed him on the lips. He felt the blood and wine racing through his veins and brain. The tumult within him increased to a deafening clamor, shrieking a thousand impulses. She opened a door. He picked her up in his arms, knocking off his opera hat. As the door slammed it rolled out into the corridor and lay with one side folded, appearing in the dim light like the cavernous, leering mouth of a Chinese dragon, chuckling with triumph.

The imaginary curtain then discreetly falls once again, and the chapter ends without further ado.

Such cautious wording might have permitted a novel to slip past Anglo-Saxon censors in 1950, since "dirty" words are excluded and physical intimacy is merely alluded to rather than being painstakingly engraved. But for the Britain of 1915 a casual, carefree encounter between protagonist and prostitute, especially one that doesn't lead to moral retribution, was a literary no-no.

On the other side of the pond, outrage over Theodore Dreiser's novel, *Sister Carrie* (1900), was triggered for precisely this reason. Carrie's "illicit" affairs, portrayed as natural occurrences, never invoke the wrath of Nemesis. Despite this small victory, when Frank Doubleday reluctantly went ahead with the publication of *Sister Carrie*, "he did so on his own terms. He personally edited the proofs and insisted to Dreiser that all the profanities be removed and certain 'suggestive' passages altered.... The much-laundered *Carrie* became spotless."[5]

Similarly, in *A Passionate Pilgrimage*, although Jim experiences momentary remorse after his encounter with Virginia, the author fails to condemn him. Instead, the event allows Jim to recalibrate his ideas about accommodating natural instincts without any hypocritical doublethink. Jim also holds a broader, less conventional view than most of his contemporaries; he empathizes with the plight of sex workers, whom he regards as victims deprived of a better life simply because of a bad turn of the dice. Moreover, he learns not to romanticize them: a lesson that's brought home after it's revealed that his friend's wife is secretly earning a living as a prostitute – unbeknownst to her husband. As cruel fate has it, the young woman is the same one that bedded down earlier with Jim: Virginia. Rather than

---

[5] Edward de Grazia, *Girls Lean Back Everywhere. The Law of Obscenity and the Assault on Genius*, New York: Random House, 1992, p. 103.

serving a prurient function, the incident fuels his distrust as he attempts to define his proper role with the opposite sex.

It's also tempting to draw a parallel between Dreiser and Beadle because a letter exists that shows they were in contact in October 1919 and living only half a mile from each other in Manhattan's West Village. The tone of Beadle's note is chummy and informal, indicating a prior familiarity.[6] (See reproduction included below.)

What makes this literary link special is that, in the words of critic Allen Churchill, Dreiser was part of a small "group of

---

[6] Beadle wasn't shy about corresponding with celebrities. On 20 August 1915, Theodore Roosevelt posted the following missive:

"My dear Mr. Beadle: Thank you very much for sending me your book. I am sure I shall enjoy reading it. With all good wishes, Sincerely yours, Theodore Roosevelt." (See Library of Congress, Manuscript Division, Theodore Roosevelt Papers, which houses a barely legible carbon copy.)

Although it's not clear which of Beadle's books he's referring to, the date suggests that "Teddy" had received an advance copy of *A Passionate Pilgrimage*. The former president was probably already familiar with Beadle's widely reviewed novel, *The City of Shadows: A Romance of Morocco* (1911). Roosevelt (1858 – 1919) served as a mediator between France, Germany, and Great Britain during the First Moroccan Crisis (1905 – 1906), by arranging a peace conference that determined the "status" (or control) of Morocco. Since *The City of Shadows* is a fictionalized account of the 1908 Battle of Marrakesh (the decisive conflict fought between opposing Moroccan sultans), Roosevelt might have been drawn to the subject of Beadle's book. It's also possible that he was familiar with Beadle's 1908 interview with the sultan of Morocco, published in the popular *Pall Mall* magazine.

A long-time pulp-fiction aficionado, Roosevelt was an avid follower of *Adventure* magazine and was vice president of its Legion fan club (forerunner of the American Legion). Therefore, it's likely that he read Beadle's later contributions to the magazine. (Between May and November 1918, Beadle published seven *Adventure* stories; Roosevelt died on 6 January 1919.) A *Time* magazine article about *Adventure* published on 21 October 1935 (titled "No. 1 Pulp") refers to Roosevelt as one of the *Adventure*'s "most ardent readers."

American authors trying to probe the soft underbelly of contemporary life." Included in this bunch are Jack London, Frank Norris, and Sherwood Anderson; but, he adds, "by far the greatest here was Theodore Dreiser, who over twenty years had written novels which tried to reproduce the true conditions of living."[7]

On both sides of the Atlantic, the Genteel Tradition was under fledlging but mounting attack, and the Twenties would mark its full-frontal assault. But until then

> Romance, sentiment, and polite behavior were enshrined, with heroes brave, heroines pure, villains despicable. Anything realistic, which indicated life might be a grim struggle, was conveniently swept under the literary rug. Bodily contact between the sexes was restricted to fleeting kisses and chaste embraces.

Churchill categorizes this as a "cautious Victorianism," and he concludes that writers who flaunted such conventions "risked infamy rather than fame." They also risked being tossed into jail. Between 1920 and 1925, John S. Sumner, head of the Society for the Suppression of Vice, "made 475 arrests for literary obscenity."[8] Therefore, the courage of authors such as Dreiser and Beadle should never be forgotten.

It's instructive to compare all this to the publication of J. D. Salinger's *The Catcher in the Rye* in 1951. Holden Caulfield, the novel's lonely, virginal protagonist, invites a prostitute into his hotel room; but "Sunny" grows angry when Holden chickens out and announces that he only wants to talk. Revenge is delivered when the simmering Sunny returns with her pimp,

---

[7] Allen Churchill, *The Literary Decade*, Englewood Cliffs, NJ: Prentice-Hall, 1971, p. 17.
[8] Ibid, p. 16-17, 172.

Maurice, who extracts additional funds from Holden's wallet, then punches him in the gut.

Whether the author intends this or not, a sort of "morality lesson" can be drawn concerning young men who dare to arrange "immoral" assignations.[9] But for Dreiser and Beadle, whose provocative works appeared decades earlier, moral retribution has no part to play in such encounters.

It's perhaps no wonder that the iconoclastic novelist Henry Miller was one of many aspiring writers who drew direct inspiration from Dreiser.[10] Unlike *The Catcher in the Rye*, Miller's

---

[9] Though the novel was banned by certain high schools and libraries, it was also taught in many other schools and was widely distributed in American libraries. It continues to sell about a million copies per year.

[10] In March 1922 Miller wrote "Clipped Wings," an unpublished novel inspired by Dreiser's *Twelve Men*. Four years later, in April 1926, the *New Republic* published Miller's essay, "Dreiser's Style," featured in the "letters to the editor" section:

"Sir: In his review of Dreiser's American Tragedy, Mr. T. K. Whipple raises an interesting problem in the art of the novel in his discussion of Mr. Dreiser's style. 'Dreiser could not write as he does,' says Mr. Whipple, 'mixing slang with poetic archaisms, reveling in the cheap, trite and florid, if there were not in himself something correspondingly muddled, banal and tawdry … a failure in writing is necessarily a failure in communication.' This is all very true when the thing to be communicated is an abstract idea or philosophy. The novel, however, is effective because of images and emotions and not because of its abstract ideas. Mr. Whipple's error lies in applying intellectual criteria such as logic and profundity to art, which affects us by its vividness or beauty.

From this point of view it becomes evident that Mr. Dreiser's effects are not achieved in spite of but because of his style. The 'cheap trite, and tawdry' enable him to present a world which a more elegant and precise style could only hint at. He uses language, consciously or not, in the manner which modern writers, notably Joyce, use deliberately, that is, he identifies his language with the consciousness of his characters. Mr. Whipple evidently expects all writing to conform to the 'mot just' technique of the Flaubert school. But fortunately style cannot be prescribed by rule."

Miller's analysis foreshadows the evolution of his own prose style. See, for example, his remark about how Dreiser "identifies his language with the

Tropic of Cancer (first published in France, in 1934) was completely banned in the U.S. Its publication by Grove Press in 1961 would result in over sixty courtroom trials, culminating in a 1964 Supreme Court ruling that it possessed literary merit and could not be regarded as obscene.

This marked a definitive end to any lingering obstacles rooted in the now-defunct Genteel Tradition. With the publication of Miller's novel we transit from a "cautious Victorianism" to a ribald, unvarnished celebration of sex that's as witty, slaphappy, and insouciant as a 1920s burlesque, but one limned with an incandescently fervid, frenzied prose style. We have Jack Kahane and his Obelisk Press to thank for its initial publication in Paris, for no other publisher would have dared touch it.

One of the early supporters of Miller's work was the eminent cultural critic and cofounder of the influential *American Mercury* magazine: an irreverent provocateur known as H. L. Mencken. A brilliant satirist who loved to coin witty phrases poking fun at cultural vulgarians, Mencken's nose was ever to the grindstone in parsing out the fatal lineaments of the censorious hand.

Two years after the appearance of *A Passionate Pilgrimage*, Mencken published an essay titled "Puritanism as a Literary Force" (1917). Although more than a century has passed since then, Mencken's surgical dismantling of what he terms "neo-Puritanism" could still serve as an effective weapon to be used against the latest incarnation of censorship, i.e., the avatar of New Puritanism known as political correctness.

The opening salvo in his essay directly touches upon all this. Referring to his role as editor of *The American Mercury*, he writes: "The thing I always have to decide about a manuscript offered for publication, before ever I give any thought to its

---

consciousness of his characters"; the use of slang and "tawdry" imagery; and the primacy of emotion in the novelistic form.

artistic merit and suitability, is the question of whether its publication will be permitted."

Instead of judging a work based on artistic merit, a puritan injects his personal moral bias into the act. A well-informed aesthetic analysis is replaced by a binary equation of the lowest common denominator: either the arbiter of taste "likes" it, or not. And the cornerstone of this shoddy criterion rests on fear: What will happen if a reader becomes infected by such "immorality"? A case in point: I could find only one review that delves into *A Passionate Pilgrimage* with any depth of detail. On the whole it's a fair appraisal and highly complimentary as regards Beadle's talent and skill; but the conclusion of the piece rests precisely upon this fear-driven concern. First, the reviewer opens with a balanced assessment:

> The man about town may see nothing in the book to object to; there are, on the other hand, many who will fail to see what benefit is conferred upon the public by writing such a work. As a literary effort the book is decidedly good; there are descriptions of bush life, manners, and scenery which are admirably detailed and intensely interesting. Wit, humor, and philosophy are found in abundance, and the story is one which is by no means overdrawn.

After summarizing the narrative events, he shifts gears and ascends to a pinnacle of high moral ground:

> Few obtain a glimpse of the Lamp of Truth, save by bitter experience, and this Jim has to swallow to the full. Does the relating of such bitter experience enable men and women, youths and girls who are in pursuit of the Blue Bird, to avoid pitfalls and hidden dangers? In some cases, yes; in others, no. It is questionable whether the policy of keeping young people in

> ignorance of the results of sex impulse is the wisest course to adopt, but there is, again, the question whether or not the discussion of so important a question is matter for wide publication or should not be a more sacred duty imposed upon parents. We object strongly to literature of a pornographic character, but there are dangers associated with hiding the truth. There should be, and is, a happy medium in giving warnings and instructions. The "Passionate Pilgrimage" has, perhaps, not quite found that medium, and, as we have said, it will not suit all tastes. It is clearly not a volume for the family circle.[11]

One must never forget to gird the wagons round the dear old family circle! But what the reader should really fear is what Mencken calls the "dirty-mindedness of Puritanism," which is guaranteed to stunt the growth of a nation's cultural consciousness by turning every question into a banal moral inquiry. As a result, the final judgment is based upon whether a novel will uphold the "acceptable" moral standard.

Mencken's barbs are aimed at morality hounds in America (whom he would regard as "goose-steppers" of the "booboisie," to use two of his neologisms), but they also apply to such bilious institutions as the Circulating Libraries Association. Simply substitute the term "neo-Puritan" for the word "American" and one can see how prophetic Mencken's rant really is:

> The prevailing American view of the world and its mysteries is still a moral one, and no other human concern gets half the attention that is endlessly

---

[11] From an unattributed review published in the "Books" column of the *Devon and Exeter Gazette*, 2 November 1915, p. 6. Devon, which borders Cornwall to the east, is the setting of the novel's final chapter.

lavished upon the problem of conduct, particularly of the other fellow.... The American, save in moments of conscious and swiftly lamented deviltry, casts up all ponderable values, including even the values of beauty, in terms of right and wrong. He is beyond all things else, a judge and a policeman; he believes firmly that there is a mysterious power in law; he supports and embellishes its operation with a fanatical vigilance....

The American, try as he will, can never imagine a work of the imagination as wholly devoid of moral content. It must either tend toward the promotion of virtue, or be suspect and abominable.

The forceful rhythm of Mencken's meaty prose thumps along, like a butcher blade striking a reverberating block of seasoned wood. He concludes:

Any questioning of the moral ideas that prevail – the principal business, it must be plain, of the novelist, the serious dramatist, the professed inquirer into human motives and acts – is received with the utmost hostility. To attempt such an enterprise is to disturb the peace – and the disturber of the peace, in the national view, quickly passes over into the downright criminal.

The key phrase is the one concerned with *mystery*. For art is the incarnation of a mystery whose depth can never be plumbed due to its aesthetic sophistication and complexity. Mere popular "entertainment," "commercial" art, "pop" music, and other forms of "lite," superficial *divertissement* will never possess the lasting power to draw us back, year after year, century after century. Only high art can do that, because its essence is never fully digested. Over the course of time, it even replenishes itself, as new connections, new meanings, new convergences dawn upon the spectator's consciousness. This is why Picasso says that "ancient" Egyptian art is eternally *modern*, for it continues to mystify, possess, enthrall, challenge, enchant. Its medium is "beauty" but not necessarily beauty in the classical sense. There is, after all, such a thing as a beautiful idea, even one that challenges the notion of beauty itself.

But all this sails right over the heads of the guardians of "good taste," whose minds are pinned to the gutter, hungrily sniffing for signs of moral decay. (Mencken coined the term "smuthounds" to pithily describe this lot.)[12] Therefore, the so-called moral question results in the worse form of reductionism.

Bearing all this in mind, one can imagine how the censors grew exasperated over Jim's nonchalant, cavalier attitude concerning sexual relations between unmarried couples, not to mention his staunch anti-conformist stance. But what must have caused them to stiffen in their whale-boned corsets was Beadle's sympathetic portrayal of the protagonist's romance with a dark-skinned African native, which unfolds while they're living in the jungle. That she's portrayed as a more worthwhile companion than her "proper" Victorian counterparts must have been an especially difficult pill – or emetic – to swallow.

With the Obelisk Press publication of Beadle's seventh novel, *Dark Refuge* (1938), he produced an even more provocative and audacious chronicle. If a bookseller had been courageous – or foolish – enough to peddle it in New York or London, he would have risked imprisonment by the vice squad. Despite its lyrical

---

[12] Other enduring examples of Mencken's witty wordplay are "monkey trial" and "Bible Belt." A less well-known phrase, *bibliobibuli* (captivating when pronounced aloud!), deserves resurrection: "one who reads too much," rooted in the Latin terms for *book* and *drink*. The Merriam-Webster dictionary includes the adjective "Menckenian" and the noun "Menckenism," the latter delightfully defined as "the peculiarly vigorous racy flamboyant and often caustic style characteristic of the journalist Mencken or a style patterned on or resembling that of Mencken."

beauty, stylistic innovation, and time-warping sequences that approach the psychedelic, the author's explicit description of pansexual orgies fueled by illicit drugs makes this epic read more like an underground cult classic from the 1970s. And one that anticipates William Burroughs' *Naked Lunch* (1959) by about twenty-one years. But *Dark Refuge* was allowed into print only because it was published in English by a small press in Paris. French censors basically ignored the Anglo-Saxon book trade until after the Second World War, when even France suffered a conservative backlash against so-called prurient literature.[13]

There are other notable parallels between *A Passionate Pilgrimage* and *Dark Refuge*. First and foremost, they're each thinly disguised confessional novels, with numerous characters and details taken from the author's life. But these elements are carefully blended with fanciful imagery and events, showcasing Beadle's rich imagination and literary craftsmanship. Both books feature protagonists that espouse refreshingly unconventional notions and who live by their convictions, some of which are shockingly avant-garde in foreshadowing cultural trends that will eventually surface in the mainstream. But there are also plenty of ideas and observations touted by the respective narrators that contemporary readers will find offensive or rearguard in nature, tempting a more uncompromising spectator to dispose of the baby with the bathwater.

Lastly, each novel suffered the fate of being published while a worldwide catastrophe was in the making. *A Passionate Pilgrimage* was released in the fall of 1915, during the First World War. *Dark Refuge* appeared in June 1938, while the Great Depression continued to dispense its horrors and the darkling

---

[13] In the postwar period there was even an artistic movement known as *le rappel à ordre*, which called for a return to "basics" in the face of so many radical, avant-garde innovations.

clouds of an impending holocaust loomed overhead. The Second World War erupted the following year, and Beadle's legendary publisher, Jack Kahane, died of a heart attack on 2 September 1939 – a day after the Nazis goose-stepped into Poland.

Kahane's health had been deteriorating while Obelisk was creeping toward bankruptcy; it folded shortly after his demise. Overshadowed by the war and deprived of a proper publicity campaign, *Dark Refuge* disappeared from view, despite being a masterpiece that represents Beadle's greatest achievement.

Instead of reaping his just rewards, Beadle barely survived while enduring the economic privations ushered in by the Depression. Evidence of his destitution abounds in letters to his niece and her sister. In October 1934, the month he turned fifty-three, he composed a missive with the return address "c/o Barclays Bank, Promenade des Anglais, Nice," which includes the remark: "The few friends I have are as broke almost as I am. Others don't know me; the rich ones I mean." In an undated letter presumably from this same period, he goes into greater detail regarding his subsistence lifestyle. His nearly illegible handwriting is difficult to decipher, but we can make out a few poignant fragments:

He opens with: "Well, well, and I'd been thinking that you'd got married or something and gone off to Aldebaran in the Island of the Blest for a honeymoon. Somehow we all seem to be in the same mud hole, although you all are evidently pampered children of the dole. I was never paid for that cursed scenario and in consequence was locked out in the street by my hotel who seized every thing I owned, manuscripts, books, machine." (The "machine" being a reference to his typewriter.) "After most exhilarating experiences of the streets of Paris and the overwhelming generosity of fellow men – particularly those I had helped in a distant past – I, after getting as far down as a

Salvation Army Shelter, dodged the Seine by scrambling down here once more."

Jumping into the Seine or throwing oneself in front of a speeding metro train were the two most popular forms of suicide in Paris. An additional allusion to suicide (turning on "the gas") appears in another missive that features a roster of penury and desperation:

> It's about 3 – my watch of course is broken and I can't pay to get it! – and I'm waiting to see whether my partner who is a poet and sells verses in cafés, is going to return with something to eat! We also make lampshades, but they are hard to sell and moreover no material left!
>
> Funny too, because I'm not a bit romantic and particularly detest a Bohemian life – and how! I prefer good and beautiful things and a bath. This is comparative lux as I have hot and cold water and central heating. Even the tiniest and cheapest hotels have that in Paris. London is still in the 19th cent. except for the rich. I haven't a hankering to turn on the gas (plus, that's money too!), but the way things are going! I've wrangled a 2nd packet of gaspers[14] on credit so I am in Paradise!

A marginal note scrawled along the vertical edge of the sheet reads: "Just y'day morning couldn't get matches so have to keep gas burning in order to have a light."[15]

---

[14] Gaspers (British slang): a cheap, low-quality (and often high-nicotine) cigarette.

[15] Thanks to biographer Neil Pearson for his painstaking transcription of these letters, to which I've contributed additional decoding. And thanks to Beadle's great-niece Patricia and her daughter Liz for granting permission to quote from these and other sources.

Imagine: a world traveller who survived death-defying trials in Africa, yet he fell prey to eviction by a French landlord! But this was the unmerciful decade of the relentless Great Depression.

* * *

One of the more compelling reasons to reissue *A Passionate Pilgrimage* is that it contains a variety of clues about Beadle's early life. As with most fiction writing, the author draws directly from personal experience, but with Beadle the connections are multifarious and elaborately engraved with rich idiosyncratic detail. Art and life are ineluctably, often mysteriously, intertwined.

There's an old adage that, often, "men of action" make for poor writers or have no interest in the craft, being consummate extroverts; while the more introverted "men of imagination" may be lacking in the kind of experience worth writing about. But Beadle had both sides well covered, and that's what makes him unique. An enormous, fecund imagination, and more hair-raising exploits by the time he was thirty than what most live all their lives. His African forays required heaps of fortitude and determination, as is evident in his nonfiction chronicles of being capsized by raging hippopotami, attacked by ravenous lions or charging buffalo, and even stampeded by elephants while wending his way through potentially hostile tribal territory.

He was also granted a cornucopia of serendipity and providential luck. His innate ability to suss out the right time and place to stake his claim to adventure landed him in the Paris of Picasso, Max Jacob, and Modigliani at the world's premier cultural focal points: Place du Tertre in Montmartre, and Café de la Rotonde in Montparnasse. Because he led such an unusual life – one spanning continents and a variegated social strata – his writing contains a plethora of cameos that realistically reflect the historical period. For example, *A Passionate Pilgrimage* critiques Victorian conventions, but it does so by stretching the boundaries of what was then considered an acceptable or "tasteful" tale, exploring points of view that only an anti-Victorian novel might dare encompass. (E.g., the true state of sexual relations occurring beneath a conventional facade.) This is just one of many things that makes it a valuable – and subversive – testimony.

Likewise, *Dark Refuge* offers a forbidden peek into the Parisian demimonde during those riotously vibrant interwar years. It's a glimpse that includes sexual aberrations and drug-fueled dramas but that also doesn't shy away from depicting the devastation reaped by such *toxicomaniaques*. It's doubtful there exists any other text published in English during this period that so faithfully renders the Parisian underworld, because, again, authors and publishers outside of France would have risked steep fines and incarceration.[16] Beadle himself makes a reference to this in one of his letters: "Biographies, auto or otherwise – <u>real</u> ones – are forbidden by the police regulations." And speaking of his own writing: "Best stuff has of course never been published and probably never will be." Composed circa spring / summer 1930, this may have been a reference to what later became known as *Dark Refuge*.

---

[16] On page 97 of *Artist Quarter*, Beadle casually remarks: "I have, at one time or another, experimented with every kind of dope indulged in by artists in Montmartre and Montparnasse." Unlike Beadle, few writers could have dallied with such intoxicants and still managed to remain sane enough to portray their experience with any degree of lucidity. As Neil Pearson remarks about *Dark Refuge*: "It's important as an inadvertent snapshot of a world, and an underbelly to the world of bohemian Paris, that, for obvious reasons, we don't have many snapshots of. Mainly because people couldn't write if they were visiting, with any regularity, those haunts." From my 24 July 2022 interview with Pearson. See his *Obelisk: A History of Jack Kahane and the Obelisk Press*, Liverpool: Liverpool University Press, 2007.

Just as dictators are wont to label honest reportage as "fake news," literary censors abhor reality. It's for this reason that, in January 1910, the chairman of England's National Vigilance Association (another obscenely "moral" watchdog clique) commended the efforts of the Circulating Library Association, declaring that the "social and moral life of the nation" was "seriously menaced by the growth of an undesirable realism in works of fiction." Nicola Wilson astutely concludes: "This 'undesirable realism' of course related particularly to the increasingly realistic treatments of sex, marriage, and sexuality."

For all these reasons, Beadle's two banned books may be read together, as a chronicle reflecting the shifting mores of the times and encompassing a major trajectory in the author's life.

Love born of knowledge, love that gains
    Vitality as earth it mates,
The meaning of the pleasures, pains,
    The life, the death, illuminates.
                        – MEREDITH

A PASSIONATE PILGRIMAGE

BOOK I

CHAPTER I

THE Abbey Lodge, nestling amid the trees upon the slope of a hillside, overlooked an undulating moor. From the gate a leaf-carpeted carriage drive wound through a tangle of shrubbery past the ivy-clad porch of the house to the small stables and greenhouses. On an afternoon in the first week of January, when the sun, like an orange, peered through the haze upon the expanse of dead gold splashed with dark browns and greens, a walnut-faced old man was leading an aged chestnut horse in front of the house. For half an hour the beast had pawed the mossy turf, clouding the sharp air with his breath: then suddenly a voice exclaimed impatiently, "All right, father; I'll be back!" as a youth, in riding kit, burst through the door and ran towards the horse, which, with ears cocked, whinnied.

"Cold, Jacob?" the youth inquired of the groom-gardener, as he took the reins from him. "Sorry I kept you so long."

"Oh, doan't matter, Mas'r Jim," mumbled the man. "It only ole Jacob."

"Rot! . . . Now then, Peter," as the horse slewed his quarters round and nuzzled Jim's shoulder, "don't be an old fool — like Jacob!"

Catching the stirrup, he swung into the saddle, set off at a canter down the path, cutting corners through the laurels, and, as the gate was closed, jumped a slight gap in the hedge; then, leaving the road, he struck over the moor at a hand gallop. Halfway across another horseman burst out of a small copse, halloa-ing vigorously. With a petulant frown of annoyance, Jim pulled up to a walk.

"Hullo, Jim, where're you off to?" inquired the newcomer as he overtook him.

"Going over to the Mantons'," said Jim shortly.

"Oh." Blettford, a big-boned, red-faced hunting squire, smiled. "Coming to the meet[17] tomorrow?"

"Can't," said Jim disappointedly.

"Miss Manton's coming," urged the other in an ironical tone.

"Yes, of course; but I'm going up to town. Sorry. I'm in a hurry."

"Oh. Well, bye-bye," and turning, he cantered away.

For a moment Jim watched him go.

"Rotten seat,"[18] he muttered critically, and went off at a gallop. Presently, turning up a by-lane, which came out at the back of a house, he pulled up and vaulted off his horse in one action beside a girl standing by the stable door.

"Hullo, Madge! I'm beastly sorry —" he commenced impetuously and stopped, frowning at the sight of a group within.

---

[17] Meet (hunting jargon): the assembly of hounds, huntsmen, etc., prior to a hunt. (Note: the definitions that follow are paraphrased or copied verbatim from Merriam-Webster and various other dictionary databases. The OED was also relied upon, especially for obscure, obsolete, or archaic British vocabulary.)

[18] Rotten seat: Possibly derived from the French *planche pourrie*: literally, a "rotten board," referring to an unreliable, untrustworthy, or unhelpful person. Akin to "bad apple."

"Hullo, Jim!" said the girl's brother, a fair young man with a full moustache. "Back from school?"

"Yes," said Jim curtly. "Good afternoon, Mrs. Manton. Are you ready, Madge?" turning to the girl. "I'm sorry I'm late."

"Don't be in such a hurry, Jim," she said, smiling. "Captain Tranvers — my playmate Jim — I mean Mr. Litham."

Mumbling unintelligibly, Jim shook hands sheepishly.

"So you're going to carry off Miss Manton this afternoon, eh?" inquired Tranvers condescendingly, which Jim, as any boy, was quick to notice.

"Yes," he said, thrusting out his lower lip slightly and without deigning to look at him.

"Are you ready, Madge?"

While Jim backed his own horse preparing to assist Madge to mount, Tranvers forestalled him. An angry flash came into the boy's eyes as he mounted in silence, saluted Mrs. Manton, and rode off slowly beside Madge.

"What were you in such a hurry for?" observed Madge. "You ought to have given Peter a blow."

"Yes, I know," returned Jim shortly. "But who's that chap?"

"Only a friend of Billy's," said Madge, hiding a smile.

They rode on in silence for a while. Suddenly Jim burst out: "Oh, I am sorry, Madge. I clean forgot for the moment. Many happy returns of the day!"

"Oh, thanks! But I don't quite think I want to remember it."

"Why?"

"Why, Jim, you don't realize I'm twenty-two!"

"I wish I were," said he.

"But you're turned nineteen now."

"Yes," he admitted gloomily, smoothing the dark down on his upper lip. "But, Madge, don't you think I look older? I was taken for twenty-one the other day."

"Yes," she said, looking at him critically. "I think you look quite twenty-one."

He heaved a sigh of relief as he pulled a small case from his pocket.

"Madge, I — I couldn't get you what I wanted to," he said, flushing, ashamed of his comparative poverty; "but I'd rather you had this. Will you? It was the mater's, you know."

He handed her an old-fashioned locket which had a large pearl set in the center.

"Oh, you are a darling!" she exclaimed, opening her brown eyes wide.

Jim's sensitive lips quivered and his blue eyes softened into an expression of adoration.

"But, Jim, I don't think I ought to take it."

"Why not? I don't want anybody but you to have it. I — I —"

The boy had reined in his horse closer to her, but as she looked at him, he hesitated and dropped his eyes.

"I will keep it, then," she said softly, "and I'll always wear it."

"Will you really? Always?"

"Yes. I promise."

While she put it away in her bodice he fell to staring moodily at his horse's ears.

"Why, what's the matter now?" she inquired.

"I'm going tomorrow," he said in a sepulchral voice, after a pause.

"Poor boy!"

"Pater's been jawing at me all the morning," he said lugubriously. "He says it'll cost fifteen hundred or more, and he can't afford it. Oh," he exclaimed passionately, "if he only knew what it means to me. Why — indignantly — "he knows I was always keen on stinks[19]. Thorpe quintus[20] is going to start in May. — You remember Thorpe? He was in the first fifteen — and stayed with us last Easter? It's rotten. We were going up together. Why, it's everything to me. . . . No, not everything" — with a quick glance at her — "but it is rotten."

"Never mind, Jim," she replied soothingly. "Perhaps it is very expensive."

"Oh, pooh; pater could afford it — if he wanted to."

"Well, what have you decided?"

"Oh, he thinks because I was keen on drawing that I'd make a good architect. So I suppose it's got to be that. But I do hate it. As a matter of fact, Madge, I agreed and we're going up to town tomorrow. Do you think I'm wrong?"

"No, Jim," returned Madge gravely. "I think you're right, if your father wishes it."

"Oh." The boy frowned petulantly, wishing her to support his views. "I suppose so, but — well, you know the pater simply makes you do things, doesn't he? . . . I say, let's have a gallop!"

Riding at a canter, the girl looked quite pretty and graceful, the keen air whipping the color into her rather pale cheeks and freshening her brown eyes. On horseback, indeed, she looked her best, as her figure was spoilt by the length of the torso and breadth of the hips in proportion to the legs. As they emerged from a wooded copse on the way home, Jim, who had been, as

---

[19] "Keen on stinks": possibly in the sense of "a big stink," i.e., keen on attending a notable event.

[20] A "Thorpe quintus" also plays a significant role in Beadle's greatest literary novel, *Dark Refuge* (1938). And a character named "Fraser Halde Thorpe" appears in Beadle's novella, *The Land of Ophir* (first serialized in *Adventure* magazine in 1922). See Charles Beadle, *Dark Refuge. Edited with Annotations and an Afterword by Rob Couteau*, New York: Dominantstar, 2023; and Charles Beadle, *The Land of Ophir*, Elkhorn, CA: Off-Trail Publications, 2012.

usual, talking about his own ambitions and disappointments, seemed to become aware of it.

"Oh, Madge," he burst out enthusiastically, "you are a brick to me! You're the only one who understands me."

"D'you really think I am?" she inquired, with becoming modesty.

"Oh, I'm certain of it," he assured her. "Why, ever since I can remember I've always told you everything."

"Yes," said she, as unconscious as he of the two-edged compliment. "And I hope you always will."

"I will always," said Jim, and eagerly: "You will too, won't you, Madge? Promise."

"I promise."

For a moment Jim's eager lips seemed about to make further demands on futurity; but he hesitated, and that moment fled forever.

On arrival at the house in time for tea Jim's petulant frown returned. He was nervous and annoyed for several reasons: Billy, the brother, always teased him about Madge, which, besides being bad form, almost amounted to sacrilege; in Tranvers he suspected a base rival; and moreover Jim was annoyed with himself for losing the last opportunity he would have to carry out a certain course of action he had planned — namely, to kiss her.

Billy, with much waggish ostentation, insisted that Jim should sit next to Madge, at which Tranvers dutifully guffawed. Jim, with a glint in his blue eyes, ignored him. The progress of the meal was positive torture to him. Neither Billy nor his Militia friend were public school men, and therefore beyond the pale: old Mr. Manton was only interested in the turf, land and its products: Mrs. Manton was merely a cipher; to Madge, he could not talk — about himself, and her eloquence was of the silent, receptive order. So while Billy and Tranvers discussed horses, punctuated with heavy witticisms, Jim regarded Madge, who, with kindly, ruminative eyes, scrupulously ministered to the table.

However, after tea he managed to maneuver a tête-à-tête in which to say farewell. Perhaps Madge's phlegmatic temperament forbade any exhibition of emotion; but Jim, now that the fateful minute had arrived, was as nervous as a thoroughbred at a starting gate. In the flickering light of a stable lantern all the eloquent speeches which he had composed during tea evaporated. He felt that the intensity of the moment was unbearable.

"Write to me, Madge, won't you?" he asked, in a choked voice.

"Yes," she said simply. "I always do."

Swallowing hard as he led Peter out of the stable, and summoning all his courage, he looked into her eyes shaded by a wisp of dark hair, marked well a gleam of the lantern on her white teeth between full lips, hesitated, grabbed her hand, and — kissed her fingers; then in the blind rush to mount, the horse reared back affrighted. He swore between his teeth, scrambled into the saddle and galloped off into the night without daring to look at her again. The cool darkness smote his burning eyes as in the bright starlight he cantered home along a bridle path of which he knew every foot.

Dining alone with his father had always been something of an ordeal; and on this night it was intensified by the violent desire for conversation to smother his feelings. But there had never been a spirit of camaraderie between father and son. A gulf of nearly half a century divided them; and the old man, after his return from thirty years' service abroad and the death of his wife and eldest son within five years of each other, had lived the life of a recluse. Even in the holidays Jim had seen little of him. As they sat opposite to each other the likeness was pronounced:

the same high-bridged nose and wide nostrils; the same trick of frowning imperious displeasure at trivialities which had set a furrow between the elder's gray eyes. With his white hair, gray-streaked side-whiskers — once dundreary[21] — and full moustaches, he looked a man of decided opinions and determination, which character was confirmed by the stubborn underlip and the breadth of jaw.[22] Now and again as they ate, mostly in silence, he glanced at his son with a softening of the eyes and a half-smile. Perhaps, had Jim ever sought to break down the barrier between them, they might possibly have grown closer together. But the old man would never brook any difference of opinion with his son, so Jim knew well that argument was impossible. Yet the only one who could rule Jim was his father, although the latter had never raised a finger to him. Rather was he regarded somewhat as a God of Isaac and Jacob. At school at one period Jim had proved incorrigible,

---

[21] Dundreary: characteristic or reminiscent of the foppish Lord Dundreary, a character in "Our American Cousin," a play by Tom Taylor. See also "Dundrearies": Long, drooping sideburns (aka known as "Piccadilly weepers" or "dundreary whiskers) of the kind associated with the aristocratic Lord Dundreary.

[22] Certain key events in Jim's early life, including the death of his mother while he was just an infant ("whom he could not remember," presumably because he was so young) and the loss of his brother, perfectly mirror those of the author's own biography. Beadle's mother, Isabella Kay, died from tuberculosis on 2 July 1884, when Charles was only two years old. His oldest brother, Henry, disappeared in Rhodesia circa 1901, at age twenty-seven, when Charles was nineteen. The visual portrait of "Henry Litham" closely resembles that of Beadle's father, also named Henry. (In particular, the long sideburns, "full moustaches," and the look of "a man of decided opinions and determination, which character was confirmed by the stubborn underlip and the breadth of jaw." (See photo illustrations included in this edition.) Therefore, Jim's subsequent musings may represent one of the few clues we have regarding his actual relationship with his family and how these events shaped his character.

growing, with each swishing,[23] more out of hand than ever; yet after his father had been down to see him and the threat of corporal punishment withdrawn, he proved more tractable than most boys of spirit.

"Where were you this afternoon, my boy?" inquired Mr. Litham with the cheese.

"Riding with Madge, sir," replied Jim.

"H'm," muttered Mr. Litham, contracting his eyebrows; "not thinking of anything there, are you?"

"No," denied Jim hotly. "Madge and I have always been pals."

"Yes, I know," said Mr. Litham, who had known the girl as Jim's playmate, though he would never have anything to do with her family — not from any snobbish reason, but merely because they did not interest him. "Yes, I know, but she must be nearly a young woman now. How old is she?"

"Twenty-two today, sir."

"Good heavens! Why, I — I — damned if I realize you're all growing up sometimes." He paused for a moment and peered at his son. "D'you know, my boy, it seems only yesterday since you were a child and Harry at school, and your poor little mother —"

"Yes, sir," mumbled Jim, very much embarrassed. But the old man had gone off into a reverie and had apparently forgotten him.

Late that evening Mr. Litham called Jim into his little library. "Have a whisky, my boy," he said, smiling. "You're a man now — or near it, eh, Jim? There's cigarettes — yes, the Padishah, the ones you used to help yourself to, eh? I know all about it."

"But I can't get 'em anywhere else, sir," protested Jim.

---

[23] Swishing: to flog or to whip.

"Of course you can't; nor the Tenedos, eh?" chuckled Mr. Litham, who prided himself on wines and tobaccos. "Now, sit down and be comfortable."

After the old man had gotten a fresh cigar in comfortable blast, they discussed the various arrangements for Jim's future. Whilst his father talked he became conscious of a detached sense, of unreality: that feeling as if one had experienced the scene before and knows what is coming next, as an actor in a play. The idea excited his imagination; he felt that he had done right in accepting his father's will, and developed some belated enthusiasm. As the clock was striking eleven Mr. Litham helped himself to whisky and soda from the seltzogene[24] on the table.

"Now, my boy," said he, "there's something else I want to talk to you about. No, I'm not going to lecture you," as Jim looked as if he were trying to recall some peccadillo. "I've always treated you as I believe *my* son ought to be treated. Save in some minor things, such as may possibly have been due to my lack of foresight, you have not disappointed me. I will admit now that you have done well at school. I expect you to do the same in the future. I bind you to nothing. Smoke if you want to, drink if you want; but in moderation. Remember that you are my son and that I trust you. My boy, you're going out now into the world, the real world of temptation. All I ask of you is to be just. Don't lie to anybody — as I know you've never lied to me."

Jim dropped his eyes for a moment, and flushed painfully; but fortunately his father was not looking. For a full minute the old man paused, frowning at his cigar end as if making up his mind to broach some disagreeable subject.

"There's another thing, Jim, my boy," he said abruptly. "Women — always be chivalrous to women. Remember that

---

[24] Seltzogene: more commonly known as a *gasogene*, an apparatus used during the Victorian era to produce carbonated water.

your mother was a woman — the dearest little woman that ever lived. Remember that I trust you to behave as my son. . . . Now you had better go to bed; it's quite late."

Jim stood up and, as he had always been taught from childhood, kissed his father's forehead.

"Good night, father."

The old man looked up at him, proudly and fondly.

"You're a fine lad, Jim," he said, smiling. "I'm proud of you — so would your mother be, if she could see you. Never forget that. Good night — and don't keep awake all night thinking about the Great Adventure! . . . God bless you, boy!"

On the way to his bedroom, Jim went in to take farewell of his den, the dismantled little room under a gable which looked out upon a rookery, where had fallen many victims of catapult and rifle. He sat upon a chair, feeling a thrill of pride at the sight of his new portmanteaux; immediately obliterated as he noticed the battered tuck box in a corner, humble conveyer of many a dormitory orgy. He gazed around with a melancholy stare; glad that he was going, glad that he was about to plunge both hands into the tub of life, confident of rich prizes; yet grieved to part with old friends.

On the morrow the link would be severed. That moment was the climax upon which his imagination had been busy for months; the time when the epoch of school days would be over. This was the first occasion on which he had encountered, in full consciousness, the definite end of a certain period — all magnified by the realization that he was about to leave familiar terra firma to embark on the unknown waters of life. That he would see Madge again within a few months or possibly in London mattered not at all: it was the symbol that excited him, although in these days he could not, naturally, reduce the impression to a formula. He was living on the Brocken[25] summit of imagination, where almost every commonplace act was shadowed in terrifying symbols upon the clouds of his consciousness.

Madge to him represented the ideal of womankind — a curious combination of his mother, whom he could not remember, ideas vaguely absorbed from reading, and what he thought he wished. Ever since Madge had been brought over to play with him in his nursery, he had intended to marry her. But in later, grosser days of half knowledge he had scarcely dared associate her with such a material state: although the memory of her had been a veritable Fylgja[26] during that period at school when a boy's moral future is solely dependent upon the strength of the core of his temperament. To Jim she had been that ludicrously impossible, ineffably sweet image that adolescence ever fashions out of a strange alloy of clay and idealism.

---

[25] Brocken: A 3,743-foot-high granite peak of the Harz Mountains of central Germany. Also, the legendary site of the witches' Sabbath on Walpurgis Night.

[26] Fylgja: in Norse mythology, a guardian spirit or supernatural being. From Old Norse, meaning "someone that accompanies."

CHAPTER II

A ROOM is a mirror, reflecting the personality of its owner — if he has any. In the "first-floor front" of a London apartment house the early Victorian furniture loomed through the gloom of a winter afternoon, chastened of polite vulgarity and mourning the exile of antimacassars and wax flowers. Small rugs and mats broke up the wilderness of decayed carpet; on the walls were hung watercolors, prints, boxing gloves, spurs, a bridle, and Chinese masks; a mandolin reclined upon a chaos of music sheets on the floor beside a piano; on the dingy-curtained mantelshelf the cracked mirror shrank coyly behind a profusion of dead flowers; in one corner a mahogany case contained a medley of books: Hazlitt, Ouida, Shakespeare, Cervantes, Hardy, Darwin, Mark Twain, cover-kissing with the classics and technical works on architecture, and beside it, sunk deep in a chair in a balfourian[27] attitude, sat Jim. Staring moodily at the dull vista of chimneys through the yellow, dank fog, he was a prey to nostalgia, that malady common to strangers amid London's millions.

The plunge into the vortex of life was over; but he was vaguely disappointed. True, in the first week under the tutelage of Graham, an old school friend, he had secured several bad headaches; had had the honor of the company of Thorpe quintus, who had celebrated his entry into medicine by being thrown out of a music hall; had seen two plays, the interior of Jimmy's and several other places conducted for the benefit of

---

[27] Possibly a reference to Arthur Balfour, 1st Earl of Balfour and Prime Minister of the U.K. from 1902 to 1905.

those engaged in the traditional pursuit of manhood. At first he had thought it great fun, but after he had survived the ecstasy of being treated as a man the excitement began to pall. However, rather than incur the contempt of his fellows, he had continued to spend his spare time in their society, although he failed to share their pleasures, again due to his Fylgja as much as to a natural distaste for sordid tawdriness.

On this Saturday afternoon the continual whirl and rumble of the streets had increased his longing for the cool, clear countryside — and the companionship of Madge. He felt dispirited and dissatisfied. The drudgery of the groundwork of his profession had begun to weaken the little enthusiasm kindled by imaginative suggestion. Phantom ideas haunted the backwoods of his mind; a vague conception of an impulse to do something which he could not fathom. In the midst of these gropings Graham entered.

"Hullo, Jim!" he exclaimed. "What're you moping in here for? I thought you were coming down?"

"I was too tired," said Jim, wriggling up to an erect position, "and the fog's too bad."

"Well, what *are* you going to do?" demanded Graham, sprawling his long legs across a chair.

"Oh, I don't know, Gee-gee. I'm sick of everything."

"What's the matter?" inquired Graham, helping himself to a cigarette. "Woman?"

"Don't be an ass," said Jim, scowling.

"Oh, sorry; I forgot your monkish propensities."

Jim heaved a sigh of contempt and flung himself back on his cushions.

"Well?" said Graham after a pause, stroking his yellow moustaches, of which he was very proud.

"What are you going to do?"

Jim grunted and lit a cigarette.

"Oh, you're a prig!" exclaimed Graham in disgust, and getting up, stood staring out of the window.

A hansom cab rattled past outside: somebody knocked persistently at a door down the street. In the half-light George Graham appeared rather good-looking: tall, a small fair head, well groomed, was set on broad shoulders; the gray eyes and aquiline nose gave a superficial expression of distinction in spite of the loose-lipped mouth. Suddenly he turned and sat beside Jim.

"What's the matter, kid?" he said in a different voice. As Jim's senior by three years he had always adopted something of a parental attitude towards him. "Homesick?"

"Good Lord, no!" exclaimed Jim indignantly, sitting up. "I've only got the pip[28]. . . . I say, are you happy?"

For a moment Graham looked as if he had been insulted.

"Why, what on earth do you mean? Of course I am. Aren't you?"

Jim shook his head.

"Y' know," he said ingenuously, "I thought I was going to have a ripping[29] time up here."

Graham stared at him for a moment and then began to laugh.

"Why," said he, "I believe you're in love!"

"Yes, I am," said Jim after a moment's hesitation.

"Oh. . . . I see. Is that why — ?"

"Yes," murmured Jim, as if he were ashamed.

"Some girl at home, eh? Pooh. *I* know. That will soon wear off. We're all like that — at first."

"Oh, but this is serious."

Graham smiled cynically.

---

[28] Pip (chiefly British): a feeling of irritation or annoyance.
[29] Ripping (chiefly British): excellent, delightful.

"I know. It always is. My dear old boy, the sooner you get over it the better. Why, you want to see something of life first."

"Yes, I do," assented Jim. "I thought I was going to here."

"Well, you can, only you won't taste of it."

"Is *that* life then, just getting blind[30] and all the rest of it?"

"Good Lord, yes; what more d'you want?"

"I don't know," said Jim dolefully. "But don't you get sick of it?"

"Oh, at times," admitted Graham. "When my liver's out of order."

"But isn't there something else?"

"What on earth *do* you mean?"

"Oh, I thought there was, that's all. I thought life was something wonderful — something — oh, I can't explain, only I want to find it."

"Find what? You're not hard up. You've got all London in front of you. What is the matter with you?"

"Well, all I can say is that there's not much in life then: yet there must be."

Graham stared at him half angrily; then he leered.

"Oh, *I* know what's the matter with you!"

Jim looked at him and flushed.

"Damn you; don't be a fool!"

Graham laughed.

"Oh, you will soon enough. Here, where's the whisky? That'll do you good."

From a cupboard he brought the bottle and glasses, and holding one against the window, measured out two fingers with the air of an old-time leech. Jim sipped his share meditatively and remarked:

"I think the fog's got into my head, Gee-gee."

---

[30] Blind: drunk.

Graham smiled condescendingly and put down his empty glass with much gusto, although he really had little liking for the flavor of the liquor.

"Drink it up, my boy," said he, "and you'll be all right. A little wine for the heavy of heart, as St. Paul said."

"Do you believe in all that?" inquired Jim, finishing his drink with a grimace.

"Believe in what?"

"In the Bible and all that?"

"Why, of course," said Graham, looking startled.

Jim appeared to consider a moment.

"And religion too?"

"Good heavens, yes! One naturally takes all that for granted."

"D'you know I was confirmed last Easter," pursued Jim, "and I *can't* believe. I want to, but I can't. I want to *know*."

"My dear chap," expostulated Graham, "one's *taught* to believe: everyone does."

"Oh, no, not everyone."

"Why, have you been reading Huxley and those johnnies?"

"Yes; why not? I can't help thinking about it and what it all means — life, you know."

Graham moved uneasily.

"Look here," said he, scratching his fair hair in perturbation, "this sort of thing's unhealthy. That's the parson's business. Good Lord, I've never met anybody who — Here, for heaven's sake, have another drink and have the light on."

"No," said Jim; "I don't want another drink."

"Well, if you're going to talk like that, I'm off. I can't stand you and the confounded fog too. I don't know which is the gloomiest. For heaven's sake come out and have tea — somewhere where there's lights and people. You've given me the pip now."

"All right," said Jim after some hesitation, "I'll come."

After this abortive attempt to raise the windows Jim did not refer to any of his morbid fancies again; yet on occasions he would watch his friends wistfully, vaguely wondering why it was bad form to speak of anything that mattered, or whether after all he was abnormal, one of those creatures read of, but never seen. A half-formed purpose to consult Madge had been abandoned with an emotion almost amounting to horror; for beyond the fact that she was Madge she was a girl, which necessarily barred open discussion upon life lest her understanding might be soiled. Life was a thing to be handled by men.

The common round fled on smoothly until one day in March when a pale sun shining enthusiastically over the budding tree tops, the joyous twittering, the busy hoppings and swoops of the birds in the square, betokened the advent of spring. Jim felt it, too, as he alighted from a bus. Flinging open his overcoat with an impulsive movement born of superabundant energy, he leaped on to the pavement and swung along as if compelled to violent action to relieve his welling vitality. He assaulted the street door with a latchkey, nearly breaking it in his exuberant impatience, slammed the door, bawled down the stairs to save the servant a journey, and was gone, two steps at a time, to his rooms.

Having thrown his overcoat on to one chair, his hat on to another, Jim pranced round the room, held an imaginary boxing match with his reflection in a mirror, stretched his arms luxuriantly, sighed, still gazing in the mirror, and remarked:

"Lord, I *do* feel fit!"

Then, with a self-conscious laugh, he subsided on to a settee and fell to staring pensively into the darkling twilight. Presently the maid bumped the door outside by way of knocking, and barged into the room with the tea tray — a plump, country lass, lacking as yet the etiolated complexion of the Londoner. She smirked at Jim, dumped the tray on the table with a crash, and proceeded to light the gas. But Jim stopped her.

"No, no," he said; "there's plenty of light."

She complied, giggled, and returning to set the tea things, remarked:

"Eh, you are a funny one, Mr. Litham!"

"Am I?" he asked curiously. "Why?"

She giggled again in comprehensive reply. Staring at her idly in the half-light, Jim suddenly became conscious that her arms, bare to the elbow, were rounded and soft. Although she had waited upon him every day for more than two months, this curious phenomenon had only just dawned upon him. He laughed as he drew in his chair and smacked her forearm.

"Maggie," he said, "you're getting fat!"

"Eh, Mr. Litham!" '

"How's your 'boy,' Maggie?"

But Maggie was the area belle of Bloomsbury. "Which one, Mr. Litham?" she giggled from the door.

After tea, Jim, making grimaces, went across to a work table and fiddled about with a T square and compasses on a drawing board. He struck a match to light the gas; but, changing his mind, lit a cigarette instead, and stood staring out into the twilight. Just then a frolicsome wind fairy rattled the windowpane (or was it the senile chuckle of the Parcae?).[31]

"Oh, hang it," he announced, "I can't work. I wonder if Gee-gee's in? I'll go and see."

Too restless to sit on the uncomfortable knifeboard seat of a bus,[32] Jim decided to walk through the Green Park to Victoria, where Graham lived. Stepping briskly along the pavement with

---

[31] Parcae: the three Fates of ancient Rome (Atropos, Clotho, and Lachesis) who determine the course or "fate" of human life. Developed out of the goddess Parca, by identification with the Moerae of Greek mythology.

[32] Knifeboard (British): a seat on the roof of an omnibus.

thoughts of a cheap dinner in Soho and a theater or hall with Gee-gee afterwards, he came to the conclusion that he had never noticed how many pretty women there were in London. Ripe lips and sparkling eyes seemed hastening on all sides to bus or train. He felt unusually happy, suppressing, with an effort, a wild inclination to dance and sing. On turning into Waterloo Place a gust of wind nearly eloped with his hat. He laughed aloud at the idea, and wondered why that particular word should have leaped to his mind.

Then he became aware of a girl some twenty yards ahead of him. She wore a small black hat with a scarlet feather, a loose dark jacket and full skirt, and walked with a jaunty swing. Obeying a sudden impulse, he quickened his stride to overtake her, wishing to see whether the face was as alluring as the figure. He drew level as she reached the Duke of York's monument and began to trip lightly down the steps. Taking two at a time, Jim glanced sideways as he bounded past her. A glimpse of a pair of demure eyes made him miscalculate the next step; he stumbled, and jumped to save himself. There was a faint squeak behind him as he managed to recover his balance. Turning in time to field her parcel bouncing down the bottom steps, he was dimly aware of a rapid, appraising glance, quickly veiled in an expression of startled shyness.

"I'm awfully sorry!" said Jim, flushing as he raised his hat. "I'm afraid I — I startled you. I slipped, you know."

"I — I thought you were going to fall" — replacing the parcel in her small muff. "Thank you ever so much!"

She dropped her eyes and for a moment they stood in mutual embarrassment. Very conscious was Jim that she appeared attractive.

"Thank you," she said again shyly.

She bent her head, holding her rebellious hat in a gust of wind as she turned to move away. Jim thought that he saw the glimmer of a smile, but he stood sheepishly for a moment.

"I say —" he began feebly.

She had reached the corner of the passage before Jim hurried after her. She hastened; he overtook her.

"I say — are you in a hurry?"

"Yes," said she. "I'm going home."

"Oh! . . . You don't mind me talking to you, do you?" he inquired after fifty yards of silent company.

She pouted; Jim thought, adorably.

"You know you oughtn't to," she said.

"Yes, but you don't mind, do you?"

No answer.

"I say, let's come for a walk" — slightly astonished at his own boldness.

"Oh, I couldn't."

"Why not? Just round the park?"

The pace had gradually slackened as they reached the southern entrance.

"Well, you know I oughtn't to!" she replied, but turned with him.

They wandered round the lake, admiring the birdlife and chatting on other desultory topics. When she glanced up at him shyly, Jim noticed that her eyes were brown. He was silent for a moment as he thought of Madge.

"Oh," she exclaimed suddenly, with a pout. "I *am* naughty!"

"Isn't it nice!" retorted Jim with an effort.

"So am I," he added, suddenly remembering Graham and smitten with an inspiration. "I was going to call on a pal and we were going to dine at the Lyon d'Or. Do you know it?"

"No," she replied absently, staring at a heron.

"Oh, *do* look at that funny bird!"

"I say," said Jim as they strolled towards the Mall, bungling an attempt at nonchalance, "I know, come along and dine with me, instead?"

"Oh, I couldn't!" she exclaimed, turning startled eyes up at him.

"Oh, do! I'm sure you would enjoy it!"

She appeared genuinely troubled.

"Oh, I reelly couldn't — Besides, there isn't time — and we don't know each other!"

"Oh," said Jim persuasively, "that's easily fixed. Here's my card."

"Oh," she said, reading it. "What a nice name!"

"Do you think so?" said Jim uncomfortably.

"What's yours?"

"Miss Cafford — Eve."[33]

"Eve? Ripping!" he exclaimed with a nervous laugh. "How appropriate!"

"How?"

"Why" — gesturing — "in the Garden!"

"Oh!" She blushed and added: "But there aren't any nasty serpents!"

"Perhaps not, but let's come and have some apples!" he retorted, and flushed to the roots of his dark hair.

"Oh," she said ingenuously, "I love apples."

"Well, now we know each other, let's get a cab."

"Oh, but I couldn't come now — not tonight!"

"Oh, do, please! It's only half-past six now; you shall be home by eight."

"Promise?"

---

[33] In *Dark Refuge* Beadle's autobiographical protagonist is trapped in an embittered, loveless marriage with a woman named Eve: a religious fanatic who considers sex to be a joyless "duty" and who refuses to engage in it once she becomes pregnant. (More on this to follow.)

"I promise."

"Oh, I am naughty!" she said, as Jim hailed a passing hansom.

They dined at the Lyon d'Or. Eve drank wine under protest: "Only one glass, please." With the generous warmth of the grape Jim forgot his natural reserve, and becoming confidential, began to talk of his ambitions in architecture, of his pater in the country, but as the latter suggested Madge he hastily changed the subject. He thought Eve charming and sympathetic; she was an excellent listener, too. In the soft lights she appeared more attractive; her nose and chin were well modeled, her mouth a trifle large, with red, hungry lips, the whole forming a longish face under a cloud of brown hair.

She worked in a hat shop. Jim cried "What a beastly shame!" when she mentioned the long hours, and felt a warm thrill of self-approbation as he decided that it was his duty to make her lot happier in any way he could. Jim asked her to guess his age. After a critical study she suggested twenty-two. Enormously flattered, he admitted that he was nearly twenty. Eve pouted and said, a trifle mendaciously, that that was her age. He felt in closer sympathy with her over this strange coincidence.

Towards half-past eight, three men came in and occupied a table near the couple. One of the party recognized Eve, who explained to Jim that he was a friend of her brother's. Jim felt annoyed, chiefly because the incident interrupted his flow of egotism. He favored the man, darkly handsome, wearing a large walrus moustache, with an imperial frown of displeasure and mentally classed him as a "bounder."[34] Ten minutes later Graham appeared and joined the group. He raised his eyebrows and grinned approvingly. Jim flushed. Somehow he hoped Gee-gee would not come over to speak to him.

---

[34] Bounder: a man of objectionable social behavior: a cad.

However, Graham became engrossed in his dinner and his companions. Shortly afterwards Jim settled the bill and put Eve into a hansom. He had become very silent, glancing at her profile surreptitiously as they rode in the cab. In the intervals of silence he had been tortured by a sense of guilt towards Madge; not for the act but — although he did not formulate the reason — because he was offending the etiquette of introductions and the social scale. At first he had tried to assure himself that the adventure could not be repeated, yet he had eagerly seized upon her hard condition in life to play the Good Samaritan. But now the trouble was serious; he was vividly conscious in his wine-flushed brain of an ardent desire to kiss her. He strove valiantly to suppress the recreant emotion. He would not see her again. No: it was advisable not to do so. Yet it would be cowardly to run away from such a small temptation. He had always imagined sins to be in the form of orthodox devils; in size, color and ferocity according to the enormity. This one was only a tiny, yellow chap whom he could squash with one finger. And he prided himself upon his strength of will. Oh, it was merely the effect of the wine, he reasoned solemnly: in the morning — Suddenly he blurted out:

"I say, do let me see you again?"

"Y-es, if you think you'd reelly like to," she murmured.

"Of course I do," responded Jim eagerly. "Will you come and have tea with me tomorrow?"

"I should love to," she declared, and looked round at him as the cab stopped under a lamppost.

"All right, I'll meet you at four."

She pouted as he opened the door and alighted to assist her to dismount.

CHAPTER III

So on the following day Jim took Eve to tea in Regent Street; and afterwards they adjourned to dinner in Soho in time for the theater. On Sunday they went up the river to Hampton Court, although the weather was chilly.

On the Thursday evening Graham found Jim at home endeavoring to work, which he had discovered to be more distasteful than ever.

"Hello, old man!" exclaimed Graham, grinning.

"Hello, Gee-gee!" returned Jim, throwing down a pencil with great enthusiasm. "I'm glad you've come."

"I say," exclaimed Graham, in tones of mock admiration, as he straddled a chair, "I say, you are going it! Thought you'd take your Nunky's[35] advice, eh?"

"I don't understand what you mean," said Jim loftily.

"Don't under—" Graham broke into laughter.

"Oh my Lord! Well, where did you pick her up, Jim?"

"What the devil's that got to do with you?" demanded Jim angrily. "And I didn't pick her up. I met her."

Graham stared at him.

"All right, Jim. No offence. But she —"

"Oh, yes, I know that black-muzzled pal of yours knows her," continued Jim at white heat. "And I suppose he's been lying. I know all about it. He's only a pal of her brother. And if you're going to talk like that you can get out of it!" Breaking a cigarette between his angry fingers, he flung it into the grate savagely. "It's damned unfair. Because a girl has to earn her own living,

---

[35] Nunky (British colloquial): an uncle.

everybody thinks he can throw mud at her. She's a jolly good little soul and works a thunderin' sight harder than you or I —"

"I believe you!"

"Shut up!" snapped Jim. "You never think for a moment what it means to a poor girl. I admire her. She's a dear little pal and nothing else, d'you understand? If I can help her in any way I'm going to, and I *won't* have anything said against her."

"But good Lord," began Graham; then grimacing at the wrath in Jim's face, he broke into a vulgar whistle. "You must be dry after all that."

Jim half smiled and offered a cigarette, which was accepted with feigned timidity.

On his return late that evening, Jim found a letter from Madge awaiting him. It was merely a note telling him that she had been in town since Monday and that he must come to see her. After a moment his delight quickly changed to acute chagrin as he realized that she had been three whole days in the same city without seeing him. From the time of his departure he had counted every day to her coming until — well, until last week. Why had she not written from home? Why couldn't he have met her? He felt deeply aggrieved and jealous, suspecting that the Tranvers fellow had something to do with it. To his mild astonishment he discovered that he was not *quite* so excited at the idea of seeing her as he had expected to be. For instance, he could sleep: whereas on every eve of his return from school he had not had a wink the whole night at the prospect of seeing Madge once more.

Having acquired a half day off for the occasion, he presented himself at the residence of Madge's aunt, in Highgate, punctually at 4 p.m. Unfortunately, Madge had not returned from a shopping expedition, with the result that Jim wore the bloom off the grooming of his frock coat and hair over an uncomfortable tea with the aunt. However, at last Madge did arrive, and Jim was content to feast his eyes upon her. To his delight she was wearing the locket he had given her; also a new dress. Naturally he must stay to dinner, as of course she could not dine alone with him without a chaperone. Several times he winced when the light shone on her brown eyes. They were so like Eve's; though even to him there seemed a wistful, caged expression in her eyes which was lacking in Eve's. Once he was half ashamed at the thought that Eve was condemned to work hard and long, while Madge had little or nothing to do.

With more than two months' town experience behind him, Jim rioted as a man of the world in the company of these two women. Madge, it appeared, had been to a play with her aunt and some friends. Captain Tranvers had fortunately been there — here Jim scowled — and had taken them all to supper afterwards. Jim immediately proposed a dinner and play, quite prepared to ruin himself for their entertainment. But as the aunt had since contracted an attack of rheumatic gout, the need of a *suitable* chaperone vetoed the proposal for the moment.

After dinner the two young people were allowed a tête-à-tête in one corner of the room, while the aunt crocheted. Jim plunged into a further account of his doings, to which Madge listened with that ruminative, affectionate look peculiar to her. Having exhausted a bowdlerized description of his friends and London generally, he hesitated a moment and then said:

"And you know, Madge — I meant to tell you in my letters, but I forgot for the moment — last week I met rather a nice girl."

"Have you, Jim?" said Madge, looking across at her aunt.

"Of course," continued Jim, bowing to the god of his fathers, "she's quite a common girl — works for a living, you know, in a hat shop. But she has eyes very much like yours. That's why I — I — er — liked her — not *like*, you know — but you know what

I mean. I think it's awfully hard lines,"[36] he went on as Madge had apparently no comment to offer, "having to work so hard — oh, awful hours. I — I — just for fun, to give her a treat, y'know — I took her up the river and to dinner — *once* — in Soho. I wish I could take you tonight. Wouldn't it be ripping, Madge?"

"Yes, it would!" said Madge with unusual energy. "But of course I couldn't."

"Of course not," concurred Jim. "But, I say, couldn't you rake out someone to act as chaperone? Do try. And I want you to come to tea and see my rooms. You must; won't you, Madge?"

"But who am I to get? Auntie hardly knows a soul."

"Oh, hang it!" exclaimed Jim with fervor. "I wish we were at home again."

"Yes, so do I, but still I do want to see something of London. And I'm going back next Wednesday."

"Oh, what a rotten shame!" exclaimed Jim indignantly. "Write and tell the mater that you want to stay longer. Your aunt wants you to, doesn't she?"

"Y-es, I should like to, but mother hates me to be away from her, Jim. You know how fidgety she is."

"Yes, but hang it, you can't be tied up to her for good!" protested Jim.

"Yes, I know, but I must go back. You'll be coming down at Easter, won't you, Jim?"

"Yes, rather, but —"

He became conscious of a strange sense of irritation against her. He wished that she would be a little less placid; show more spirit, even if it were in opposition to him. And as he gazed at her the extreme orderliness of her hair vaguely annoyed him.

---

[36] The OED defines this as a strict or inflexible policy, belief, or stance. Also, an uncompromising adherence to such a policy.

The next moment he was distressed, as if he were guilty of lèse-majesté.

However, after a long consultation with Aunt Ruth, who raised many objections, which were attacked and overridden by Jim with great vigor, it was arranged that on Saturday they should visit Jim's rooms after tea and that she would chaperone Madge to dinner at a quiet restaurant; although she could not be made to comprehend why anybody wished to dine out when there was a very good dinner at home.

Accordingly the following day Jim rang up Eve on the 'phone to tell her that he would be unable to keep their appointment as an aunt, with whom he had to dine, had arrived from the country. But Eve had evidently heard of rural aunts, for she replied:

"Oh, you are naughty, Jim. Do your aunts come to town *very* often?"

"Don't be absurd!" retorted Jim, vastly indignant at her perspicacity.

"O-oh, don't be cross, Jim," she replied. "I was looking forward so much to seeing you again."

"Were you really?" he inquired, completely mollified, and made another appointment.

It would take so long to explain everything, and she wouldn't understand, he complained to his unquiet conscience afterwards, wholly oblivious of the platonic gospel he had preached to her.

On the morning of *the* day Jim solicited Maggie's extra attentions to the dusting of his rooms, whereat Maggie desired to know if Jim's young lady was coming, which he haughtily denied. But Maggie could not conceive of a world in which nice young men did not have nice young ladies, and said so. Nor when, without instructions, she brought in tea for two, could she be made to understand that he had *not* been disappointed, proffering her sincere sympathy that perhaps the "young leddy" might turn up after all. At half-past six, when Madge and Aunt Ruth arrived and were admitted by the admiring Maggie, Jim rushed from the room in festal attire to welcome them. The aunt sat in state in the most comfortable armchair admiring the room and the floral decorations which Jim strove to infer were the customary order of his habitat, while Madge inspected his household gods under his depreciatory guidance. Much enthusiasm, however, was damped by her practical mind as, sweeping the top of a picture frame with one finger, she observed: "Really, Jim, you ought to make them *clean* your rooms occasionally."

"I do," said Jim dolefully. "I told them only this morning."

"Good gracious," commented the aunt, who thoroughly concurred with her niece's spirit, "what must the room have been like before?"

After this captious criticism, which Jim as a right-minded young male resented, he somewhat sulkily suggested that he should send for the cab. Scarcely had Jim's hand released the bell rope than Maggie appeared, very smart in cap and apron, and intent upon taking stock of the visitors. As they drove to the restaurant Jim struggled hard to erase the impression that the visit had not been a success by remembering that as "she" had spoken, it must be right, resolving that he would take Maggie severely to task. But the dinner, in spite of his single-handed efforts, seemed to flag; for all of which he felt himself responsible. Afterwards, on reflection, he decided that the presence of Aunt Ruth had been to blame.

On the Sunday he rose early, to Maggie's astonishment, and went to Highgate to attend church and dine. During the sermon shadows of the old doubts returned. He looked curiously at those about him, feeling an overwhelming desire to confide in someone. Aunt Ruth was staring fixedly at the pulpit, her usual prim air of conscious righteousness magnified. By her side, too, Madge's eyes were in the same direction. Calm and contented, full of deep thought, reminding him of something which he could not recall. Then in a second the likeness flashed into his mind — a cow chewing the cud on a summer afternoon. He flushed with angry scorn of himself, and tried to fix his mind on the monotonous voice of the vicar. Yet control his attention he could not. Questions leaped to his mind as trout at flies in a Scotch pool. A sense of guilt and a shadowy fear that a thunderbolt might strike him for impiety, haunted him. Again he glanced at Madge. How cold she was! She was never troubled with these insane queries. When they were together she would be able to soothe and calm his mind. His thoughts flew off at a tangent. He recalled the night he had said "Goodbye" to her and the expectations he had had of life. Life! What a disappointment it had all been. Of course he did not know exactly what he had expected — something great and moving. Yet here he was, well launched in the midst of life, and nothing had happened. Everything jogged on monotonously — unless those things which his circle of acquaintances considered worthwhile were the salt of life. He shuddered at the idea, and moved in his seat as if he were afraid of contaminating Madge beside him. What did he want to do? He did not know; merely a blind desire to reach out to capture the shadow of something he could not see. It was there, he knew, that great Something in life. But what? He felt Madge's eyes reproving his restlessness. Madge? Yes. No: it was something that he and Madge must find together; or perhaps he had to search alone. He remembered imagining himself a knight and that he was bidding farewell to Madge ere he set forth in quest of the Holy Grail. Suddenly he hungered for someone in whom he could confide. He felt as if his Ego were battering at the walls of his consciousness for expression. The terrible sense of child-loneliness possessed him.

He felt as if Madge and all the people around him had suddenly been removed to a million miles away: he could see them receding across eons of space, straining his lungs in vain attempts to implore them not to leave him alone in icy, desolate misery. . . .[37]

"And now to God the Father . . ."

The minister's words and the shuffle of the congregation recalled him with a jerk. He caught Madge's eye and smiled. To his surprise she stared a moment and whispered:

"What's the matter, Jim?"

"Nothing," he replied, and dived for the hymnbook, feeling half ashamed and half frightened.

To his annoyance Madge was engaged to dine out on the Monday and Tuesday, so that he did not see her again before she left for home. Always had he been mentally sore after any of these attacks of "unhealthy broodings," as Graham called them. He spent these evenings with him. On meeting Eve on the Saturday afternoon he was really glad to see her again, or rather was flattered by her frank delight. When they were dining together in a new, little restaurant they had discovered in Soho, he was startled by a passing thought which was prompted by the lack of conventional restraint and by the soothing vanity that upon Eve he was conferring a favor, whereas in the rarefied atmosphere of Madge upon her high pedestal, he felt chilled. In the comparative proximity of the two the strange likeness, and

---

[37] Compare this to the cosmic imagery of the narrator-protagonist whirling through intergalactic space at the conclusion of Beadle's *Dark Refuge*. According to psychologist Carl Jung, such symbolism (appearing in archetypal dreams and fantasies) is symptomatic of emotional isolation and withdrawal from the mundane world. It can also be symptomatic of a traumatic sense of abandonment experienced after the death of a parent in early childhood or adolescence. In any case, without an authentic human connection, there can be no "grounding" upon the earth.

yet utter dissimilarity, was the more apparent. He divined, but could not articulate, that Eve seemed to understand him as a man better than Madge could. It was apparent in many small ways: little acts in which Madge would have disappointed him, Eve seemed to comprehend and do instinctively. And yet but a little while since he had felt and said, that Madge understood him better than anyone. But that was different somehow. The expression in Eve's eyes, too, was different: deeper and more sympathetic, seeing more into common motives than Madge. And with Eve he felt more inclined to enjoy himself than to fall into his moods of abstraction and tendency to metaphysics generally, usually concomitant with the proximity of Madge. He felt jollier with the one, and happier with the other. Oh why, he reflected, could they not be one! And straightway, consistently with semi-educated snobbishness and his exaltation of Madge, he felt that the thought was an insult to her.

On the following Sunday Jim had promised to meet Eve and have a jaunt to Kew. But all day there had been a deluge. He could not telephone to her home to postpone the appointment, so he was compelled to meet her; and as there were no tea shops open in London on the Sabbath, he hesitatingly suggested that she should come to his rooms. She assented. They took a hansom and drove there. Suddenly Jim became very silent as they approached their destination. For some absurd reason he half expected to see Madge awaiting him in the room. Of course she was not there; so leaving Eve, who discarded her hat and coat on entering, he went below instead of ringing, and very agitatedly instructed Maggie to prepare a special tea for two at five o'clock, whereat Maggie wanted to know whether it was for Jim's "financy." He indignantly denied the charge and returned slowly upstairs, pondering an excuse to meet Maggie outside the door and carry in the tray himself, fearing comments she might make on beholding another "young leddy."

Although he had never found the time hang heavily in Eve's company, the half hour seemed to be a small eternity. Acutely conscious on a sudden that her eyes were very soft and her lips very red, Jim showed her his "pots" and other treasures. An interest which she developed in the very picture on which Madge had laid the charge of filthiness, made him more uncomfortable than ever. Eve's hair, too, had a knack of tickling his face as she bent beside him to examine a photograph album.

However, at last Maggie's feet and heavy breathing were heard outside, and the tea arrived. Eve withstood Maggie's bold scrutiny, and presided over the table very charmingly. As the afternoon wore on he became more and more self-conscious. Towards seven o'clock, after an abortive attempt to play the mandolin with nerve-twitching fingers — which Eve pronounced "lovely"! — he suggested that it was time for dinner. As he helped Eve into her jacket, assisting to guide the refractory balloon sleeves, he, inadvertently, pulled a strand of her hair. She cried out and pouted. Jim smothered an apology on her lips, her head seeming to fall back to meet him. It was a long, lingering kiss.

Jim released her. He apologized abjectly. Eve seemed covered in blushing confusion. She caught him by the arm appealingly.

"Oh, Jim, *why* did you kiss me?"

"I tried not to," he said truthfully. "Really I did."

"Oh, why did you!" she cried in distress. "No man has ever kissed me before."

For the fraction of a second a sense of proportion hovered in his mind, but it was drowned as he looked into her eyes, earnest and steady. She plucked at his arm as if compelling faith.

"You *do* believe me, don't you, Jim?"

"Yes," he said solemnly. "I do, Eve."

She clung to him for a moment. As he released her she pouted. They went out of the room in silence.

CHAPTER IV

ONE of the many verities masquerading as a cynicism is that two things which a man never forgets are the first kiss and the last. To the soul of Jim there came in that first full kiss a tumultuous intoxication, far surpassing any dream of bliss. He was fearful as his imagination seized upon it hungrily. All that evening he was unusually silent, conscious that now Eve stood as a symbol of something wholly different. The thought of Madge made him wince, knowing himself guilty and fearful of his weakness. The little, pale yellow devil of temptation grew into a huge purple monster. With an effort he endeavored to readjust his perspective, and determined that it should not happen again. But that very evening while driving Eve home she looked at him, pouted, and — he kissed her once more.

That was Easter week. On the Thursday he was thankful for the excuse to go home. By the time that he had reached the fresh countryside, things seemed to assume a normal air. Yet those haunting kisses refused to be banished; even in the very presence of Madge they returned, driving him to an ecstasy of remorse. And Madge too seemed altered. He tried to hate himself because it was so. They rode for miles as they had used to do, but it was all different. A phantom wall seemed between them: the kisses. He loathed himself for looking at Madge's lips and wondering . . .

No more was he troubled with those "unhealthy breedings." He even felt self-conscious under his father's eyes, which seemed to be ever peering at him questioningly. Then in rarer moments of reaction Madge appeared to him to be a being of more ineffable superiority than ever: and himself unworthy to be near her — all because of two kisses and an imagination!

However, the few days of the holidays were soon over. Jim arrived back in London. At first he refused to see Eve, contenting himself with Graham. But on Saturday he met her and by mutual consent they went to tea at his rooms.

So for a month this idyll pursued an innocent course, what time the first rapture abated and Jim began once more to hypnotize himself into the belief that his motives were of pure chivalry: after all, he argued, there was no harm in a kiss, such might surely come under the category of the platonic. Then on the receipt of a sarcastic note from Graham, he unwisely sought to make amends for his desertion by spending an evening with them. But their bawdy leers were too much for his dignity and tender conscience. He did not repeat the experiment.

During this period, by force of necessity for his peace of mind, he developed the popular faculty of thinking in separate compartments: *id est*, never to commit the error of leaving the doors of the mind open, lest, peradventure, reason stalk into the chamber of sentiment, or duty enter the bedroom of desire.

Although Eve continued to be the pensive maid, salted by a charming coquettishness which had so enchanted Jim in the first instance, there were moments when her delicious habit of pouting childishly merged into petulance, mystifying him to the point of irritation. And some phrase, innocently meant he was assured, constrained him to warn her solemnly of the influence of the evil minds of her associates in the shop. That he was in love with her he resolutely refused to admit: merely a platonic affection, he repeated with the insistency of an incantation. This theory of pure chivalry he was pleased to propound to Eve with pathetic emphasis and frequency, dilating upon the pleasure it gave him to see her enjoying herself after her arduous labors; whereat Eve would thank him prettily — if with a thought of sarcasm unperceived by Jim through the fog of his self-complacency — and pout. Then as Jim, if opportunity served, kissed her to prove his consistency, her eyes demurely observed the universe through the fringe of his dark hair. He even accomplished the meritorious feat of reprimanding himself while actually enjoying the erethismic[38] thrill which her kisses gave him: and the nearest approach to lucidity he attained was to argue that he was unable to break off the intimacy because it would cause her pain. Throughout he was consciously proud of the fact that he always thought of her interests to the exclusion of his own; indeed, so tough was this conviction that he succeeded in stretching it to the point that, on the rare occasions when he permitted the memory of Madge to intrude into the mind chamber[39] dedicated to Eve, the painful qualms resulting were resolved into martyrdom on Eve's behalf.

However, as surely as the tides obey the moon, there came a night during which Jim watched the gray dawn percolating slowly through the dingy windows; sleepless hours spent in

---

[38] Erethismic (obsolete): a term translated from the French as "excited or irritated." From the noun *erethism*: abnormal irritability or responsiveness to stimulation. (From French *éréthisme*, from Greek *erethismos*, irritation, from *erethizein* to irritate; akin to Greek *ornynai* to rouse.) Beadle must have been fond of the word; it reappears in his story "Black Velvet," published in *This Quarter* in 1932. There, he portrays "The jazz of the jungle muted to the yapping of curs, cries of children, bleating of goats, lowing of cattle; and ululating in staccato, shrill notes, round and yellow, velvety, erethismic as a woman's caress." (More on "Black Velvet" and *This Quarter* below.)

[39] Through the creation of a witty conceit, the narrator of *Dark Refuge* is able to enter the "brain chambers" or "skull chambers" of the chief protagonists in the tale. The references in *A Passionate Pilgrimage* to "mind chambers" and to the multiplicity of the self and its various ego states shows that Beadle was already preoccupied with such concerns as early as 1915.

futile recriminations, alternating with a faint disgust ever swamped in wondering delight.

The memory of Madge seemed swept to a distance; still his ideal, but too ineffably holy for him to dare to gaze upon. In the morning he was due home for Whitsun.[40] He did not want to go; he dared not go. Until he saw Eve again his mind was in a turmoil. He did not know what he thought or felt. Then he did not care. He refused to think of Madge or anything. The influx of passion swept him away as a straw in a millrace:[41] on the flood he was reduced to a primitive young savage accepting without thought the gifts the gods were pleased to send. Madge's letters were left unanswered; in fact he succeeded, while under the potent spell, in banishing every troublesome thought from him; abandoning his ideals and fancies, he tacitly agreed with the views of Graham and his friends. He looked on the world and women with different eyes. After all, what did it matter? Every teaching of his fellows at school and since, even history, classic and modern, taught that every man had a mistress.

Then followed halcyon days during which Jim dallied in a trampled by-lane of love, never doubting, never thinking, never caring: drunk in his worship at the shrine of Eros. Prosaic study had ever been irksome, so little wonder that the charms of his first inamorata proved too much for mundane resolutions. Work became of secondary importance; more joy was there in the house of Jim over one lingering kiss than in the solving of ninety and nine architectural problems.

---

[40] Whitsun: relating to Whitsunday, from Old English *hwīta sunnandaeg*, literally, white Sunday (probably from the custom of wearing white robes after being baptized during this season). Whitsunday is also known as Pentecost.

[41] Millrace: a canal in which water flows to and from a mill wheel. Also, the current that drives the wheel.

But this inebriated phase lasted barely six weeks. If moral scruples were still drugged, those fanciful ideals of his youth and kin to his temperament began to stir sluggishly. A pale phantom of the old desire for fullness and understanding of life arose and beckoned fitfully. When alone moody contemplation of Madge afflicted him. Remorse for his treatment of her seized him. He felt that she was still the ineffable being of his youth, but that he had fallen beyond her ken or sympathy.

Then towards the end of June the immutable law of cause and effect completely awakened him from uneasy slumber, and a vision of the future was conjured up with nightmare realism. One twilight evening as he was seated at his table making a half-hearted attempt to work a light knock at the door aroused him. He turned in his chair and sighed, as Eve, who now had the entry to his rooms at any hour, came in. Sitting on the edge of the table beside him, she opened a side drawer and helped herself to a cigarette.

"You are a naughty darling," she said, blowing smoke. "Why didn't you ring me up?"

"I didn't promise," protested Jim. "And I must get *some* work done."

"Oh, twiddles!" she exclaimed. "You know you'd rather come to me, wouldn't you, you silly ole darling?"

"Yes," said Jim sheepishly.

"Pooh!" she pouted, "and I could have got off at seven! I waited for you till nearly eight, then I thought I might as well come along and cheer you up — and you need it, too! What's the matter, Jim? You look as if you'd dropped a suv'rin and found a tanner! Lemme come!"

She planted herself on his knee and soothingly caressed him. They sat chatting for some time.

"I say, ole boy, I've got some news for you," she said suddenly. "Can't you guess?" as he looked enquiringly. "Why, you soppy ole thing!

Gimme a kiss and I'll tell you!"

Stooping, she imprinted a long kiss on his ready lips: and then, pulling his head on one side, whispered in his ear. He started as if someone had struck him.

"Good Lord!"

Almost roughly pushing her off his knee, he got up, walked over to the fire, and leaned against the mantelshelf.

"Good Lord!"

Greatly perturbed, he began to pace up and down. She sat on the vacated chair, and watched him in interrogative silence.

"Jim darling," she said presently, "what's the matter? Why d'you keep away from me?"

He made no answer, but continued the march, his thoughts in a whirl. She pouted and made childish grimaces, but as this failed to draw him, she rose and pulled him to her.

"Kiss me!" she commanded.

He obeyed, almost mechanically. Pushing him into a big armchair, she knelt at his feet.

"Don't worry, ole boy, it's all right! We can easily get married!" An expression of anxiety flitted across her face. "You *will* marry me?" she demanded.

"Er — I don't know — er — yes, of course," he began incoherently. "Oh, Eve!"

"Don't be potty," she said, a trifle sharply.

"Oh!" as he frowned, "if you're going to be cross and nasty, I'll go. You make as much fuss as if" — threatening tears — "Oh, I don't know — I —"

"All right, Eve, I'll pull myself together — only, you know —" bending towards her — "it was a surprise! *That* never entered my head."

"Well, isn't that like a man!" she pouted. "Why, what did you —"

"Why," he interrupted, naively, "did *you* expect it?"

"Why, you naughty ole thing, of course I did."

His eyebrows arched in surprise, and his face became serious. She nestled into his arms and began to weep softly. Although depressed and fearful, he comforted and kissed her as she insisted that he should do. But as soon as he could persuade her to go, he escorted her home.

On leaving her with renewed promises, he turned towards the park trying to grapple with the unexpected. The effect at first seemed as if some bandage which had blindfolded him had been suddenly removed and that the light dazzled him. Why had he been such a fool? Why had he not foreseen? What was he to do? Fellow pedestrians flitted past him like ghosts. Everything seemed unreal. He narrowly avoided being run over by a van, and for a moment regretted that he had escaped. He crashed into a lamppost at he raced along, and was a homicidal maniac for quite fifty seconds as someone's laugh rang in his ear. . . .

The very first thought that had entered his head when Eve had spoken had been of his father. Good God! He literally gasped at the idea of telling him. No; that was unthinkable. Yet he was in honor bound to marry her. Of that there was no doubt. . . . In a great, throat-burning wave of emotion came the thought of Madge. Now that the blinding scales of passion were gone the memory of his old adoration returned overwhelmingly. He had defiled himself and lost her for good. How could he have been so mad, so utterly insane? Oh God, it was bitter! He had ruined his life before he had started. On a sudden he recalled his wild protestations that life had been disappointing, too placid and monotonous. He had not realized then that he was only wading in knee-deep; but now the strong current had swept him out into midstream, and he felt that he was nigh to drowning.

Finding that his legs had brought him home, he rushed up to his rooms and flung himself on the bed. With the light burning, he smoked cigarettes feverishly, trying to determine what he should do. That his father must know nothing was imperative. He was dependent upon him for the next five years at the least. Well, marriage would save her name at all events. He must pay the price. And even if he could not settle everything now, that did not remove the necessity for reparation. Yet — Madge . . . He loathed himself. . . . Suddenly, as an idea thrust into his mind by an alien force, came a fragment of the marriage service — to love and to cherish.

Love? Did he love her? Good heavens! He hated her. Had he loved her? He had always been fond of her — and — his mind fled the question. Yet they had perpetually sung the lovers' litany. He revolted at the memory, but he could not deny it. Love! No, no, no, he had only loved Madge. Always had. Always would. *That* was love: not the other — not Eve's. Yet, persisted memory, he had sworn to Eve that he loved her. He groaned aghast — in the astonishment with which one contemplates actions in a dream. And what a criminal fool he had been to Eve as well as himself. Oh! If he had only thought. But he forgot that youth disdainfully refuses to think: if not, how could one be young? He had some vague idea of the civil ceremony at the Registrar's Office. One had simply to give notice, pay the fee, sign a book, and it was all over. Tied up together for life! At the thought he shuddered. That, however, he decided, was what they would do. He would take a day off for the purpose. Surely he might have a holiday on such an occasion? He smiled dismally at the thought. He had often stolen days for less auspicious events. With a sigh he remembered THE CAREER which had been mapped out for him. He had in imagination already designed the brass nameplate and office.

Even yet he had not realized the full meaning of what this alteration in his life would entail: a terrific sense of calamity felt, but not wholly understood. The dominant idea was that having committed an injustice, he must make amends without counting the cost to himself. Married! The very terms seemed strange and unnatural. He had vaguely imagined that state as being exalted and noble. And with Madge — Oh God! . . . He winced and stared dully at the gas jet. . . . Presently his thoughts appeared to go on again from the same point, as a machine rewound. What difference could the mechanical register of names in a book and payment of a fee possibly make in one's feelings? Or even the Church ceremony? Yes — that was more or less solemn. A ceremony? Yes: but how could that alter one's sentiments? The question kept recurring with irritating persistence. Real marriage must be an ideal state. Ah, with Madge . . . Then the corollary was that it was the person that mattered: not the ceremony. Surely, for what possible difference could a metal ring and the term "my wife" create? It was legal. Legal! He was to marry in order to make it legal. He had experienced married life, but that was not legal. He must have a license to be considered respectable — as has to be bought to keep a dog, only that it cost a penny more. He shuddered at the thought.

"Then my father —" He stopped short, not daring to finish that thought. Jim had always held his father in such high veneration: almost as a god who could do no wrong. Yet now Jim felt that even his father had dropped many degrees in his estimation. Sick and appalled by his own thoughts which had run amok, he lay sleepless till the dawn.

CHAPTER V

TOWARDS four o'clock of the following day Jim disconsolately jostled his way along the Strand and turned up Bedford Street. On the corner he halted irresolutely, the dank drizzle of the midsummer day dripping from his hat and mackintosh. He surveyed a passing vegetable barrow and two bibulous walking-on[42] gentlemen of the Maiden Lane fraternity with gloomy indifference; stared moodily at the shapely leg of a chorus girl high-stepping into a hansom as if she were the apotheosis of all his troubles, and walked with dragging feet up Henrietta Street past a window which bore the legend:

"Births, Deaths, and Marriages."

Feeling that every passerby must know the full details of his mission, he slunk on, casting a sidelong glance at the inscription. The two latter epochs of human life he had regarded as in the far distance: now they both seemed to have been suddenly brought to unpleasant proximity. He found himself wondering why "Marriages" had been placed last; surely they ought to have been written in the correct order — Births, Marriages, and Deaths? But perhaps it was an omen, a

---

[42] Walking-on: an obscure term that had me completely stumped, finding absolutely no trace of it until I consulted with Beadle's great-niece. According to Patricia, the sentence refers to the once-disreputable Covent Garden / Maiden Lane area of London: a red-light district then known for its prostitutes. "Walking-on gentlemen" would refer to the men who were loitering there. (The phrase is probably the equivalent of *kerb crawling* or *cruising*.)

warning. He considered the question with grave-faced concern, attempting nonchalant interest in an adjacent shop; then sauntered back to the entrance, and halted again. The somber, businesslike exterior of the Registrar's Office seemed to dissolve all his honorable intentions. Feeling as if he were on the brink of another world, he dreaded the act of stepping off familiar terra firma. However, sticking out his nether lip in the effort of determination and casting furtive glances up and down the street, as a novice entering a pawnbroker's, he wheeled round jerkily and marched in.

Through the office counter window he saw a prosaic-looking clerk in spectacles and tallow hair. A sudden uncontrollable nervousness took possession of Jim. He stood staring stupidly at the clerk. "What on earth does one say?" he wondered. Why hadn't he thought this out before? "Please, I want to get married" seemed foolish; besides, he *did not*. The clerk smiled encouragingly and said, "Good morning!" Jim mumbled something inaudible and hesitated. With an effort he regained control, and looked less like a sheep going to the butcher's shop.

"Oh, I just wanted to enquire about a license," he said. "A marriage one, don't you know," he added flurriedly,[43] fearful that the clerk might misunderstand, and wondering why one should not have to take out a license to be born and to die; all these events seemed equally unavoidable and spontaneous.

"Oh, yes," answered the clerk, smiling dryly. "Will you just step into the room — the next door on the right?"

Jim paused a moment in doubt, as if he suspected a trap, and then did as he was bid. He found a plainly furnished room, containing a long businesslike table and leather-covered chairs. Presently there came to him an elderly man, gray of moustache and hair, bespectacled and kindly, to whom Jim repeated his

---

[43] Flurriedly: in an agitated or confused manner.

careless inquiry. The official smiled a benign smile, seeming to Jim reminiscent of a physician's bedside manner.

"Oh, yes," he said suavely. "What age is the lady?"

"Nineteen," said Jim unsuspiciously.

"And you are about nineteen, too?"

"Oh," said Jim, flushing, "I — I was only inquiring."

The blue eyes behind the spectacles seemed to read the secrets of his soul, as maybe they did, well-versed from long experience in the ways of a young man and a marriage license.

"Nineteen," amended Jim guiltily, "last January."

"Then, of course, you have the lady's mother's consent?"

"Oh," murmured Jim, and after a moment: "Oh, I could easily get that."

"And your people are living?"

"Er — yes; my father," Jim admitted reluctantly, foreseeing the next statement.

"And you have his consent, too?"

"Well, no — that is, not yet. But — er — can't we get married without that?"

"I'm afraid not," smiled the recorder of the Three Gates, and gently propounded the English law concerning minors and marriages.

Crestfallen, yet with a strange sense of relief flooding his mind, caused possibly by a sudden burst of sunshine, Jim departed after shaking hands with the sympathetic official as if he were a benefactor.

In the evening Jim diffidently informed Eve of his experience.

"You *are* a fool!" she retorted, with a greater display of temper than he had ever seen before. "I'm twenty-fo— I mean, why didn't you say you were twenty-one — and me, too?"

"I — I didn't think of it until it was too late," protested Jim, feeling that he had been an accomplice in the law's refusal.

Eve pouted and softened suddenly.

"Oh, Jim darling, you are naughty," she murmured to his coat collar. . . ." I know what," she added, looking up.

"What?" said Jim gloomily.

"We can go to Scotland!"

"But Gretna Green's[44] been done away with."

"Oh, you are naughty. I don't mean any ole Gretna Greens. If you're there you've only got to say you're married before witnesses and you are! . . . Darling, we *will* go, won't we?"

"But that can't be right," protested Jim, to whom the idea that a canny nation like the Scotch could be so lax in such a serious matter seemed absurd.

However, on consulting a Whitaker's Almanac he discovered that her statement held a grain of truth; that, at any rate, youth was not a bar to matrimonial infelicity. So it was settled that they would make the pilgrimage to the land of Burns, who, had he been alive, would doubtless have been able to give Jim other and more potent advice.

During the week he worked in a half-hearted and desultory fashion. The alteration in his life and the probable consequences weighed heavily on his mind. Although steadfastly adhering to what he had considered to be his duty, the thought of what might have been tormented him.

On a Friday evening, one week before the date appointed for the trip to Edinburgh, Jim sat after dinner staring moodily into a warm July twilight, smoking cigarettes. Work was impossible; the whole affair preyed upon his mind. He was really pining to pour forth his soul to someone in sympathy with him, although he neither knew it nor would have confessed it. Consequently,

---

[44] Gretna Green: a village in southern Scotland, on the English border, that was a common destination for eloping couples seeking to wed under Scotland's more lenient marriage laws. From 1754 until 1940 these marriages were legally conducted by blacksmiths who were colloquially known as "anvil priests."

he felt ill-humored, restless and miserable. Reticent and sensitive by nature, he feared the possible flippant remarks of an unsympathetic critic who would not understand. Several times he had been on the point of confiding in Graham, but shrank at the critical moment.

As he sat puffing a cigarette, Maggie's shrill voice was heard at the door. Graham walked in. Relieved that someone had come to distract his thoughts, Jim welcomed his friend warmly. Graham commenced talking of the superlative charms of a new dancer at the Empire. But gradually Jim resumed his moody contemplation of the chimney tops against a splash of smoky russet red. Graham ceased to chat. For a short while he sat and watched Jim's gloomy face. Presently he leaned forward and tapped his friend sharply on the knee, saying:

"Come, Jim, wake up!"

Jim started nervously: he appeared to have forgotten Graham's presence.

"I'm awfully sorry, old man. What were you saying about La—la—? I've rather a rotten memory."

Graham laughed.

"Jimmy, you ass! What the devil's the matter? Now," as Jim made an irritable gesture, "don't lose your temper with me. Now, then, be sensible and let off steam. It'll do you all the good in the world."

Jim kicked a hassock maliciously.

"Yes, that's splendid!" commented Graham. "Kick that rather than me!"

Jim smiled faintly, realizing vaguely that he was behaving like a peevish schoolgirl.

"I'm sorry, Gee-gee. I don't think I know what is the matter with me. I feel cross, miserable; and to tell the truth, I don't exactly know what I do want, except —"

He paused. Graham drew his chair nearer, and leaning forward, looked him straight in the eyes.

"Well — except what?"

Jim dropped his eyes and showed further signs of peevishness.

"Nothing, I tell you; absolutely nothing."

"Now, old man," commenced Graham firmly, "pull yourself together. You must think that I'm blind, man! Look me in the eyes! That's it. Is it . . . woman?"

Jim averted his eyes.

"I thought so. Who is she? . . . Not Eve?"

Jim sullenly nodded his head.

"I'm a fool," he declared impressively.

Graham thought the remark obvious.

"But somehow one doesn't like to — Oh, you know what I mean."

Graham nodded. Still apparently interested in the twilit sky, Jim poured out the whole story from beginning to end. Graham sat smoking, silently watching the speaker. Now and again he would nod and smile faintly, patronizing Jim from the stupendous height of his superior world knowledge. When the recital came to the point regarding the journey to Scotland, Graham whistled softly and appeared about to interrupt. However, he refrained, until Jim wound up with the phrase:

"Thank heaven! I've got that off my mind."

"And thank heaven you've told me," added Graham.

"Yes, I'm glad, old boy," began Jim gratefully.

"Wait; you don't understand."

"Don't understand what?" enquired Jim.

For a while Graham sat staring anxiously at the window as if he hoped to find some assistance there.

"Oh, damnation!" he muttered.

"Well, don't you think that I am doing the right thing?" queried Jim.

"No; damned if I do! . . . Look here, Jim," he continued, sitting up, "you're in the devil of a mess — far more serious than I ever imagined. Of course I knew that you were *very* pally with her, but this possibility never entered my mind — although," he added reflectively, "I don't know why it shouldn't have. I used to rot you until you turned rusty. Still, I never thought you'd be such an ass. Yet I — well, ifs are no use; we've got to face facts. The first thing to do is to get you out of this hole. Now, I don't —"

"Yes, yes," interrupted Jim, impatiently, "but I don't understand what all —"

"Be quiet and listen."

"But I cannot see —"

"No, of course not. . . . Oh Lord!" He stood up and stared into the empty grate. "Well, it's this. Eve has tried this game before."

"What! Good God!" Jim exclaimed excitedly, jumping from his chair.

"Sit down, or I won't explain." Jim sat on the arm of the chair. "You know Herbert Greener?" Jim remembered the man with the walrus moustaches whom he had seen in the restaurant during his first dinner with Eve. "He was the man. This occurred five years ago. She was nineteen then. I won't go into the facts of the case — these should be enough. Of course he wasn't a fool; he refused to marry her, and he paid for her to go away for a time, but it turned out an Arabella trick.[45] How on earth it's been possible for you to have been so blind, is a

---

[45] Arabella trick: a reference to Arabella Donn, a character from Thomas Hardy's novel, *Jude the Obscure*. The daughter of a pig farmer, Arabella tricks Jude into marrying her by pretending to be pregnant.

mystery. I ought to have warned you; but hang it, Jim, I didn't think you were such a fool."

Jim was now pacing up and down the room.

"I don't believe it!" he exclaimed suddenly. "If it had been any other man but you, I'd —"

"Oh, rot!"

"By God, I mean it."

"Well, whatever you do, you certainly can't marry her."

"I *will*," commenced Jim, "if I —"

"You won't!" said Graham emphatically. "You must not and *shall* not marry her. Good God, if you were tied to a woman like that you'd either go mad or end by shooting yourself and her. Don't be such a fool, old man."

Jim continued to pace up and down in silence.

"Heavens!" he muttered to himself. "I have been a fool, but by God I'll do it. I must — it can't be true. I won't believe it."

Graham, watching him anxiously, laid a hand on his shoulder. Jim shook him off roughly.

"Oh, for God's sake, leave me alone! . . . Hell!"

"Jim!"

Jim ignored the appeal and angrily threw a chair, which had gotten in his way, to the floor with a crash. Graham appeared to be debating with himself; and then, apparently having made up his mind, he slipped in front of Jim, who scowled portentously and tried to step round. Graham sidestepped. Jim swore.

"Look here, Jimmy," said Graham quietly, "I've got a confession to make to you."

"Confession? Me?" snarled Jim. "What the — oh —" sneering — "s'pose you mean that all this" — he waved a hand — "is a damned lie — for my benefit, eh? Acting the martyr to save the innocent boy. But what the devil's it got to do with you, anyhow? Damn it, leave me alone and don't tell lies about a woman you —"

"Wait! Let me tell you —" commenced Graham patiently.

"Oh, go to the devil!" snapped Jim, and broke away from him. "I'm going out."

"You won't go out until I've finished," said Graham, and walked to the door.

Jim angrily crushed a straw hat on his head.

"Well, what the devil is it?"

"This," said Graham slowly, looking Jim squarely in the eyes. "Two years ago Eve was my mistress."

"What!"

Jim stared in blank incredulity.

"You — Oh, rot!"

"Why not?" demanded Graham. "I didn't want to confess it, but —"

"Good God! Is that true, really true? You swear it?" exclaimed Jim.

"Yes," said Graham, holding Jim's eyes fixedly, and then, with a shadow of effort, "I swear it!"

Jim stared for a moment.

"Oh, Christ!" he ejaculated, and jerking his hat across the room, flung himself into a chair, where, holding his head with his hands, he muttered thickly: "Damn! . . . Oh, damn! . . . damn!"

Graham made no comment, silently watching.

"Why didn't you tell me before?" demanded Jim suddenly.

"How could I?" returned Graham quietly, and sat down in a chair. "How could I? That was some time ago, and when I saw you with her that night I only thought — well, hang it, a fellow can't do a thing like that. I shouldn't have told you now if I hadn't — hadn't been so fond of you. You know as well as I do, that a fellow can't tell things like that about a woman even — Besides, I never dreamed you'd want to marry her. A fellow doesn't marry a girl of that type. She never tried anything like that on me. I suppose she thought you were soft enough to marry her — and —"

"My God, yes, I am soft!" exclaimed Jim, jumping to his feet. "I wish to God I'd never met her — nor you either. Oh God, what will the pater say! Heavens, I don't know what to do!"

"Well, the best thing is to let her know that you won't marry her and go away for a holiday for a while."

"But what am I to tell her?"

"Good heavens!" exclaimed Graham, starting to his feet in alarm. "Don't tell her I told you, will you? Swear you won't do that! Why —"

"Good God, of course I shan't. But what shall I say?"

"Tell her that you know about Greener."

"But then she'll guess that you told me. Does she know that you know that, too? . . . Or anything else?" added Jim, bitterly.

Graham did not reply.

"And my father? Oh God, I don't know what to do."

"If I were you I'd tell him everything."

"Oh," said Jim with an impatient gesture, dropping into a chair again. "That's utterly impossible."

"Yes, you must, Jim. He'll understand."

"No! No! *That's* out of the question. You don't know the pater. He'll never forgive me. Oh, my God, what a fool I've been!"

"Nonsense," remarked Graham; "your father's a man of the world."

"I tell you he'll never forgive me. I know him — you don't. I know what I shall do," he said abruptly, looking up. "I'll clear off."

"Clear off?" echoed Graham. "Where, and why?"

"I don't know and I don't care. Why should I stay?" he demanded. "I hate and loathe my work — always have done. My father will never own me now. Everything is against me. I can raise about fifty pounds somehow or other. I was doing that for Scotland. I'll tell her tomorrow. Damn!" he cried again, hysterically, "what a fool I've been! I hate her! — shut up — I — I suppose she thought I was a soft young fool; so I am. Oh yes, I know the meaning of many things now. No one need know I am going. I'll pack the few things I want and tell the landlady I'm off for a holiday — then she'll find I'm not such a fool."

He raved on, worked up to this pitch of excitement by a revulsion of feeling. Graham sat quiet, making no effort to stem the torrent of self-reproach, and the bitter denunciations of the cause of his trouble. Jim had lost sight of the fact that a short while previously he had desired anything but marriage, although he honestly intended to force himself to the act. Now by a common mental process he felt that he had really wished to marry her because he honored her, but on the very verge she had been proved a traitress. As Jim refused to pay any further attention to him Graham went away, promising to think over things carefully and to give him further advice on the morrow.

After Graham had gone away Jim resumed his march up and down the room. At length he sat down and resumed his moody stare into the darkling shadows. For a long time he struggled in mental turmoil, until tears began to course slowly down his cheeks.

He was too perturbed to analyze his emotions. He did not doubt for a moment that what he had heard from the lips of Graham was true; although a surge of hatred and loathing rose at the thought of him. Many words and actions of the accused girl came back to him with a rush. Then the question of his flight obsessed him, a dominant desire to get away from everybody and everything. Where should he go? The first country which came into his mind was South Africa. He remembered some glaring posters advertising some steamship company — the Goldfields, they called it.[46] Ah! that would be the place for him. Perhaps he might be lucky and make a fortune. Others had; why not he? Yes, he would go to South Africa. He had always hated his present work. Now he would be free. Exactly what he expected to do and to find there did not enter his head. He remembered having heard of Mounted Police.[47] If the worst came, he could join them. Should he write to his father telling him? No, he thought not; he had always had an exaggerated idea of his father, and he never for a moment supposed that he would do other than curse and disown him.

Memories of his childhood came back to him when his father used to visit him at school, gravely pat his hand and give him a tip. He had always seemed so stern and immaculate. He could

---

[46] Beadle's great-niece Patricia informed me that Charles and his brother Henry joined the South African Police, to fight in the Boer War. She also said that London was rife with recruiting posters back then, which were displayed on the streets and in the Underground. According to family legend, Charles enlisted after seeing one of these posters. Patricia added that, after Charles' mother died, he was raised by his sixty-seven-year-old maternal grandmother, Catherine Owens, who was "wealthy and blind." Catherine died on 22 July 1890, about three months short of Charles' ninth birthday. He was said to have forged a stronger bond with her than with anyone else in the family. We can only guess at how Beadle bore the brunt of this second "maternal" loss. (Telephone conversation with Patricia and her daughter Liz, 6 November 2022.)

[47] Beadle was employed by the British South African Police from November 1898 until about 1902. "Parental Government required me to become a consulting marine engineer; but a congenital dislike of work and a gaudy poster persuaded me to learn poker, to starve in Cape Town where I held down a waiter's job for four hours and to join the British South African Police." Note the mention of a "gaudy poster" (see prior footnote). Source: Beadle's autobiographical sketch in *Adventure* magazine, "The Camp-Fire" column, 3 July 1918. (Also featured in Arthur Hoffman, ed., *The Camp-Fire*, Norwood MA: Steeger Books, 2023, pp. 102-103.) See also Beadle's commentary in *Adventure*'s "Ask Adventure" column: "The Rhodesian Mounted Police," 18 September 1919.

never possibly understand. It had always been: "Never forget you are my son." These words ultimately gave him the impression that other sons might fall, but that he, being his father's son, must never fall — and now that he had, no forgiveness would be possible. As useless regrets crossed his mind the tears welled in his eyes once more. Struggling hard to repress such weakness, as he considered it, he caught up his hat and rushed out of the room. At the street door he encountered the postman. Snatching at any chance of action to distract his mind, he opened the letterbox inside the door and held up the contents in the light of the hall. The sight of Madge's large, prim handwriting struck him like a blow in the face. He threw down the other letters on the hallstand and hesitated. In answer to the double knock of the postman Maggie had appeared. Holding his head on one side to hide his eyes, Jim rushed past her and up the stairs. In the room he tore open the envelope. The intake of his breath whistled as he read the opening sentences at a glance:

> "Dear Jim,
> Why haven't you answered my letters? I have such good news. Do you know I am engaged to be married to Mr. Blettford? Mother and father are so pleased. I am coming up to stay with Aunt Ruth again next week, and Mr. Blettford is . . ."

For a moment he stood, his eyes staring, his lips open and quivering. The letter fluttered to the ground. Then he walked stiffly into the next room and flung himself on his bed. That Madge should be perfidious was the last straw. No man had ever had such a cruel blow dealt him by fate. In common with many minds in an overwrought condition, he seized upon the opportunity with the ecstasy of martyrdom to wallow in delirious agony, feeling in honor bound to make the most of the pain. He could not weep. He remembered that in moments of crisis tears are denied . . . .

At length, physically exhausted with the ebullition and strain of the past days, he dropped off to sleep in his clothes, the gas burning all night.

CHAPTER VI

To Youth life is a drawing in black and white, crude and out of perspective, lacking the subtleties of light and shade. Although buffeted about in a maelstrom of emotions, hatred, disgust, remorse, the past appeared all the sweeter for the loss. Jim was assured that he had drunk the bitterest dregs of the cup of life: for what worse could happen to a man than to find his ideal blasted, his love untrue, and best friend false? But by the time he rose from bed the keenness of his grief and remorse was dulled. Already he felt a momentary glow of excitement at the idea of adventuring abroad. His decision to leave England had plucked on the strings of another chord of his temperament — Romance. But immediately he strove to banish the emotion, feeling that it was an act of impiety towards his own martyrdom. Yet he was up long before his usual hour, extracting some satisfaction from the haggard appearance of his face in the mirror; and proceeded to pack with the slapdash energy of a desperate man, careless of existence. To Maggie's gaping astonishment, he requested her to tell her mistress that he would be leaving that day, immediately, as he had been called away on urgent business.

"Lor, Mr. Litham!" she exclaimed, letting bacon grease drip on the tablecloth. Her mouth opened and shut like a trout on a bank in a futile attempt to find words. "Lor, Mr. Litham!" she added again.

"Yes," said Jim tetchily. "Mind that grease! And tell Mrs. Hobbs that I'm in a hurry."

Maggie stared for a moment at Jim's irritable face.

"Lor!" she remarked darkly, "some people are 'igh and mighty, to be sure."

"Oh, shut up!" adjured Jim, and pushing his plate from him, scowled, seeing in Maggie merely one of the accursed sex who had deceived and ruined him.

By the chance that he had lately received his quarterly allowance he found that he could muster some sixty odd pounds. After he had had an interview with his landlady, during which he had fended her kindly curiosity with sullen civility, under the impression that he had been haughtily dignified, he drove to the office of the Cape Mounted Rifles in Victoria Street. There was no recruiting in England; but, they assured him, he would probably secure acceptance at Cape Town. Disappointedly he went on to Cook's, and purchased a ticket for the next boat to the Cape. Then, after a visit to an outfitter's, where a bland assistant persuaded him to buy some utterly useless impedimenta, he returned to take away his luggage. As he turned into the street he saw Graham walking up. Without hesitation Jim turned aside and waited round the corner until Graham had called at the house. In his rage and black despair Jim was obsessed with a hatred against everybody, particularly against Graham and Eve. Yet, with the thought that he might never see Graham again, he stared hard at him as he passed in a flood of yellow sunshine a few yards away, stifling regret.

Fortunately the boat was due to sail from London on the morrow,[48] but in order to avoid everybody he had determined

---

[48] There are numerous references to London in Beadle's pre-1914 biography (the period covered in *A Passionate Pilgrimage*). After his birth at sea aboard the Merchant Marine vessel SS *Cilurnum* (his father was the ship's captain), Beadle was raised in the family residence in West Hackney, a district in the London Borough of Hackney. Circa 1906, at the age of twenty-four, he was elected as a Fellow of the Royal Geographical Society (FRGS) in

to move immediately. With what he conceived to be Machiavellian cunning he requested the landlady to tell any inquirers that he had gone home to Derbyshire, and, after loudly instructing the cabman to go to Euston, drove to an obscure hotel.

He had intended to keep an appointment with Eve that evening and scornfully to tell her his decision; but as the time approached his courage oozed. He knew that she would weep and feared accordingly. However, he compromised by ringing her up on the telephone, and cowardly administering the congè[49] over the wire. At the sound of her voice his determination weakened, but after a halting attempt, he blurted out:

"I've found out — about Herbert Greener. . . . I can't marry you. . . . Goodbye," and dropping the receiver on to the bracket, fled in a moist panic.

After he had prepared a letter to his father — to be posted on board — he felt that he had passed the Rubicon. Never having had to labor for his daily bread, he had an elastic idea of the value of money; so much so, that it was in his eyes a great act of self-denial and commendable prudence when he decided to travel third-class. So with forty pounds, some loose silver (which he did not trouble to count), an assorted and useless kit (which included a huge Colt revolver), a colossal inexperience

---

London. The following February, he was also elected to London's Royal Colonial Institute. He embarked from the Port of London aboard the SS *Agadir* on 23 April 1908, heading for the Moroccan coast. His name is the first to appear on the ship's passenger list, in the First Class section. Beadle lived in Morocco from 1908 until about 1911, at which time he returned to Hampstead, London. In 1914 he was again elected Fellow of the Royal Geographical Society. But by 1914 he had expatriated to France. On 14 March 1914 he married Sylvia Hornsby at the British Consulate General in Paris, while the couple was residing at 4, rue de la Grande Chaumière.

[49] Congè: in the sense used here, taking formal leave; farewell.

of the world and a sublime confidence in the favor of the gods, he found himself aboard ship amid a crowd of fellow voyagers. The noise and excitement, the weeping of odd children and the maudlin men, offended him. In disgust he looked around the third-class saloon with its rows of painted iron pillars and frowsy people. An individual in uniform, whom he took to be a head steward, stood near him. He touched this person on the arm and haughtily demanded to be shown his berth. The man brushed him aside and walked away. Scowling, Jim walked up to another official, who immediately told him to "go to blazes." Rendered speechless by a combination of offended dignity and lachrymose distress he fled on deck, undecided whether he would report the man for insolence, change his ticket for first-class, or not go at all.

However, he found a quieter spot behind the steering gear box, and fell to watching the preparations for departure with jaundiced eyes. The sight of the bustling activity of the docks and the hoots of the steamers in the river brought back his sorrows. But the perfidy of Eve and Graham, and the wrath of his father, were all in the giant shadow of the greater tragedy of his broken faith in Madge. The former were material disasters, as it were; the latter the blasting of the great ideal, the Goddess whom he had set upon the highest pedestal. Even in the greatest moments of bitterness after he had decided that he must pay the price his honor demanded, there was, besides the satisfaction in fulfilling his code, the glowing knowledge that his Fylgja was there, guiding his inner, secret self, grand and infallible. Also at the back of his mind had been the hope that, in some way impossible to foresee, one day he would redeem his faults and be fit to kneel at the feet of the apotheosis of divinity. But after she had failed him nothing mattered. Oh, it was bitter; but still more galling to think that her ineffable virtues were to be wasted on a thing like Blettford. Scornfully

Jim remembered him, a hulking, pudding-faced man, fifteen years older than she, whose only idea in life was foxhunting: and even then the fellow couldn't ride. There was the taste of the oleander. Jim would not have cared — so much — had she chosen someone of whom he could have approved: someone better than himself — though Jim in these days would have been hard put to it to find such a one.

Eve and Graham had receded comparatively into the distance. No thought of what they might feel or think occurred to him: even his father seemed remote. All these appeared to belong to another world, some other existence. The only real fact to him was that *he*, Jim, had been grossly deceived and injured, that she whom he had deigned to clothe with impossible attributes, had deigned to worship as a Goddess, had wantonly trampled upon his most sacred feelings by being human. Even when the crisis had occurred with Eve he had not thought for a moment for her feelings: he had intended to make reparation, not for her good, but because the arbitrary code of his honor demanded that he should do so: otherwise he would lose self-respect for himself. Of two evils choose the lesser: rather than offend the majesty of his own opinion of himself he would wreck his worldly prospects.

As Jim stood gazing from the summit of his own egotism upon the bustling world beneath him, he became conscious of that sense of unreality again, as one acting in a play. That gray, misty atmosphere above the grimy warehouses held the past: down beyond that muddy, swirling river was the genesis of a new epoch. A strange optimism gripped him for a moment. He felt that he was setting out to find something. The idea excited him. Yet the next moment he noticed that the gangway had been withdrawn, the ship's bow was leaving the dockside; they were off! And straightway as his eyes sought the mist of London a great longing suddenly welled within him for the old familiar things: his rooms, Graham, Eve, his father, and the Compleat[50] Ideal. . . . A difficulty in swallowing assailed him: his eyes burned as the thought occurred that he might never see any of them again. He swore inarticulately, and, turning back, began to pace up and down the deck, utterly oblivious of the crowd, wrapped in the cloak of his own tragedy.

The ship was clear of the docks and swinging into the crowded river. The sun came out in a sudden burst of glory. He paused by the rail and stared down the misty river. What was down there waiting for him? Life was worth living. Why? The hope of finding — what? A passing wave of panic shook him. He longed for one intense moment to get back to that gray shore of belching chimneys behind which lay all he knew. Then he set his teeth and, his underlip slightly protruding, gazed steadily down the river into the misty Unknown. . . .

---

[50] Compleat: having all the necessary or desired elements or skills; that which has no deficiency.

BOOK II

CHAPTER I

FIVE years had passed: years of kopjes,[51] bush and veld, of wet night rides and of rides sun scorched, of hunger and thirst, of smoking kraals, venomous Maxims,[52] and flying niggers;[53] and

---

[51] Kopje (South African): a small, usually rocky hill, especially on the veld.

[52] Maxim: the first automatic machine gun (1884), invented by Sir Hiram Maxim (1840 – 1916). Also called Vickers gun.

[53] In his Introduction to the 2007 edition of Beadle's *The City of Baal*, John Locke discusses the significance of racial epitaphs in Beadle's fiction: "Slaves represented cheap labor. They also represented the contempt of Europeans for different people – dark-skinned *and* non-Christian – without which they couldn't have justified depriving them, as a matter of law, of freedom. But even after moral outrage back home led to the abolition of the slave trade – after three centuries – functionaries in the field retained the contempt, clear from the language of Beadle's characters. Early in 'The Cave,' the first story here, a British police trooper describes a native as a 'fool nigger.' 'Nigger' and similar racial epitaphs occur occasionally in the dialogue, a natural consequence of Beadle's authenticity. Most of Beadle's characters are Englishmen in the employ or ex-employ of the Empire, and the word 'nigger' was common in the British Empire as a description of dark-skinned peoples. Of note, the epitaphs do not appear as verbal abuse from a white to a Black. Instead, they are descriptions shared between whites, a seeming affirmation of their common understanding of racial superiority ...

Today, 'nigger' is generally, and somewhat dramatically, regarded as the worst thing a white could ever say to a Black. The word has attained a political status well-elevated above its weight at the time Beadle was published. Evidence of this is found in the editorial conventions of *Adventure*, the magazine where all but the last of these stories appeared. Beadle's characters curse incessantly, indicated by the long dashes used to

of the dull routine of an outstation life in the Rhodesian Mounted Police.[54]

Jim had been to school again: had received some education in the finest college in the world. He had learned many lessons: bitter lessons in poverty, in endurance without complaint, control of temper; had had some of the orgulous[55] pettiness of caste knocked out of him. And above all he had discovered that he was not the godlike creature he had fondly but subconsciously imagined himself to be. Nights in which he had lain awake with a saddle for pillow, and watched the miracle of the procession of the heavens, had sobered his egotism a little and had awed him with the stupendous splendor and immensity, crushing his vanity sorely and squeezing out thoughts which frightened him. He began to see the world in a different light and learned to laugh at himself occasionally. And in the solitudes some of the old moods which Eve had nearly suffocated, came back to him. He could think of Madge, too, now, without a feeling of resentment against her; but he had never quite contrived to understand why she had married Blettford: nor had he forgotten that the man couldn't ride! He

---

censor oaths in the dialogue. It's clear from the context that the reader was being shielded from 'damn,' 'hell,' and like terms. 'Nigger' is never censored, suggesting that religious-minded readers were considered worthy of being shielded from offense, but that African-Americans, in that era of Jim Crow, or whites sympathetic to African-American causes, were of no concern.... the censorship in *Adventure* was the magazine's policy, and not Beadle's preference.... As we would expect from pulp stories, he betrays no agenda beyond the desire to tell a good story.... Beadle's understanding of native beliefs and practices do not suggest the thoughts of an ignorant or jingoistic man." See Locke's Introduction in Charles Beadle, *The City of Baal*, Castroville, CA: Off-Trail Publications, 2007, pp. 10-11.

[54] See illustration provided in this edition of a uniformed Beadle mounted on a horse in South Africa.

[55] Orgulous: proud.

had even succeeded — after two years — in writing to her, although he was nervous lest she had heard the real reason why he had left England. However, she had replied, and he learned that she had had a son and heir. He did not answer for six months after that; and finally the correspondence died a natural death as such do. But he never forgot her.

On the road to Bulawayo[56] Jim had written to his father, and had received in reply a sympathetic letter chiding him for being inconsiderate and foolish in not having given confidence when easier circumstances might have been arranged. "However, my son," the letter had continued, "as you have made your bed you must needs lie upon it and not complain," adding whimsically: "I am remitting you £100 which may tend to soften the mattress." Veld life was not conducive to the study of women, hence Jim's views were still in a chaotic state. In appearance he had broadened out and acquired the lithe, swinging walk of the veld man; the blue eyes seemed lighter in contrast to the tanned features, which bore deeper lines, and the silky black moustaches. A man who goes through a frontier life usually develops into a candlewaster[57] or a man; he who retains his lamblike qualities will remain a lamb forever and aye.[58]

Upon receiving his discharge from the Police he had settled upon a grant of land from the Company, and for a twelvemonth

---

[56] A city in Zimbabwe. John Locke has identified references to Bulawayo in three of Beadle's stories: "The City of Baal": "Daycomb got a commission and is down at Bulawayo." "The Gifts of Diamonds": "Harry Martin, whom you'll remember in Bulawayo." "The Land of Ophir": "we sold out to a Bulawayo company and went in together trading"; "We wandered all over the shop from Bulawayo to the Nile."

[57] Candlewaster: one who consumes numerous candles as a result of staying up late at night while engaged in study or in acts of dissipation. A bookworm.

[58] "Ever and Aye": from Psalm 136: "Forever and aye, the mercies of the Lord endure forever and aye." Also rendered as a sea shanty.

followed the precarious life of a native trader. But, his knowledge of agriculture being a negative quantity, and having discovered that his allotted portion consisted mainly of a series of stony kopjes, he eventually accepted a comparatively generous offer from an enthusiast, and journeyed to the Golden City[59] with great hopes of making a small fortune. However, as he was wholly unsophisticated in the gentle art of I.D.B.,[60] Gold Bricks, jumping claims, rigging of markets, and other specifics for the embryo millionaire, he promptly fell a victim to a suave gentleman of Hebrew extraction on the "chains,"[61] who relieved him of the bulk of his capital.

So upon a day Jim contemplated the future; which act showed that he had grown up. Indeed, the prospects were none too rosy. Although many thousands of cigarettes, and almost as many ideals, had ended in smoke since the London days, he had not learned much of use in commerce; town is no Eldorado to the frontiersman. Few friends had he in Johannesburg, and of patrons, none. So after his kind, his thoughts turned to the veld from whence he had come. Yet, as he sat and smoked in the open verandah of his rooms in Standard Buildings, overlooking

---

[59] Johannesburg was sometimes referred to as the Golden City. In his essay "A Decade of Christmas Dinners" (published in the December 1914 issue of *Badminton Magazine of Sports and Pastimes*), Beadle describes a Christmas spent in Johannesburg (circa 1902-1903). See further references to this essay below.

[60] I.D.B.: illicit diamond buying.

[61] The chains: possibly a reference to "the trains." In the context of railway engineering and surveying, "chains" refers to a unit of length measurement (equal to 66 feet, or approximately 20.12 meters). The measurement was widely used in railway construction and surveying during the early twentieth century, particularly in British and Commonwealth countries such as South Africa. Later in the novel, when Jim is about to board a train, Biddy advises him to "Have a good time and gamble on 'the chains.'"

Eloff Street,[62] no vestige of a practical suggestion would materialize.

Eye-sealing clouds of dust arose from the parched street beneath, smothering everything and everybody in a gritty, gray coat. The jingle of passing rickshaws and rumble of wheels merged into a gallimaufry of sound through which penetrated, to a keen ear, the heavy, thrudding pulsation of batteries on the distant mines. A Negro's belly laugh, the thick voice of a Zarp[63] shouting in Dutch, and the sharp jingle of a bicycle bell, floated up distinctly. At a long distance a mine hooter[64] began to blast the hot, dry air, repeated and echoed along the reef.

Throwing away a cigarette stump, Jim rose moodily to repair to a café for tea when a footstep sounded behind him.

"Jimmy, darlin'," said a voice, "are ye there?"

"Hullo, Biddy!" he called to the newcomer. "Come in! Where have you dropped from? I thought you had gone to Delagoa Bay?"

"No, darlin'," said Biddy, lounging against the lintel. "It's meself that's stayin' to comfort ye. Ye see, there was a woman in it, an' women are the divil, the darlin's! — and sure an' I ought to know."

"I believe you!" laughed Jim. "You're an authority. I've got the hump," he continued. "I —"

"The divil fly away wid yer hump," announced Biddy cheerfully. "Listen, I've got an idea —"

"Oh Lord! another?" said Jim plaintively. "Your ideas are like fusees — pff, bang, flare, hell of a stink, and ends in smoke."

---

[62] Eloff Street: the first street to be surveyed in Johannesburg, named after Jan Eloff (1859—1939), the first civilian commissioner.
[63] Zarp: acronym for the South African Republic Police.
[64] Mine hooter: a shrieking instrument that blew several times a day, announcing work shifts in the mine. It was also used to alert miners to underground accidents.

"Not bad, me son — for an Englishman," said Biddy, stroking a red shaven face. "But what are ye goin' to do? It's no use twiddling your thumbs — that won't feed ye nor the gurrls."

"Hang the girls!" responded Jim. "I can't stand a petticoat."

"Ah, darlin'!" said Biddy soothingly, "ye've never been properly eddicated. It's meself that'll coach ye, and I'm a master. Now look ye here, my bhoy, I'll tell ye what we'll do. It's no use ye lookin' for a job, for you wouldn't kape it if ye got it. We'll out-Jew the Jews!"

"Eh?" exclaimed Jim, sitting up.

"We'll buy watches, cheap jewelry, oleos, and sell 'em.[65] Make over a hundred percent, me bhoy."

"What's oleos?" enquired Jim listlessly.

"Cheap picture things," explained Biddy lucidly. "Vant to puy a vatch, ma tear? Vera sheap vatch!"

Jim smiled disdainfully and caressed his moustaches.

"It's bully, I'm tellin' ye! We can sell 'em to the aristocrats of Fordsburg[66] and suburbs. Yes, I know what ye're after thinkin' — that it's not the thing. I know. But this isn't the old country and it doesn't matter a damn what ye do here. . . . Besides, me bhoy, there's shent per shent in it!" he exclaimed, and launched into technical details.

---

[65] In his 1918 sketch in *Adventure*'s "Camp-Fire" column, Beadle writes: "saw Boer War in B. S. A. P. [British South African Police], Morley's Scouts ... and Stock Recovery Dept. After Peace held various jobs from three days to a week — in a news office, a bar, hawker, insurance agent — and peddled cheap jewelry for three months (and made money!); served in Transvaal Customs and became Asst. Compound Manager to the Witwatersrand Native Labor Association." So these rich descriptions of hawking jewelry probably owe their vividness to Beadle's actual experience. In a letter to his niece Isabel written in the 1930s he writes (with typical Beadle modesty), "I am about as much use selling things or getting orders as a monkey on the wireless."

[66] Fordsburg: a municipality in Johannesburg, established in 1888 on land owned by the Ford and Juppe Estate Company.

Finally Jim agreed to try the scheme, but protested that he could never induce anybody to buy an article they did not require, which only invoked a fresh storm of multiloquence.

Jim was accordingly initiated into the mysteries of the peddler's pack. Gorgeous gilt watches, bracelets and brooches with 18 ct. stamp[ed] on were procured from a snuffling gentleman with a large paunch and a small sense of humor. These were, as Biddy explained, particularly suitable for the belles of Fordsburg; photographs of the Queen and Royal Family for patriotic miners — not a few, and small samples of genuine jewelry for the more select of prospective customers.

On the following morning, Jim, carrying a worn bag containing his stock, attired in oldest clothes, red scarf carelessly round throat, boots carefully burst at the seams for the occasion, looking like a stage Apache, presented himself for Biddy's inspection.

"H'm," said Biddy, surveying him with disapproval, "distressingly respectable; won't do at all. Phwat the divil d'ye mane by a ring? Away at once!" Jim dutifully obeyed. "H'm — clean hands — that won't do — dirty 'em. And phwat's the matter wid yer face? Why, ye goat, ye — ye mustn't shave — or if ye will, shave at night when ye're goin' a-courtin'. Look at mine," stroking a night's yellow bristle. "A clean face would spoil the artistic whole. Cultivate a persistent whining tone, and as ye can't speak Oirish dhrop yer aitches. Now, come along; we'll drink to the schame and I'll give ye final instructions. . . .

"Mine's an Oirish and milk, darlin'," to the barmaid. "Sure an' it's pretty eyes ye've got entoirely. Phwat's that? Yes, an' another for me friend. Here's to the purtiest gurrl in Johannesburg," raising his glass to the girl with an amorous look. "Sure I'd sooner have a kiss from those lips than all the whisky in the worrld — liar that I am (*sotto voce*). James darlin', women are the divil for money and blarney. If ye've got both ye've got any woman in the world, an' if ye've only got blarney ye've got ninety percent. Shovel it on by the hodful, and they'll squirm and love ye for it. Never ye mind how unreasonable it is — just shovel it on, I'm telling ye. Ye see, man's a rasonable animal and woman's an onrasonable animal, and so the more onrasonable ye are the more they'll adore ye. They think it's agin nature for man to be onrasonable. Women is the essence of onrason. Loving 'emselves they love onrason; so the more a man's onrasonable, the more they love him, for ye see they're loving themselves reflected in the man — hence both parties are delighted, the spectators amused, and everybody's happy — that's why love is the finest pastime in the worrld. Av coorse the neglected swain isn't amused, but then nothin' in this worrld is perfect — not even love! Never thry to tell a gurrl why ye love her — she don't want to know, and ye don't know yerself — ye see, that's the exception to the rule. If man was wholly rasonable he'd never love a woman — divil a bit I — an' then the worrld wud come to an end. That's why the Creator put a flaw in man's rason — just to kape things goin', as it were. And Jimmy, never — never take a woman as a humorous subject — if ye do she'll never forgive ye. She thinks she's a serious subject — and so she is — to man, bedamn! A man swearin' he'll love a gurrl to all eternity is one of the funniest sights this side of Hades — but she can't see the humor of it — divil a bit — even when he isn't the first. Ye see, she takes herself seriously and therefore takes him seriously. James, me bhoy, never be serious — it's the greatest calamity that ye can meet. When ye commence to take anything seriously then the end is at hand, as a serious somebody said in the Boible. Jimmy darlin', I'll leave that maxim to ye, and when ye die ye should mention it in your will, bequeathin' a rich legacy unto your issue. Immortal Will! Begad, he knew more about women than any man I ever met. D'ye know, Jimmy, I believe he was an Oirishman — and that ye thaves of Englishmen stole him as well as our liberty. However, I'll forgive ye — ye was born onlucky. Speaking of luck — phwat's that? Well, have another drop. Yes, ye must; I've got to get wound up, else I'll forget all me blarney for the gurrls. Hello, Norah! just to see those purty fingers fluttering like the burrds in springtime, we'll double the last evint, only go aisy with the cowjuice, there's a darlin'. Now, James, 'pithness ith pithness, ma tear.' We start work in Fordsburg; you take one side of the street, and I'll take the other. Talk to every gurrl over six and under sixty as if ye were dyin' of love for her. Call 'em all the nice names ye can think of — if your eddication's been neglected I'll write ye a list. If they spitfire at ye, smile and call 'em an angel — and don't forget to put yer fut in the door. Keep on talkin' — don't give 'em a chance to get a word in — once ye do ye'll never get yer lead again. Remember it's a woman ye're dealin' with, an' once ye get inside — don't go out until they've bought somethin'. If they can't find cash, I'll guarantee to get it out of 'em. Be careful, darlin', for they're cuter than snakes. If she offers — er — a kiss for a bangle, even if she's pretty, don't do it — unless ye want to badly, and then don't forget to calculate the cost value of the bangle and the number of kisses."

They tramped, Biddy talking continuously, to the selected street in a district adjoining the mines where in lines of mean brick houses, reminiscent of the East End of London, dwelt the poor whites, Dutch and British. Biddy promptly attacked the first house on the left, leaving Jim to try his prentice hand on the other side. Jim felt very uncomfortable and all Biddy's valuable advice deserted his memory. At last he summoned up courage to give a single knock. After a while, there being no sign of a response, Jim knocked with bolder mien. A mysterious voice sang out:

"Nothin' today, thank you."

Jim peered around, and being unable to locate the owner, knocked again.

"Go 'way," sang out the same voice; "don't want nothin' today."

"This is a promising start," mused Jim. "I suppose I'd better move on to the next house. I wonder how Biddy is getting on." He looked across the street and saw his partner at the door of the second house. Biddy's knee was against the lintel, supporting the open bag; his hands were occupied in manipulating, to the best advantage, a display of bangles and brooches whilst he talked loquaciously to a dark matron and two daughters, the latter evidently dazzled by the combined effects of the clinquant gawds[67] and Biddy's "gift of the gab."

He noticed the amused expression on the matron's face and the eager smiling faces of the girls, whilst Biddy's musical laugh floated across to him. He felt a trifle envious, and with more determination approached the next house. At his knock a young woman opened the door.

"Er — good morning, madam," said Jim. "May I show you some jewelry?"

The woman stared.

"Nix ni," she replied, and began to close the door. Jim stood silent and angrily watched the lock snap. Turning to retreat, he saw Biddy standing close by, laughing.

"Oh, ye he-goat, that's not the way I told you! Why didn't ye put yer fut in the door? She was all right; I could tell by the gleam in her eye."

"Tell what by her eye?" enquired Jim tetchily.

---

[67] Clinquant: glittering with gold or silver, and hence with metallic imitations of these; tinseled. Gawd (variant of *gaud*): a plaything, toy. Also: something gaudy; a showy ornament, a piece of finery; a gewgaw.

"Why, that she'd flirt, even if she wouldn't, or couldn't, buy. Me bhoy, I can spot 'em by instinct! Ye can always tell by a woman's eye whether she'll flirt immediately or whether it'll take time. They're all the same — only a matter of time and degree. Now did ye see those darlin's over the way? Well, I sold 'em two bangles at a shilling each. I asked eighteen pence and they offered me a bob — just like a woman. They cost us a tickey[68] each — so there's three hundred percent, me bhoy. Adopt the Oriental trick in this game, Jimmy; ask three times as much as you'll take. They like it. They're as pleased as Punch if they think they've struck a bargain. Now come along with me, my bhoy."

He ran lightly up and gave a vigorous rat-a-tat at the next door, which was answered by a lusty woman of thirty odd with lank cane-colored hair and large red hands.

"Top o' the mornin' to ye!" began Biddy in his richest brogue. "It's a foine spring we're after having. In the springtoime young man's thoughts lightly turrn to thoughts of love," looking her straight in the eyes and stepping inside the door at the same time. "But it's not love I'm tellin' ye about at all, at all," opening his bag, his eyes still on the woman; "but the adornment of the female form divoine."

With an extra ardent look he produced a gilt wristlet watch before the astonished and half-mesmerized woman's eyes.

"Now!" suddenly swooping on her unoccupied hand, "just see for yer purty self what an iligant setoff it is to yer tiny wrist."

Jim, nearly convulsed with laughter, watched Biddy straining the trellis bangle to its largest capacity over the woman's enormous paw. "Beauty unadorned," continued Biddy to fill up

---

[68] Tickey: a South African threepenny piece, replaced by a five-cent coin in 1961.

the time, "I never believed in until I met you, darlin'," with an amorous look at the woman, who flushed under the storm of unaccustomed flattery.

"Oh, but I —" she began, as Biddy paused to push the bangle over the thumb joint.

"Divil a word, me darlin'," said Biddy instantly; "just listen to me and I'll make yer gurrl friends drown thimselves with invy. Now if ye had a waist belt," producing one, "it wud just match your purty frock. To any other I'd say improve yer figure, but shure that's impossible wid yer purty self."

The woman with heightened color hurriedly said, "Oh, come inside," and turning, entered the front room, shouting in a cracked treble: "Maria! Maria! Come 'ere! There's a man with some lovely jewil'ry."

"Now, me bhoy," whispered Biddy, "we've got 'em!"

Two girls of sixteen and twenty respectively came rushing into the room with their hair in curlers.

"These are me sisters," said the woman by way of introduction.

Biddy, hat in hand, made a sweeping bow.

"How d'ye do, young ladies? It's meself that's charmed to meet beauty!"

The girls giggled. Biddy rattled on, never pausing for a moment, covering the table with variegated samples. Taking up a brooch, he would, with superb audacity and supremely ridiculous compliments, insist on fastening it in a girl's bodice, and then swiftly produce a hand mirror, which he carried for that purpose, for the girls to admire themselves in.

Each of them fell in love with different samples of feminine gewgaws, but could not pay for them till the end of the week.

"Shure," said Biddy to the elder woman, "that's nothing at all, at all! When yer father comes home he'll ne'er refuse such a purty darter."

"It's me 'usband," simpered she.

"Shure an' it's meself can hardly belave it — lucky man that he is an' all."

"That's the way to bait 'em, my bhoy!" whispered Biddy as they bowed themselves out. "Just ye take a lesson frim that, James."

CHAPTER II

TRADE was brisk. Jim, under Biddy's tuition and banter, overcame the remnants of his priggishness, and developed a zest in the pursuit of what he now considered a profitable and highly amusing jest. He could never hope to attain to Biddy's natural fluency and power of persuasion, but still he contrived to dispose of a goodly number of trinkets per day, now and again securing orders for expensive items of jewelry. Their clientele was growing apace. Later Jim cheerfully admitted that Biddy's business acumen was not at fault, and that this method of "keeping their end up," as Biddy expressed it, in the struggle for existence, also very delightfully coincided with the immutable laws of natural selection. He found their short business hours of eleven till four most agreeable to his indolent tastes. To Biddy's disgust, Jim insisted upon shaving every morning and washing his hands; and had, unobtrusively, mislaid his artistically dilapidated footgear. Biddy's cute blue eyes quickly observed the sly move; he diagnosed the case immediately.

"Vanity, James, me bhoy," said he. "Shure the gurrls are at the back of it."

Once on a warm summer afternoon Jim knocked at a small red-brick villa in Jeppestown,[69] where lived two old maids who had invited him to tea and given him a commission to match some table silver. Immensely amused at the deferential manner

---

[69] Jeppestown: a suburb of Johannesburg, established circa 1886 by L. P. Ford and C. E. G. Jeppe, who, along with his son Julius Jeppe, formed the Ford and Jeppe Estate Company.

in which they always treated him, he had returned to deliver the order. Jim had discarded any attempt to mutilate the King's English with his shabby clothes, and as, unfortunately, he had the innate knack of tasteful dressing, his appearance was somewhat incongruous in the guise of a peddler. He was "ushered into the front room by a trim little maid, and, having disposed of business to the old ladies' great satisfaction, proceeded to sip tea and chat in the conventional manner as he would have done to two maiden aunts.

He had just lighted a cigarette at the especial request of the elder of the twain when a ring at the door announced a caller. He jumped hastily to his feet with the intention of hurriedly retreating, but his hostess refused to permit his departure. He felt painfully conscious of his peddler's bag, and savagely kicked it under the sofa as, dimly, he heard someone say:

"Claire, dear, this is Mr. Brown — Mrs. Icksburg."

With a distressful lack of originality, Jim had given this name. He made a polite bow and, as the advancing vision held out a small gloved hand, murmured: "How d'ye do!" He blushed furiously, darted a hunted look towards the door, as if contemplating sudden flight, and then back again to the visitor, who, he observed, was smiling delightfully.

"One or two lumps, dear?" he heard Miss Maitland saying.

At first Jim could only see the door and the vision — now he could only see the vision. On a sudden he became conscious of the cigarette in his hand. His eyes still upon her, as if fascinated, he mumbled: "Oh, forgive me!" — and arose helplessly, wondering where he could dispose of the cigarette.

"Oh, no, don't, Mr. Brown!" she protested, showing a set of pearly teeth to Jim's admiring gaze. "I really enjoy — er — the scent of smoke."

Jim murmured his thanks and resumed his seat on the sofa. The younger of the two old dames had commenced knitting and chatting to the visitor. For what seemed an eternity, Jim sat smoking and wondering what on earth to talk about, suffering all the pangs of nervous shyness which most men, after a long sojourn in a womanless wilderness, experience. He noticed the new silver upon the sideboard and almost prayed that his hostess would not refer to it. He could scarce keep his eyes from the charming figure clad in cream dress and flowery summer hat, who to an unbiased eye appeared as a petite young woman of prepossessing manner, her short Irish nose, small mouth and dimpled chin bestowing a piquant expression to her pallid oval face. Whenever she looked towards him he would bashfully avert his eyes.

"Er — I believe that you're a stranger to Johannesburg, aren't you?"

Jim became aware that she was addressing him.

"Er — yes — I mean, no!" he stammered; "that is, I've been here only a few months. I've just come — returned from Rhodesia, you know. Was in the Rebellion,[70] but of course that's all over."

---

[70] Genealogical research conducted by Patricia revealed that Charles "Marmaduke" Beadle enlisted in the British South African Police, Matabeleland Division, Regimental Number 1019, on 26 November 1898 and was discharged (along with his brother Henry) on 18 July 1901. Upon discharge he had a different regimental number, one indicating that he'd transferred to a division in Mashonaland. For his service in the Anglo Boer War, Beadle was awarded the Queen's South Africa Medal. During this period he received various other decorations and service awards. I also uncovered a document entitled "Roll of individuals entitled to the South Africa Medal and Clasps, April 1901" that includes Trooper Charles Marmaduke Beadle, who served in the National (Waldon's) Scouts and Orange River Colony Volunteers, Nesbitt's Horse, Regiment Number 1014. His great-niece has speculated that Charles may have created this fake middle name ("Marmaduke") in order to enlist a second time. In *Dark Refuge* the autobiographical narrator despises his own given name ("William") and asks: "Why hadn't I been called Marmaduke?"

"Really? How interesting! I had a brother who was at Salisbury then. I wonder if you knew him?"

Jim had not met him, but the subject served to break the constraint; his extreme nervousness abated and he chatted with more semblance of ease on conventional topics.

"Oh, Claire, I quite forgot," interrupted his hostess. "Mr. Brown has succeeded in matching that old silver of father's. Isn't it good of him?"

Jim swore mentally and flushed hotly.

"Really, aunt, how very fortunate!"

"Yes. Mr. Brown is in the jewelry trade; he brought us some samples."

Rather a nice way of putting it, thought Jim.

"Indeed; now that's very lucky. I am in need of some jewelry. If Mr. Brown could spare the time, I should be really obliged if he will bring some for my inspection. It will save me a dusty journey and the bother of selecting. Will you, Mr. Brown?"

"Oh yes, certainly, with pleasure," said Jim rather eagerly.

"Thank you so much," she smiled. "Perhaps I had better give you my card."

Opening a small reticule she proffered the conventional pasteboard.

"Oh, thanks," said Jim, and gave her one in return; then he turned a dull brick color with embarrassment as he realized that the card bore his correct name and address. Raising her eyebrows slightly, she smiled at him.

"So very good of you, Mr. — er —" — Jim trembled — "Brown. Will eleven o'clock tomorrow suit you?"

"Oh, yes, certainly," smiling gratefully. "Thank you so very much," he added with emphasis; "I — er — must be going. Good afternoon, Mrs. Icksburg. Good afternoon, madam."

"Oh, Mr. Brown!" called Miss Maitland, "you've forgotten your bag."

Feeling excessively foolish, Jim grabbed his bag, at the same time shooting a quick glance at his prospective customer. He went out with a vision of a laughing pair of soft blue eyes.

That evening Jim was unusually silent. He was nervous and conscious that she attracted him — and — so had Eve. Next morning, however, in spite of misgivings, he presented himself at her residence in Doornfontein,[71] punctual to the minute.

"Oh, yes," said the maid to his enquiry, "the mistress expects you. Will you come in?"

Looking exceptionally neat and spruce, Jim was ushered into a room at the rear, where he found Mrs. Icksburg lying full length upon a sofa, clad in a white morning gown and reading, or pretending to read, a novel.

"Oh, good morning, Mr. — er — Litham!" she said, laughing mischievously as Jim blushed. "Oh, you needn't have feared. I wouldn't give you away, you know. Now, what have you got for me?" she cried archly, jumping off the sofa. "Something nice, I hope."

"Oh — er — I didn't know exactly what you would like," said Jim, frowning slightly.

"Oh, well, let me see!"

Jim opened the bag, which she promptly seized and overturned on the table.

"Oh, dear, what a lot of rubbish!" she exclaimed. "Haven't you got anything better than that? Why, that's not so bad," picking up a small silver bird brooch, "if it were in gold."

"Oh! I could have it made in gold if —"

"Of course you can. Come here," she commanded. "Isn't that beautifully made?"

____

[71] Doornfontein: an inner-city suburb of Johannesburg, located east of the city center.

As Jim bent forward to inspect the wonder, he felt his heart thumping like a steam hammer. He pretended to be interested in the piece of metal, but his eyes wandered, sheep-fashion, to her face, to find her employing the same method of observation. He smiled and she laughed simultaneously.

"Tell me, why are you doing this sort of thing?"

"What sort of thing?" obtusely, his eyes devouring her form.

"Why, stupid, this silly jewelry business! Who on earth put that silly idea into your head?"

"Well — it pays — as well as anything else."

"Well, you shouldn't, you — . . . Do you know my husband?"

"Only by sight," said Jim.

He remembered a portly gray-haired man of between forty-five and fifty, with a fleshy face and hard eyes. Jim wondered how she had married a man so much her senior; she could not possibly be more than twenty-four at the most.

"At least I suppose he is your husband."

"Oh, yes," she said, and inconsequently: "Let's look at those trinkets of yours again!"

She fingered the things aimlessly, and at length selected a brooch at random.

Jim remained silent, busily packing his bag.

"I — I'll bring you the brooch — on — Friday," he announced nervously.

"Oh, very well . . . if you like. I don't care."

He looked at her.

"Mayn't I?"

"Oh, certainly!"

After this visit Jim was more than nervous: he was alarmed. He knew he would go again and that he might fall in love. He tried vainly to remind himself that she was the first attractive girl with whom he had ever spoken since he left England. All the vivid memories of Madge and Eve came uppermost in his mind. He would only make a fool of himself. Yet — yet it seemed rather hard, as well as absurd, that he should never dare be acquainted with a pretty girl again. And an impulse springing from a deeper cause urged him on: the insatiable craving to find the ideal. Perhaps she might be! He was torn between the hope of being able to fill that aching void and the fear of being disappointed and hurt again. So on the Friday he went — without the professional bag. She received him very demurely; the brooch was satisfactory, of course. As she was about to set out upon a shopping expedition, he timorously offered his escort to town. On parting he received permission to call; gradually he became accustomed to drop in to tea.

Several times he experienced a slight pricking of conscience, but persuaded himself that there was no harm; in fact, he began to be sure that he was really in love with her, and unconsciously to place her upon a platonic pedestal — only this time he did not use that adjective, but he meant the same. The visits became more frequent, until a daily tête-à-tête was an established habit. A common phenomenon was that the emotions awakened by her aroused the old moods of imaginative doubt and desire for knowledge which, save for those occasions when the mind was stirred by the weight of vast solitudes or the pageant of the heavens at night, had been dormant. He began once more to delve into the abstract, to demand something great and wonderful of life: to seek. She reciprocated — to a slight extent. Her friendship, too, softened his manner and refined his thoughts. Biddy soon noticed the change, and as usual chaffed him about the "gurrls." Then for the first time during their acquaintance, Jim exhibited a flash of temper, at which the Irishman laughed immoderately. Jim decided that he ought to stay away from Mrs. Icksburg, and did so — for two days.

One afternoon three weeks later Jim sprawled luxuriously in an armchair in Mrs. Icksburg's drawing room, smoking cigarettes and listening to a dreamy excerpt from Greig.[72] Presently Claire ceased playing, and, swinging round on her music stool, sat pensively watching him.

Jim produced his case of cigarettes.

"Oh dear, no," said she, smiling, "not those nasty clumsy things. Have one of mine? . . . Jimmy!"

Jim gave her an ardent look, and she laughed merrily.

"Now, sir, light it for me."

Jim did so with a trembling hand, and sat in a chair beside her.

"What's the matter, you silly boy?"

"Nothing," said Jim, trying to look unconcerned.

She exhaled a long whiff of smoke and laughed till the tears came.

"What's the joke?" he enquired, frowning, at which she went off into another peal of laughter.

Leaning suddenly forward, Jim burnt her dress with his glowing cigarette.

"Oh, you silly!" she cried. "Look what you've done!"

"I'm so sorry," said he penitently.

"Well, don't do it again; throw away the cigarette," she commanded. "I can see you're not smart enough to pay homage to two divinities at once."

"No," said Jim, obeying; "I'll worship Lady Nicotine at home and you here."

"Splendid! I declare you're improving. . . . What's the matter with your tie? It's climbing up the back of your neck. Bend your head and I'll arrange it for you."

"It's jealous," said Jim, with his head between her arms. "It wants to leave me for you."

---

[72] Edvard Hagerup Greig (1843 – 1907): Norwegian pianist and Romantic era composer, who used folk music in his compositions.

"Naughty boy!" she cried, pinching the back of his neck. As she withdrew her arms, Jim suddenly made a dive with his lips, but she was too quick and successfully dodged the onslaught.

"Oh, you wicked boy!" she exclaimed. "How dare you? I believe you wanted to kiss me! Get farther away from me — you're not safe!"

She laughed nervously.

"Oh!" said Jim; "I couldn't help it."

"You confess it — you wretch!" she cried, standing up and stamping her foot. But her blue eyes laughed all the time. "Still —"

A maid entered and placed a tea tray upon a side table. Claire began to pace up and down the room, while Jim, leaning against the mantelpiece, lit another cigarette and watched her.

"I suppose you've often wondered why I married him?" she began abruptly, when they were alone. "I didn't want to — I had to — my people thought him a good match — *mariage de convenance*, you know. . . . I don't know why I started this subject, though," coming to a halt in front of him. "It sounds wicked, I know, but I *hate* him. He never understands me; all he thinks about is money — money. I hate it!" she cried vehemently. "I do so want to confide in somebody. Girls are all the same. They think because you've got a rich husband that it's everything."

She flung the stump of her cigarette away angrily, marched to the sofa and threw herself upon it. Jim followed her and resumed his seat.

"You mustn't think about it. Let me light another cigarette for you?" hurriedly avoiding her eyes.

She smoked for a while. He watched her. She rose to her feet. Jim rose also.

"Oh, Claire!" he exclaimed suddenly, and folded his arms about her.

"Oh," she sighed, "you —"

The remainder of the sentence was suffocated as his lips again met hers.

"Ah!" she cried, pushing him from her. . . . "Don't!"

Claire made him release her, and going over to a mirror, rearranged her hair. Then she returned and sat upon the table.

"Jimmy, you're a naughty boy. I mean it. You must never kiss me again. I am horribly weak with you — you wretch! No, sit where you are, sir! I really ought to smack your face and never speak to you again; but —" she blushed — "well, I simply can't."

"I am sorry," said Jim humbly. "I couldn't help it because — I love you, dear."

"But, Jim, you mustn't!" she exclaimed, and, suddenly sitting down, buried her face in her hands. Jim stood nervously picking at the tablecloth and staring absently out of the window. Presently he became conscious that she had removed her hands, and was watching him. He questioned her with his eyes.

"I was wondering," she replied, "if you *really* love me."

"I do, Claire. Why, dearie, don't you know I do?"

"I do — I don't, and it isn't of course. Sometimes I think — oh, I don't know."

Jim looked bewildered.

"Oh, you are so dense! Can't you understand, Jimmy?" she asked plaintively.

"Understand what?"

"Oh, how stupid men are, Jimmy!" He came and sat in a chair next her.

"Do try and understand. . . . Oh, I do so want you to, Jimmy," very solemnly. "Tell me truly, do you really love me? Don't fear to hurt me. Tell me — for God's sake, tell me!"

"Yes, Claire," he said with sudden emotion, kissing her hand; "I do, I really do."

"As you would — oh, as you would if — if I were not married? Swear it."

As he gently took her averted head between his hands, her eyes were swimming with tears. He kissed her on the forehead.

"I do, Claire; I swear it" — and he meant it.

"Ah, but will you always, Jimmy?"

"Always and always," averred Jim solemnly, unconscious that he was beginning once more to chant the Lovers' Litany.

Her eyes brightened; she sighed contentedly. For a while they remained silent, he holding her hand a tight prisoner, until both had recovered their composure.

"Jimmy," she said dreamily, "I do love you. Oh, more than you can ever guess. I know that it's wicked, but I cannot — oh, I cannot help it. It's not fair. I never understood the meaning of love before — the inner beautiful meaning. Fancy! when they wanted me to marry him I didn't know, I didn't understand. He seemed such a nice old man — like father; and then he was rich. . . . He could help father so much and buy me beautiful clothes and things. I thought — or I didn't think at all — I was only seventeen. I simply didn't know. I thought that — that it would — would be like living with father. Oh God, it's cruel! Why didn't they tell me? Why didn't I know? I would sooner have killed myself. Then I hated him and loathed everybody — life. Everything settled down into a dreary misery. He knew that I hated him — said so and laughed. He treated me after that as a child or as part of the furniture — to sit at table and look pretty. He never understood me. He's so coarse. All he thinks of is money — and whisky — ugh!" she shuddered. "He hates music. Calls it a damned row. He doesn't understand, never appreciates — anything — that really matters. . . Thank Heaven, I've made him hate me! — from the very first. Since then we've lived our own lives — separately — apart. Later he let me know — did so because he thought it would hurt me, I suppose — that he had a mistress. Oh, I could have killed him! I wasn't jealous; good gracious, no! but I felt the insult. I heard men — his friends — laughing about it. Oh, I thought all men were brutes. I hated them and thought that I always should. Then I saw you, dear. Even now I can't understand it. I thrilled when I saw you. I couldn't sleep. I couldn't think of anything but — of you — your eyes — your face haunted me. Then I thought — oh, I don't know what I did think. I simply wanted you — longed for you. I knew that it was wicked — but I didn't care. I felt that I could walk the universe to get you. I knew that you wanted me — and oh, I was mad. But it seemed so hard. I suddenly knew what love was, and — Oh, I simply couldn't resist. I know I'm very wicked, but I don't care. I don't care what happens as long as I have you. . . . Life's so different since you came. The sunshine looks brighter — the birds sing sweeter. I hardly noticed them before. Yet sometimes when you're away — an awful doubt comes — doubt of you — supposing. . . . No, I won't suppose anything, only that I've got you!"

Leaning forward, she seized and passionately kissed his fingers.

"Oh, don't!" he exclaimed.

Snatching them away, he kissed her full on the lips, afterwards sinking back into the chair.

"You, too," he said suddenly, "have altered everything to me. I started life wrong. . . . I made a ghastly mistake —" He stopped abruptly.

"Yes?" gently stroking his hand.

"Shall I tell you?" he said brusquely.

"Yes."

"It's hard to explain to you, dear. . . . You see, I — I had always loved, or thought I'd loved, a girl I knew since I was a child, but

I thought she was — oh, an angel. You know the sort of thing a boy imagines. Well, then I went to London and met another girl. She was a — a poor girl who had to work for her living, you know, and I meant to be only a friend to her. Of course I thought all sorts of silly things. Well, she — I — I thought that I had wronged her." He began to speak rapidly — "I was going to marry her — a friend opened my eyes. Then I heard that the other one was going to marry somebody else. After that I came out here; but they distorted my views of life and women. Of course it was silly, but I was young, and hearing things from others, I jumped to the conclusion that all women were the same — at least, nearly all. Yes. . . . But when I first met you, you dazzled — hypnotized me. Then cynical thoughts arose. . . . I thought — forgive me, dear — that perhaps you were the same. Oh, my darling, you cannot understand. . . . Yet I don't know. . . . You have taught me — so different. Changed the perspective of the whole universe. And yet — it's only a month since I met you. Good Lord! it seems absurd — four weeks to change one's views of the whole scheme of things!"

"Don't!" she exclaimed, starting away from him, "or I shall begin to cry."

"We're getting too deep into things — taking things too seriously, don't you know," he said. "A good many — an Irish pal of mine preaches that gospel — the evil of taking things seriously; and I'm not so sure that he's wrong. Look, between music and — love, our tea has got cold!"

"Oh! I don't want such mundane things when I've got —" Her eyes finished the sentence.

"Nonsense, Claire! Such things are necessary, although personally I've often thought how ripping it would be if we could only dispense with eating, drinking, and other sordid affairs of life. There we go again, wandering far into the land of the impossible. Don't look so serious, Claire. I love to see the laughter in your eyes."

"I'm not serious, boy — only — deliriously happy."

"Don't, Claire; such cannot last."

"Why not, Mr. Cynic? Well, if you insist upon sordid things we may as well have them hot, and — now I come to think of it, I'm dying for a cup of tea. I suppose I shouldn't be a woman if I wasn't. Strange, isn't it? How we're tied up by little conventionalities! If one doesn't conform to the popular idea one's condemned as eccentric — crazy — whether you have money or no. I often feel a wild desire to throw off such shackles and be original — be less of a sheep. Oh, what a weird boy you are! With you I'm always wandering from the concrete into the abstract. Yes, Simmons" — to the maid — "some fresh tea, please. . . . Her proper name is Tulip," she continued when the maid had departed. "Father's Russian and mother — crazy, I should think. I can't say Tulip and look at that lanky, rawboned figure; and Brechkowsky imperils my front teeth. So I call her Simmons."

"That reminds me of the Chinese chestnut," said Jim, laughing. "An Englishwoman in China engaged a manservant. 'What's your name?' she inquired. 'Wan Lung Ah Foo,' came the bland reply. 'Oh horrors!' she exclaimed. 'That's too long and I couldn't remember it. I'll call you John. You savee?'[73] 'All litee, me savee,' said John. 'What you name?' 'Mrs. Corbett-Browne,' she replied with dignity. 'Mith Corlet Blown,' repeated John. 'Me no savee him — me call you Sammy — savee?'"

* * * * * * *

---

[73] Variant of *savvy*: to know or to understand.

Next day Jim lunched with Claire. They chatted on various topics of local and personal interest. There had been a series of burglaries of late which were supposed to be the work of kaffirs.[74]

"Do you know, Mr. Litham," she said for the benefit of the maid, "I am dreadfully scared that they'll pay us a visit. You can see," indicating the window, "that a man could easily get through the hedge into the garden. I only hope that if they do they won't tackle my room. I should be frightened to death. Unfortunately, it's the one nearest the hedge. I shall certainly shift to another bedroom if another house is attacked. Have you ever been burgled, Mr. Litham?"

After lunch, while titivating her hat at the hall mirror, she suddenly exclaimed:

"Oh, I don't care! . . . Jimmy, come to dinner tonight? There are six others, and you'll make up the eighth for two sets of whist."

Jim hesitated: he was thinking of her husband.

"Now don't refuse, or I shall be angry; you *must* come. There, that's settled. Only don't forget that you knew me in Cape Town," she laughed. "You know Cape Town, don't you? That's all right, then," as Jim nodded, smiling. "Dinner seven. Don't forget, there's a good boy! No! Au revoir."

Jim went away feeling supremely happy, but horribly guilty.

At seven-fifteen he arrived in immaculate evening dress. He discovered that the other guests, a married couple, two men and two girls, had arrived. They were waiting dinner for him. His hostess, he thought, in the soft light and low bodice, looked

---

[74] Kaffir: An offensive term for a Black person, used especially in southern Africa; or for a Xhosa: a member of a Bantu people inhabiting the eastern part of Cape Province, South Africa.

absolutely ravishing. She smiled as he greeted her, and whispered in his ear:

"Welcome, Mr. Brown, the peddler!"

He had, with considerable trepidation, expected to meet her husband. It was not until dinner was nearly over that he learnt from conversation that Mr. Icksburg was still at Kimberley; moreover, that he spent the greater part of his time traveling upon his large business interests. Jim was soon very much at home, becoming, under the benign combination of champagne and his inamorata's brilliant glances, quite witty. One of the men was middle-aged; the youngest was the fiancé of one of the charming girls, and all were friends of the Rand miner magnate.[75]

Jim began to long for just one kiss. The eyes and wine had driven all petty scruples from his head. After they had rejoined the ladies the whole party wandered for a bit on the lawn smoking and chatting. Although many possibilities presented themselves, Claire kept aloof with a most provoking laugh in her eyes. Presently they settled down to whist. To Jim's delight, he cut Claire for first partner, but so absorbed was he in watching her that she at last was constrained to whisper a caution to him.

---

[75] Rand: also known as the Witwatersrand: a ridge of gold-bearing rock in the Gauteng province of South Africa, which was the site of a major gold rush that began in 1886. This led to the rapid development of gold-mining in the region and to the rise of wealthy industrialists known as "Randlords": mining magnates and financiers who controlled the diamond and gold mining industries roughly from the 1870s to World War I. The Randlords amassed enormous wealth and influence through their control and played a significant role in shaping the economic and political landscape of South Africa. As noted above, circa 1902 Beadle was employed by Transvaal Customs as Assistant Compound Manager, Witwatersrand Native Labor Association. Source: *Adventure*, 3 July 1918.

Midnight had arrived ere the guests rose to depart. Jim was in the hall with the last of them, who, to Jim's annoyance, insisted upon giving him a lift in his cart as far as the Wanderers'. He badly wanted a moment alone with Claire. Suddenly he found that he had forgotten his cigarette case. He ran back to find it, hoping that she would invent an excuse.

"It's not in there, Mr. Litham," she called; "I saw it on the table on the verandah. I'll get it for you."

She did, with the consequence that they met outside.

"Give me one kiss," pleaded Jim, as she dodged his first attempt.

"No, sir; not *now*."

She whispered in his ear.

"Good night, Mr. Litham," she said aloud.

Jim was very preoccupied as Faulkner[76] drove him into town. He had been startled by the quivering of her pedestal and strove to console himself. A line of Kipling occurred to him:

"I couldn't do such 'cos I loved her too much,
But I learnt about women from 'er."

Yes, that was true, Jim told himself. He dismounted at the top of Wolmarans Street, and, bidding Faulkner "Good night," stood irresolutely in the gloom of the tall trees.

Yet — why shouldn't he take the sweets the gods were pleased to send him?

---

[76] It's highly unlikely that Beadle was referring to author William Faulkner (né Falkner; 1897 – 1962), who was only eighteen years old in the fall of 1915 (when reviews of *A Passionate Pilgrimage* appeared in London). And William Falkner did not become "Faulkner" until 1918. (Note the alteration in spelling.) Faulkner's first publication, a poem titled "L'Après-midi d'un Faune," appeared in *The New Republic* on 6 August 1919.

"Biddy's right. Women *are* the devil," he informed the silent street, and set off into the darkness at a great pace.

CHAPTER III

JIM had arrived at crossroads. In a cursory analysis of himself he had suddenly discovered, as he had remarked to Claire, that his views of the world had changed, or rather that they were changing on certain points, which accounted for his mental confusion. Up to then he had adopted opinions formed from his small experience of women. This was natural, as everything is comparative. He had had a vague idea that there were good women, but that they were few and far between. The teaching of Biddy and other cynical men of the world coincided, more or less, with his very limited experience; therefore he had accepted their view as being the truth, not in the least acceptable because inevitable. On the evening of the dinner party he had been convinced that he was wildly in love with Claire; then the fact of what he had considered her weakness, of her stooping from the pedestal, had shocked him; for Claire had very nearly attained the position of Madge in his estimation. But he thought of Eve. Well, he was not such a child now; he was a man of the world. Yet, although he had found that his emotions towards Claire were so near akin to his worship of Madge, he had feared that they would be destroyed. However, he had reasoned, it was only in accordance with his and others' opinion of women; consequently there was nothing unusual. To his utter astonishment he discovered that she had not fallen in his estimation; there was no suspicion of self-loathing; he loved her more passionately and yet more tenderly than ever. . . . Then the solution flashed upon him. He really loved her. He had never loved Eve. He hadn't supposed that he had; not his ideal love. But in the past he had decided that there was no such thing as love. . . . Well, now everything was so different. Poor darling, what a miserable and unkind fate had dealt with her. He understood so much now; and sympathized. . . . And Claire was so different. . . . He lay awake nearly all night attempting anew to solve these problems, to label and arrange his emotions.

*　*　*　*　*　*　*

"Boy," said Mrs. Icksburg over tea one afternoon a few weeks later, "I want you to do something for me; will you?"

"Why, certainly, girlie. What is it?"

"Promise?"

"Well, how can I —"

"Because I want you to," — looking into his eyes. "You must; won't you?"

"I . . . all right . . . I promise, girlie. Now what is it?"

"You must give up this horrid life. No" — as he frowned — "you must; you promised, remember."

"Oh, Claire, hang it! Besides, I must settle on something first."

"Why don't you try the stocks?"

"Thanks," he laughed. "I've tried it."

"When? Did you lose?"

He told her.

"Oh, you silly boy! Now let me be your oracle. I'll give you the tip what to buy and when to sell. Trust me, Jimmy. I'm not a business woman, but I know that." Jim looked doubtful. "Oh, you are stupid!" she continued, frowning. "Can't you see? Oh, that's just like you men, you always think that a woman cannot understand business. They understand a good deal more than you think they do. I know because — well, I know."

"Oh!" exclaimed Jim, the solution dawning upon him.

"Well?"

"Nothing."

"Oh, boy, what's the matter with you? You're as dense as — as can be. Oh, I could smack you[!] Now you are to do as I tell you[.] Go tomorrow and cover as many Valley Deeps as you can afford. They're below par now, but they're going up — when they touch fifteen, sell."

Jim smiled at her glib market jargon.

"I don't know," he said slowly. "You made me make a blind promise, but —"

"I won't have any 'buts,' boy. You've got to do as I tell you. . . . Now!" looking into his eyes. "Promise!"

"I have promised, girlie."

"Promise you'll keep it?"

Her lips hovered above his.

"Oh, yes! I'll promise anything if —"

* * * * * * *

The fact that, against his inclination, he had promised Claire to profit financially by her private knowledge caused Jim considerable misgivings. There was nothing exactly wrong in it, but he felt that it "was hardly playing the game." However, he had promised, and so had kept his word; but he had from the outset determined that it should be once, and once only. Having given up peddling, he had now to decide upon another method of providing bread and butter. He could not come to any satisfactory choice — in Johannesburg, at all events. To leave Claire would be terribly hard. But would it not be the best course for both of them? His emotion denied, but his reason acquiesced. He really loved her, he told himself. Well, that being the case, was it not better to sacrifice a little than cause her ultimate disgrace? He felt that the present state of affairs could not last for long. He was in a dilemma. If he stayed the situation would, he was sure, lead to a divorce, which he really wished, although the fact that he was not in a financial position to marry and keep her did not escape him. Finally he decided to leave her. When he had an assured income he would return and force the hand of circumstances. This, he argued, was the most reasonable plan. Once having made up his mind, he refused to deliberate any further; he knew his weakness.

"Claire," announced Jim one afternoon from the depths of a long chair, "if Valley Deeps turn up trumps, I'm going away."

"Going away? Boy! Why?"

"I think I shall go back to Bulawayo and —"

"But why, Jim?"

"Because — because I think it's best, girlie."

"Are you — don't you want to see me anymore, dearie?"

"Good Lord! That is just the reason. I want to see you too much. Much as I hate it, I think that I ought to, Claire; I really do. If you were only free and I could marry you, it would be so different, girlie; but as it is, this will only end in trouble. It doesn't matter for me; it's yourself I'm thinking of, dear. I love you so, the last thing I wish to do is to bring disgrace upon you. Can't you forget me, girlie?"

"No," she answered slowly, after a pause. "Of course I cannot. Do you think a woman can so easily forget when she loves?"

"Nor I you, dear; but what I wish to do is the right thing. I don't think it right to allow this to go on. All the punishment would rest upon your head. I love you, Claire dear — that you know — and shall always do. It is because I love you so much that I am going to leave you now. Don't make it harder for me! Girlie, don't you understand? I think — I know that in the end I shall love you more — or respect myself more — for love you more I cannot."

"But, oh, boy! it will hurt — a wound that will never heal."

"Don't you think that I, too, shall suffer? But, Claire darling, will you wait — till you are free, and then I can marry you?"

"Wait?" She spoke eagerly. "Wait? Do you mean that? Will you wait for me, dearest boy? Oh, then, that — that will soften the pain — so much."

"Yes, Claire, I will wait, even if it's years and years, because I love you so. My love for you will never die."

"Nor mine for you, my dearest darling."

A dust devil, whirling from the street, rattled the windowpane like a senile chuckle as he raised her hand and kissed it.

"Oh, my dearest boy, I'm so happy '."

"Are you, girlie? I'm not. I'm so miserable."

"You don't understand," she said gently. "I mean that I'm happy because I know, now, that you really do love me — the love I've dreamed of — the ideal love."

There was a pause.

"Do you know, Claire, that it seems rather rotten to — well, wait for another man to die." He stared absently. "I've seen many die and killed a few niggers, so I suppose that after all it's very absurd. Many fellows wait for their people to die to come into money and all that sort of thing. . . . This is far higher — less sordid — than that. Good Lord! what rot I'm talking. Forgive me, dear, if I hurt you. Do you know," he continued, smiling, "I believe that I must have inherited a small chunk of nonconformist conscience from some ancestor. It's queer how absurd ideas like that float into my brain at odd times. I suppose it's a sort of incipient madness like that which causes criminals to go and make silly confessions."

"I don't care in the least if it's wicked. He has been far more wicked to me. He's certainly nearly ruined my life. We're not trying to hurt him; because of his wickedness we've got to wait. Oh, Heaven knows how long! . . .You don't know — can't imagine the torture he has caused me."

"I must go, girlie!" he exclaimed presently, jumping up; "it's nearly six."

"Who is she?" she chaffed.

"A crowd of fellows," said he, laughing; "so you needn't be jealous. Au revoir, darling! . . . Tonight?" he whispered, as he kissed her.

* * * * * * *

About half-past nine one morning, having leisurely dressed and visited the P.O. Box in the same building, Jim proceeded to breakfast. One letter was from Claire with the laconic word "Sell." Calculating that his broker ought to be down town, Jim rang him up on the 'phone, instructed him to sell, and learned that he stood to make a comparatively rich profit. "No wonder these blighters[77] in the know make money!" reflected Jim. "Why, if I were to — No! I won't; I'll go, as I said I would. Come in. . . . Hello, Biddy! . . . The very man. Say, Biddy, we're in luck. I've just sold Deeps at eighteen and four-fifths. — That's £1,500 each. Eh, what?"

"Bedamn, it's millionaires we are entoirely! Come and have a bottle of the 'bhoy' to celebrate the event?"

"Wait a moment; I want some money. . . . How's pithness, my boy?" Jim inquired as they entered the street.

"I've turned it down, Jimmy. No; seriously, it doesn't suit me delicate constitution. I'm goin' to try to be respectable, but" — with a prodigious sigh — "it'll be terrible hard work. No, bedamn," he added, "I won't. I'll go back to the profession."

"The what?"

---

[77] Blighter (slang, chiefly British): A contemptible or unpleasant person; often used as an extravagant substitute for "fellow."

"*The* Profession, darlin': actin' for a living instid of livin' by an act — of a damned Dutchman."

"Didn't know you were ever on the stage, Biddy?"

"An' ye didn't know I was a gintleman of manes, an' a cab driver, an' a quill driver, and a professional liar for a paper, did ye? It's rememberin' the things I haven't been that worries me. But pretinding to be someone else is the finest of all: 'cos then ye find out what a devilish fine chap ye are yeself. That's why actors are God's own people: He made 'em first and then made the world for 'em to live in; but even He couldn't make it good enough for 'em."

They entered a restaurant, sat down, and ordered wine.

"Biddy," remarked Jim, with the second bottle, studying his wine glass, "supposing — just supposing a man loved — a married woman and — and that she loved him." — Biddy smiled gently. — "And — her husband was a beast" — unconsciously Jim spoke maliciously. "Old, you know, and a — a beast," he repeated.

"It's always like that," Biddy murmured.

"What's that?" enquired Jim, looking up.

"Nothin'. Is the girl pretty?"

"Oh, awfully pretty." Jim's eyes softened absently.

"Yes, they always are, the darlin's —"

"Eh?"

"I said that they — er — the girl in your case is pretty."

"No! no! I'm only *supposing*, you know — supposition —"

"Yes, av course — supposition," agreed Biddy, with the faintest inflection on the word.

"And," continued Jim, "they loved one another — you understand?"

"Ah, yes, I understand."

"And they are — were," corrected Jim — "both young —"

"And handsome," supplemented Biddy.

"No-o!" said Jim, dreamily critical. "I don't think the man is — er — that is, was."

"They usually are — in books."

"Yes, yes, in books" — grasping at the new idea. "This is in a book."

"Av course!"

Jim paused and abstractedly sipped his wine.

"And the man loved her — really loved her, and she really loved him."

"So you've said," dryly.

"Eh?"

"Go on."

"And they loved each other," he repeated lovingly. "And do you think that — that — that he ought — to go away — for her sake?"

"If he really loves her, and if he's wise, he will go away."

"That's what I thought," murmured Jim softly.

"And wait — events," concluded Biddy, smiling.

Jim frowned and relapsed into dreamy abstraction.

"A toast!" cried Biddy after a while. "Here's to Her —"

"Eh?" said Jim, looking bewildered. "Yes, here's to — whom?" he finished, suddenly cautious.

"Your girl — the suppositious girl!"

"Ah, yes. Here's to her!"

They clinked glasses and drank standing.

"Biddy," said Jim presently, "have you ever been in love?"

An expression of pain flitted across Biddy's eyes as he murmured:

"Yes — once — long ago!"

Jim looked enquiringly; after a pause Biddy said very quietly:

"That was fifteen years ago — she, too, was married. Like you — your suppositious case — and I went away."

"Ah!" said Jim thoughtfully. "I see."

Biddy remained silent, staring vacantly at the bottle of wine.

"And she?"

"Died."

"Strange," observed Jim; "so like my — suppositious girl."

"No!" said Biddy, suddenly emotional; "nothing strange. History repeats itself. Same little tragedies — same little comedies year after year; same little mistakes — century after century, age after age. The Everlasting Cycle. . . . Damn!"

CHAPTER IV

ALTHOUGH an impulsive temperament oftentimes leads a man into trouble, it occasionally jerks him away from temptation. Once Jim had made up his mind, he always acted in a hurry, with the result, in this case, that he did not dally long enough for Claire, who had not taken his decision in earnest, to weaken his resolution to leave Johannesburg. Now she strove to keep him near her, and grew angry at what she was pleased to call his desertion. The subconscious reason of this anger was the fact that Jim would not, or could not, understand that she merely desired to play with the emotion of grief caused by the suggestion of losing him; just as a cat is prompted to allow a rat to escape a few inches, and then, as anticipatory disappointment at losing the prey pleasantly thrills her, to dart a lightning paw to recapture the victim. Such is human nature, the inherent passion for playing with emotions, pleasant and otherwise; for this reason a woman purposely quarrels with her lover, the huntsman extracts joy in flirting with danger.

However, the effect was to cause Jim to hurry his departure, conscious of his weakness and prompted by an unwritten law of the males that one man may not tamper with the property of another man, unanimously, if mutely, denying the "property" any opinion or desire at all, no matter in what circumstances; as well might a man's horse or dog wish to change owners. Also, although Jim would not admit it even to himself, the owner, in the portly person of Mr. Julius Icksburg, whom Jim had not met as yet, was arriving in town that week: not that Jim feared him physically, but in the fact that he as a man — a point of honor Jim would have called it, quaintly enough — would have been ashamed to look him in the eye, feeling that he had poached upon another man's preserves. So the following day, after an emotional farewell to Claire in the early morning, he was dining with Biddy, amid the glare and bustle of the station restaurant.

"Have you really decided on your next move?" Jim inquired as they attacked the cheese. "Wish you'd come along with me, old boy?"

"Wish I could, too, but I'm too old for wild and woolly adventures, me son!"

"Rot! You an old man at forty! What are you going to do?"

"Sure and how the divil do I know? Have a good time and gamble on 'the chains.' Might bring off another long shot. I'm often lucky when I don't care whether or no."

"Oh, hang!" exclaimed Jim. "I don't want to go in the least. I'm sick of everything. When there is a chance one can't take it. Everybody always on the watch to get the better of you. A good pal's so rare, Biddy, and now — oh, life's rather rotten, after all. What do you really think of life, Biddy?"

"Life is what you make it — leastways, more often what ye livin' makes it. Life strikes me as being some sort of gigantic joke, and the only protection is to take it as such and enjoy it as a joke. In the main, av course, there is times when — when ye can't quite see the point, but perhaps t'other Johnny's got a keener sense of humor than we have. Sometimes we've got to do things we don't like, then it's no joke; but when we watch the other fellow being made to do what he don't like, then we laugh like the devil — that's human nature. When the Gods started gathering materials for the making of mankind, he who shoved in the whacking dose of human nature must have chuckled and anticipated some fun. Bedamn! perhaps they sit up there and play us off one against the other like a marionette outfit."[78]

"Yes," said Jim. "But it appears to me more like a child playing around with a vast box of bricks trying to form a particular pattern — making a mess of it and wiping it out and starting afresh. At one time, I used to believe in the orthodox beliefs, and now — well, I don't know whether I do or whether I don't. Some things seem so utterly incomprehensible. I used to believe until I started to think about it. One does when stuck away in the wild. But, once think, and then there are the impossible questions one wants answered, and I always did want to know why. Anyhow, the effect of thinking of the terrific primal forces made me wonder whether we are of so much importance. Still, I suppose I'm wrong — perhaps there is a God who looks after us and I'm wrong to question. Still, I was made that way. 'Did the hand then of the Potter shake?'"[79]

"The wisest thing, me bhoy, is not to think. Nobody can solve these problems. We simply don't know. So what's the use of howling about it?"

"Yes; but, Biddy, if you take religion away altogether — well, there doesn't seem much to live for — I mean, to be good for. And, besides, it keeps people good. Without it many would be so unhappy!"

"Why unhappy, me son? That's childish. Because you take away a false something — an imitation — a doll which you've been used to, you must needs weep and howl like an ill-trained child. Why unhappy?"

---

[78] Throughout the narrative the Irishman resembles a sort of Harlequin figure poised to tweak the reserved personae of his staid Victorian counterparts. But Biddy may also personify Beadle's evolving life-philosophy, especially as later limned in *Dark Refuge*.

[79] Attributed to Omar Khayyam (1048–1131), from Edward FitzGerald's 1859 translation titled *Rubaiyat of Omar Khayyam*.

"Oh, it's not exactly that — it's — oh, something. But the other — tendency to evil."

"Tendency to rubbish! Shure, I'm not a saint although I am an unbeliever; but, bedamn, I'm straighter and less of a rotter than many of your —"

"All right, Biddy" — smiling; "don't get hot."

"Well, that does irritate. All the sects are the same. Believe in what I say or be damned. A man can be just as straight with or without a religion. He'll do exactly and be exactly as his faculties dictate."

"Well, you may be right, Biddy. Who knows? as you say. But all the same I don't like the idea."

"No, nor does the child like the idea of parting with its doll; and a little while afterwards it wonders why on earth it liked it."

"Maybe!" Jim paused to light a cigarette. "Well," he said reflectively, "I don't know which or who's right, but there does seem to be a kink in mankind generally, as if the Creator was only in the experimental stage."

"Bedamn, that's more than likely. Experimental or developing stage are much alike. We're all so damned imperfect — woman especially. Yet I don't know," he added, lighting a cigar; "we say women are the devil. So they are in the main. But man ain't a paragon, is he, Jimmy?" with a twinkle. "There's always two sides to a question. Women do things just because they can't help it; and, damn it, so do we. Fact is, some primitive strain in man wants an angel on a pedestal to worship, and then because he finds the angel to be very much the same as he is, simply flesh and blood, he stamps around cursing everybody and brands women as fiends incarnate. Few women do anything they shouldn't do purposely, with malice aforethought; simply do it because — they can't help it — the darlin's! So human too.

As one studies human nature the more compassionate one becomes."

"Do you really think that all women are — well, wicked, Biddy?"

"H'm, I don't know. Some are really good, I suppose. I thought that one was, but then any man sees only one side of a woman and — one never knows — everything. Pope or somebody says that all women are rakes at heart — and, bedamn, he's right, I think. He meant that as human nature simply. Dame Nature is a sad rake."

"It's awful to think that no woman is really good," observed Jim.

"I don't think so. Some women — many women — will do deeds of noble sacrifice far higher than man and perhaps never sin; and after all sin is mostly what we've agreed to consider wicked. Bedamn! more often than not, a real sin, a sin against nature and happiness, is masquerading in the pure white wings of a conventional virtue. But personally I think there's a devil of a lot in opportunity and the right man. Men are always so content to be a devil and at the same time expect the woman to be an angel. Have you ever met a man who was an angel?"

"No," said Jim, laughing.

"A woman?"

"Er, don't know. I knew one. . . . I mean I've met some who looked like angels."

"Looked? Did you know her? 'Tis them I mean. . . .Well?"

"No-o."

"Lucky man! 'Ware wire when you meet another!"

"And man's? What's man's character?"

"Hasn't got one, bedamn! Man is, as I've told ye, reasonable, and reasons out plans, works and deliberately does wickedness, partly because he likes it and partly to profit himself. Yet with all man's forethought and ingenuity I've known women to make a bigger mess of things by sheer — couldn't help it. Search where ye will, ye'll never find a man or a woman, however bad, without some good in them; hard to find sometimes, I'll admit, but it's there somewhere. And *vice versa* — however good, there's a strain of wickedness somewhere; usually easy to find. Now, Jim, for thirdly and lastly take this advice — never wholly trust a man nor a woman. The man will usually let you in to profit himself; the woman because — she can't help it. You probably won't act up to it. We never do, and that's the pathos and bathos of life. Here we go paddling through the centuries making ghastly mistakes, slowly gaining a little wisdom by the time we are ready for the grave and too late to profit by it; and yet we cannot, and most cases don't try, to let posterity profit. They shuffle blindly along the same old trail, stubbing their toes and hurting themselves as their forefathers did before 'em. And so, I suppose, we shall go on for all Eternity — or until the child gets tired of his box of toys and — sells it, I was going to say — but perhaps he has become tired long ago and sold it — to the devil. That would explain many things. There goes your second bell! Waiter! it's the bill I'm after havin'. No! me son, my shout."

The train was already drawn up beside the platform, the electric dynamo throbbing like the heart of a sentient animal, ready for her long flight to the Cape and Bulawayo. Jim found his seat in the Rhodesian portion, labeled, and the compartment, to his delight, unoccupied.

As they stood talking on the verandah of the carriage one or two casual acquaintances upon the platform bade him a cheery farewell. The approaching departure was emphasized by the environment. Jim became preoccupied, having in his mind's eye a pair of blue eyes moist with tears. He felt as if he could not start; he wanted to jump on the platform and refuse to go. At last the whistle sounded; friends made a rush off the cars, the guard waved his lantern, and with a jerk and a groan the Cape Limited gathered way.

"Goodbye, old boy," said Jim, shaking hands.

"Goodbye and every good luck, me son! Wish I was coming — now."

"Well, come — quick! Jump!"

"No, sonny!" — laughing. "Not now. Ta-ta! Be good — as you want to!"

Jim hastily began to smoke. Rain had commenced. As the train rattled past the Doornfontein level crossing he waved the glowing end of his cigarette towards a slender figure under an umbrella, who answered with the feminine handkerchief.

"Goodbye, girlie!" he muttered, with a lump in his throat. "Even the Gods themselves do weep! . . . Damn! What an emotional ass I am!"

Whilst indulging in gloomy and sentimental reflections the train drew up at Elandsfontein Junction[80] to await the Pretoria section. Jim alighted and marched up and down the platform, watching the lights and bustle. At length he observed the advancing headlight of the Pretoria train. "Considering all things," he said, addressing the night at large, "and the dampness thereof, I think I'll have a drink for the good of my soul." As he emerged from the bar he ran into the arms of a Pretoria acquaintance.

"Hello, Litham! Where are you off to? Come-and-have-a-drink?"

Jim agreed, glad to escape his own company.

"Bound for Bulawayo," he explained later.

---

[80] Elandsfontein, now known as Germiston: site of a railway station in Johannesburg.

"Are you? Good!" exclaimed Hubbard. "Friend of mine going up to meet her fiancé. Might do the civil. Rather pretty girl," he added by way of inducement.

"Oh," said Jim, without enthusiasm, "certainly."

Upon their return to the car they found Mrs. Hubbard talking to his prospective protégée, who leaned out of the window of a ladies' compartment next to his own. "How do you do, Mr. Litham?" said Mrs. Hubbard. "Miss Lyston — Mr. Litham!"

Jim, looking up, beheld a pair of large yellowy-green eyes regarding him quizzically.

"How d'you do!" she said quietly, nodding, without offering to shake hands.

Jim became conscious of her mouth, of medium size with sensitive lips puckered slightly at the corners, appearing ever ready to twitch with amusement. He felt slightly annoyed, ready to resent her seeing him as a humorous subject. For a long while he was unconscious that she had any features save her eyes and mouth.

"Litham's bound for Bulawayo too, Violet," observed Hubbard to his wife. "He's going to look after Joan[81] for us."

"Oh, how good of you, Mr. Litham. — You are in luck, dear! — Mr. Chandler, an old friend of ours, was to have escorted her, but unfortunately he had to leave for Natal on business. Joan insisted upon going, nevertheless. She's very obstinate; aren't you, Joey?"

But Joan did not reply, having found something of interest down the platform.

"There goes the bell, Litham! You'd better jump in," exclaimed Hubbard. "You're half an hour overdue as it is. . . . Goodbye!"

---

[81] "Joan" is modeled at least partially upon Beadle's wife, Sylvia Grace Ellen Hornsby, who died on 13 September 1915 at the age of twenty-four, around the same time that *A Passionate Pilgrimage* was published. The original edition of the book is dedicated "To My Wife."

Again the Limited started with a jerk, a screech, and a chorus of "Goodbye"; and the passengers began to settle down for the night.

"May I make myself useful, Miss Lyston?" inquired Jim, looking into her compartment, which was shared by a middle-aged woman.

"Oh, no, thanks," she replied, struggling with a bundle of rugs.

"Let me unfasten those for you?" — advancing.

"Oh, please don't trouble," she answered acidly.

"What the deuce is the matter with the girl?" thought Jim. "Nonsense. Allow me!" and quietly he persisted in performing the civility

"I'll just lay them out for you."

"Thanks very much," she said in a softer tone; "but I'm not going to sleep yet."

"May I lend you any magazines?"

"I've altered my mind; I shall go to sleep," she decided frigidly.

Without any remark he stood on the seat to pull out the folding bunk.

"Don't trouble, please, Mr. Litham; I'll sleep on the lower."

The other occupant had already stretched herself upon the opposite seat.

"Well, good night, Miss Lyston!"

"Oh, good night!"

"Good Lord! what a bad-tempered little wretch!" he muttered as he returned to his own compartment to lie awake and sentimentalize over Claire.

* * * * * * *

Next morning Jim awakened at daybreak. The train was rumbling along at a steady speed, now and again rattling across a culvert through the undulating country of the Free State; a dreary, monotonous immensity. At about 8 a.m. he knocked at Miss Lyston's door. She was up and ready for breakfast. On their way through the swaying cars to the dining saloon the golden sunlight set her uncovered hair in a copper flame and revealed a slender, sinuous figure, immature.

"I'm afraid," she observed during breakfast, "that I was rather grumpy last night. I'm awfully sorry."

"Not at all," he replied conventionally.

"You didn't appear too pleased with yourself, Mr. Litham." She glanced at him mischievously.

"Well, that was tit for tat," said he, laughing. "I wasn't aware of it. I apologize."

They stopped an hour at Bloemfontein,[82] which proved to be the destination of the other occupant of the ladies' compartment.

"Much nicer," observed Miss Lyston. "Now we can chat uninterruptedly."

They spent the afternoon sitting on the carriage stoep[83] watching the surrounding country, whilst Jim endeavored to describe Rhodesia. He began to find that her big eyes had a strong attraction for him, and little by little he thought less of Claire. During the evening they became more intimate and amused themselves with cards. She did not object to Jim's cigarettes in her compartment, and in fact, after considerable fencing, smoked one herself. Her hair, ruddy brown in the shade, developed a knack of caressing Jim's face; at first, it

---

[82] Bloemfontein: now the capital of South Africa's Free State province. From 1902 to 1910 Bloemfontein was the capital of the Orange River Colony; in 1910 it became the Judicial capital of the Union of South Africa.
[83] Stoep (South African): a veranda.

caused him to think of Claire, then he only thought of Joan. Her ankle, too, he observed when she lay quite naturally at ease upon the seat, was fine and slender. It was really very fortunate, he thought, to have such an undeniably pretty girl to help him kill time on the monotonous journey. Once, when both stooped to pick up a card, her hair became unfastened shower upon Jim's face. He kissed her.

"How dare you, Mr. Litham?" she cried angrily, her eyes flashing green. "I thought — you must never — take such a liberty again. I mean it."

"I'm awfully sorry," apologized Jim with a doleful look. "I couldn't help it. You looked so damned pretty."

"Now, you make matters worse by swearing," she said, with a futile endeavor to maintain her stern look, as she deliberately let down the rest of the hair, which fell to her hips.

"By Gad! You have magnificent hair!" he exclaimed admiringly.

"Have I?" she enquired with a pout of disdain. "It makes my head ache. You must excuse me. . . . I have to recoil it, you see."

"Certainly," said Jim. "Please go on recoiling it. I rather like it."

"What impudence!" she exclaimed. "Will you kindly retire whilst I finish my toilet?" she added, with her chin in the air.

"Certainly," said Jim, with equal hauteur. "Good night."

"Oh, good night."

Half an hour later, Jim, sitting on the rail of the car verandah, smoking, was surprised to see the door open and Joan emerge.

"Isn't it a fine night, Mr. Litham?" she observed serenely. "And what glorious stars!"

"Very," said Jim dryly, looking at her.

"Do you know anything about them?" she continued, unheeding.

"A little," conceded Jim.

"Tell me," she demanded, moving closer to him so that he caught the perfume of her hair. "Tell me all about them, and — do you think that anybody will see if I have a cigarette?"

"I don't think so," he hazarded, smiling.

Hardly had he commenced his astronomical observations than she shivered, remarking:

"Oh! it's too chilly; don't you think so?"

"Shall I get you a wrap?"

"No-o, I don't think so."

"Shall we go in?"

"No-o" — pouting.

"I'm afraid I'm boring you?" he observed.

"No. . . . No, really you're not."

He resumed his topic.

"Let's go in!" she suddenly exclaimed.

"What the devil's the matter with her?" commented Jim to himself, as they returned to her compartment.

"Shall we play cards?" he suggested.

"No-o."

"Well, what shall we do?" he asked in desperation.

"Oh, read to me, will you?"

"Certainly," said Jim, ready to oblige, although he hated reading aloud.

"Oh, I can't hear properly with the horrid noise. I'll sit here" — plumping down alongside. "You don't mind if I rest my head, do you?" she said, glancing over her shoulder.

"No. Why should I?"

Gradually she leaned against him, as if in the effort to hear. Outwardly unconcerned, Jim read on. She pillowed her head against his arm.

"There, that's comfortable!" she exclaimed with a sigh, as if her action were the most natural thing in the world. "Now go on reading."

Jim, biting his lips, resumed the magazine story. Once or twice he stopped to rub his face.

"What's the matter?" she enquired innocently.

"Your hair tickled my face."

"Oh!" with raised eyebrows, "does it? I never thought of that. Shall I move?"

"Oh, no; it's all right."

When he had finished the story he remarked:

"Shall I read another?"

"No — how funny!" she exclaimed inconsequently.

"What's funny? The story?"

"No."

"Well, what?"

She laughed.

"Why — your heart keeps going thump, thump, thump, all the time. I've been listening to it. Does it always go like that?" her big eyes upturned.

Jim swore beneath his breath.

"Yes, of course it does."

"Ooh!"

Jim moved his arm and lit a cigarette. The arm returned and enveloped her waist.

"I didn't say you might," she observed placidly.

He exhaled a cloud of smoke by way of answer.

"Do you hear?"

"Yes."

She slipped her head farther down and looked up at him laughing, her red lips showing pearly teeth.

"Do you hear? Take your arm away!"

"I won't."

Suddenly she saw something in his eyes; with a bound she was up and seated on the opposite seat.

"You dare!"

"You little devil!"

"Ha! ha! ha!" she rocked with laughter. "Oh, how funny you are!"

"Damn!" said Jim, suddenly thinking of Claire. "I'm going. Good night."

A silvery, taunting laugh came floating down the corridor as he made for his own compartment.

"Women *are* the devil!" he muttered, as he flung himself savagely into a corner.

Thump, thump, thump, on the partition, and a gurgling laugh.

"Damn the little devil!" he ejaculated.

Thump, thump, thump.

"What the deuce does she want now?" he thought. "Anyone would think I was made of cast iron."

Thump, thump.

"Oh, I suppose I'll have to see what she wants."

By the time he reached her compartment he opened the door with trembling, eager hands. She was sitting in a corner, one leg on the seat, her mouth twitching.

"Oh, I'm *so* sorry to trouble you, Mr. Litham," she mocked. "I want another pillow. . . . Will you spare me one?"

He fetched one without a word.

"Thanks ever so much," she said sweetly. "Would you mind getting down the rugs? . . . Thanks! . . . It is so good of you; and you might fasten the window for me, will you?"

Jim did so, violently.

"Isn't there anything else I can make you do?"

Jim's lips noiselessly formed one monosyllabic word.

She saw and laughed musically.

"Good night," she said.

"Good night," he replied, opening the door.

She caught him by the arm.

"Well, perhaps," she murmured, holding up her head with pouted lips and laughing eyes[.]

He paused irresolutely. As he made a movement towards her she skipped back to the window.

"No, sir!" pointing a finger at him in derision.

"You little fiend!" he exclaimed, and turning, left her.

Jim went in to breakfast next morning without calling her.

"Good morning, Mr. Litham! I hope you slept well?" she remarked casually, as she sat down to breakfast.

"Oh, splendidly, thanks. I hope you did too," said Jim, parrying determinedly.

During the morning she exerted herself to be more than usually alluring. Now and again Jim would catch her looking at him with laughing derision which maddened him.

At Kimberley the Mail waited two hours. He took Joan for a drive in a Cape cart. He had not visited the town before, so that they both found considerable interest. During the afternoon Jim avoided a tête-à-tête, remaining on the verandah or reading in the library car. At dinner he noticed that she had made a few alterations in her costume, which tended to increase her natural charm. Jim forgot all his resentment; and he did not surprise any more derisive smiles. After dinner they remained upon the stoep as usual, talking; a few passengers were upon the opposite car platform.

"Where are you going after Bulawayo?" she enquired.

"I don't know exactly," said Jim. "I may go on to Salisbury, or more probably Victoria."

"Are there many white women up there?"

"No, very few; but I shan't stay in either town — beyond civilization."

"What, where there are no women nor fellows?" she asked.

"Yes, only niggers."

"But what makes you do that?" she insisted. "Surely you prefer whites to blacks?"

"Oh, it isn't that. I want to get some shooting and make money, you know."

"Poor old boy; I feel quite sorry for you."

"Don't look at me like that," he said suddenly.

"Why not?"

The last of their fellow passengers had left the verandah. She sat upon the rail holding on to a guard.

"Silky!" she exclaimed, running her hand through his hair; "and *so* thick!"

"Oh," said Jim; "don't!"

She laughed lightly.

"Why, you silly?" she said, stroking his head.

Jim slowly allowed his head to rest on her bosom, where it remained without protest; he sighed contentedly. She continued to stroke his hair; he to smoke. She bent her head and lightly kissed his hair, too lightly for Jim to notice.

"Come!" he said thickly. "Go in to bed. This is not good for either of us; you know it."

"Good night, Jim," she said after a pause, and left him.

He returned to his compartment and took off his collar and tie. He looked at his watch: only nine o'clock.

He leaned out of the open window staring into the night. A light rap sounded on the partition. He hesitated; he went. She was stretched at full length, with the rugs over her.

"Come and talk to me," she said plaintively. "I can't sleep. . . . No, read to me."

He picked up a magazine at random, and sitting opposite, began to read in a nervous and uncertain voice.

"Oh, hang it! I can't read tonight," he said, looking up.

"Can't you? Well — let's talk."

"All right!"

A pause.

"Why don't you talk?"

"What about?"

Their eyes met; hers amber clouded.

"Oh, I don't know!"

A pause.

"I — I think — I'll go," he said huskily.

"Will you?"

"Ye-es."

He rose and sidled towards the door, apparently unable to remove his eyes. He paused, and then advanced and stopped again. Neither spoke; both were hypnotized. He advanced another step; he stood over her. One hand opened and shut convulsively. On a sudden she sprang to her feet.

"No, no," she whispered. "Go!"

Jim drew back, breathing hard.

"Just one!" he pleaded.

She shook her head and moved away from him.

The train dashed across a culvert with a roar. Jim stepped back to pass her, with lowered eyes. He looked up at her and pleaded again, the words drowned in the roar of another culvert. She gestured for him to leave her. A violent jolt of the carriage threw him off his balance. Thrusting out her hands to fend him off, she caught him in the left eye with her finger. The pain was momentary, but intense.

"God!" he exclaimed, and fiercely caught her up in his arms and held her, raining kisses on her face and neck.

CHAPTER V

ON the following morning the Mail was traveling through a monotonous undulating country of scrub, broken here and there by a rough boulder-strewn kopje. Sometimes when panting up an incline, half-nude yellow-brown children and men from some adjacent kraal trotted alongside the carriages in the brilliant sunshine, offering bottles of milk or ground nuts for sale.

About half-past eight, Jim, looking very grave and preoccupied, made his way along to the dining car. Erewhile Joan joined him. She appeared nervous, and her eyes were slightly red. Neither looked at each other as they exchanged greetings.

Afterwards they adjourned to their carriage stoep and sat silent, Jim smoking, watching the rolling panorama of scrub and age-worn kopjes. The train, running comparatively swiftly down a slight incline, had just passed a ganger's[84] hut, when over the sea of bush a distant rooftop glinted in the sun[.]

"There!" exclaimed Jim at length; "that's Fig Tree[85] at last."

---

[84] Ganger (chiefly British): foreman of a gang of laborers.

[85] Fig Tree (also spelled Figtree): a railway station and small settlement in Mangwe, a district in the Matabeleland South Province of Zimbabwe. Figtree Train Station still exists and is located 37 km from Bulawayo on the railway line to the south. Additional information may be found in this account from 1907: "After entering Rhodesia the bush and grass country is occasionally varied by outcrops of granite boulders piled up in quaint-looking koppies. At Mangwe we come into the theater of the campaigns against the Matabele in 1893 and 1896. 'Fig Tree' station was one of our posts, and from the train you can see the Matopos away to the southeast, and the Inugu Mountain, one of the enemy's strongholds, rising like a dome

"Oh, I see — above those trees, the tin roof?"

"Yes. Only a few minutes now."

They looked at each other. Joan signaled him to follow her.

"Jim," she said with an effort, when they were alone, "I want to talk to you seriously."

"Yes."

"You must promise, solemnly promise — to do something I particularly wish."

Jim hesitated.

"Surely you can do that?"

"Yes, I will. . . . I promise."

"Thank you! It is that from now you must not know or recognize me."

"Oh!" protested Jim.

"You promised, mind, and I shall hold you to it. I've been very wicked and foolish," she continued, looking out of the window. "I'm more to blame than you are. Yes, I am. You're only a man. All men fall in love with a pretty girl. Yes, I know I'm pretty. I knew immediately I saw you — that I should like

---

among the other hills." Robert Baden-Powell, *Sketches in Mafeking and East Africa*, London: Smith, Elder, and Co., 1907, p. 77.

The abbreviation FRGS appears before the author's name, indicating that he was a Fellow of the Royal Geographical Society. Beadle was also elected to the FRGS in 1906, when he was twenty-five; and he was familiar with the work of this best-selling author (who also created the international Scout Movement, also known as the Boy Scouts). In the 18 September 1919 "Ask *Adventure*" column, in response to a question from a reader, Beadle writes: "The Rhodesian Mounted Police are the British South African Police with headquarters at Bulawayo and Salisbury, South Rhodesia. Baden–Powell wrote a book on them in the early days" (probably referring to the 1901 publication of *Notes and Instructions for the South African Constabulary*). In 1899, during the Second Boer War, Lieutenant-General Baden-Powell successfully defended the town of Mafeking during a 217-day siege. Thus, both Baden-Powell and Beadle were in South Africa at the same time.

you. I told you. You know I did. I meant to tease you, but — oh, I didn't realize — everything. You know what I mean. I couldn't resist teasing you. It was so tempting, like — like playing with matches."

Tears began to well in her eyes.

"Oh, Joan, don't! I was a brute beast."

"No! no! for heaven's sake don't touch me. You'll make me cry then. Oh, I have been wicked and foolish. He does love me." She looked at him through her tears. "Oh, why has Fate been so cruel? I've never allowed any man — except him — to kiss me, and now, just before —"

Jim smiled inwardly, despite the tragic circumstances.

"Oh," she cried, dabbing her eyes with a handkerchief, "swear that you'll never know or speak to me again? For God's sake swear it!"

"I swear, if you wish it."

"Oh, what a fright I am! Go! For heaven's sake, go!"

He seized her hand and kissed it.

"Goodbye, Joan. I only wish —"

"Oh!" she cried, and seized him. "Kiss me once more. I can't resist you — once more — just once. Oh!"

Breaking from him, holding him at arm's length, she gazed intently at him, her whole soul in her eyes, as if she would engrave every line of his features in her memory. Then she drew his face to her, the tears welling afresh, and kissed him madly, passionately, on eyes, face, ears, mouth, crying afresh between every kiss:

"Go! Go! Go! Go!"

She almost flung him from her and threw herself on the seat, sobbing.

He remained standing, helpless, not knowing what to do.

"Go, darling — oh, do go!" she sobbed.

Again he seized her hand, and, kissing it vehemently, left her.

"Good Lord!" said Jim to himself as he packed his rugs, feeling miserable and trying to swallow emotion. "What a strange creature I am! In love with Claire" — he smiled dismally — "and now just as bad over this one. I don't understand it. I must be in love with both of 'em. Man's a polygamous animal, I think."

At length the train ran through a few outlying bungalows and drew up in the Bulawayo station, a mere space of cleared veld before a line of corrugated iron offices, in which some dozen white men in khaki and drill,[86] and a few white women, were lost amid the crowd of natives in all manner of costumes, from cast-off European clothes to the humble loincloth. Jim had dragged his rugs and impedimenta to the far end of the car in order to avoid meeting Joan. He placed his goods in charge of a nigger porter, and as he walked up to the luggage van he saw Joan greeted by a tall, bronzed man whom she kissed effusively. Jim saw the glad look in his eyes and shuddered. "Poor devil!" he muttered. As he passed them on his way back Joan deliberately shifted ground in order to keep her back to him.

"Yes, I had a bad night, Harry," she was saying.

"Weren't you lonely, little girl?" the man asked affectionately.

"I was, rather," she replied, pouting. "The train was very empty — only some grumpy men who —"

"Good Lord!" thought Jim. "I don't understand. Women *are* the very devil."

* * * * * *

Jim put up at the Maxim Hotel, and spent a week idling about calling on old acquaintances. At the Police Camp few knew him;

---

[86] Drill: a durable fabric made of twilled cotton.

nearly all his old comrades had gone their various ways: civilization, the veld, fever and war.

Several times he passed Joan with her fiancé, but she looked serenely through him, apparently unaware of his existence, which caused Jim much troubled thought.

"I'm hanged if I understand women," he told himself in confidence; then after an emotional storm, in which he lashed himself into a frenzy of self-abasement, he found that, as nearly all hatred is a reflex of some action of our own, he was extremely angry with Joan. He wondered when the wedding was to be — and pondered. A woman who could treat her fiancé, poor devil, like that! Yes, he had been weak — horribly weak — behaved as a brute and a cad — yet she had tempted him and — well, he couldn't help it. She shouldn't have teased him. She should have known that he was only flesh and blood. He thought of Claire — and then felt indignant and angry with Joan again. She had done him an injury, he felt, and certainly it was her fault because she had tempted him. Women had no right to — Besides, now she even refused to recognize him. He thought of the man. Of course, had Jim known. . . . Well, yes, he remembered that he did know, but — she had tempted him. There was no pardon for that. He smiled as he thought of Biddy. Yes! Biddy was right. Women were the devil. But erewhile he began to concur more fully with Biddy; men, too, sometimes did things because they couldn't help it. Queer, complex creatures — men and women!

BOOK III

CHAPTER I

"UGH!" yawned Jim, sitting upon the side of his bed in the tent, some six months later, "this is an ungodly hour to get up. What time is it, Miêville? — Damn the skeeters!"

"Three of the clock and a fine moonlight night," said Miêville, scratching. "She's been up about an hour. Isn't it glorious? . . . Jaha, coffee ready?"

Jim, anxious to leave Bulawayo before Claire's letters undermined his resolution, had thought himself fortunate in meeting Bernard Miêville, a tall, brown-bearded man, with soft, sleepy eyes, who was something of a mystery in Rhodesia. He had been on the West Coast and in most parts of the world too, and easily persuaded Jim to join him on a trading and shooting trip through Upper Barotse[87] and out through Angola. Under his languid manner Jim had found an ideal veld partner and charming companion.[88]

---

[87] The Barotse floodplain runs along the Zambezi River in Angola, extending from Lukulu in the north to Nangweshi in the south.

[88] In his July 1918 "Camp-Fire" column Beadle provides some background info on his first story published in *Adventure*, "The Christman," which appeared the previous May. "The scene of 'The Christman' is laid on the upper waters of the Zambezi: in fact, the exact village is indicated. The story was founded — or rather suggested — by an incident which happened on my trip. A bearded gentleman — as described in the story — arrived at Livingstone from nowhere in particular with a wonderful tale of hidden jewels and buried Ivory in the southern Congo. A prospector named Poindextre fell for it and financed the *safari*. Just after they had gone we

As they were seated round a huge wood fire, drinking coffee and eating boiled eggs and biscuits, the men struck camp and packed the canoes. They had camped upon a wooded islet in the Kabompo.[89] In a neighboring pool a school of hippopotamus had disported themselves all night with many grunts and splashes, sometimes crashing about among the reeds and trees, but never approaching very near the large fires.

"He's a noisy, cheeky beast," said Jim, referring to an abnormally loud grunt close at hand. "He's been inquisitive and talkative all night. I've half a mind to give a four-fifty Express[90] just to teach him better manners."

"I haven't had much sleep either," observed Miêville. "A syndicate of five skeeters inside my net kept me amused whilst

---

heard that our bearded friend was wanted for murder and robbery in Cape Town. The next thing was that Poindextre was found nearly dead with blackwater fever in a native kraal. His charming partner had abandoned him in the bush, taking guns and outfit. Natives had found him. He recovered, came down to Livingstone, had a relapse and died. 'Miêville' was never heard of again."

[89] The second-deepest river in Africa, the Kabompo is one of the principal tributaries of the upper Zambezi. Beadle's adventures in this region are featured in a lively essay titled "Our Trip Down the Zambezi," which appeared in the May 1907 *Wide World Magazine: An Illustrated Monthly of True Narrative, Adventure, Travel, Customs and Sport*, pp. 276-283. The article chronicles a 1904 expedition to Chikoti, Zambia (a "prospecting and hunting trip along the upper reaches of the Zambezi and its tributaries, the Kabompo and Mombeji" (the latter most likely being a phonetic renderings of local dialect). On the return trip described in the piece, they embark "a little above the junction of the latter two rivers."

[90] "Fifty-four Express: a type of large-bore rifle cartridge, developed in the late nineteenth century. It was designed for hunting big game, particularly in Africa and India. Express rifles were known for their high velocity and flat trajectory, making them a popular choice for long-range shooting in open terrain. "Fifty-four" refers to a .54 caliber projectile.

they chewed my face. I killed all but one, but their pals are having revenge now. Just look at 'em, in clouds."

"Yes, my neck and hands are simply chawed up. Come and let's get underway; there won't be so many in the open river."

The high wooded banks cast deep and mystic shadows upon the silver-tinted water as the canoes glided, ghostlike, into the gloom, to reappear with the moonbeams glinting upon the wet paddles as they rose in unison, propelled by six stalwart, half-nude figures, one in the bow and five in the stern. In the wake at some distance followed two more spectral boats — the baggage canoes. Miêville's clear tenor voice floated out across the water in a passionate love song in Italian, accompanied by the thrumming of a guitar and the gentle swish of the paddles. Now and again the splash of an otter or water rat, or a wild call of forest life, echoed across; or, very occasionally, the loud snort of a playful hippo would cause the paddlers to increase their pace.

"Ah," said Jim, exhaling smoke, "this is heavenly!"

"Yes, it's very fine," admitted Miêville; "it just lacks one thing."

"What's that?"

"A pretty woman."

Jim laughed, thought of Claire and saw Joan's eyes.

From a distance came a long, moaning wail.

"Hark!" exclaimed Jim; "a lion!"

An owl hooted in the forest; a crash of reeds and undergrowth sounded as some large beast moved upon the bank.

"Primeval nature," said Jim.

"As it was in the beginning —" suggested Miêville.

"Absolutely. This is real beauty. Makes one think, think how utterly puny and insignificant man is, and how beastly conceited. Someday — who knows? — we shall have a beastly snorting steam launch here. Man arrives and brings with him that horror — civilization — with all its attendant horror sprites, smoking factories, screeching engines, tin houses with vile liquor, brothels and vice. It does one heaps of good to get away from it all and see how grand nature is before man dabs his vandal paw around. Look at those stars, at the Cosmos, and at us ants painfully crawling about on the face of the earth, shouting to one another how great we are! — to keep up our courage, I suppose!"

"Quite true," said Miêville; "how utterly insignificant we are in the scheme of things. Tom, Dick, or Harry takes it into his head to think that he's committed a sin, and immediately rends the air with his cries; thinks the Creator will be so grieved about it; imagines all his visionary band of angels weeping for him; doesn't realize that he is an atom — one of many million billions. Why should he flatter himself that the Creator ever thinks of him? The sooner he realizes his proper place in nature the better. But he won't; he's too conceited and thickheaded. If people only would see straight, they wouldn't waste time howling about sins. It's just savage hard nature — every living thing for itself, the universal struggle for existence, and the survival of the fittest. The man who talks about sin, moral responsibilities, and such rubbish, goes to the wall."

"No, I don't agree with you there," said Jim. "I admit man's place in nature and the proper recognition of such, but not the other. That's simply the primitive idea; we've developed and should be above that now. It should be for the benefit of the race in general or the community. I discard the primitive struggle for existence as limited to the prehistoric individual. There's no reason because one used once a primitive gut mouth that we should endeavor to use the same now. Physical nature has developed other and more accomplished methods; why should that not apply to mental development?"

"That sounds pseudoscientific, my young Ulysses, but wait until you've been in the hands of a modern Polyphemus[91] and his merry crew. Tell me, have you been so impressed in your experience with the fact that the other chap is thinking or doing things for your benefit, or the community's benefit; or, in fact, for anybody's except his own? You know that you haven't. I'll admit that there may be a few exceptions — fools who go to the wall for their trouble; but can you or I afford to be quixotic and tilt at windmills? Life is too short, remember, and say what you will, nobody can rely on any other."

"True in some ways," said Jim; "but still I don't agree with you. Circumstances force many from acting as they would or from trusting others. Still, the other *is* the higher ideal. You would argue that a man has the right to beat another by any means?"

"Yes, decidedly; otherwise he'll go under."

"No, I certainly don't think that; my idea is simply play the game. The motto of 'Do unto others, etc.' is, I admit, impracticable in this world. 'Do unto others as they do unto you' is far more reasonable. No matter how you argue on your side, Miêville, you know as well as I do that there are many things which, damn-it-all, a fellow can't do, don't you know."

"H'm," said Miêville, his teeth gleaming in the moonlight; "I don't know. A man can do anything — if he is determined."

"Oh!" said Jim, slightly irritated; "you're in a cussed mood tonight. I'm often sick and tired of everything, and feel like doing anything to get on — get money, to be able to have the power to follow up ideals, and — and other things."

"Women?" smiled Miêville.

---

[91] Polyphemus: a one-eyed giant Cyclops, who traps Odysseus and his shipmates in a cave and begins to eat them. Odysseus induces the Cyclops to drink a potent wine; once the beast passes out, the men blind it in order to escape.

Jim frowned and proceeded:

"But yet I know that I couldn't and wouldn't do many things; neither would you or any man."

Miêville laughed shortly.

"Bah! youngster; you don't know the world — as I know it."

Jim remained silent, staring across the river.

One of the paddlers, squatting down for a spell, asked for a cigarette, which Miêville gave him. As he crouched, the flare of the match lit up the man's face of polished mahogany, inset, cunning soft eyes. A loud splash sounded alongside the bank amid the mystery of the overhanging trees, followed by a piteous, half-human cry.

"What the devil's that?" exclaimed Miêville.

"A croc got a monkey, probably; poor little beast," said Jim, who knew the laws of the wild.

Miêville strummed idly on his guitar.

"Strange thing, life," observed Jim. "I don't understand it."

"Really?" remarked Miêville sarcastically; "who does?"

"Looking at this Jim gestured largely — "always makes me wonder what it all means. Why we're all here? What for? Why?"

"Why!" Miêville mockingly echoed. "The everlasting, eternal question asked since the world began. Even the wolf and the dog ask it when they howl at the moon — the unsolvable problem. Sometimes I think, when I can spare a few thousands, of building a Babylonian garden full of the rarest and most beautiful plants and flowers, and on the summit erecting a gigantic white marble pillar, having upon the top the note of interrogation sculptured in the finest black marble to stand against the sky. Black as a weak effort of mourning for the unsolvable problem, the sadness of countless millions."

"What a queer fellow you are!" exclaimed Jim.

"Queer? Why again. Nothing queer — only another personality — another side of me." He laughed. "I hardly know myself how many 'me's' there are. Every person is a plurality of individuals. Trying to guess which individual is going to turn up next is such a devil of a puzzle sometimes."[92]

A floating object, gleaming in the moonlight a few yards from the canoe, suddenly jumped into life, and with a swish of a huge tail and a flash of wicked eyes, disappeared.

"Lord! Crocodiles, Moonlight, and Philosophy. What a mixture! The Cynic and the Saurian! Ha! ha! New musical comedy. Listen!"

With a clever impromptu accompaniment he improvised to a lilting tune:

> This happened once upon a time
> When the world was growing old, Sir.
> There lived a certain sour young man,
> Whose eye was dour and cold, Sir.
>
> He preach'd that every man was vile,
> And women rakes at heart, Sir,
> Because he couldn't steal the plums,
> Nor the jam within the tart, Sir.
>
> Mister Cynic was his name,
> Of which he was so proud, Sir;
> And as he strutted round the world
> He blew his trumpet loud, Sir.
>
> Then idling 'pon a summer's day,
> He spied upon a rock, Sir,
> A-basking in the warm sunshine,
> A most gigantic croc, Sir.

---

[92] The multiplicity of the self as expressed through various ego-states — past, present, and future — is plumbed in depth in *Dark Refuge*, where the narrator uses the expression, "my quondam self."

"Howdy, Mister Saurian? —
Why d'you waste the day, Sir,
In sleepy bliss and sweet content,
When your wife has gone astray, Sir?"

"Is that so?" grinned the crocodile;
"Why make this awful pother?
There're many pebbles on the beach —
I can easily find another."

But the Cynic plied the crocodile
With questions rude and snappy.
Until he made that reptile's mind
Quite worried and unhappy.

"For ninety years and more I've lived
In wet and warm content, Sir;
Why must you now disturb me? —
Get you gone, before you're sent, Sir."

But Mister Cynic having caused
Another soul to doubt things,
With keener zest pursued his task
Of egging him to flout things.

Then Mister Saurian's tail, in wrath.
Rose swift with deadly aim. Sir;
Swept Mister Cynic off the earth —
Just Nemesis to blame, Sir?

Green and moldy now he lies
In water-hole mid reeds, Sir,
Providing fam'ly Crocodile
With luscious, dainty feeds, Sir.

His epitaph might read like this; —
When Skepticism mars your bliss,
Impart it not to guileless souls.
Lest you, too, rot in water holes.

"Very good," applauded Jim, laughing. "Why don't you appreciate your own moral? I suppose, like most of us, you can give good advice but are careful not to follow it, eh?"

"Did you ever meet such a rara avis who did follow his own advice?"

"No, I can't say I have."

"Nor will you. He belongs to an extinct genus, like the disinterested politician, the faithful husband or wife, the man who never told a lie, and other fabulous beasts. Faithful, I mean, in thought or desire, for all sin is a child of opportunity by desire. How many would be virtuous if they had the opportunity? I hold that a man is just as guilty who would but couldn't. The opportunity is lacking. Take the negative sins and virtues. The would-but-couldn'ts versus the could-but-wouldn'ts. Poor little could-but-wouldn'ts, you wouldn't be able to find them in the enormous mass — hunting for a needle in a haystack! A man may say in such and such a case he could but wouldn't, but why? — because he daren't! Another multitude to join the would-but-couldn'ts — the could-but-daren'ts. Very virtuous, isn't it, to refrain from sin because of fear. A man sees and desires the wife of another. He would, but he daren't — he notes the muscular arm of the husband — he might be caught — Ha! ha! — or he fears what the neighbors would say! Supposing all source of fear were removed — the husband off the earth and the neighbors too — would any moral consideration for his own wife or for her restrain him? Devil a bit! Then the religious person who refrains from a tempting sin because he fears hellfire: or resists something that hasn't much attraction because he thinks he's going to get a disproportionate reward in Heaven afterwards. Very virtuous! A man hates another and desires to kill him, but he doesn't — why? Because he fears that possibly the man might kill him, or if he doesn't the law would. Moral consideration. Wrong to take another's life! Bah! Fear only. I don't believe there's a streak of real virtue or moral responsibility in ninety-nine percent. Watch how indignant a man is at the idea of another man seducing his wife! Oh! the high moral tone! — the wickedness of the other man! whilst in the same breath he plans to seduce that other man's wife. It's true, Litham, I'm only talking from life as I've seen it. Adultery — the attentions of the other man to your wife! True love — your attentions to the other man's wife!" Jim winced. "Ha! ha! caught you, have I?" laughed Miêville. "Of course," feigning gravity, "I quite understand — exceptional circumstances — the husband's a brute, etc. — he always is."

"Damn you! Shut up!" said Jim, half savagely.

"Had enough? Well —" sweeping a chord on the guitar, he sang:

"Could I be true
To eyes of blue
If I looked into eyes of brown?"

"Pinked[93] you again, eh? Well, cheer up, you can console yourself with the assurance that women are just as bad as you are. It's just human nature, that's all. The most interesting study, for we're all so much alike. You're always safe to touch on the raw if you prod the human nature of a man. Study human nature, Litham, until a man or woman is like a stringed instrument to you; watch them respond, vibrate, shriek or laugh

---

[93] Pinked: (a) to pierce or stab; (b) to wound by irony, criticism, or ridicule.

as your fingers caress the strings of their nature. Love, too, is a harp — each woman a different string: so play skillfully on many and the result is harmony, perfect and sweet. Byron, Burns — any poet knows that. If you pluck on D sharp the whole time the result is monotony. Most amusing occupation in the world, I assure you."

"I should think that with the knowledge you seem to have, your appearance and accomplishments, that — that you're a devil among women."

"You flatter me, Litham," with a mocking smile.

"How old are you, Miêville?"

"Forty-eight. How old did you think?"

"Oh, about thirty-five."

"Again you flatter me. I'll tell you the secret of a long life — maybe it will be useful to you."

He stopped and laughed softly.

"Now, listen. Never worry yourself with moral or any other responsibility. Take your fun where you find it, as the Kipling fellow has it. Study human nature. It will both amuse and profit you immensely. Don't drink bad liquor or eat too much meat — it coarsens the fibers. Take ample sleep, exercise, and enjoy every moment of life as I do. Then you'll live long, bar accidents, as I have done with youth and vitality. I've enjoyed all my life, every moment of it; and when unkind Fate decrees my end, I'll die anywhere, happy in the thought that I've had a good time and regretting that it can't last longer. Ah me, I'd like to find the Philosopher's Stone or the Elixir Vitae — life is so very amusing. . . .Hullo! There's old Sol coming up for his daily task. I'm going to have a snooze."

A sudden exclamation from the bowman caused Jim's eyes to follow his outstretched arm. "By Gad! Miêville! Quick! Look!"

They were passing a flat across which a kudu, with his long horns flat on the withers,[94] raced for his life, pursued by three yellow dogs flying at his heels, tongues hanging, occasionally uttering a short, coughing bark.

"Splendid sight," said Jim.

"Yes," agreed Miêville, as the hunters and hunted disappeared in the shadow of the forest. "Splendid example, too, of life — of the survival of the fittest and the struggle for existence. Modern civilization — the Wolf Pack! Well, I'm going to have a snooze."

* * * * * *

At midday they reached the junction of the Lunga River.[95] Jim and Miêville from the top of the bank shot an eland and zebra respectively, for the sake of the meat for their men, who, overjoyed, promptly overloaded the baggage canoes. Walking for a while along the bank the country seemed alive with game — puku in herds, so thick that they resembled a sheep ranch.

"Stupid beasts," remarked Miêville, throwing a clod of earth at a whole herd standing stock still some sixty yards away. The clod broke before them, at which they turned, and, cantering for forty yards, turned and stood again, peering inquisitively over their shoulders. Miêville and Jim returned to their canoe as the flats gave way to thick undergrowth and forests. About five they arrived in sight of a large, stockaded village built upon the right bank.

---

[94] Withers: the ridge between the shoulder blades.

[95] The Lunga: a tributary of the Kabompo River, which is a tributary of the Zambezi.

"This is Sepopa's," said Jim, after consulting Gambai. "Better camp close and send Gambai with preliminary gifts and greetings."

"Well-built people," observed Miêville critically, watching the crowd of warriors clad in skins, with hair combed and oiled into a mass standing a foot above the head. After a lengthy palaver they landed and pitched camp, to the amusement and wonder of a large crowd of women, children and men, who quickly gathered to observe the white men. A tall man, bearing a conspicuously Semitic cast of feature, with ivory bangles and leopard-skin loin covering, harangued the crowd and Gambai. He, it seemed, was the Chief's eldest son, and from the many scars upon his body and face, evidently a great warrior. The Chief was ill, Gambai interpreted; Mateka would receive the presents and bring them his father's orders.

"Give him half a bale of the spotted bafta,[96] Gambai," said Jim. "We don't want to be mean, but that's quite enough for a start."

Mateka professed great indignation. Were they eaters of fish? (A term of opprobrium applied to the Marutse.)[97] A noisy and

---

[96] Bafta (variant of baft): a coarse, loosely woven cloth, made from wool or cotton, originally of Indian manufacture. It was mostly used for manufacturing sacks or for wrapping goods. But it could also refer to a type of garment or material used for various practical purposes, such as covering or protection. "Spotted bafta" suggests that it was imbued with a design featuring spots or dots.

[97] The Marutse, also known as Marutse-Mabunda, inhabited a kingdom in southern Africa during the nineteenth century. They occupied the fertile valleys of the Barotse country bordering the Zambezi, from Sekhose to about 150 miles south of the confluence of the Kabompo and Liba rivers. A considerable kingdom composed of various tribes and territories, it was connected to the Mabunda kingdom to the north, which was governed by the Marutse royal family. One notable monarch mentioned in the historical sources was King Sepopo, who expanded the kingdom's territory. Note that

violent altercation ensued, from which Mateka departed grinning, carrying off an extra present of a sheath knife. Later he returned, hungrily watching the heap of trade goods. Sepopa, his father, demanded the instant appearance of the white men, who were to bring much muti (medicine), for he was very sick.

"No," said Jim, "I'm damned if we go. This is taking too high a hand altogether. Tell him, Gambai, that we are tired and would rest. Tomorrow we will bring medicine to cure the Morena."[98]

Mateka at first refused to accept the message, but finally went away scowling.

"Mustn't be too cheap?" remarked Jim; "although they could easily murder us or lug us off in fetters. The great game of bluff, you know."

Late in the evening two skinny goats, some fowls and eggs arrived with the Chief's greeting.

"They're coming to their senses, I see," said Miêville, laughing.

At five in the morning another messenger arrived from the Chief to summon them.

"Go to the devil!" said Jim angrily, when they awakened him. Miêville smiled dreamily behind his mosquito net and dozed off to sleep again. At eight an angry discussion again awakened them.

"Oh, damn it," said Jim, sitting up, "I suppose we'll have to go — they'll never let us rest till we do. Umzilo, get breakfast."

---

here, In the narrative, Mateka's father is called "Sepopa" (note variation in spelling).

[98] Particularly among certain Bantu-speaking peoples, the word "Morena" typically refers to a chief, leader, or ruler. A title of respect and authority, it's bestowed upon one who holds a position of leadership.

After running the gauntlet of inspection of men, women and children, mangy curs and half-starved goats in the village, they arrived at an inner stockade with the usual ornamentation of a dried skull or two. Inside was a small square mud house with a mud fence built around it, a thatched roof forming a verandah. Upon a pile of skins reclined a gorbellied,[99] pockmarked man, ivory bangles actually imbedded in the flesh. Behind the Chief, holding an ivory-handled fly-switch,[100] crouched a nude young maiden. Mateka, who accompanied them, saluted by laying the palm of his hand upon his forehead; at which Jim, noticing, whispered to Miêville, "Arab salutation!" Mateka spoke rapidly to the Chief, who grunted in reply.

"He says," interpreted Mateka in broken Serutse,[101] "that he is pleased to see you. He is sick. Give him medicine." "Concise," chuckled Miêville; "I like a man who knows what he wants. Fever, I should say. Ask him what's the matter," observing the flabby underlip and hollow eye sockets.

"He says that sleep hath not come to him for days, and that he cannot eat."

---

[99] Potbellied.

[100] Fly-switch: flyswatter, aka a fly-swish or fly-whisk.

[101] I was unable to find a linguistic reference to Serutse (perhaps not surprisingly, since Africa is host to between 1,250 and 3,000 languages). But based on a translation of phrases that appear later in the text, Serutse is probably synonymous with Setswana (Tswana), a Bantu language spoken in Southern Africa. I also found a nineteenth-century map featuring a town named "Serutse," located about 160 miles southeast of Bulawayo (20s09, 28e36) in modern-day Zimbabwe (the country forming the northern border of South Africa, formerly known as Rhodesia). See *The Geographical Journal*, London: The Royal Geographical Society, 1893, appendix section, map subtitled "The routes of Frederick Courtney Selous, 1872-92." There's also a "Seretse" (note the variation in spelling) located in South Africa, in the Free State province.

"Eaten too much, I should say," eyeing the vast paunch. "Insomnia, I think. Tell him we'll send him some medicine."

"Now that indaba's[102] finished let's get to business," said Jim. "Gambai, shout for the presents."

At that moment a maiden, attired in the royal leopard skin, entered the stockade; a retinue of some six Mamböe[103] girls followed. Tall, perfectly proportioned, her coal-black hair fell in a wavy, tangled shower to her waist; the pad of her small feet and the lithe, sinuous motion of her body appeared as a bronze statue of a Greek nymph under the awakening touch of Aphrodite. She seated herself upon a native stool under the verandah, her maidens squatted at her feet.

"The daughter of the Chief, Gambai?" inquired Jim.

"Nay, Amethlokadi" (eyes like the sky), he answered, "the Mogwai" (Chief's sister, ranking as Chieftainess).

"How would you account for Arabs down here?" asked Miêville of Jim, who was still staring at her. "Too far south, isn't it?"

"No, not necessarily. Many Arab traders farther south than this. She's of Arab extraction sure enough — probably from Madagascar. Look at the straight hair, hawk nose and the eyes — hardly a trace of Negro in her. Probably her father settled amongst these people, and by wealth, or superior cunning, or both, became Chief."

Two of the Marutse appeared in the enclosure bearing bundles of calico, sugar, tobacco, and a Winchester rifle with ammunition.

"Tell him that we give him these as a present; that we want six canoes and men to travel as far as canoes can go on the river, for

---

[102] Indaba: a council or meeting of indigenous peoples of southern Africa, assembled to discuss important matters.
[103] Mamböe: possibly a reference to the Mambwe, an ethnic group of East Africa located primarily in northeastern Zambia and Tanzania.

which we will give him another rifle, and presents to all the men."

Mateka had pounced upon the rifle, which he handled greedily. Reluctantly he passed it to the Chief, who suddenly seemed wide awake. He grunted rapidly to his son, who, with another savage, helped the corpulent Chief to his feet.

"He wants to try it, cautious brute," observed Jim.

"He says, can you shoot with the gun?" interpreted Gambai.

"Yes."

Again a series of grunts, whilst his arm pointed through the gate of the enclosure, where, by a hut, sat a man mending a spear.

"He tells you to kill that man outside."

"Well, I'm damned!" observed Jim. Miêville laughed outright. "No! Tell him I don't kill people for pleasure."

The Chief scowled; Mateka laughed.

"Morena sayeth, cannot a man kill his goat if he so wishes? That man is the goat of the Black Elephant."

"Well, I won't," said Jim. "Tell him to bring a goat — a real goat. I'll kill that for him."

After an angry discussion a goat was sent for. As it was driven through the gate Jim placed a bullet behind the fore shoulder in a workmanlike manner, which simple feat raised a chorus of approving "Oughs."

"Well, the Morena agreeth?"

"The Morena demands two rifles."

"No: one."

"The Morena would know why you would go up the river? There are many elephants here."

"We do not want ivory. We go to the sea."

"The Morena sayeth: 'Thou hast two tongues.'"

"Oh. Tell him we go to our camp."

"The Morena desires you to eat with him. Wilt thou enter the house of the Black Elephant?"

"H'm," remarked Miêville, "I wondered how much longer he would keep us here in the broiling sun. Litham," he added, as he sat upon an overturned calabash, "look there," nodding towards the dark end of the hut, where in the gloom something gleamed dully.

"Good God!" exclaimed Jim, walking up and examining a crucifix of solid silver and gold. "How do you think this got here? Monks never got as far as this, surely."

"No, I don't think they did. Probably some loot from Angola."

"Gambai," said Jim, "ask him where — no, what is this?"

"He says that it is a great ngaka.[104] That his father's father brought it from the country of the white man."

"That," said Jim, "means white settlements — monks. Ah, here's a drink!" as two old men came up with gourds and some eggs.

"Great Caesar!" gurgled Jim, with his head in a huge calabash of sour milk, "this is good. Ah! finest thirst quencher under the sun. Hallo! What's 'Fatty' up to?"

The Chief had had his pile of skins brought inside, and was now upon his knees, kissing the crucifix.

"Gambai, ask him why he does that."

"The Morena says that his father taught him to do so as his father had taught him."

"Did he teach him to say anything?"

"No, only to kneel and kiss."

"That's interesting," said Miêville. "Evidently this savage's grandfather, or perhaps great-grandfather, was converted by the monks in Angola, and has simply taught his son the ceremony,

---

[104] Ngaka: a word from the Setswana language spoken in Botswana and South Africa meaning healer, doctor, or medicine man.

the ceremony and nothing else. You can see he hasn't the remotest idea what it all means."

"Simply a great fetish to him. Gambai, do all the tribespeople do this?"

"No, only the Chief; and when he is dead his son, the next Chief."

"Degenerated into a sort of royal prerogative," suggested Jim.

The Chief had returned to his skins. After a long deliberation he grunted rapidly to Mateka. Mateka's face brightened as he made some suggestions, but fell again as his father solemnly wagged his head.

During the afternoon Mateka returned, demanding the medicine for his father. He also opened negotiations regarding the men and canoes, insinuating that if it were made worth his while he would use his influence with his father. Finding, however, that nothing much offered, he calmly announced that the Morena had already arranged for the men and canoes on condition that two more rifles were given him, for which he would remit any payment to the men. This after an argument Jim refused to do, although he knew that it would amount to the same thing in the end. Mateka rose and departed sullenly.

Although by sunset that evening they had given up hope of settling terms with the fat chief that day, he sent for them, and suddenly consented to have everything ready to start next morning. Overjoyed at this withdrawal of obstruction, they threw in the extra rifles, which Sepopa hardly troubled to acknowledge, rolling sulkily upon his skins. But by virtue of his experiences with natives Jim felt vaguely uneasy, and half suspected a trap. However, the Barutse[105] canoes were paid off

---

[105] "Barutse" refers to a subgroup of the Lozi, a Bantu ethnic group found primarily in western Zambia, particularly in the region known as Barotseland, which encompassed parts of what is now western Zambia and eastern Namibia.

to the men's satisfaction; the only old members of the party remaining with them being Gambai, the guide, and their two Matabele[106] servants, Jaha and Umzilo. At daybreak Mateka appeared. Officious and insolent, Jim saw that the man could easily make serious trouble. He presented him with another old Winchester. This satisfied Mateka's soul for the time; it was *the* article for which he had been angling ever since they arrived. As usual on such occasions, it was midday ere the canoes were loaded, various petty but excited disputes settled, and the journey commenced.

During the following day a good deal of time was lost negotiating a small series of rapids. The pair went off on the fresh spoor of elephant, but did not succeed in sighting them within reasonable distance from the canoes. The next day Jim felt rather unwell, but concluded that it was a touch of the sun or the effect of the heat. That evening they camped at a particularly fine game spot, and Jim, always enthusiastic, seized his gun immediately the canoes ran aground, and started off on the hunt; but he soon returned complaining of feeling faint and weak.

"I think I'll have a stiff brandy," he said, and told Umzilo to find the case of Martell kept for medicinal purposes. Naturally the effect of the stimulant revived him, and after fifteen grains of quinine he felt quite fit and well. At dinner he suddenly found that the food repulsed him.

"What's the matter?" said Miêville, noticing him staring disgustedly and making faces at his plate.

---

[106] Matabele: a Bantu-speaking ethnic group mostly located in southwestern Zimbabwe. They originated as an offshoot of the Nguni people from Natal (now part of South Africa) in the early nineteenth century. The Matabele migrated northward in the 1820s, later settling in what is now southwestern Zimbabwe.

"Ouf! I don't know. I'm off my food. Ugh! I believe I've got a touch of malaria," he muttered, feeling his hot, dry forehead.[107] "Umzilo! bring the box of muti! This," he exclaimed, holding up a clinical thermometer, "will tell me all about it. Lord! I am thirsty! Jaha, bring me another cup — bottle — any bottle — only quick!"

Presently he examined the small tube, laughing noisily.

"Say, Litham," observed Miêville, looking sharply at him, "you're a bit lightheaded, aren't you? What temperature?"

"Hundred and four, point two," said Jim, laughing uproariously again. "I — I think I'll turn in, eh? Damn!"

He stood up, swayed giddily, and sat down on the bed in a heap.

"Give me another fifteen grains of quinine and ten of phenacetin,[108] Miêville, will you? And what else? Oh, yes, I know, some calomel. . . . Pile on all the blankets, old man, and tell Umzilo to bring me oceans of hot tea," he said when he had been assisted to scramble into bed. "Don't wobble so," he cried petulantly, after a while. "I mean — the tent. . . ."

---

[107] Beadle was probably writing from direct experience. In the 18 September 1918 issue of *Adventure*, in the "Ask *Adventure*" column (in which writers answered questions sent in by readers), he penned a missive titled "Diseases of East Central Africa." There he states: "Health conditions between Lakes Tanganyika and Victoria are fairly bad. Malaria, spirillum, blackwater, and sleeping sickness are the principal diseases." After including minute descriptions of each illness and the horrid symptoms they entail, he concludes: "But still[,] don't run away with the idea that the country is fatal. I've lived there and the only thing I collected was malaria and not much of that."

[108] Phenacetin (also known as acetophenetidin): a white crystalline medicinal compound, formerly used to ease pain or fever but withdrawn because of serious side effects.

CHAPTER II

PERIODS of semiconscious nightmare followed; his body appeared to be inflated with gas, and only by clinging desperately to his bed could he prevent it floating to the top of the tent: he experienced the horrors of Dante's inferno, roasting in flames and freezing at the same time. An agonizing thirst afflicted him which could not be assuaged. There were blurred impressions of someone handing him cups of hot tea; then, after a long period of dreams, he moaned and shouted for water, but no one came near him. He felt irritated by the silence, although he was too ill to reason. . . . There was another blank phase. . . . He grew dimly conscious that he was sitting on the floor of the tent, holding something weighty in his arms. He wondered vaguely how he had got there, and what he wanted to do. It was dark save for the eye of the moon peering through the flaps of the tent door. He sat quiet, trying hard to collect his wits. His brain seemed to be the mechanism of a clock, yet as light as swan's down, and the wheels flying madly round and round. If they would only keep still a moment he could think, but they whirled on the faster. . . . A few shadows passed across the moon, an owl hooted dismally and the persistent yapping of a jackal irritated him. . . . Where was Miêville . . . and Umzilo? Umzilo ought not to have left him. A frenzy of exasperation shook him.

"Miêville! Umzilo!" he shouted in a hoarse whisper. Oh, damn it, why wouldn't they come to him? He was so thirsty. He wept with peevish impotence. Then it occurred to him to wonder why he was still sitting there. He became aware that his fingers were wet and sticky. He threw off the oppressive weight in his arms and turned to scramble to his feet. Something hard hit his head. He grabbed at it. It appeared to be a stick. The silver streak of moonlight revealed a spear. He thrust it from him. Why the devil couldn't Umzilo see that the men kept their dirty things out of the tent. Where *was* Umzilo? He shouted again, and, standing up, swayed and fell against the table. The motion caused a dozen steam hammers to pound within his head: his forehead seemed about to burst. He clutched at the tent pole for a moment. . . . He heard himself laughing and flew into a weak passion. What on earth was he laughing at? His tongue was parched with thirst, his throat burning. His hand struck something cold. He clutched hold. It was a water bag hanging on the pole. He tore it down and drank greedily. For a moment he felt much better and quite strong: and his anger against Umzilo grew. He would rouse up the lazy brute and teach him not to disobey orders. He essayed to step boldly back to the tent door, but his feet felt so extraordinarily light. They would not go where he wanted to place them. Dizzily he caught at the canvas flap and dragged it open. Outside in the moonlight, squatted around a fire, were a dozen natives. What were the fools doing at that time of night? Jim waved a hand and screamed:

"E-eh — WEN — a! E-eh Um-ZI-lo!"

The voice was not very loud, but it aroused them. Simultaneously their heads turned towards him with the ludicrous effect of puppets worked by a string: then with a unanimous, smothered yell, they leaped to their feet and fled into the bush. The action, instead of surprising him, produced a wave of homicidal rage. He grabbed dizzily for the spear, tripped and sprawled over the bed. . . . For a few moments the concussion bereft him of his unstable senses. . . . Then he found that he was lying on his stomach with his head hanging over the bedside. Opening his eyes he stared in front of him at an object in the moonlight from the open door. Slowly, within ten inches of his nose, he became aware of the face of Umzilo, which appeared to be grinning at him. He was too exhausted now for anger. He could only wonder dimly. Then it gradually dawned upon him that the glazed eyes were those of a dead man: and following the line of his body he saw that the front of the tunic shirt, which Umzilo had worn as a uniform, bore a great black patch . . . and his fingers and hands were bloody. As the horror of realization penetrated his mind he drew up his body in a convulsive movement. The feathery clockwork in his brain seemed to whirr into infinity. . . .

* * * * * * *

Once more a brief gleam of sanity dawned slowly. He was lying on the bed and somebody was near him. It was Mateka, who, Winchester in hand, was standing over Jim as he lay tangled in blankets on his bed.

"Mateka? Mateka?" repeated Jim, glancing at him, and hugging his pillow.

"The Black Elephant —" began Mateka, whilst a crowd of warriors peered curiously at Jim.

"Elephant," frowning. "Oh, don't be silly! I haven't got your damned elephant," he added, in sudden access of passion catching at the word. "I — oh — what's the matter with your face — oh! Ha, ha, ha!"

He lay still for a while, his eyes wandering feverishly. Then he began to babble again in delirium.

* * * * * * *

With dawning consciousness, after a long and dreamless slumber, Jim began to sense the presence of someone.

"Where am I?" he muttered, endeavoring to concentrate his thoughts. "I thought that — why, this is a native hut! And who the deuce are you?"

He peered perplexedly into the darkened interior, dimly descrying a pile of calabash pots alongside a cane partition, and beyond by the door, patiently squatting, a young girl, whom he vaguely recognized as the Mogwai. Not understanding English, she made no reply, probably thinking that he was still under the influence of the evil spirit. He raised himself upon his elbow and took stock of his surroundings anew.

"Strange," he thought; "this must be Sepopa's kraal, I suppose, but how the devil did I get here? Where's Miêville? I remember going sick, but I — yes, I dimly remember something about Mateka and a crowd of niggers, or was I dreaming?"

A pair of dark, gazelle eyes were still incuriously watching him. Perhaps recognizing the light of sanity in the white man's eyes, she spoke as if to test him.

"Dumella!"

"Sabona, Intombizan!" he said in Sintibeli.[109] "I mean Dumella, Mogwai!" he added in Serutse.[110]

As if satisfied that he was really awake and sane, she arose, her figure outlined against the light of the door.

"Drink, O white man," she said, smiling and handing him a bowl of curdled milk. He drank long and thirstily.

---

[109] "Sintibeli": Beadle is probably referring to "isiNdebele": a Northern Ndebele language also known as "Sindebele," which is spoken primarily in Zimbabwe. (It's also called Zimbabwean Ndebele, North Ndebele, or Matabele.) In isiNdebele, "Sabona, Intombizan" translates to "Hello, young girl" or "Hello, young woman."

[110] "Dumella": a greeting in Setswana (Tswana), equivalent to "Hello" or "Greetings." "Mogwai" is a term of address used for an elderly person or for someone respected in Setswana culture. (Similar to "Sir" or "Madam.") From this we may conclude that Beadle's "Serutse" language is actually Tswana (also known by its native term, Setswana).

"Thank you," he said in broken Serutse. "Tell me, O maiden, what hath brought me here? Where is the white man, my brother, Monepi?"

"Nay, I know not," she answered, "for my eyes have not seen him."

He was silent for a while.

"Know ye aught that has happened?"

"Mateka, the son of the Black Elephant, spake before ye left here. He put evil into the heart of the Black Elephant.

"Oh," mused Jim, "I begin to see light. I wonder where the devil Miêville is, or Gambai or Umzilo. — Knowest thou he of the Marutse, Gambai?"

"Ow! Truly. He is within the village."

"I would speak with him."

She departed, and after what seemed an interminable period, during which Jim came to the conclusion that Miêville must be somewhere in the village bound or guarded, Gambai, escorted by two fully armed warriors, entered, and squatting on his haunches, saluted by clapping hands, in the Marutse style. His captors gravely sat by the door.

"What meaning hath this?" enquired Jim in Sintibeli, which Gambai understood, and replied, brokenly, in the same medium.

"O, Inkoos,[111] many strange things have happened. We are the captives of Sepopa, the offspring of swine, the father —"

"Never mind his personal attributes," interrupted Jim in English. — "Tell thou me all that thou knowest. I have memory of the camp at the place of many gazelle, where the sickness came upon me."

---

[111] "Inkoos": a term that means "chief" or "leader" in several Southern African languages.

"It is done. When the evil spirit entered into thee, thou didst call loudly, even as the hyena crieth, and thou didst fight with the strength of bulls. For three days wast thou —"

Jim whistled.

"For three days! Art sure?"

"Even so. Upon the fourth day when the sun was low a strange thing happened. . . . Ow."

He paused.

"Ow," concurred Jim with interest.

"Even so. But whilst thou wast in the hands of the Mosi-oa-Tonya[112] (the evil spirit of the Victoria Falls), I, Gambai, heard the sons of dogs talk concerning ye. And they laughed and spoke of ye making good sport for the children of Sepopa. Then I knew what was in the black heart of the eater of offal and feared for ye. And on the fourth day when the sun was newly born I spake with Monepi. But he laughed and said that I had dreamed this thing, *I*, Gambai of the Marutse! Ow!" — He grunted in contemptuous disgust. — "Then did Monepi call Singubulu and bade him prepare one light canoe for the hunting, which was done. And he called Umzilo and Jaha to bring their guns to go with him, but Umzilo would not leave thee. Then did Monepi place his tent, very much food and many blankets in the canoe, saying that should they kill elephant they would not return until the morrow: and together with Singubulu and three paddlers, did they, Monepi and Jaha, depart. But I knew what was in his heart and told Umzilo.

"And all day did we sit by thy tent with our rifles, listening for the coming of the children of Sepopa. We knew that Seluka

---

[112] In the Lozi language, "Mosi-oa-Tunya" means "The Smoke" (*mosi*) "that Thunders" (*tunya*): an indigenous name for the Victoria Falls of the Zambezi, located on the border between Zambia and Zimbabwe. This poetic term refers to the impressive amount of billowing mist and roaring, thundering noise produced by a massive discharge of water.

and his people would not outrage thee, for their hearts were as water at the Mosi-oa-Tonya. Sometimes didst thou sleep, and many times asked for water, which we gave thee.

"Then the sun fled on and was swallowed up: and still we watched together until the birth of the moon. But Seluka and his people appeared to sleep in their camp. Then leaving Umzilo that he should watch by thee, I crept and lay beside the fire. Everything save the voice of the forest was still. And after the moon had fled high there came the sound of paddles, very faint, and silence again. There was whispering among the people of Seluka, and knowing that the time to die had come, I rose, but something struck me and knew I nothing . . . Ow!

"When again I knew myself was I fast bound in the power of Mateka, offspring of dung. Slowly the moon died and the voice of dawn spoke. I heard them talking that Seluka had killed Umzilo from behind the tent, but that none dared go near ye for fear of the Mosi-oa-Tonya. Wrath, too, was Mateka, because Monepi had escaped, for they had orders not to injure thee: they desired to take us all alive. . . . Ow!

"And afterwards did I tend ye and wash ye, for much blood was there on thy body. Then did they bring ye here unto Sepopa, even I as well; but after Monepi have many canoes gone. . . . Ow!

"And Umzilo I buried in the manner of his people, for they are brave and he had the heart of a lion; moreover he loved thee well, Amethlokadi, even as do I. . . . Ow! So was it."

He ceased abruptly. Jim remained silent, piecing together the phantom-like memories of his delirium and wondering whether Miêville had really deserted him as Gambai suspected. He concluded that Gambai was mistaken. Miêville had never shown the white feather on any occasion: yet a logical query was that Miêville, arguing that both would be massacred if he stayed, had taken the opportunity to save his own life if he could. Jim turned to the two Mamböe and asked in Serutse whether they had had any news of his brother white. They had not, but were confident that he would be taken, as their canoes were fast and well manned. At any rate, Miêville had rifles, and he and Jaha would put up a good fight for it. Jim hoped that neither would consent to be taken alive.

He dismissed Gambai and lay back on his bed sick with the knowledge of the various deaths by torture, of the ants, the crocodiles or worse, which awaited a white captive in the hands of such peoples: for he did not doubt for a moment what the orders for them to be taken alive portended.

CHAPTER III

SOME extract of meat which Mateka, not knowing the contents or their use, had, with a few other articles, permitted Gambai to secure, proved invaluable to Jim's convalescence. His temperature was below normal, but he rapidly recovered his physical strength. No one except Gambai and the girl came near him, and neither could give him any news of Miêville. Anxiety for his own fate began to tell upon him, although he tried hard not to think, to be philosophical. Yet the idea that he was being allowed to get well in order to provide more sport, haunted him. Well, as it was decreed, so be it. He hoped that he would meet his fate like a man, but he shuddered — he had an intimate acquaintance with native ingenuity.

Lying almost on a level with the floor, his eyes lit upon the Mogwai industriously blowing the fire to boil water for his beef tea, which she had quickly learned to do from watching Gambai. From outside in the yellow sunlight came the occasional bleat of a goat or screech of a bird, breaking the hot silence. Again he fell to wondering what his fate would be — perhaps she had some idea.

"O Maiden, come hither!"

She ceased blowing and came softly into the cool shadows.

"Knowest thou, O pretty one, what is in the heart of the Black One?"

"Nay! O Amethlokadi. I am but a maiden; know I the mind of the Black Elephant?"

"Tell thou me, thinkest that he hath an evil heart towards me?"

"Nay, that cannot be; for hath not the Black One given thee to me, Haiwani, his sister?"

"Eh? What's that?" Jim sat up, startled. "What sayest thou?"

"Even that thou art mine," she said, in simple surprise. . . . "The Black One was wroth with thee, and would have put thee to the death of the crocodiles, but I loved thee and claimed that he would give thee to me according to my right. He would not; but yet he did so, for I spake and said, 'These are foolish words, O Black One, for the white man hath great knowledge of medicines and of guns. He gave thee water that hath made thee whole. Wouldst thou cast away good medicine?' And he saw that my words were words of wisdom, and because I, Haiwani, sister of the Black One, loved thee, therefore he called to all the chiefs of the village and spake, saying, 'Know, O my people, that I, the Black One, the Bull Calf, give to Haiwani, Mogwai, the white man, Amethlokadi. Know that, for I have said it, and see that none harm him.' And so," she concluded, with naïve logic, "thou art mine."

Jim had listened to the recital in silence. What did it mean? He glanced at her. She was regarding him reproachfully.

"What sayest thou?"

"I — er — truly my words are words of praise, little one. Thou hast saved my life from the crocodiles," he said slowly; "what wouldst thou that I might repay thee?"

"Are thou not my man (husband) and I thy handmaiden (wife)? Hath not the Black One spoken?"

"Good God!"

He stared at her, whilst she, with her sloe eyes, gazed at him affectionately. His knowledge of native ways, and her expression, did not leave him in any doubt regarding her meaning. He felt that she expected him to say something, but his mind was chaotic.

"Er — hast thou the meat water?" he enquired, to ease the situation.

"I will fetch it for thee," she replied.

Suddenly Jim fell back on the bed shaking with laughter. The relief from the probability of being eaten, or roasted alive, made him hysterical — a sob and a laugh got mixed and almost choked him. But realization quickly sobered him. He had to choose between a death by torture in some form, or — living with a young, savage queen whose barbaric beauty would have attracted most virile men. The crisis found him weak in body, and therefore in mind. He thought of Claire — and groaned. Yet it was a case of life or a hideous death. Should he even offend his queenly captor it might mean the crocodiles. The lady or the crocodile? The thought of "the Lady and the Tiger" made him laugh hysterically. Which would Claire have chosen for him? An unkind thought suggested Claire in his place. He frowned and wondered why he was so silly. That was not a fair analogy. He was a man: a woman is different. The lady or the crocodile? persisted the query, which suggested Miêville's "Cynic and the Saurian," the last verse but one of which ran in Jim's mind:

> "Green and moldy now he lies
> In water-hole mid reeds, Sir,
> Providin' fam'ly Crocodile
> With luscious, dainty feeds, Sir."

"Ugh!" murmured Jim and shuddered. That decided it. He could not die like that. Claire would surely understand? He shrank from the question, and hesitated no longer. He wanted to live, strenuously desired life; the problem was the future.

Haiwani glided in, bearing a cup of beef tea. She placed the cup on the floor and sat beside him. She looked at Jim; he looked at her and smiled nervously. Deliberately placing her arms around his neck, without the slightest trace of embarrassment, she pulled him to her until her hair hid him from view.

Jim looked at her with a new light in his eyes.

"O little gazelle, thou art very comely."

"A bird singeth within my heart," she answered. "Thou, O beloved, art like unto the young lion."

She smiled gloriously.

"My bronze Goddess," murmured Jim.

CHAPTER IV

IN the late afternoon he ventured out of the hut. He found a circular enclosure of some thirty feet wide, formed by a high, mud palisading supported by tall stakes, with fire-hardened points protruding. At the gate squatted, with sphinxlike gravity and patience, two fuzzy-haired warriors armed with fishhook-bladed spears. Jim was still groggy on his legs and was glad to retire to his lowly couch. During the evening, when the fire threw flickering lights through the smoke which percolated through the grass roof in lieu of a chimney, he talked with Haiwani, who reclined upon a pile of skins beside him. Once a clamor of voices arose, breaking the sultry quiet, echoed and answered from the village by men and dogs. From Haiwani Jim learned that the warriors had returned with Miêville. Jim received the news with a cold shudder of horror. Haiwani, in answer to a question, replied indifferently that it was a matter for the Black Elephant, and when Jim pleaded for her intervention, threw up her head, and withdrew.

During the next two days Jim saw nobody save Haiwani and Gambai. On every occasion on which he began to plead or to protest on Miêville's behalf, Haiwani's sloe eyes flashed dangerously. If he persisted she left him to his own devices in jealous displeasure. Early on the morning of the third day the rhythmic pulse of drums awakened him. With sudden cessations of some few minutes they continued all day. Jim guessed what they portended. He was left to himself until sundown, when Haiwani returned. He grew angry against her and still more wroth at his own impotence. She proceeded to make him beef tea without comment. There was a markedly wild glint in her eye, and a strongly controlled temper was displayed in every line of her supple body. Jim did not know that all day she had been pleading and arguing with her brother, Sepopa, for Miêville's life, and had failed. Suddenly the drums grew to a frenzy, and there broke out savage yells, accompanied by the piercing, prolonged shriek of the women.

"Good God! I can't stand this!" exclaimed Jim to Haiwani. "O little one, I will it that we go yonder — I would look once more upon the face of Monepi!"

Angrily Haiwani shook her head until her black mane rippled blue lights.

"Send thou the guard[, if] thou wilt. I cannot escape."

"Nay!" she exclaimed abruptly, watching him. "I will go with thee and I alone. Thou has given thy word, O my beloved, and I alone will look upon the face of the Black One. Come thou!"

They walked out under a deep, sapphire sky brilliantly studded with stars. At the entrance she dismissed the guard with an imperious gesture. Together they made their way round the deserted village. Haiwani led him to a large ant heap from the top of which, lying upon a skin, they looked down upon the savages dancing. Haiwani placed her arm round him in a protective, motherly manner.

A large, irregular ring of fires threw fitful and uncertain shadows upon nearly nude figures. The men were following one another in a circling, stooping, shuffling dance, like a fantastic game of follow-my-leader, crooning a long chant to the pulse of the drums. The women, moving in a contrary direction, were within the circle, intermittently screaming in unison. Half in the shadowland beyond sat Sepopa upon his stool of state, upright and uncomfortable. Jim's eyes, searching eagerly, could find no trace of Miêville.

For some while the dance continued monotonously. Now and again a man, worked up to a state of irrepressible excitement, would spring out of the line, yelling horribly, leaping high in the air. . . . On a sudden the enormous circle, without warning, broke, merged into an indistinguishable mass, and as quickly formed again into a ragged line of warriors, the Chief as the center point. The drums ceased abruptly. For a portion of a minute the silence appeared appalling. A misguided cock crew. . . . With a rippling splash of sound the drums recommenced, with a more rapid and exciting throb. A single tenor voice chanting rapidly was just audible. Then with a thudding crash of spear against shield, feet against earth, came a tremendous shout — "Ow-ough!" — drowning the shrill and piercing cries of the women. The mass of nude limbs, flashing eyes, spears glinting in the flickering firelight, the maddening, quick pulse of the drums, and the terrific thundering warrior chorus, caused the heart to leap quicker and every hair to bristle. Here and there a warrior, springing out from among his fellows, would crouch behind his shield, give another mighty leap, throwing sand in the air, then a rush — a stabbing action, vicious hacks at an imaginary enemy; each a pantomime of fierce fight, triumph and capture of the enemy's womenkind. Faster beat the drums, louder screamed the women, higher leapt the warriors; the frenzied mob seemed possessed by a legion of devils. The scene amid the many flickering fires under the light of the new-risen moon peeping over the tree tops, placid and cynical, appeared a veritable inferno.

Jim began nervously to fidget and twitch. Haiwani's arm tightened around him.

"My God!"

He half rose as his eye caught the gleam of white metal in the moonlight near Sepopa. He saw the large silver crucifix upon a tree, and — naked and bound — Miêville.

Sepopa had discarded the chair, and reclined upon his usual pile of skins a few yards from the victim. He had the case of

Jim's brandy beside him, and occasionally he lifted a bottle, swallowing neat spirit.

Jim could not detect any movement of life in the gleaming white figure; the distance was too far to be certain. As he watched, fascinated with horror, a body of warriors, racing forward, threw themselves face downwards before the crucifix. Almost immediately springing to their feet, they began to caper and leap, gradually increasing in frenzy and activity. Three of them suddenly snatched burning brands from a fire, the light of which more distinctly revealed the figure bound to the tree. Jim could see the white of eyes which, to his excited imagination, now seemed to move.

"Oh, if only I had my rifle!" He began to mutter and murmur, swearing and blaspheming unconsciously. One of the savages thrust a burning log on to the white flesh and bounded away, shrieking with laughter. Jim screamed and tried to spring to his feet. Rapidly the fiendish gang circled and leaped round the doomed man; louder roared the warrior chorus; still more frenzied beat the drums.

Sepopa, in drunken frenzy, threw a bottle into the nearest fire, scattering the ashes in a ruddy shower. The ivory bangles gleamed in the light. He showed his teeth in savage laughter, and attempting to rise, fell upon his back, where he lay kicking his ponderous limbs and sprawling like an elephantine baby.

Another warrior, springing before the white figure, slashed with a spear at the abdomen. A bloody gash remained.

"God! They're going to mutilate him!" screamed Jim. A ruddy mist suddenly enveloped the central figure and the yelling fiends. Jim saw and knew only that scene. He forgot that he was still weak, unarmed and alone — forgot everything. Only mad, blind rage and desire to kill possessed him. He fought like a maniac with Haiwani, but she, lithe and active as a leopardess, overpowered him. At length he lay weak and panting, eyes glaring, in her arms.

"Be thou quiet, Beloved," she gasped; "wouldst thou kill thyself? Naught can save him." And she added, "Not even I could save thee if those dogs saw thee."

He looked again. The body was crisscrossed with livid gashes.

"Oh, my God! I can't! I can't. Christ! If I only could!"

He hid his head on Haiwani's breast and sobbed. Once more he looked and cried as in pain. A fit of trembling seized him.

"Come thou," said Haiwani.

She raised Jim tenderly. Half carrying him she led him down the ant heap, and away into the ghostly shadows.

CHAPTER V

JIM had returned to the village sick with rage against the natives, Haiwani included. Haiwani was very patient with him. For a while Jim brooded to himself, and finally dropped off to sleep on a mat, exhausted. Gently Haiwani took his head and pillowed it against her bosom. For a long time she sat nursing him by the flickering fire. Now and again she would watch his face anxiously, smoothing the hair from the flushed forehead. At length she gradually released herself. Throwing back her luxuriant hair with a toss of her head, carefully she picked Jim up in her powerful arms and deposited him on his bed.

Next morning Jim awoke in delirium. For five days Haiwani refused to leave his side, tending him with lavish care. Gambai imperiled his life by arguing with her. He maintained that he knew more of the white man's medicine than she could possibly do. With suspicious eyes she consented to allow Gambai to give Jim medicine which he had seen his master use. Fortunately it was quinine. But Haiwani, to make sure, concocted various compounds of herbs which, if they did no good, failed to do any harm. For long hours Haiwani would sit holding Jim's hands, cooling his fevered face with soft, cool fingers, ministering to his demands for drink. She did not seem to need any sleep. The tall, graceful figure in leopard skins hovered like a dusky angel around the lowly bedside. She would turn with tigerish eyes upon anyone who dared to enter the hut or make a noise without. Undoubtedly Jim owed the quick return to health to her — if not his life.

During his second convalescence, he still continued to contemplate the manner of Miêville's death. He could never decide whether Miêville had succeeded in taking a quicker way or had suffered torture. For a long while Jim's mental attitude to his position was undecided. He would lie on a pile of skins for hours brooding over his captivity. Then Haiwani would come and crouch beside him, intently watching his every expression with her large, luminous eyes. An arm, jingling with ivory bangles, would stretch out and smooth his hair. She would imprison his hand and dumbly smother it with kisses. A want had only to be half expressed and she would do it, or cause it to be done. At times her devotion overwhelmed him. Yet other times he would remember and brood afresh. Her attitude was not all one of doglike devotion; she would develop a matchless imperiousness. Then against his will Jim would admire her immensely. He objected to being guarded. Haiwani asked him to give his word not to flee. He refused, still contemplating the idea of escaping and avenging Miêville's death. The next day in the courtyard he noticed that the guards were withdrawn. He questioned Haiwani. She was lying at full length by his side regarding him. She took his hand and kissed it as she answered softly:

"It is my will."

"Have I not told thee that I shall flee?"

She brushed rebellious hair from her face, looking him passionately in the eyes.

"Dost thou hold me as a feather in the wind?"

"Nay, but thy people are not my people, and I would —"

She flung his hand away and sprang to her feet, drawing the skins about her.

"Thy people," she cried scornfully, chin in air, with flaming eyes. "Thy people! What are *thy* people to me? What are *my* people to me? As dogs are to a lion. And thou . . .? Go thou! Where thou wilt. I have given the Black One my life for thee! Take it and go!"

Her eyes filled with tears. She turned and fled towards the open country.

For a moment Jim hesitated, bewildered: then he followed and found her lying in the long grass, sobbing. Jim felt a brute, and suddenly realized how she must love him. Kneeling by her side attempting to console her, he experienced a revulsion of feeling and fell to kissing her madly, bitterly blaming himself. Haiwani turned, a wild joyful light playing through her tears, as she hid her face on his shoulder. They returned to the village — the scrubby bearded white man in tattered and worn khaki suit, and the skin-clad queen of the wilds, both chattering and laughing like children.

This incident was the turning point in Jim's mental position. He felt that he liked her awfully — loved her in a way. She was only a savage. Yet although there was Promethean fire in her passion, her delicacy was vestal in natural simplicity. In hours of passion he was sure he loved her and was happy. At times he would suffer keenly from ennui, and a desire to meet congenial countrymen and — Claire. On occasions he became aware of the strange mental trick of thinking of her and seeing Joan's eyes. Then he would curse — and wonder; albeit he could never wholly master the vagary. Yet what did it matter now? The future held — what? He felt afraid to tackle the problem and tried to give up hope, to force himself to be content to retrograde into the primitive state, to be Haiwani's husband. Jaha had perished with Miêville, only Gambai and himself survived.

Partly because it amused him and partly because he feared to lose his mother tongue, he taught Haiwani English, which she soon spoke fairly well. She was never tired of inquiring about European customs. Women's dress she could never understand. Jim dressed her hair in European fashion — after a style. Immensely amused, Haiwani wore it for a whole day. With her willing help he studied the language and customs of the country — principally the latter. Jim shaved every morning; it filled up time. Sepopa having no use for soap, Jim had retained his own supply for himself — and Haiwani. Jim being lathered by Haiwani was a sight for the Gods — a fine advertisement wasted.

The uneventful life in the heat and solitude would have had an enervating effect on an unimaginative mind, but with Jim it had a contrary effect, inasmuch as the absence of the thousand and one events of civilized life, or even the companionship of another man, threw him back on himself, spurring his imagination in order to alleviate the ennui of his existence. The brilliancy of the tropic nights developed a greater fascination than ever. Many hours he spent lying on his skins in the courtyard staring at the glory of the constellations, wandering amid the millions of other worlds and systems, trying to meditate upon infinity until his mind reeled. The effect was conducive to a philosophical acceptance of his fate: and a further crushing of his own conceit. What counted the torturing to death of Miêville, of Jim's soul struggles towards something he could not define, of a thousand million puny humans' uplifted voices in the relentless cycle of the Universe? The realization that the whole world had seemed to stand still because of his petty troubles, forced a laugh at the sheer absurdity.

Sometimes it seemed as if he were upon an altitude watching, with a comic sense of pity, himself darting anxiously hither and thither like a disturbed ant: and the insect seemed so terribly in earnest as if really endeavoring to accomplish something vitally important, that he was constrained to wonder what it was all about, what the puny little thing, which was himself, did want? . . .

In memory he saw his schooldays — and his life; remembered Madge and all she had been to him; and suddenly he perceived clearly that there had been a persistent struggle percurrent the whole time. Even in the Rhodesian days had been the feeling that someday he would meet his ideal in spite of his youthful cynicism. The thought gave him the heartache for Claire. Thank Heaven he had found that ideal at last. Yet had he? The flickering doubt he sternly repressed. But, no matter how he would deny it, there was something in Haiwani which was not in Claire. It was too subtle to define, although Claire was a mental companion which Haiwani could never be. Strange. He evaded the point. No, Claire was his ideal, he told himself hastily, with a ghost of his old sense of lèse-majesté, which brought in its train the longing for her and her environment; then followed a paroxysm of grief — to be forgotten in Haiwani's arms. Haiwani, quick-witted, soon noticed that another woman occupied Jim's thoughts.

"Thy heart is sore, my beloved," she would sometimes say. "Thine eyes would gaze upon the men and women of thy race; is it not so?"

Which Jim would deny strenuously. Why he scarce knew, save that he had grown to love her more than ever for her devotion.

Some five months after his capture news came of a strong party of whites four days' journey down the river, which immediately prompted the thought that he might successfully reach them if he chose. The temptation was great. He arose in the night, secured a quarter of goat, his rifle and cartridges, and crept down to the river. There were plenty of canoes. He stepped into a small fast one. He sat still for a while.

Then he said, "No — I can't. She's only a savage — but — damn it — I can't."

He returned and resumed his place beside Haiwani. He kissed her and discovered that she was awake and weeping; she threw her arms around him, sobbing, and nearly choked him with kisses. Her life would have paid forfeit had he gone.

Most of his time was spent in thinking, talking to Haiwani, and mending his clothes. As books were of no import to Sepopa or Mateka, he had been allowed to retain his small stock, each of which he had read many times — particularly the advertisements. Sometimes he would go out shooting with Mateka. The latter had become a very good shot, after Jim had taught him not to raise his back sight to increase the speed, and a few other necessary details. He seldom saw Sepopa. All the natives seemed to look upon Jim as Haiwani's private property, and therefore to be respected — which sometimes amused him, and at others made him sad. He often wondered what had happened to people he knew. Perhaps he was reported dead. What would Claire — and others — think and do? He wondered if Joan were happy with her husband, and hated her because he thought she might be. He failed in an attempt to send a letter. Sepopa had an unholy fear of punitive expeditions, of which he had heard some vivid accounts.

One morning, awaking at dawn and having as usual bathed with Haiwani in the stream, he was lying upon a couch of skins at the door of their hut in the native manner, smoking cigarettes. He had long ago finished the little tobacco which Gambai had saved from the marauding fingers of Mateka, so Jim now endeavored to solace himself with native tobacco, adapting leaves of a Gibbon's "Rome" as cigarette papers. Haiwani reclined near him engaged in the gentle art of *dolce far niente*.[113]

---

[113] *Dolce far niente*: Italian expression meaning the "sweetness of doing nothing" or of being idle.

From without the palisading came the hum of the life of the village; cattle lowing on their way from the kraal to their pastures; a child's laugh or a cock crow, whilst above all floated the monotonous thrum of a drum from the far end of the village, which had commenced at the first streak of dawn.

"Now, Haiwani," said Jim, waving a huge clumsy cigarette, "I am about to hoist Nero with his own petard."

Haiwani wrinkled her brows in an attempt to solve the hard words and unfamiliar names.

"To the flames," added Jim between the preliminary puffs.

"Neelo?" repeated Haiwani; "me no unnerstan."

"Nero," said he, rolling over laughing to pull her hair, "was a big King — Chief — who lived — the Morena," relapsing into the vernacular, "O pretty one, who lived once upon a time. He had great strength. Those of his children who would not believe in his gods he would burn in the flames. These are the words of his doings. I burn them in my mouth with the savory leaf. So his spirit I burn with them! Now do you see the joke?"

Haiwani still appeared doubtful.

"Yes," said Jim, "that's the worst of explaining a weak joke. — What meaning hath this thing?" referring to the drums.

"It is the Initiation, O Jeemy," replied Haiwani. "Suliwa, the daughter of Maruwi, hath come to the time of womanhood. She with many others go to the bush this day."

"By Gad!" exclaimed Jim. "O Haiwani, I would see this thing. Many are they of my people who have heard of this custom of thy kindred, but few are they who have seen. They speak many things concerning it, and I would see that they are double-tongued."

"Nay, that may not be, O my man, for it is forbidden that the eyes of any male shall look upon these things."

"I will it, O Haiwani."

"Even so, thy handmaiden may not obey thee."

"Oh hang it," said Jim to himself, "I must see this. — O my gazelle, listen, it is my will and desire. Thou art the Mogwai, and I, Amethlokadi, thy man."

"Even so. Before the rising of the next new moon will there be the Initiation of the youths — that shalt thou witness."

Jim remained silent.

"Tell me, O Haiwani," he asked at length, "art thou of the Initiated?"

"I am, yet am I not, for mine eyes have seen, yet my body hath not."

"What meanest thou?"

"I am Haiwani, the Mogwai. It is the custom that they of the children (family) of the Black One see all things, yet do not as they of the Mamböe. They are not as we."

"But why so?"

"Nay. I know not. It is even as our father was taught by his father before him."

"Tell thou me, O my handmaiden, what doth happen to those of the unlearned ones? Who are they who teach and what do they teach?"

"They, O Amethlokadi, of the teachers are the Mothers of the tribes. They who are taught are the flowers ripe for plucking."

"Yea, even so."

"It is the custom to await the time that many are ripe — even as it is now. Then, they of the to-be-initiated lay hands upon the fattest bull of the herd, which dieth and is their food. A place within the bush apart from the eyes of man, is prepared by the Mothers of the tribe. The maidens are taken by the hand and led away into the appointed place. They are anointed with the sacred oil prepared by the doctors, after which are practiced the rites. Then they are taught from the lips of the Mothers of the tribe all that a woman should know, even of the duties to their man; that which is forbidden by the customs of their tribes; **the** dangers of the witchcraft and of the evil spirits, that they may be wise and profit by the wisdom of their mothers before them. For one moon are they within the circle of the Initiation."

"What do they during this time?"

"They are taught, O Amethlokadi, even as I have told thee, the preparing of food, the knowledge of children, and all that a woman should know. Also they are taught the dances of their tribe; the dance of Death, the dance of Initiation, the dance of Victory, and the dance of Pleasure."

"And when the time is that they return unto the haunts of men?"

"Then are all things of their maidenhood burnt that they may not suffer from the evil eye of him who might possess them. And when that they are come to the village is a great feast proclaimed, and much dancing wherein the initiates dance the dance of Pleasure, for they are women and fit mates for men."

"And then it is that they depart into the houses of their men (husbands)?"

"Even so do those who have been bought in the past. Others are they —"

A prolonged series of yells and women's shrill cries, mingled, floated across.

"What meaning hath that?"

"It is even as I have spoken — the killing of the bull."

"Then thou hast not, O Haiwani, eaten of the full Initiation?"

"Nay, as I have told thee."

"For what cause is it forbidden to the children of the Black One?"

"Nay, I know not. It has been ever so."

"Strange," reflected Jim; "perhaps it may be the effect of some lost teaching of the monks to the original possessor of Sepopa's crucifix. — "Tell thou me, O little one, what reason hath the ceremony of the horns of the bull?"

"Again I know not. It is the custom."

Jim diligently rolled another cigarette with the aid of Gibbon, and enquired:

"And little wise one, tell me what reason is there in the giving of knowledge in the Initiation?"

"If thou hast a young dog thou takest him to the river to show him that the water is deep, to teach him to know the danger of the crocodile, so that he may take heed that he doth not fall in, or swim where they may eat him."

"True again, another point to thee and thine, O Haiwani. Truly thy ancients were wiser than my people."

Haiwani remained obdurate in her refusal to attempt to assist Jim to satisfy his anthropological curiosity; but by her influence the connivance of one of the Fathers of the tribe was obtained. When the stated time had arrived all the lads of the village of the age of twelve or thirteen departed for the mystic ground amid much drumming and dancing. Provided with food and water, Jim had been guided by Maruwi during the previous night to the appointed spot and his body hidden in a convenient antbear[114] hole, the mouth of which was covered with light-green brushwood permitting a clear view through the interstices.

The bear hole was situated on a slight rise of ground overlooking a small glade in the forest in which a skeleton hut had been erected. For a long while Jim lay half asleep, listening to the noises of forest life. A hyena, scenting the message of an alien presence, came sniffing within a few yards. Imitating the barking of a dog (as a precautionary measure), Jim scared the cowardly brute, who, loping away for fifty yards, sat on its haunches and serenaded him with eerie, mocking howls. Many times he heard the grass rustle close at hand as some jackal or

---

[114] Antbear: aardvark.

other forest beast slunk away, after a nasal investigation which proved that the anticipated dinner was very much alive. Several of them retired to the background and joined the chorus of lamentation.

Just after the glorious flush of dawn in the east, the hyena ceased its vocal efforts and departed in disgust, followed by the jackals. Then the birds took up the refrain; so that Jim was not without entertainment, although he began to get impatient for the actors to arrive. He wanted to smoke; but as he dared not he compromised by chewing the leg of a boiled chicken. A honey bird, quickly noting his presence, came to an adjacent tree and, twittering excitedly, invited him to loot the hive on share terms — the long-standing compact between the bird and man. Jim feared that the bird's sporting invitation might betray his presence should any of the natives arrive on the scene. At last, sweet tooth, wearied of futile chatter, flitted away, almost immediately to be replaced by another bird, who implored Jim in shrill tones to, "Go-wa-ay! Go-wa-ay!"

The tree tops were silhouetted in indigo against an ocean of molten copper by the time that his ears caught the sound of distant chanting. "At last!" he thought, indulging in a final stretch of his already cramped limbs, and snuggling down well into the hole. Soon a line of woolly heads appeared through the trees, and, led by seven Fathers of the tribe, some fifteen youths filed into the clearing. Forming up in a circle they proceeded to execute a slow, shuffling dance to the throb of the hand drums, manipulated by the old men in the center. The lads were smeared from head to foot in yellow ochre, giving a weird and ghastly appearance. The chanting of the masters, now and again, became intelligible to Jim, who gathered that they were invoking the aid of the spirits to avoid the evil eye.

The performance was continued monotonously for some two hours; then the circle of initiates subsided on their haunches, whilst the eldest of the seven harangued them from the center. At the end of each speech, which seemed to consist of several verses, a round of applause, or chorus, was given by the youths, accompanied by a short gentle tattoo on the drums. The rapidity of the language only permitted Jim to catch the gist, which was a flowery and involved lecture upon the duties and faculties of men, to their chief, their tribe, and their women. The lads were nude, Jim noticed, and had apparently brought no food, nor sleeping skins. Again about midday another dance, more fantastic and longer than the last, was performed; at the end of which all of them seemed on the verge of exhaustion under the influence of fanatical excitement. Then, in unison, the Seven commenced a wild and weirdly plaintive chant, working gradually to a frenzy, leaping and gesticulating, whilst the young members crouched low upon the ground, emitting low grunts "Ought! — ough!" in time with the crescendo measure of the drums. At length when the whole mass seemed charged with uncontrollable excitement, they suddenly sprang to their feet, yelling, gesticulating, leaping madly round and round the center Seven, who still chanted yet more rapidly and fiercely. . . . Abruptly the drums and chant ceased; the frenzied circle dropped flat on the ground, eyes rolling, panting and sobbing. . . . Afterwards followed the rites of lebollo.[115]

* * * * * * *

At somewhere about midnight Maruwi, leaving the exhausted devotees asleep under the skeleton hut without any covering or food, crept to Jim's place of concealment and

---

[115] Lebollo: a Sesotho word meaning "initiation." In Basotho society it refers to a rite of passage involving circumcision and indoctrination into tribal ceremonies.

whispered to him to return. Painfully Jim crawled out, and was compelled to sit and stretch his cramped limbs before he was able to walk back to the village.

During the month of the Initiation period, Maruwi would, upon his return to the village every night, report progress and describe all that had happened during the day. In brief, Jim learned from the old man that, besides the constant lectures upon the laws and each man's duty to his tribe, they were, after the first week, forbidden any food or clothes at all; armed with spear, bow and arrows, they were forced to stalk and kill game to provide food and clothing for themselves, with the consequence that, although some of them succumbed during this test of endurance, the survivors were warriors and men. Should any cravenhearted among them seek help at the villages he was immediately speared.

"When a man hath a garden," elucidated Maruwi, "doth he not destroy the weeds and uproot the sickly and weak in order that the whole may be a garden of strong trees and bear much good fruit?"

Jim discovered it was the custom to destroy all weakly or deformed children at birth with this object in view. At the end of the month the survivors of this Draconian law were again harangued at the place of initiation by the Seven, the yellow ochre washed away, and a ceremony of purification performed; finally all articles of the past were burnt, and the "men" raced back to the village without once turning to look upon the flaming huts and contents, for fear of the evil eye. A great feast was then prepared to welcome them into the tribe in their new status. Forever afterwards the members of each initiation formed a sort of club or freemasonry lodge, each sworn to help and assist the other more than any man. A chief or Induna would always, in after years, appoint his brother initiates to offices in his gift. This freemasonry also extended throughout his tribe and allied tribes, so that a native could travel throughout the length and breadth of the country and receive equal share of food and shelter from every village or camp that he might pass through; he need never starve, unless the others were starving at the same time.

The ethical laws of the tribe, Jim found, unlike many tribes, were strictly and rigidly enforced, the whole result being a physically fine, clean, stalwart race.

CHAPTER VI

ONE afternoon Jim was seated upon the bank of the river in the mottled shade of a tree, idly throwing clods at the smiling stream, a habit which he had contracted during the ten months of exile. A little way up the bank a Mamböe was engaged in placing basket fish traps. Haiwani appeared through an opening in the bush, swinging down the footpath with her easy, panther-like stride. She bore something in her hand. Jim looked up and smiled as Haiwani stood over him.

"Well, little gazelle, where hast thou been?"

"Honey for my lord," she smiled, subsiding beside him amid a musical jingle of ivory bangles.

Jim made room on the pile of skins for her, and together they fed on the robbery of an adjacent hive, laughing and playing like happy children. Jim had taught her to improve the natural beauty of her hair. Hours had he spent in brushing the long tresses himself.

"Here, little baby," he said, holding out a finger with a blob of honey.

She gobbled it up, showing her pearly teeth. Laughing, she leaned suddenly forward and kissed his lean, tanned cheek.

"Ugh," cried Jim, "nasty sticky thing." He patted her cheek with honeyed fingers, both laughing and teasing. "Now we're both in a lovely mess! We will wash, little one."

He attempted to rise, intending to go to the river edge, but she pulled him back.

"Nay," she said, one shapely finger to lips. — "Ho, man!" she called to the bush, "bring thou me water!"

Presently the fisherman appeared, bearing a calabash of water. He placed it at her feet and withdrew. They rinsed their hands together. Having made a cigarette by the usual method, Jim settled down to smoke. The brazen sun, sinking in the heavens, began to filter through the underbranches of the trees. Haiwani, her back against a pad of skins, drew Jim to her and arranged her lengthy tresses to shield his face from the sunspots; together they sat under the canopy of her hair: she content to watch and stroke him, he to lie and smoke.

"Life, Haiwani," remarked Jim at length, "is a funny proposition."

"Life ees what, Jeemy?" she replied, smiling down at him.

He glanced up at her, smiling, too. She kissed him.

"Well, little gazelle, it's — untranslatable — both the phrase and life. Dost understand, little one? What meaning hath life? We know not."

"Do not the wise men among thy people know?"

"Nay, Haiwani, no man knoweth. One man sayeth it is thus, and another man sayeth it is so."

"It is ever so with our people. One man sayeth that a white man is a god, another sayeth he is a devil. Truly I have had the thought that thou art a God, O my Beloved, for thy wisdom is great."

"My gazelle, my wisdom is naught. I am truly a frail God."

"Nay, thou art indeed my God."

"You mustn't be so blasphemous," said Jim, in English, laughing. "The wise white men sayeth that thou shouldst not liken any man unto God, for he is a jealous God and would punish thee."

"That thy great God is jealous of a man! Surely that cannot be; if that were so then truly he cannot be a god, for no God could be jealous of his own making? Who hath said this thing? Dost thou have faith in it?"

"Nay, Haiwani, I am not of the wise men. They read these sayings in books, therefore they know."

"How can that be? Are the books made by thy God?"

"Nay, they were made by men who are now dead."

"How did they know these things, these men who are dead?"

"They write that God himself hath told them."

"How dost thou know that these men speak the true word?"

"We know not. The wise men say that we must believe."

"Dost thou believe?"

"Nay, I do not, little one."

"Then it is thou who art wise. Shall a man believe all that he sees in words? If the God hath spoken to these men why doth he not speak unto men of this day?"

"Again, I know not."

"Thou art even as I have said, a God, for thou art wise."

"What dost thou believe?"

"Nay, I believe naught, for naught know I."

"Then thou art a Goddess on thy own saying — and a deuced logical one," he added in English.

"I know that I love thee more than all that can be, O Amethlokadi. I know that I am alive, that water and food a man must have or he die, yet what else know I except that a man dieth? I have heard, truly. I have heard that thou wert a devil. I have seen thee and my heart telleth me that thou art a God. How then can I believe what my ears have told me, seeing that they lied concerning thee?"

"Solipsism," mused Jim aloud, the invariable habit of a lonely exile. "Strange how many minds, both cultured and untutored, seem to fall on that theory. Well, after all, I don't know. I suppose it is as someone says — each man sees in the Universe round him what each man brings the faculty of seeing; therefore logically as Nature endowed him with those faculties how can a man be blamed for his opinions? Oh, I don't know what I believe, to be honest. I wonder how many are really honest in their expressed opinions — or even with themselves. I think the majority deceive themselves — subconsciously, perhaps. Well, anyhow —"

"What thinkest thou? When thou dost speak so thy thoughts are hid from me."

"I did but think on the foolishness of men, and sometimes I speak to myself."

"So dost thou in thy sleep, Beloved; often thou talkest much, and many times hast thou cried a word, Jo-on."

"Eh!" he exclaimed, startled.

"And at others — Claire. Tell me, she is of thy race?"

"Claire? Who?"

"Nay, I know that Claire is a woman," she sighed. "So thy eyes long to rest upon her?"

"Thou speakest foolish words, little one," said Jim, rising. "Come thou, let us return!"

"Nay, I speak what is in my heart. I know that thou wouldst return to thy people."

Jim was silent.

"O my beloved," she said. "I love thee well, that thou knowest."

"Aye," he said, "I know. — Often I wish you didn't," he thought.

"Thou lovest me?"

"Have I not told thee a thousand times?" he said evasively.

"Aye, thou dost not love me with the love that thou wouldst give to one of thy own race. That is true!"

He made no reply.

"Yes, I know that is true — my heart hath ever told me. Yet why?"

"I know not," said Jim.

"O Amethlokadi," she said at length. "Thou wilt return, for I love thee, this very night."

"What meanest thou?"

"Truly. This night, when the moon hath risen, thou, with Gambai and a slave, wilt return down the river unto thy white brothers."

Jim's face brightened, which Haiwani observed and sighed.

"Nay," he said, after a pause, "that will I not do — without thee."

"Thou must have no thought of me, thy handmaiden, for I love thee and would give thee joy; yet I know that thy heart pines for — thy white brothers. Therefore shalt thou go."

"Nay, I will not without thee."

So arguing they returned to the village. Jim felt his heart bound at the idea of returning, but at the same time felt ashamed and would not acknowledge it. Haiwani had food prepared secretly and warned Gambai. But Jim remained obdurate and Haiwani, overjoyed, kissed him; he fell asleep within her arms.

But during the night she awoke him.

"Arise, O my beloved, for it is time."

"Nay, I will not go, Haiwani, even as I have said."

She drew him to her and kissed him fiercely.

"But if I too go with thee?"

* * * * * * *

Before the first cockcrow, the pair, accompanied by Gambai and two slaves, were gliding rapidly down the ghostly stream. On the fourth day, by paddling and drifting day and night, and with the aid of the swift current, they were upon the broad waters of the Zambezi — safe from pursuit. Jim had not stopped to consider the future of Haiwani. He had assured himself that whilst Haiwani's life would be imperiled by his escape he would never consent to go; but now, having that one obstacle removed, he was too much overjoyed at the prospect of freedom to reconsider matters. Now the excitement was over and freedom near, this problem confronted him. Haiwani never hinted at any opinion upon the subject: she apparently considered that wherever Jim went she would naturally go; yet, thought Jim, she knows or guesses of Claire.

Late one afternoon they arrived at Mungu, near Lealui,[116] where they had heard a trading station had just been established. Alighting from the canoe, Jim gladly toiled in the deep sand up the hill, where he startled a suntanned man, smoking a pipe and gazing morbidly at the vast plain beneath.

"Good Lord!" he exclaimed, staring at Jim as he stood in marvelously patched clothes and skin sandals. "Where the devil have you sprung from? And what — who are you? Why — Heavens! It's Litham!"

Jim briefly explained to the man, whom he had met on the outward journey, over a whisky peg which half intoxicated him. "I'll tell you the yarn later," he concluded; "it's too long now. I should like a bath if you don't mind. And — oh — you might send a message to — er — the lady I mentioned. You won't mind if we —"

"Lord, no, my dear fellow; of course not. Hullo! Here's your man, I think."

"Well?" turning to Gambai, who had suddenly appeared on the verandah. Jim paused in the doorway.

---

[116] Formerly known as Mungu, Mongu (spelled with an "o") is the capital of Western Province in Zambia. Mungu was the capital of what was then known as Barotseland. Mongu is also the home of the Litunga, king of the Lozi people. Lealui (aka Lialui) is located 14 km west of Mongu and is the dry season residence of the king. Barotseland was incorporated into Zambia in 1964.

"O Amethlokadi, Haiwani, the sister of Sepopa, sendeth thee greeting and saith — 'Go thou to the woman of thy race. I love thee, but I would that thou wert happy. Fare thee well.'"

"What meanest thou, Gambai?"

"Nay, I know not, Morena; thus said she, and saying, departed on foot and forbade any to follow her."

Suddenly a thought flashed into Jim's mind, and without a word he tore down the hill to the canoe.

"Where hath she gone?" he cried to the Mamböe.

"The path which leadeth by the swamp."

Hatless he ran, and finding her footprints, traced them to the edge of a swamp pool.

He was too late.

By the body he knelt and reverently kissed the still warm lips.

. . .

"Do you mind," he said to his host afterwards, "if I remain in my room? I'm not hungry."

"Not at all, old chap," the other replied, who was pining for company; "not at all."

"You see," said Jim gravely, "I want to be alone."

CHAPTER VII

NOBODY, to Jim's surprise, had surmised that the party had ever met any trouble; indeed, everybody had concluded that they had continued on to the Congo and out by the Coast. No letters or telegrams awaited him; the Postal Authorities had returned all as having no address. One of his first inquiries had been for Joan, whom he heard had left for England immediately after her marriage. Jim suffered a pang of unreasonable disappointment at not receiving any word from Claire, and, with his usual impetuosity, rushed to Johannesburg. He arrived at Long's Hotel five days later, mentally in sackcloth and ashes one moment at the tragedy of Haiwani, and the next in joyful excitement at the prospect of meeting Claire. He had sent a sheaf of wires from Bulawayo announcing his return to civilization and demanding news. At Johannesburg he received a cable from home announcing the death of his father, and consequently a considerable legacy.[117]

It was a long time since he had seen his father, and although he felt grieved, he was not sufficiently hypocritical to try to persuade himself that the money was at all unwelcome on that account. In fact, both incidents were forced into the background by the absence of any reply from Claire. With a jumble of these affairs in his mind, he drove out to Doornfontein. A strange European maid answered the ring, and to his enquiry replied that the present occupier was a Mr. Foster. She stared curiously

---

[117] Upon the death of his father on 19 March 1906, Beadle received a substantial inheritance, including assets that would have gone to his brother Henry, which allowed him to finance his African expeditions.

at him when he enquired whether Mrs. Icksburg was still resident in Johannesburg.

"Oh, no; she left some time ago."

The maid opened her lips, as if to add something further, but evidently changed her mind suddenly.

"Oh, perhaps they have gone to Europe," suggested Jim.

"Perhaps," said the maid in a noncommittal manner.

"You see, I've been away up country for some time," said he, by way of explanation. "Thanks."

More puzzled than ever, he returned to the hotel. Later, he went off to the Rand Club with the intention of inquiring from Faulkner, the man whom he had met at the first dinner party, but refrained, fearing that he might in some vague way compromise Claire's name. However, walking up Loveday Street debating about it, he met Faulkner.

"Oh," said Jim casually, after inquiring after people whom he had scarcely known, "and how are the Icksburgs?"

"The Icksburgs?" echoed the other. "Haven't you heard? Oh, I forgot, you've been up in the wilds somewhere. Why, man, she bolted with that Scotch fellow, McDermott. The old man — why, what's the matter?"

"Oh, nothing," said Jim thickly, "nothing."

"Nothing! You look very white about the gills. Come-and-have-a-drink? You weren't hit there, were you?"

"Lord, no!" said Jim indignantly. "I scarcely knew her. I —"

"H'm," said Faulkner, watching him keenly. "Well, come along."

"Who was McDermott?" enquired Jim after a while, with attempted nonchalance.

"Oh, a South American Scotchman. I believe they've gone there. The old man took it very calmly. Said it was a good riddance."

"The cad!" exclaimed Jim.

"Cad? Why? Think he did the best thing. He's getting a divorce. Of course she was much younger than he, and — well, I wasn't surprised."

Jim had never liked Faulkner; now he thought that he positively detested him. He bade him an abrupt good morning and returned to the hotel in an access of temper against everyone. He sat down disconsolately upon his bed. "What a fool I've been," he soliloquized, "to even imagine that Claire would wait. Well, only another and convincing proof that Miêville and others were right. Women are the devil. But Haiwani!" He had forgotten her. The Bronze Goddess! She, the savage, had been the finest and best of all. If she were not dead he would return straight to her. With his foolish faith in Claire he had practically caused her death — murdered her.

"Damn women!" he said vindictively. "Oh, I don't know what to do. I'll get drunk. I feel like painting things red. . . . No, I won't — it'll make me ill. I wonder what the other fellow, McDermott, was like? Oh, what a fool I was! Why didn't —" He snapped his fingers at his reflection in the mirror. "You're a damned fool!" he said solemnly.

CHAPTER VIII

NEXT morning Jim awoke dissatisfied with himself and the world in general. Everything seemed to turn to a bad taste in the mouth. He fell to cursing Claire, Joan, and women in general, save Haiwani, whose memory he had now set upon his very best pedestal, contemplating with morbid fascination his life with her and her sacrifice to free him for — what?

The "boy" came in with morning coffee and drew the curtains. A bleak, rain-sodden sky depressed him. Life seemed empty. If only Haiwani were alive, by God, he'd go back to her. A great loneliness laid hold upon him. All civilization was false and rotten. He would return to the veld, where things were close to nature, passionate and true. A house seemed like a suffocating trap. He must get away from the dreary wilderness of bricks and mortar, away to the freedom, the masterfulness of the wilds. He sprang out of bed determined to carry out the inspiration on the instant. A knock at the door interrupted him.

"Hullo, come in!" he cried, sitting on his bed wondering who the visitor could possibly be. The door opened.

"Good God, Biddy!"

"Is it Jimmy? Bedamn, me son, you're getting so thin I hardly knew you, and you're as black as a nigger."

"How did you know I was here?"

"Sure I came in for 'a hair of the dog' and they told me."

Jim smiled. Biddy sat down on the bed.

"Just the same old Biddy, doing the same old things."

"Sure and why not? Phwat the divil d'ye mean be not writing? I wrote ye, but me letters, like the cat, came back. Where have ye been?"

"Oh, it's a long story. I'll tell you after a bit. Gad! I'm glad to see you again, Biddy; I've got the hump."

"Have ye, now? It's the gurrls again, I'll warrant."

Jim sighed.

"Yes, you're right; and what's more, I'll agree with you this time. Women are the devil."

"Ah! Ye've been larning things, have ye? Well, let's have it."

Two hours later they were sitting on the verandah, watching the brilliant yellow sunlight glinting on the burbling gutters.

"H'm," said Biddy, sampling a third whisky and soda. "I wrote and told ye what had happened — gently, mind."

"Why, did you guess?" said Jim quickly.

"Av course I did. D'ye remimber a fairy story ye told me?"

"When? Where?"

"Why, just before ye left — supposin' this and supposin' that." Biddy chuckled.

"Did I? Oh, yes, I remember something about it. I was awfully queer then, wasn't I? I've learnt a whole heap since I left you, Biddy. Dear little Bronze Goddess!"

"H'm, well, ye'll find others."

"No, that I won't. I swore this morning that I'll never look at a woman again."

Biddy cackled with laughter.

"I mean it!"

"Jimmy, ye haven't learnt as much as I gave ye credit for."

"I'm not rotting. I tell you, I mean it," said Jim, his eyes on the street.

"Well, I shouldn't twist my neck trying to ogle the pretty girl in the rickshaw."

"Don't be absurd," said Jim loftily. "Er — what are you doing now, Biddy? I've been yapping about myself so much I've even forgotten to be polite."

Biddy's blue eyes twinkled.

"Good for ye, me bhoy! Well," he said, striking his chest, "it's a stage manager I am, bedamn! Leonard Merton's Company No. 2, and the leading lady and meself is going to make a match of it."

"You married!" exclaimed Jim incredulously. "I thought you had too much sense."

"Ho! ho!" chuckled Biddy. "Hark to the voice of the Cynic! I'll bet ye don't wait till ye're my respectable age."

"I," said Jim severely, "shall never marry."

"It'll be the death of me ye'll be, Jimmy. What a terrible pitiful case it is. And so young! So innocent! Poor dear! Is it the heart or the liver ye feel most? A little sea voyage for ye, Jimmy; for the air and the gurrls. I'll give ye a sure cure: take one pretty gurrl, dilute with moonlight, evening kit, and southern seas. One dose every evening on the upper deck under the lee of a boat. To be well shaken before taken — most obstinate cases cured in a week."

"Oh, rot!" said Jim, laughing.

"Well, what are ye goin' to do? Ye're a landed proprietor, a bloated plutocrat seemingly."

"Oh, it ought to pan out about enough for a single fellow to live on comfortably, but I'm going back to the wilds. I'm —"

"It's a lucky fool ye are, Jimmy!"

"Rot! I know something now. I'm no longer a fool," said Jim. "I'm absolutely fed up with civilization — everybody stiff and formal, hollow and artificial. Yet perhaps it isn't exactly that. I suppose I've got the Wanderlust or the Call of the Wild. It's the best life, after all. I wish I'd never come back. Ugh! Fancy getting up every morning at the same time, meeting the same people, doing the same things all one's life!"

"Oh, bedamn, it's not so bad as all that! Life's quite amus—"

"Life? This isn't life!" exclaimed Jim emphatically. "Yet — oh, I don't know what's the matter with me."

"Fall in love again, I'm tellin' ye," said Biddy, laughing.

"Can't. Besides, I don't believe in love. I think I shall go to the Far East[118] for a change."

"Do, darlin' — for a change — of gurrls."

"Oh, for heaven's sake, leave the girls alone."

"Practice your own advice, me son — if ye can! Come along and have dinner tonight: then see my show."

* * * * * * *

---

[118] In 1905 Roger Pocock, a veteran of the Boer War, created a civilian group known as the Legion of Frontiersmen. It served as an unofficial intelligence gathering group, whose purpose was to prepare its members for war and to maintain peacetime vigilance. References to Beadle appear in Pocock's diary, which is housed at the Bruce Peel Collection, University of Alberta. (The men appear to have been friends.) One entry dated 6 March 1908 states that Beadle was "just back from Borneo" (i.e., the "Far East"). Beadle also records his visit to the Far East in an essay titled "A Decade of Christmas Dinners," published in the December 1914 issue of *Badminton Magazine of Sports and Pastimes*. (The text is structured around various locations where he spent his Christmas holiday over the span of a decade, circa 1900 – 1909.) Beadle's Far East episode includes the following: "Through the trees of the maidan was a vista of the lights of steamers and junks in the harbor beginning to twinkle, eddy and surge. Outside in the broad road was a motley throng: women and men in rikshas, gharries, and open landaus with silver-mounted harness and woodwork in which sat the bland figures of Chinese merchants; a few odd coolies on foot, a turbaned policeman, a solitary motor car, Malay girls in brilliant scarlet and yellow head cloths and sarongs, sedate Japanese, and a trio of British tars." (Sailors whose clothing was often stained by the ship's pine tar, which becomes sticky at a relatively low temperature.) Beadle also mentions Borneo in his 3 July 1918 "Camp-Fire" column: "Went to Dutch Borneo, rubber planting. Afterward returned to go to Morocco; penetrated into interior in disguise during rebellion." In the same column he writes "My infancy was spent around Siam and the farther East: early memories, fire-flies mosquitoes and ayahs." Until 1939 the Kingdom of Thailand was known as Siam. An "Ayah" is a nurse or maid native to India. Presumably Beadle's stay in Siam was connected to his father's work as a ship captain.

Jim lay late in bed next morning. After midday he leisurely bathed, dressed, and wandered round to Biddy's rooms. That eminent individual he discovered in a purple dressing gown, lolling in a rocking chair, discussing[119] whisky and soda.

"Morning, me bhoy," said he; "have a hair of the dog that bit ye?"

"Ugh! No," said Jim, straddling a chair. "I feel liverish still. Biddy, I've been thinking."

"Bad habit, darlin'. I've warned ye against it."

"Biddy, I'm an ass."

"True for ye, Jim. I congratulate ye on discoverin' the truth."

"No, but I am."

"I'm not denyin' it."

Biddy with tenderness drained his glass. He sighed regretfully as he replaced it on the table.

"Ah, that's good liquor, Jimmy. Good liquor was invinted by a merciful Providence for the solace of man. Man unfortunately, as I told ye, sometimes becomes unreasonable, then he drinks bad liquor, which agin is ginerally caused by a woman, which agin brings proof that the root of all evil is woman. Not but that woman is sometimes an angel, which is a paradox, which agin is life."

Biddy, with a leg over each armrest and cigar in full blast, prepared to uphold his reputation. Jim smiled.

"Life, I'm tellin' ye —" recommenced Biddy.

"Do you jaw your blessed company like this, Biddy?"

"Phwat's that?" catching at a new topic. "Av coorse I do. You know the old saw — a woman, a dog, and a walnut tree. Well, add the profession to it and ye'd —"

"Oh, shut up," said Jim.

---

[119] Discuss (British; facetious, rare): to eat or drink with enthusiasm.

Biddy obeyed.

"It's yourself that wants the flure. Well, get along with it," he encouraged.

"I wasn't in love with Claire," said Jim abruptly.

Biddy winked approvingly at his cigar tip.

"There's no such thing as love!"

"Oh?"

"Love is the root of all evil — the greatest enemy of mankind, accelerated by the fact that they will not realize it nor attempt to understand it. Dumas says 'cherchez la femme,' and it's true. I don't mean any disparagement of women. Love rules the world, they say, too. And a perfect example of maladministration, say I."

Jim paused at the end of a gesture, like Ajax defying the lightning.

"H'm," murmured Biddy, chewing his cigar. "Go on, darlin'."

"Yes," continued Jim firmly. "It's merely sexual attraction. A particular female catches your eye and then certain nerve centers become irritated, so to speak, which cause palpitation of the heart and other physical phenomena, which have a very stimulating effect upon the imagination, with the natural consequences that the object becomes in the patient's eyes all that his imagination dictates — his ideal. In exceptional cases it remains for long periods, but it is most distinctly transient. It is really simply the method of nature for the continuity of the reproduction of the species. The worst of it is that we are not taught these things, and the mental and physical phenomena not being understood by the patient, serious consequences often ensue. This" — with a gesture of scorn — "is dignified with the name of love! Love! A temporary hallucination at the most: therefore there is *no* such thing as Love.

"One may talk rot about higher planes, affinities, mental companions, and all that, but no one ever wanted to marry a girl to carry on a scientific or debating society. I was as much in love with the Bronze Goddess — poor little Goddess! — as it is possible to be, and didn't know it. I thought that I was in love with Claire for the simple reason that she was far away, and when I saw her here I only saw her at intervals; hence that fact allowed me to clothe her with idealistic charms and — er — virtues — for want of a better word. I — I daresay this sounds rather boring to you because you've found it out before, but it's quite a revelation to me."

He paused out of breath.

"No, Jimmy, it's very interestin'. You're bearin' up quite well. Many people go through life without recognizing any of the plain patent facts of life. There's no necessity to howl over these broken ideals — for ideals they are. Every man and woman is born with these painful and unnecessary ideals; they always haunt at the back of things. But the sooner ye get rid of 'em, the better for ye. It's painful, I know — like carving out the vermiform appendix without an anesthetic. And yet I like to think, or try to think, that she was — you know who I mean — that she was the ideal. It's just the ghost of the old complaint. She might have been — there may be but —"

"Maybe," said Jim. "I've gone through a little hell on my own coming to these conclusions —"

"So does everyone."

"Well, I'm not going to make an abject ass of myself again by allowing my imagination and romantic emotions to run away with me again. Romance is very nice and exciting, but I mean to have the curb on it. I've learnt a whole lot, by the Lord! and I mean to benefit by it. One thing my conclusions have taught me is to be very tolerant of others. With Claire, for instance, I now do not feel bitter or cynical, because I can understand. Her life with him was hell on earth. She was young and full-blooded. Well, the natural law demanded a mate for her — and nature found her one — first myself; then when I had foolishly — or wisely, I think for my own sake — gone, nature was just as strong. The other fellow came, and — well, the force of attraction was too strong for her. I felt I wanted to kill him — just the primitive instinct — as a bull would fiercely attack another of the same sex who dared to approach the herd of cows: the Call of the Wild in another phase, the natural instinct stronger than artificial morals. I know now, and understand. Those same laws have, of course, worked equally within myself, but I was — like many others — too blind to see, as in — well, other cases."

Biddy smiled.

"I'll admit that knowledge of these things has mitigated or wiped out the agony of unrequited love, and all that sort of thing. Still, there's an ache left — but it's not for Claire — an ache of regret for a life a little more empty and futile; but it won't hurt so much. But, by God, I'll never look at any woman again."

"Bedamn!" said Biddy. "I'll wager —"

"I won't. I swear I won't!" retorted Jim passionately. "And in time — in time — I've nearly accomplished it now — to be utterly indifferent, which will mean freedom from care or pain. And I'll adopt your outlook on life, Biddy. But, anyhow, here's to Lindsay Gordon:

> 'In all this world there's little worth a sigh
> And nothing worth a tear!'"[120]

"But, ye omadhaun,"[121] exclaimed Biddy, clinking glasses, "there's a whole world of things to laugh at!"

---

[120] Paraphrase of a stanza in "To My Sister," by the British-Australian poet Adam Lindsay Gordon (1833 – 1870): "On earth there's little worth a sigh, / And nothing worth a tear!"

---

121 Omadhaun (chiefly Irish): fool, idiot, simpleton. From Irish Gaelic, *amadān*.

BOOK IV

CHAPTER I

YET Jim lingered on in Johannesburg, ever voicing his weariness of all things civilized and his intention to return to the wilds. In Biddy he found a subtle solace for the bitterness in his mind; to whom he clung tenaciously, as a nonswimmer swept away in a winter flood. To him Jim poured forth babbling denunciations of the perfidy of women and the falsity of the world at large. Biddy listened patiently, chaffing sympathetically. Sometimes when Jim felt constrained to apologize for a lengthy harangue Biddy retorted: "Good for ye, Jimmy darlin': the poison's coming out."

Biddy introduced him to several of his company with instructions for his subjugation. They failed miserably. As one of them explained: "Oh, my dear, he's impossible; he won't give me a chance to get near him, and sneers every time I tickle his face with my hair, and — oh, he's horrid!" In these days Jim was like a rudderless ship, he was inclined to drift any way the wind blew; and had it not been for Biddy's cunning hand and unfailing sympathy, Jim might have made an abject fool of himself over wine and cards. However, Biddy weaned him away from the misanthropic idea of burying himself in the wilds, and endeavored to persuade him that he ought to return home to attend to his affairs, and to try the recipe of moonlight and girls. But Jim laughed scornfully, and said that there was no need, as he could arrange everything by post.

Believing that he was accepting things philosophically, he sometimes worked himself into a fury against Claire, quite convinced that all women were alike, and that he had really lost inclination towards the sex; although the more he thought of Haiwani, the finer the character she assumed. Subconsciously he felt that he could not rest without an ideal upon a pedestal, even if she were only an Egeria[122] in imagination. Haiwani had saved his life, and he never ceased to reproach himself bitterly for having, he considered, murdered her. But it really depended upon the mood of the moment. If the surroundings were pleasing, then all had been for the best; if a fit of discontented depression held him, he savagely accused himself of the murder of Haiwani, and cursed the moment when he had consented to return to civilization.

Although he tried hardly[123] and laboriously to play the selected role of misogynist, his natural virility rebelled. The impulse of sex once conjured from the flagon of innocence was as difficult to recapture as the fabled jinni. To his angry disgust, he would find that some particular girl attracted him against his will and reason. He would storm and curse, chanting his formula of love like an incantation against evil. Painfully aware of the effect, Jim, unlike so many, knew and recognized the cause. He conquered — for the time being; but only at the cost

---

[122] In Roman mythology Egeria was an oracular water nymph who imparted wisdom and prophecy in exchange for libations of water or milk deposited at her sacred groves. She was said to be the divine consort and advisor of Numa Pompilius, the second legendary king of Rome (following Romulus). But given the context of Beadle's novel — as well as its title — it's possible that he's simultaneously invoking the memory of the pilgrim Egeria (also known as Aetheria): a fourth-century Hispano-Roman Christian who conducted a pilgrimage to the Holy Land circa 381/2–384 and who composed an epistolary chronicle of her travels. Her untitled letter is now known as *Itinerarium Egeriae* (Travels of Egeria), but it's also referred to as *Peregrinatio Aetheriae* (Pilgrimage of Aetheria) or *Peregrinatio ad Loca Sancta* (Pilgrimage to the Holy Lands).

[123] Hardly (archaic): with force: vigorously.

of many agonized hours and much vexation of spirit. The more he mortified the flesh, the more bitter he grew against the world. The higher the blasted ideals have been, the more intense the bitterness; hence the mere human vegetable retains the veneer of smug optimism. After some four months of restless misery in Johannesburg and Durban, during which he developed a peevish temper, a soured sneer, and ugly lines around one corner of his mouth, he determined to return to England. But there came rumors of impending war. Jim nearly prayed in gratitude, and immediately hostilities broke out he rushed off to volunteer.

Then for three years Jim forgot his doubts of gods and women in the primitive excitement of man hunting and killing. He emerged with a commission and a D.S.O.,[124] won not by bravery but by foolhardiness, that much vaunted quality of which popular heroes are made, upspringing from sheer stupidity and lack of imagination, or crazy recklessness. Then flushed with the lust of blood he raced across to the Far East in time to witness the Russo-Japanese war.[125]

With the lapse of time and the absence of opportunity the demon, that legacy of Adam, was lulled to sleep, which Jim mistook for the silence of death and rejoiced accordingly. His hatred and unacknowledged fear of the opposite sex grew into tolerant contempt of the woman feminine and admiration of the masculine woman. He reverted, unconsciously, to his old idyllic theory of platonic friendship; with the result that one woman, with whom he became mentally intimate, fell in love with him,

---

[124] D.S.O. or Distinguished Service Order: British military decoration that recognizes officers for their distinguished or meritorious service. Established by Queen Victoria in 1886, it's usually awarded to officers above the rank of captain.

[125] Japan declared war on Russia on 8 February 1904. Beadle had turned twenty-two the previous October.

destroyed her husband's happiness and her own, what time the unsuspecting Jim serenely pursued his way, supremely oblivious to the trail of broken hearts; that is, he despised the physical and worshipped the mental.

After the excitement of battle and licensed murder Jim's mind had fallen a victim anew to the clamoring hosts of doubt. His virility, after finding an outlet in the physical activity of war, sought issue in thought. He began to study life in a detached sense, read extensively, and became appalled at the complexities of the problem he was seeking to solve. He wandered restlessly from country to country, punctuating periods of life research by odd hunting and exploring adventures.

*   *   *   *   *   *   *

At last upon a day in April he arrived at Tilbury.[126] As the train approached the terminus he gazed with mild astonishment at the wilderness of roofs. He had expected to be rather excited, but the gloomy atmosphere and absence of sun depressed him: and the metamorphosis of London into a hooting, roaring pandemonium of traffic bewildered him. However, he spent the first evening in company with a party of fellow passengers who had arranged a farewell dinner, and continued on to Derbyshire the next morning.

The familiar country station did not seem to have altered in the least. But the little, redheaded stationmaster, who failed to recognize him at first, had grown balder and stouter; and Jacob, who had brought the dogcart, was as gnarled and hardy as an old oak. To Jim's eyes everything appeared on a smaller scale: the fields and coppices were diminutive, the bracken-covered moor had shrunk; the countryside was merely a series of tiny

---

[126] Tilbury: a port town in Thurrock, Essex.

gardens, fenced and restricted with boundaries, giving an irritating sense of being fettered.

As he drove Jim learned from Jacob the local news: that the widow who had been his father's housekeeper had married and taken a small "public"[127] about seven miles away; that Peter had broken his foreleg seven years ago and had had to be shot, at which Jim felt a keen pang of regret; and that Mr. Blettford had just bought a pair of new carriage horses, and Mrs. Blettford's second boy had nearly died of pneumonia last winter. At the mention of Madge, Jim had felt a queer thrill. The environment and Jacob's garrulity had brought up the past so vividly that it seemed but a few months ago.

"How many children has Mrs. Blettford now, Jacob?" he inquired after a pause.

"Foive, sir; three boys an' two gal twins a year laast Michaelmas."

"Oh my Lord!" groaned Jim and relapsed into gloomy silence. The news hurt him: the ghost of the Compleat Ideal stirred about him. That *she* should have children like a charwoman!

The sky was leaden, and had been threatening rain all day. Rather depressed and disappointed, Jim at last drove through the laurel bushes and pulled up before the old ivy-clad porch — home.

An aunt, who, since his father's death, had lived at the Abbey Lodge, welcomed him, which he resented somewhat, feeling her to be an alien presence. On the first opportunity he went up to his old den, now used as a box room.[128] But the environment conjured up the ghosts of his youthful ideals who came clamoring about him: it seemed as if he were a stranger meeting himself at nineteen. He fled.

---

127 Public: a "public house," commonly known as a pub.
128 Box room (British): a room in a house where things are stored.

Unable to break his mood of depression, he found dinner with his aunt almost more irritating than he could bear. There was nothing in common. He felt as if he were talking to a child. She would persist in recalling his father's last days; what he had said, and how he had wished to see his son once more.[129] Vaguely Jim wondered why people would be so morbid. He alone knew how much he had cared, and these unnecessary details only aroused a combination of remorse and resentment for the things they had both left undone.

After dinner he excused himself from discussing affairs of the estate, and, having a horse saddled, rode out on to the moor, straight from the table. The clouds had cleared away, leaving a bright, starlit sky. Almost unconsciously he had taken the familiar bridle path. When he realized the direction he pulled up, smiled cynically, and turned towards the Blettfords' place. Riding up to the front of the house, he saw the buxom figure of a woman inside the open French window of the dining room. She turned her head at the sound of hoofs on the gravel — Madge. She looked straight at him, and he at her — taking in the matronly figure, the same placid eyes and pallid complexion; but the face had broadened considerably, confessing to more than a suspicion of a double chin. He urged his horse a few paces towards her, amused that she did not recognize him. She appeared perplexed and moved away.

"Madge!" he called, "Don't you know me?"

She looked round in surprise and stared.

"Jim!" she exclaimed. "Why, I didn't know you. — Harold" — to someone behind — "here's Jim Litham. Ring the bell and

---

[129] When the author's father, Henry Beadle, died in 1906, he was survived by two older sisters: Mary Beadle (1846 – 1918) and Sarah Emily Beadle (1848 – 1908). When I spoke with Beadle's great-niece Patricia, she said she believed that Charles was "cared for by Henry's sister Sarah Beadle and by Catherine Owens, Charles' grandmother."

send someone for his horse, will you? — Why, Jim, I am pleased to see you," she continued, crossing the lawn towards Jim, who had dismounted. "Gracious! you have altered. When did you come home? We heard nothing about it. Of course we thought you would have come long ago, after —"

"Yes, of course," said Jim, shaking hands; "but I — I was up country and then the war broke out, you know."

"Hullo, Jim!" exclaimed Blettford in a hearty voice, following his wife. "So you've come home at last, eh? Ah, my boy, you've missed some of the finest runs since old Teckford broke his neck. . . . Come along in."

Relieved of his horse, Jim entered the house. There were several other local people who knew, or had known, him. Although they intended to treat him as a species of lion, the effect was as if he were that beast in reality and that they were half afraid he might roar, bite, or do something that was not good form. Blettford had grown much stouter, a trifle noisier if possible, and a little redder in the face. He was very proud of his children; and Madge, to Jim's disgust, insisted upon taking him up to the nursery to see them. With mixed feelings Jim obeyed, and looked in tongue-tied embarrassment at the cot containing the twins.

"Very nice," he said at length, at which even Madge smiled.

After this ordeal he was requested to give some account of his wanderings, which he evaded after admitting the bare facts that he had been in the War and Japan. Somehow he felt very ill at ease and wished that he had not come at all. While he fended polite queries, his mind was occupied in considering Madge. Now in the light of a traveled man he realized only too clearly that she was a homely, healthy woman with no pretensions to beauty nor to mentality; in fact, hopelessly mediocre in every respect. Even though his memory of her had told him something of the truth during the years, the actual ocular and oral demonstration was needed to impress the fact upon his mind. For the moment his bitterness against the world was increased: how could he have been so blind as to magnify a very worthy but ordinary girl into a Goddess? That was a typical instance of what that insane hallucination called Love would do, he reflected. He looked at her afresh as he pretended to listen to an account of an extraordinarily fine hunter which Blettford had nearly bought at a sale. She was just the same as she had always been really. Her dark coils of hair were "just so," as he put it, not a hair out of place. Her eyes were as placid as a millpond. No temper or coquettishness had ever been there. Impossible to have aroused the flash of Haiwani's eyes in Madge, or the tantalizing twinkle of Joan's. — He felt annoyed with himself for thinking of Joan. — He glanced around the room. Every "damned thing" in the place was "just so," he thought, in a spasm of irritation. Madge's calm personality pervaded the house. He rose protesting that he must leave, but Blettford boisterously refused to allow him, and Madge aided him by remarking that she could not spare her "old playmate."

Jim frowned quickly at the appellation, and yet was pleased.

When he had arrived he had wanted to have a chat with Madge tête-à-tête, but when an opportunity offered he avoided it. What could he talk about? Madge could never have dreamed of all she had meant to him, of the turmoil and struggle which had gone on within him. However, while two of the guests were at the piano and the talkative Blettford elsewhere engaged, Madge cornered him.

After some desultory remarks she said:

"Well, Jim, are you really glad to be home?"

"Yes," he said, after a moment's hesitation, thinking that she would not understand if he told the truth.

"You've changed a lot," she pursued. "You look harder, Jim — and you're going gray! You don't look happy either. Are you?"

"Why, of course I am," said Jim ironically.

"I am glad of that," she replied, simply. "Because I thought sometimes that you might not be. You must be so lonely."

"O Lord, no," said Jim. "Why should I be?"

"Ah, Jim, you think you're happy, but you're not really."

"I am," he asserted.

She shook her head and smiled.

"You can't be. I wish you were. I am so happy, deliriously happy." — Jim winced. — "Why don't you marry, Jim? You won't know what happiness is till then."

"Oh, pooh," said he uneasily. "I shall never marry. I — I don't believe —" (in love, he was going to say).

"Believe what?"

"Oh, that I shall ever meet *the* girl, don't you know."

"Oh, nonsense! There's lots of nice girls. . . . Let me find you one, Jim?"

"O my God, no!" exclaimed Jim. "I beg your pardon," he added, and felt that she was indelicate in referring to a wife as one would to a dog or a new piece of furniture.

"Well, you won't know what true happiness is until you do," she persisted. "Why, I wouldn't change one of my darlings for all the gold in the world: children are the greatest blessings God can give you. I've often thought of you and wondered if you had got married. Sometimes I quite expected you to bring a wife and children home with you when you did come, although I thought you'd have written and told me that."

"Yes, of course I would."

"Well, you're going to stay at home now, aren't you, Jim?"

"I don't know, Madge; really I don't. I — I've got to go back to London in a few days, anyhow."

"Oh, Jim, I *am* sorry. But you'll come over to church and dinner tomorrow, won't you? Quite like old times."

"Oh — I never go to church now, Madge."

"Jim!"

"Oh, I haven't been for years."

"I am sorry. Why not?"

"Oh" — evasively — "one gets out of it up country, you know."

"I wish you did, Jim," earnestly.

"Sorry, Madge, but I can't," he said, half smiling; "and I'm afraid I can't very well desert Aunt Marianne either. You must forgive me. I expect I'll be down again soon."

"Oh, Jim! . . . But won't you be here on Tuesday for the meet? Harold will never forgive you, if you don't."

"But I haven't got a mount now."

"Oh, we'll mount you."

"I'll see."

At that moment, to Jim's relief, Blettford interrupted to ask his wife to accompany him on the piano. So while he roared his perennial hunting song, Jim was left in peace to stare at Madge and ponder. The fact that she had said she was happy, which was true, disturbed him. Blettford was happy too, and obviously adored her. Strange. Blettford was a fool, reflected Jim, a boisterous teddy bear of a man: and Madge was — well, mediocre; but they were both undoubtedly happy. Jim frowned and sighed wearily. Madge had merely existed and had become happy. Blettford had led the ordinary life of a young man of his class in town and country, and had been made happy: while he, Jim, had furiously sought the blue bird without success. Of course the solution was simple enough: the less one required the more easy it was to obtain. Neither of these fortunates had ever been galled with imagination, that curse of the Gods, mused Jim morosely.

Then he suddenly perceived how good her influence had been over him in his youth. He was now in a position to realize what she, as a Fylgja, had done for him at school. A wave of emotional gratitude towards her welled within him. He wished in that moment that he could believe in love, and marry such a woman as she was — followed immediately by the bitter conviction that such a one would bore him to tears. Ah well, it seemed an unjust world and little hope for him.

Yet Madge was a good woman; which led him to the cynical reflection that virtue was lack of imagination.

When the other guests had gone he was moved to tell her how much she had been to him. However, he refrained, knowing that she could not understand. She insisted upon her husband lending him a coat to ride home, as the night was chilly. Jim protested that he did not need one.

"Good Lord, of course you do!" roared Blettford. "You'll be down with pneumonia riding round at midnight in nothing but a boiled shirt. Have another drink before you go, too. Yes, you must."

Jim drank a glass of brandy and turned to go, feeling as if he were an outcast leaving the warmth and comfort for the hedgerow. They escorted him to the door.

"Goodbye, Madge," he said, taking her hand.

"Good *night*, you mean, Jim," she said, laughing. For an instant he hesitated, and then, as years before, bent and kissed her fingers.

CHAPTER II

LIFE in London amused Jim for a few weeks, but when the novelty had worn off, it had the opposite effect. The few people whom he had known had disappeared. He wrote to Graham, but not receiving any reply, concluded that he, too, had gone abroad. He managed to unearth one man whom he had known before slightly, who introduced him to many others; but they all seemed vaguely out of tune — nothing in common. All of them had their own particular hub around which they gravitated with irritating monotony.

Jim quickly realized the truth of the fact that he was far more lonely amid the teeming millions of London than ever in the wilderness. Conventionality and narrow-mindedness jostled him on every side.

One day he was stricken with an attack of sentimental curiosity in the shape of a wish to see and stay in his old rooms. After alighting from a taxi, he sauntered on past the house, noted that the blinds appeared as he had remembered them, and that the house was a shade more dingy; then he wheeled about and knocked sharply on the familiar door, which was now a dirty blue. As footsteps sounded within, he expected to see Maggie of the soiled apron and smutty face; but a tall, hawk-faced woman in rusty black silk sharply inquired his business. Jim frowned annoyance at the disappointment, and inquired if the first-floor rooms were to let. They were, and grudging permission was granted to view them. As he mounted the stairs and entered the sitting room in the wake of the rustling skirt, he experienced an eerie expectancy of seeing Eve rise eagerly from the old armchair by the fire, as she had so often done before; or of Maggie busy with dustpan and brush. But the walls had been repapered with a majestic gold-and-red design, and the room furnished with polish-smelling Tottenham Court Road furniture; only one of the old mirrors remained to gibe in a cracked leer at Jim. The wish to occupy the old rooms died, and he smiled at his own mawkish sentiment — so unlike him of late years! He inquired the rent and raised his eyebrows to learn that the price had risen a hundred percent. The beadlike eyes of the woman brightened as she noted that he did not protest. He asked after Mrs. Hobbs, but the thin lips acidly assured him that she did not know who Mrs. Hobbs — with a generous aspirate — might be. Jim became suddenly annoyed with himself, the reflex action of the emotion discharging itself against the landlady. He thanked her curtly, said the rooms would not suit him, and was conducted in stony silence to the door.

Outside Jim stood for a moment pondering upon the imbecility of mankind and of himself in particular. Then hailing a taxi he drove west, wondering what had happened to Eve — not that he cared a straw, he was convinced, but merely out of idle curiosity as to what had become of her. Probably married and settled down as a model of respectability, he reflected with his favorite sneer. However, the jaunt had done him no good; it depressed him and revived with intensity his ever-present resentment against life, against the constant aching for some object to make life really worth living. He had an appointment to lunch with some people, but sent a wire instead, snatching upon the conventional lie which he had used as a text for a mental homily upon the rottenness of humanity. He fell to quoting Omar Khayyam with malicious emphasis. He lunched alone and miserably. He had not had such a fit of depression for many months, and cursed himself for giving way to the weak sentimentality which he was assured had brought it on. As he sat in the smoking lounge afterwards he saw Lascelles, a man whom he had met in England and abroad, enter. Jim's first impulse was to avoid him, but he was really rather pleased when Lascelles recognized him and came over. Jim was in a mood when he would have been grateful to be spoken to by a thug.

As Lascelles had nothing to do, they sat all the afternoon drinking liqueurs and chatting. They decided to dine together, and accordingly met at a well-known restaurant about half-past seven. Deferentially the head waiter greeted Lascelles, with whom he appeared to be on terms of intimacy. When the wines had been chosen with much deliberation, for Jim had now become something of a connoisseur, he stared about him with a peculiar expression of amazement.

"What's the matter?" inquired Lascelles, a trifle tetchily, pulling at his dark moustaches.

"Oh, nothing in particular," said Jim. "Only the chatter and lights always half mesmerize me — for about a month after I return to civilization. It's wonderful, all this —" he gestured vaguely — "until it wears off. Has an intoxicating fascination about it; the wine, the lights, fancy foods, as if it were the only thing worth living for."

"It is!" exclaimed Lascelles.

"Oh, rot! It only lasts a little while and then bores one to death. Although it's worth a spell in the desert to get that strange thrill of excitement. *You* miss that."

"Oh, do I? It's life to me."

"Yes, but you can't appreciate it."

"Why not?"

"Because you have it always. Every pleasure is haunted by satiety and boredom."

"Well, what is worth living for?"

"God knows," said Jim, suddenly morose. "I don't."

"Well, what's the use of hypercriticizing everything?"

"I don't know," said Jim, and laughed. "Still, other people are interesting. They never fail one. There's so many of 'em. Look at the couple at the next table. Stout old girl's simply laden with diamonds; the fellow's thundering good-looking, but looks terribly bored. Wonder what relationship they are?"

"Husband and wife," said Lascelles, after observing them keenly.

"Oh, rot! She's old enough to be his mother."

"True, but it's as I say. Notice the air of proprietorship about the old girl, and the long-suffering air of the man. He talks to her spasmodically with the tail of his eye on the pretty girl beyond. Married her for money. Obvious. Dining her out by way of penance. Common enough."

"Oh Lord!" exclaimed Jim, "I could do many things, but not that. I'd —"

"H'm," said Lascelles, laughing cynically; "I'll admit I've done the same."

"Oh! I'm sorry," said Jim. "Have I put my foot in it? Matter of fact, I thought —"

"Oh, I don't mind. I like being candid — sometimes. What were you going to say?"

"Oh! well, I — your wife is deuced pretty —"

"Thanks!"

"And obviously very fond of you. It never occurred to me."

"Yes, she's a dear little woman. I wish," he said callously, "she wasn't so fond of me. I feel a bit of a rotter sometimes."

"Really?"

"Well, hang it! I look after her — amuse her — take her out occasionally and that sort of thing."

"And the others?"

"Well, why shouldn't I? Others do. Besides, she's my wife, and — well, a fellow can't treat a wife like a mistress, you know."

"Why not? What's the difference?" demanded Jim. "One's licensed, the other's not."

"Oh, my dear chap, I've respect for my wife. One — oh, dam-it-all! — one can't have fun with one's wife. There's no disrespect to her in my affairs with other women. Any decent man — well, debauches himself with other women rather than his wife. You know well enough that there's the beast in every man."

"Yes, by God, I do!" exclaimed Jim, and drank his wine at a gulp.

"Well, there you are!" retorted Lascelles triumphantly. "You're a bachelor, so —" He smiled suggestively.

"Even if I *am*, your inference doesn't follow. I hate women!" exclaimed Jim heatedly, "and never have anything to do with them."

"Oh, rot, my dear fellow! If you married a good pure woman —"

"And debauched myself with others. *Yes*, go on."

"You'd have your respect for her sex return."

"Oh? Really?"

"It's only because you starve yourself that you're a misogynist — if you really are! You know how Kipling puts it? —

> 'For a man must go with a woman,
> Which women do not understand;
> But they that say that they do
> Are not of the marrying brand.'"

"Damn Kipling!" exclaimed Jim furiously. "That's all damned tommyrot.[130] The fact is you're merely a selfish beast. You're

---

[130] Tommyrot: utter foolishness; nonsense. From *tommy* (simpleton; tomfool) + *rot* (English dialect). A relatively new term at the time, it was first coined in 1884 (thirty-two years before the first publication of this novel).

frightened to reveal yourself to your wife. — I'm speaking generally. — You want her to think you an ascetic saint. But supposing she did the same?"

"Oh, my *dear* chap, no decent woman —"

"Has feelings or passions or any other damned thing?" concluded Jim. "Lord, you sicken me. You can make as much a beast of yourself as possible, but she — You only *condescend* to marry a *pure* woman. It's all rank and rotten Egoism, Vanity. If a man's a beast he should marry a beast woman, and so neither would be in danger of losing respect for each other. What really happens is that a man with natural passions marries a like woman. He, with his slimy vanity, is frightened to show that he is passionate and goes to other women, and she, often enough, is starved into a lover's arms; then tragedies galore!"

"Oh, that's all very fine in theory," conceded Lascelles, "but you know yourself that a man doesn't marry a girl who's been another man's mistress or his own. *You* wouldn't."

"I never intend to marry at all, but if I were to do so, I would — if I loved the woman. Good God, do you realize what your dictum means? That men place physical charms — sensualism — as a pearl above price, above all intellect, brain, character?"

"Well, we do!" asserted Lascelles doggedly. "From the dark ages and before we've always extolled virtue. — 'A virtuous woman is more precious than —'"

"Damn Solomon! He was nothing but an old sensualist. The trouble is you fill yourselves up with other people's opinions. You won't think for yourself. You take any old saw and hug it to your breast if it suits your inclination without testing the truth of it at all."

"Well, others do, and that's good enough for me!"

"Sheep!" snorted Jim, as indignation choked the wine in his throat.

"And as far as I'm concerned," continued Lascelles angrily, "I'm satisfied. So shut up. I hate jawing about these things."

"Naturally."

"And you've made me hot and angry and spoiled the damned dinner. Phew! What shall we do this evening, you, with your crazy ideas?"

"Oh, anything you like," said Jim disgustedly.

"Empire?"

"Yes, if you like — it's near and there's an American bar."

It was nearly ten o'clock by the time that they arrived at the music hall. They were unable to find a seat, so viewed the show from the promenade, the world-notorious human mart,[131] thronged as usual with hard-eyed women in extravagant salacious costumes and dresses lasciviously plain.

---

[131] Promenade: both in Paris and in London, the music hall promenade had earned a well-deserved reputation for being a "notorious human mart," especially in the late nineteenth century (by which time music halls had begun to replace the earlier venues known as dance halls). For example, in his classic text on Montmartre, Nicholas Hewitt writes: "The two key spaces in the music halls were the promenade and the bar. The promenade, which ran alongside the dance hall, allowed the male visitor to observe the dancers and to accost, or be accosted by, available women." There, the male gaze met – on equal terms of ferocious intensity – an ardently lewd female gaze. In addition, the bar offered a "social space which facilitated encounters between bourgeois men and working-class women," just as Beadle describes here. In a class-conscious society such as Britain, the appeal of an erotic nexus freed from distinctions of social class can hardly be overestimated. Hewitt adds that while "the dancers at the Opéra ... could be visited backstage only by the most privileged," "the rise of mass entertainment in the last two decades of the [nineteenth] century effectively began to democratize this power relationship." "Public participation in the dancing, and the close and informal contact offered by the promenade, removed the mystique of the Opéra," leading to (as depicted in the paintings of Degas) a "more popular access to pleasure." Nicholas Hewitt, *Montmartre: A Cultural History*, Liverpool: Liverpool University Press, 2020, pp. 77, 82.

"For heaven's sake, come and have another drink!" exclaimed Jim at length. "This sight and the stink of patchouli sickens me. God, I've seen this sort of thing in every quarter of the globe, but I think this is the limit. Their eyes are enough to haunt the egoism out of any man; they make me think of Dante's inferno."

"But, my dear fellow," drawled Lascelles, coolly eyeing an adjacent woman with the expression of a butcher criticizing a sheep, "it's common enough. We couldn't do without them."

An unusually attractive young girl, with soft, pleading eyes and a sinuous figure, glanced under her lids at Jim, who returned the look unconsciously, and then hated himself.

"Damn women!" he muttered.

"Oh, come on!" exclaimed Lascelles, smiling at Jim. "You're getting overheated."

They sat drinking steadily for half an hour. Jim felt his spirits brighten in inverse ratio as his sight clouded. He eyed the women about him with growing compassion.

"Look at that poor little devil in the corner there!" he said to Lascelles. "She looks so lonely and miserable; her life must be a hell."

"Ask her to have a drink."

As Jim walked over to her, she smiled.

"Say, little girl, will you have a drink?"

"Yes, little boy, I will," she answered pertly.

He sat beside her and ordered a drink. Lascelles brought his glass over.

"Rather rotten show," said Jim awkwardly.

She laughed.

"Isn't it?"

"Oh, I don't come here to see the show."

Jim frowned.

Another blonde girl strolled up and looked at Lascelles tentatively. He eyed her deliberately. She smiled. "Come and have a drink, fairy," he invited as she sat down beside him.

"Are you boys going to take us to supper?" enquired the last comer after a while.

Jim raised his eyebrows at Lascelles, who nodded.

"All right, come along."

"Rather a nice pair," observed Lascelles to Jim as they passed out. "Quite above the ordinary. Like yours best."

Jim frowned.

They drove to the Majestic. Even under the combined influence of burgundy and champagne, conversation flagged. Lascelles, livening up, took to telling risqué stories, at which Jim laughed dutifully.

"I say," Jim said awkwardly, to his vis-à-vis, "do you know you're a very pretty girl?"

"Oh," she said indifferently; "I have to be, you know."

Unconsciously Jim drew away.

"What's your name, dear?"

"Virginia," she replied.

Jim smiled at the incongruity. Her manner of speech struck him as above the ordinary and aroused his curiosity.

"What were — what did you do before — er —"

"I? Oh, I was at home with my people. Father is the pastor at — but don't talk about that, please," she said.

"I say, what the dickens made you take to — er — this?" he asked tactlessly.

She laughed shortly.

"What do you want to know for?"

"Oh, because — because I think it is a beastly shame."

They remained silent for a while.

"Well, because you — you men made me. A fellow deceived me. Of course I didn't know; how should I? I was perfectly innocent; I was only seventeen. My people disowned me and turned me out. I lived with a fellow for a while and then he got tired of me. What else could I do? I hate my father. . . . Oh, it was cruel!"

"The cad!" exclaimed Jim. "How old are you now?"

"Twenty-one. . . . And you" — she burst out passionately, "you — you men make us what we are — then you laugh and sneer at us. And your women draw their skirts from us. It wasn't my fault. I simply didn't know. I wish I could die."

She regained her composure suddenly.

"I'm sorry," said Jim humbly and lamely.

She laughed.

"Why, silly boy, don't take any notice of what I say. I get the blues sometimes."

"Well, have some more fizz? That always cures the hump."

"Yes, thank you," she said, as the waiter refilled the glasses. "I like to get drunk, because —" She shrugged her shoulders.

Jim changed the topic. He drank thirstily. Presently a few lights were extinguished as a hint: they arose to go. Lascelles mutely asked a question with his eyes. Jim refused to see. Lascelles and the other girl entered a waiting taxi.

"Good night, old boy!" sang out Lascelles.

"Good night," replied Jim.

"Come on," said the girl, "I can't take you home, but we can get a room round the corner."

Jim, pulling his opera hat over his eyes, walked beside her. His brain was befogged. Struggling to think, to reason, he was only conscious of an awful impulse that clogged his brain, and drew him relentlessly to follow the girl. Somewhere in the backwoods of his mind an angry and fierce disgust fought violently with an unchained beast. It was as if someone were shouting to warn him of a nightmare danger, but he could not hear in the press and clamor of a thousand shrieking devils. As she passed in front of him in the flare of a light above a small hotel door, he dimly admired the curve of her neck and figure. She seemed so lithe and attractive. What had he been talking to Lascelles about? What did this brazen-faced woman, with debauched monkey eyes under a cloud of metallic yellow hair, want?

"Ten shillings," someone was saying.

"That's for the room, dear," the girl prompted him.

He brought out a handful of silver and gold from his trouser pocket, which Virginia took, gave a half-sovereign to the ogre woman, and handed the rest back to Jim. He followed her up some narrow, evil-smelling stairs. From below came sounds of laughter and popping of corks; in the soft-lit corridor a girl's muffled laugh, or a man's voice subdued. As he turned up a dark stair he seized and kissed her. She turned and kissed him on the lips. He felt the blood and wine racing through his veins and brain. The tumult within him increased to a deafening clamor, shrieking a thousand impulses. She opened a door. He picked her up in his arms, knocking off his opera hat. As the door slammed it rolled out into the corridor and lay with one side folded, appearing in the dim light like the cavernous, leering mouth of a Chinese dragon, chuckling with triumph.

CHAPTER III

THE greater the humiliation the more dumb is the agony, the more crushing the misery. With the glaucous dawn of day came merciless sanity, dragging in its wake a host of emotions, the leader and chief of which, although naturally he did not recognize it at the time, was wounded vanity. That dragon of which he had grown contemptuous through a long period of iron-held abstinence, had lain in wait for him, and upspringing at the first moment of weakening control, had full slaked its thirst and yawned with strength anew. The general contempt of mankind, and women in particular, was fanned into a fierce and bitter hatred by blasts of self-loathing and dread of the awakened monster, the magnitude and strength of which terrified him. The rest of the day he remained in his rooms, tortured and miserable.

Lascelles called at midday with an invitation to lunch. Jim groaned with suppressed rage and refused to see him. All day he fought with the clamoring impulses within him, stronger and keener with the passage of years of sex starvation. All the philosophy of the negativists swarmed to his mind, epitomized by Omar:

> "Perplext no more with Human or Divine;
> tomorrow's tangle to the winds resign.
> And lose your fingers in the tresses of
> the cypress-slender Minister of Wine."[132]

---

[132] A quatrain attributed to Omar Khayyam, from the Edward FitzGerald translation.

Yet, that way lay . . . Torn between the awakened duality of man's nature, he went once more through the valley of the eternal struggle, deeper and denser than of yore, as is the penalty of Life. All the old doubts and questions were aroused by the tumult within him. With no God nor Faith, nor any prop to aid, with no promise of reward nor punishment, he fought hardly and long.

In the later afternoon he wandered out alone, just an ordinary man of a gloomy countenance and despondent mien, jostling his way through the teeming millions, with all the mythical devils of Hell tearing at his vitals. Something, a native obstinacy, thwarted for a while the craving to drink, else . . . At length, unable to bear his misery any longer, he sought dinner in the nearest place. As he turned in at the portals something familiar arrested his attention. He glanced round. It was the Lyon d'Or. The first impulse was to curse and rush out. But he checked himself and, smiling savagely, deliberately selected the favorite table of sixteen years ago. As he smoked and drank red wine, visions of the past came up to him. He recognized that the mysterious force of Sex had driven Eve, Claire, Joan, Haiwani, Virginia, and himself like chaff before the wind. Poor fools! they were all thrown about willy-nilly by this immutable law, fiercely blaming each other and themselves for what was as much out of their power of control as the moon or the tides. Haiwani. . . . She had been the truest, the most perfect and natural woman. And Joan. . . . Somehow the others seemed dim and shadowy, only Joan's eyes, even across the gulf of years, seemed bright and distinct. Had she — had they all been tortured on the rack of sex? What was the use of it all? What did it all lead to? Why! why! why! Was he to be ever tormented, was there no escape nor peace? Why shouldn't he give way to the universal persecutor and satisfy it by finding a mate? Yet he hated women for the very weakness. Why? He would do as others did, as Lascelles, and not worry about problems. Yet . . . What was this subtle refusal to give way? Was it merely obstinate vanity? He began to think it was. He had an ever-present idea that he was searching for something. What! The Truth? But what idiocy! What was the truth? An abstraction. Good God! If he merely asked the simple question: What am I, the Ego? it was unanswerable. So why ask anything? Why, one couldn't prove the existence of matter except through the senses, which were not infallible. Therefore, if he couldn't prove that he was himself, how . . . He continued to argue in this strain until he found difficulty in deciding that he was alive at all. . . .

Yet when, with an effort, he came down to mundane affairs, he discovered that his existence was sufficiently proved by the dull ache of resentment against the eternal struggle caused by an attractive young girl who had just entered the room, and towards whom he was conscious of a desire to know. There was a young man with her, in whose eyes, as he watched the girl, Jim noted the expression of a sickly calf, which is popularly termed love-light. He smiled cynically, wondering how they and others all about him were faring in the fight against the incubus of sex.

He ordered black coffee and fell to staring at the mildewed wallpaper. What was he to do? Life was not worth living, yet — he did not want to die. He wanted to live and to go on seeking. Seeking what — Truth? Something seemed to chuckle sardonically. He grew angry with his own mind. Pushing his cup away with a clatter, he rose to go. But where? Out into the streets, lonely streets filled with "monkey-minded men"[133] and wistful-eyed women? To the house of friends to hear some idiot

---

[133] Monkey-minded: a phrase attributed to Buddha, used to describe the restless nature of the mind, especially when lacking discipline or focus.

of a girl wailing sentimental songs about love — (ugh! the word infuriated him); or to a club to hear inanities chattering about horse racing, or telling smutty stories? He sank down again, ordered more coffee and wine, and damned the girl who was seated near him for having a musical laugh. He glanced at her. She was dark and tanned. He became conscious that she was vivaciously describing some place where she had evidently been staying. Something about fishing boats — going out through a rocky entrance at sunset, craggy cliffs and seagulls. "Only a few artists there — no one else — and some of them such funny freaks." . . . Jim smelled the very sea and heard the gulls. Poor little fool, she little knew the torture of life before her. But anyhow she had given him an idea. He would flee from this city of harlots and pimps for the pure sea. Presently he heard the name of the place which sounded so attractive — Polperro. Tre, pol, and pen — it must be in Cornwall.[134] He decided on the instant to go there. Within sound of the eternal song of the surf he could find peace — and freedom from the plague of women.

When any strong emotion or strong intoxicant enters the chambers of the mind, reason flies out of the window. During the long rush through the pure country air towards Cornwall, Jim became sober; that is, his mental equilibrium was restored. Life is very much like a tightrope, requiring the skill and practice of a Blondin[135] to maintain the balancing pole of reason

---

[134] In Cornwall, place names and surnames abound with the prefixes *Tre*, *Pol* and *Pen*. So much so that we have this rhyming couplet, first recorded in 1602 by Richard Carew in his *Survey of Cornwall*: "By Tre Pol and Pen / Shall ye know all Cornishmen." In Cornish "Tre" refers to a homestead; "Pol," a pond, lake, or well; and "Pen," a hill or headland. Hence, Polperro: a village in south Cornwall known for its fishing harbor.

[135] Charles Blondin (né François Gravelet; 1824 – 1897): French acrobat and celebrated tightrope walker, who crossed Niagara Gorge on an 1100-foot

against the blasts of physical drugs, alcohol, morphia, cocaine, on the one side; and mental drugs, hatred, passion, avarice and vanity, on the other. So often is it that, say, a drunkard, clutching madly at the pole of reason, recovers, but with the momentum sways, like a pendulum, past the mean of sane reason on to the side of emotional intoxication, such as is afforded to a teetotal maniac; or another, attaining the balance of reason, being weak-minded and afflicted with vertigo, is drawn irresistibly to one side or the other; such are they who, without the prop of Faith, would lose all control over their passions of lust, avarice, and hatred.

The descent into Avernus[136] had had a good effect upon Jim. It had sorely wounded his vanity and taught him that he was not, as he had begun to boast, immune from the universal impulse to mate. It also marked an epoch in his mental growth: made him less intolerant of the weakness of others, and more compassionate. Afterwards he felt calmer, stronger, and became less sure of the need of, and merit in, mortifying the flesh. On a sudden he awoke to the fact that for long, through misconception and wrong interpretation, he had had the impertinence to pose as superior to himself, to have occupied the ludicrous position of reproving nature, of an unexpressed desire to teach the Great Architect how to run the universe. When this thought took shape the humor of it made Jim laugh, and he felt humbler and happier. Then arose the corollary that that being so, and the yoke of sex a great and good thing, how should it be used. He began to perceive that the fault lay with Man, not with Nature; that when Nature threw two beings

---

rope on 30 June 1859. Blondin performed this feat numerous times, often with spectacular variations. During one crossing he cooked and devoured an omelet; on another, he performed blindfolded.

[136] Avernus: a volcanic crater near Cumae, Italy that cradles Lake Avernus. In ancient Roman times, it was believed to host a portal to the Underworld.

together for a definite purpose, man stepped in and said that they should live together for the rest of their lives without consideration of their happiness — hence yoked misery. That two persons should continue to cohabit after passion had died, seemed to Jim to be wicked; it aroused an acute sense of disgust. But that was the Law and the Custom.

Musing on these problems, Jim arrived at five on a gray, drizzling afternoon at Looe;[137] and was driven through hilly, narrow roads, between high bramble and shrub-covered hedges yellow-splashed with primroses, into an old-world village nestling in the depths of rugged green hills which reminded him of the kopjes of Rhodesia. Through the driving mist, sweet laden with the myriad scents of spring and the tang of the salt air, the rolling brush-strewn combes[138] opened up green and inviting.

Night came up quickly as Jim discussed[139] a homely meal at the Ship Inn. Afterwards, plugging a pipe, he strolled out to make his obeisance to the sea. On emerging from the inn door he found himself in inky, velvet darkness. Overhead the irregular hilltops towered in indigo silhouette against a dull murk, through which struggled gamely two distant stars. Away up the narrow street a tiny shop window on a level with the ground shone a dull, deep yellow. Footsteps sounded in the darkness. A shadow passed the yellow splash of light. Now and again the shuffle and mutter of cottage inmates, or belated feet clattered on the cobbles against a steady murmur borne on the wind — the voice of the sea. Jim stood, inhaling with his smoke the salty peace and quiet. On a sudden a voice, some way off in

---

[137] Looe: a coastal town in southeast Cornwall.

[138] Combe (British): a deep narrow valley; or a valley or basin on the flank of a hill.

[139] Discuss: as noted earlier, a facetious and rarely used term meaning "to eat or drink with enthusiasm."

the clinging darkness, began to sing; other sounds, seemingly too full and melodious for human throats, joined in full-throated melody, like a fugue upon an organ.

Jim stood quiet, drinking in the harmony and air. Then close to him came the mutter of voices, a sound of a kiss, a girl's subdued giggle, and simultaneously the distant singers, breaking into raucous shouts of laughter, launched into a popular music hall refrain. That indeed was like life, thought Jim, and swore as he walked on up the street. Everywhere the mating instinct, the rustics, the birds, the fishes; all the world seemed throbbing with the impulse and he alone stood aloof, paying the penalty in isolated misery. He felt that he was wrong, not in himself, but through the wrong attitude of the conventional mind, the monkey mind which had shaped his views to the common mould that all sexual intimacies were ugly and disgusting. Logically, he reflected bitterly, they ought to be ashamed of their own existence, as they were naturally the product of the action they affected to loathe and despise. A memory of his childhood came to his mind, the memory of the awakening of sexual curiosity and the deliberate lies of those about him. How could parents, he wondered, expect to retain the respect of their children when from the first they showed to them that they were liars, and, moreover, ashamed of ever having had a hand in the creation of their offspring? . . . He began to perceive that having swung to the other side of the pendulum, having denied Nature instead of abused her, as most men did, she was exacting a penalty just the same. He knew that mind and body would be the cleaner and saner for a mate, a true mate. Yet he could not deliberately, consciously seek her; the idea was revolting.

He stumbled on up narrow cobbled streets, whitewashed cottages ghostly in the velvet darkness. The odor of fish and tarred nets caught his nostrils. He saw through a break in a line of buildings the glint of water, broken by shadowy masts; above were daubed a few yellow blobs of lighted windows around the base of an indigo-shrouded hill which loomed with ragged summit against a patch of star-plashed sapphire sky. On again, passing a dim form which growled "G'noight, zur," until he came to a seawall in front of spectral cottages, nestling at the base of a hill, steeper and more rugged than the opposite one. Over the wall a lamp on the end of a quay, a massive stone forefinger stretching to meet a stone thumb as a protecting hand against the fury of winter seas, shed a yellow circlet upon the counter of a smack[140] and cast dancing points of yellow-green upon the ripples of the glaucous harbor water. Farther on the muttering lather of foam caressed the rocky base of a jumbled mass of rocks which, with four short jagged stumps protruding against the sky, seemed like the antennae of a colossal snail, crouching, like a guardian dragon at the entrance of a Fairy Cave. Beyond stretched the darkling infinity of ocean and sky, welded together by a dull murk of mist through which double-winked the light on the Eddystone Rock.

As Jim leaned on the seawall he became aware of a denser shadow stealing as noiselessly as a bat between the lesser darknesses of the opposite cliff. A man's voice echoed across; a silvery rippling rattle; the musical creak of spars and sails sinking, as gracefully as a swan alighting, to rest, as the harbor light gleamed upon the bow of a smack, gliding towards the yawning mouth of the harbor.

The glamour and poetry of the scene enveloped Jim and acted as an anodyne to his misery; he felt that here was perfect peace and calm, where all slept happily in the arms of nature, each following the appointed way, sublimely oblivious to ideals,

---

[140] Smack: a sailing ship (such as a sloop or cutter) used chiefly in coasting and fishing.

untroubled by a perturbed mind. Jim thought of the fishermen of Galilee, and, wishing that he was as one of them, saw, for the first time, the exquisite poetry of the Biblical story. Leaning on the wall with the clammy sea fog caressing his face, he began to appreciate the beauty and rarity of the teaching of the Christ, and that in his anger and disgust for the pharisaical followers he had blamed the gentle philosopher rather than the dull witted and self-serving multitudes. And, as Jim pondered, the association of ideas conjured up the memory of a crucifix glinting in the flickering light of fires which gleamed fitfully on the body of Miêville, around whom devilish gnomes whirled and slashed against the gloom of an African forest.

CHAPTER IV

JIM's first conscious sensation next morning was of a multitudinous sound of squeaking, harsh screams, kittenish wails and cries. Sleepily he wondered what the uproar might be, until a shaft of golden sunlight shot through the small chintz-curtained window and awoke him. He sprang out of bed with the clean alacrity born of sleep in fresh country air, and, hurriedly dressing, made his way out.

The ebb of the tide had left glistening mud and sand in the inner harbor, where hundreds of seagulls hopped, flew and fought noisily over fishy tidbits, about the naked hulls of the fishing fleet dry-propped in serried rows. He paused upon an old stone bridge which spanned a tiny stream flowing from the combe, to view anew the village under the searching light of day. Upon the east side the houses, mostly built of slaty stone, some gray and others whitewashed, were flush with the harbor where green sea moss marked the high-water level; their roofs were weather painted and seagull splashed in haphazard order, seeming rather that they had grown out of the rock than been built: higher still, separated by a broad daub of green, were modern villas, alien vicious spots. Upon the opposite side, beyond a stone quay, a rugged line of cottages ended in a huddled mass; all appeared as a flock of gray sheep hurrying to the entrance of a pen. Amid soft-tanned grays and greens was the blue sign of an old-time inn, shrinking unobtrusively behind a bold, stone cottage which had resolutely planted itself in the middle of the quay walk. Over the roofs a few other cottages, one outstanding in whitewash, grew out of the green hillside, their walls and outhouses blending with the living rock so that the line of demarcation vanished: all a soft and subtle harmony.

As Jim turned to move on he was amused by a strange, somber figure of a gray-haired woman, a stumpy bundle of black clothes, who had taken up a stand beside him on the broad wall of the bridge and was busily painting in watercolor. He glanced from the picture, which in form and color was without trace of talent, to the woman's expressionless eyes set in an insipid face. The hopelessness of her attempts — she looked as if she ought to be in a kitchen — and the fact of her age, saddened him for a moment. The sight was both ludicrous and pathetic. Across on the quay side another woman, young and comely, was already setting up her easel. On the way out to the mouth of the cove he observed four other women artists ensconced in odd corners.

Beyond the last line of whitewashed cottages outstaring upon the gray mass of the jagged, diminutive peninsula, now strangely plashed with yellow, green grass patched and streaked with broad layers of pale maroon strata of rock, the path began to mount where sprouted some mushroom villas such as might have been transported from an ultra-artistic suburb of London. Seeking for a place from which to bathe, Jim noted the sharp, foam-seething rocks, like serried masses of stone razors upended, all a wondrous harmony of grays, indigos, orange and pale maroon. A blue-guernseyed fisherman, mending a tawny net spread upon a grassy slope, advised him to go to Gigan Cove, and staring with bucolic indignation at Jim's appalling ignorance, broadly instructed him.

Jim continued on past the dwarfed lighthouse along a nettle-kissing path, beside potato and strawberry patches hardly snatched from the rugged hillside, and came down and out upon the weed-draped rocks, which, at low tide, appeared as bared fangs of gnarled teeth. In the emerald-clear water of the tiny cove floated long strands of seaweed like women's hair. At the extreme seaward edge he found a foam-washed ledge overhanging deep water. Erewhile he was venting his bottled displeasure of the flesh and the devil in the sapphire arms of mother ocean. Reaching an outlying rock, he disturbed the complacent meditations of two seagull lovers by clambering with difficulty upon a knife-edge of rock, encrusted with needlepointed barnacles.

As he sat viewing the rugged slopes, thickly carpeted with acres of pink and white sea thrift, the age-worn cliffs and the sea-blunted rocks over which the gulls wheeled in foam-white streaks, a blob of blue broke through a wall of green, the figure of a woman coming down the steep and slippery path. Jim watched with reluctant admiration her sure-footed agility as she sprang up and down over the jumbled foot rocks. She disappeared behind a ledge, to emerge, after a brief pause, in bathing costume. Resenting her intrusion and wondering where she thought she would find shallow water for her "hen dipping," as Jim phrased it, he was almost constrained to shout a warning as she halted upon the very ledge from which he had taken off. To his astonishment she raised her hands — as a *man* would do! — and dived with scarcely a ripple. As Jim saw her strike out to seaward he swore: "Oh, damn the woman!"

Slipping back into the water, he began to return with a rolling overhand action; then suddenly self-conscious, imagining that she would think that he was showing off, altered to a modest breast stroke. He saw that she was swimming straight towards him. Swearing, he turned over on his back and floated. He began to feel numbed in the fingertips. Turning to look, he saw that she was swimming about a few feet from the rocks. Savagely fuming, he determined that he could not endure the cold any longer, and swam back, wondering how long the "fool of a hen" would keep him shivering on the rocks. He clambered up and, turning his back to her, perched in the sun. Presently he heard an exclamation near him, and saw her emerging from the water. She paused in the act of standing erect and stared. As he looked he was aware of a dim stirring of memory. The brilliant sun lit up her tanned face and large eyes; her sea-darkened hair hung in dank wisps across her forehead and neck under the blue rubber cap. Vaguely conscious of a faint resemblance to someone whom he could not identify, he turned his head, hoping that she would continue on and leave him to dress. Then came her voice, nervous, with a suggestion of echoing laughter.

"Jim!"

Startled, he wheeled about and stared at the dripping figure silhouetted against the sapphire sea. The mobile mouth puckered into a smile.

"Don't you know me?"

The smile and the voice stirred the sleeping memory cells into furious activity.

"Joan!"

For a moment they remained, each outstaring the other as if endeavoring to summon wit to cope with the unexpected, smiling a trifle fatuously.

"I always knew that I should meet you someday," she said, which broke the frozen constraint.

"Good Lord!" exclaimed Jim, and came towards her. "I *am* glad."

"Thanks!"

She laughed, which brought up the decade-old memory of her as vividly as one of yester-eve. He looked at her anew and saw that she had altered, and yet was the same. Her mature figure was as supple and her movements as sinuous as of yore. The complexion had lost the clarity of early youth and the sun revealed deeper moulding of character lines; the mouth puckered more, and the dimple of the cleft chin was emphasized. There was too, although Jim did not notice it at the time, a suspicion of pain in the greeny eyes, in which, however, there still lurked the gleam of laughter.

"Good Lord!" exclaimed Jim again.

"You seem distressed," she observed, and sat down on the rock, trailing one bare foot in the water.

"Oh, no, I'm not," protested Jim, and sat beside her, forgetting to shiver. "I'm very startled. I never dreamt of seeing you — here."

"Nor I you!" she said, and at the time Jim did not remember her first sentence.

"But I didn't know you were living in England?"

"And I didn't know you were living in England!" she mocked him.

"Oh, but —" he smiled. "Still laughing at me?"

"Of course. Should I cry?" Her mouth twitched with amusement, the old trick which used to annoy him. "I suppose you think that I ought to treat the occasion with due solemnity. — Just the same old Jim!"

"Well —" he commenced, thinking of what had passed between them and wondering how he ought to treat her.

She laughed.

"The sun's almost as warm as — South Africa," she remarked, watching him under her lids.

"Yes — almost."

He dropped his eyes and stared out to the horizon. He felt awkward and knew that she was laughing at him.

"Been long in England?" she inquired. "You're not as talkative as you used to be."

"No," shortly. "Only landed in London a month ago. . . . Have you been here long?"

"Where?"

"Oh, dammit, in England."

She chuckled.

"Just the same old Jim!" she repeated. He frowned and she went on: "Oh, nearly — how long is it since we met, Jim?"

"Over ten years," he replied. "But I thought women didn't like referring to the flight of time."

"Aha! Still a cynic?" He did not reply. "Well, I've been in England — off and on — just over ten years."

"But when —"

He paused, wanting to ask what had happened to her husband. A sudden side memory came of how he had been unable to banish the memory of her eyes for years. He wondered. There were the eyes, and he felt that he still detested her; although he *had* often wanted, longed to meet her again.

"He is dead," she said quietly. "Nine years ago."

"Then you're a widow!" Jim exclaimed with a palpably, but unconsciously, exultant note in his voice. He glanced up and saw that she was gravely watching him.

"No, I haven't married again. I don't believe in marriage."

"Neither do I!" he exclaimed forcibly.

The dimple in the corner of her mouth returned.

"We're agreed, then — for different reasons."

"Why different reasons? Nobody but a fool would try to make two people always live together who're — who're—"

"Tired of each other?"

"Well, if you like to put it that way."

"So that's your pet hobby, is it?"

"What should make you suppose that?" he demanded irritably.

"Ah, you've been thinking, have you? You didn't do much thinking when — in those days."

"Didn't I?" He smiled. "D'ye know" — he wanted to say Joan, but dared not — "I don't think I did."

"Do you still keep on thinking?"

"Oh, heaps!"

"Bad habit!"

He smiled, thinking of Biddy.

"But what do you really do now?" she inquired.

"For a living?"

"Yes."

"Oh, nothing. Got a small income now."

"Made a fortune in Rhodesia?"

"Oh, no! Had it left me, you know."

"Oh! Another one of 'em."

"What?"

"Parasites."

"Parasites!" indignantly. "Why?"

"Of course you are, if you don't do anything at all."

"Well, what do *you* do?" demanded Jim.

"Oh, I paint!"[141]

Jim's lip curled. She laughed outright.

"Oh, you are delicious," she assured him. "You're funnier than ever you were!"

Jim tried to smile — unsuccessfully.

"Well, you don't call painting a living?"

"Why not?"

"Well, you don't make money by it, or do any good."

"Is making money the only thing in life? Besides, as a matter of fact I do make a little money — I have no other. The second question is rather deep, isn't it?"

"Yes, I suppose it is," conceded Jim. "I only arrived last night, but I've seen dozens of your tribe."

---

[141] Beadle's wife, Sylvia Hornsby, is identified as an artist on their marriage certificate. According to a 1911 Kensington census, her mother, Teresa Ashwell, was also a painter. The artistic bent seems to have run in the family. Beadle's niece Isabel, with whom he held a lengthy correspondence, made her living as an art teacher and pursued commercial illustration.

"Dozens?"

"Well, four or five in one street. They seemed very busy."

"Yes — poor souls."

"That's what I thought; but —"

"Come!" she exclaimed, feeling her hair, wisps of which gleamed copper in the sun. "I'm going in for breakfast."

"Wait for me," called Jim as she disappeared behind a rock ledge; "I've got to dress."

"Can't!" she shouted back.

"Where will I see you after breakfast?"

"Can't," she said, emerging with a blue wrap thrown over her bathing costume. "I've got work to do. Just the effect I want."

"Oh," said Jim, and frowned. "Well, when shall I see you?"

"I don't know," she shouted, hurrying over the rocks.

"Damn her!" said Jim to himself, as he watched her, a blue daub amid the green. "She's like all women. She thinks I'm going to run after her; but I won't."

* * * * * * *

Left to himself, Jim found that he had a deal to think on. He had imagined that if ever he did meet Joan the occasion would be difficult for both of them; that she would probably be angry or sentimental. He had been quite prepared to be remorseful. But she had merely laughed at him, and seemed as elusive and flippant as ever. Then he remembered her first statement, that she had always known that she would meet him, had been afterwards flatly contradicted. What did that mean? He smiled cynically as he deduced that she was in love with him, had searched and longed for him. "At first a woman loves her lover, then she loves love," Rochefoucauld had said.[142] Well, Jim had been her first lover, so, ergo, she had always loved him. At first man, reflected Jim sagely, loves love, and then he loves women, and finally a woman. Feeling rather pleased with himself over this epigram, he made his way back to breakfast, convinced that the old longing to meet Joan and the memory of her eyes was inherent sentimentality emphasized by romantic glamour. Jim decided that he was completely heart-whole.[143] He acknowledged that she attracted him, but explained that as merely sex impulse. Accordingly he sallied forth determined that he would not seek for her, and that when — not if! — when they met again he would be prepared to offer her platonic friendship.

Entirely oblivious to the fact that the pertinent debate upon the whys and hows of the Universe had ceased, and that only Joan occupied his mind, he mused along the cliff edge, trying not to acknowledge that his roving eyes sent a small thrill of expectation at the glimpse of an easel. After an hour's stroll along the upper and lower paths of the west side, he decided — merely, of course, to obtain another view — to explore the east cliff. An easel set amid a white and pink carpet of sea thrift drew him as far as Lake Rock, to discover a bespectacled woman of gloomy mien. At lunch he was inclined to be captious with the food.

---

[142] La Rochefoucauld's aphorism reads: "In their first passion women love their lovers, in all the others they love love." (François de La Rochefoucauld, *Maxims* (1665; trans. J. W. Willis Bund and J. Hain Friswell in 1871), maxim #469. In his satiric narrative poem, *Don Juan*, Lord Byron renders this as "In her first passion Woman loves her lover, / In all the others all she loves is Love" (*Don Juan*, canto III; composed between 1818 and 1823).

[143] Heart-whole: (a) heart-free; not emotionally attached; not in love; (b) sincere, genuine, wholehearted. Beadle is using this term in the former sense.

However, towards the late afternoon he espied Joan at work upon the harbor quay. Solely out of curiosity to see what sort of work she did, he wandered down with a great assumption of indifference. As he approached she appeared too engrossed in her work to notice him. He had ample time to subdue the slight shock of pleased surprise which her appearance in a simple white jersey, with sleeves rolled up displaying tanned arms, and copper head aflame in the sunlight, gave him. He stood for a moment watching her; then he looked at the canvas. At the first glance he felt puzzled; to his surprise, masses and blobs of pigment, which seemed to have been hurled on to the canvas, grew into fishing boats actually gliding through live water shimmering with light, wet water which revealed rocks and seaweed in its pellucid depths. The more he looked the more there seemed to be. He was conscious that there was much that he could neither appreciate nor understand.

"Well, Jim, what d'you think of Polperro?"

He looked up to find her regarding him with an amused smile.

"Splendid — unique. I didn't think there was anything like it in England."

"There's very few, if any: although they've nearly spoiled it."

His eyes wandered back to the picture, which appeared to fascinate him.

"I like that immensely."

"Do you? Then I am more than rewarded."

"Oh, don't," he said, flushing. "I know I'm not a critic, but I can see that's good. It looks more — more — what's the word? — harmonious than the actual view."

Joan chuckled.

"Yes; as Whistler said, 'Nature is catching up!'"[144]

Jim smiled.

"Well, you know what I mean."

"Of course I do: and thank you, Jim," she said, beginning to pack her brushes and palette. "I always knew you had an artistic sense. But I hope it's not the worst form?"

"Worst form? How?"

"Oh, well, don't you know that there are two forms of the artistic temperament? The creative and the noncreative — merely appreciative. Poor wretches, the latter are often a living hell to themselves. . . . Here, carry my box for me and the easel, and as a reward you shall come to tea."

"Oh, thanks," said Jim, loading himself up. "I was going to ask you."

As they walked up the rough path to the road they passed another woman busily painting in watercolor.

"There, that's one specimen of what I mean. She has a touch of the artistic temperament, but no creative power. Otherwise, she is seeking self-expression. Denied her proper métier, she is led by that fatal touch of the artistic. She will never do anything. She never can. That's where the tragedy lies. *But* it satisfies her to a great extent."

"I don't quite follow," said Jim. "I put it down to lack of the sex satisfaction."[145]

---

[144] When James Whistler was told that his painting was beginning to resemble nature, he quipped: "Yes, Madam, nature is catching up."

[145] Possibly a reference to Freud's theory of sexual sublimation. The first edition of Freud's *Drei Abhandlungen zur Sexualtheorie* ("Three Essays on the Theory of Sexuality") was published in 1905, just a decade before the appearance of *A Passionate Pilgrimage*. Beadle was well aware of Freud and his theories; in *Dark Refuge* the narrator engages in a surrealistic dialogue with a character who declares: "Freud's a fool!" (And in a letter penned to his niece circa 1930, he writes: "I think Freud must have suffered from a sexual frustration at the age of two and then recovered from it: otherwise

"Quite right; it is. But she wouldn't attempt art if she could satisfy her natural proclivities. She feels the inclination for self-expression common to everyone, but is denied that one way in which she could attain that end, and attempts another for which she has no power. . . . Here, Jim, this way!"

A square slate-stone house was built just within the shorter quay. With the first floor on a level with the road, it seemed to cling to the rock like a limpet, the lower windows staring upon the harbor waters, the back formed by living rock. At one side, through a break in a wall, she descended some steps and into a moss painted, wooden porch which led into the studio. Around the bare walls and floors were scattered canvases of all sizes, which Jim immediately began to examine.

"Let your curiosity wait," exclaimed Joan, and handing him a box of matches, pointed to an oil stove in a corner. "There, get busy, and I'll get the tea things."

"Why on earth don't you get somebody to cook meals for you?" he grumbled, disconsolately viewing grimy fingers.

"Because I prefer decently made tea," retorted Joan.

Erewhile they smoked cigarettes and watched the slowly rising tide through the windows where the seagulls circled round and over again, like a detached shower of gargantuan snowflakes. Joan did most of the talking, which Jim afterwards noticed was confined to any general topic; at each occasion upon which he had attempted a personal note she fended him off adroitly. Although during tea he had several times become

---

there's lots of basic truth in his theories – yes, quite lots.) But the concept of psychic sublimation wasn't invented by Freud. In 1873 Nietzsche employed the term *Sublimierung* in his *Philosophy in the Tragic Age of the Greeks*. There, in his analysis of linguistics and cultural dynamics, he employs it in a broader, deeper, more sophisticated manner than Freud. And Nietzsche continued to elaborate upon his sublimation concept throughout his later work.

aware of her attraction, the thought was immediately forgotten. He decided mentally that she would make a most perfect platonic friend — to him: although he could easily imagine any other man falling a victim to her physical magnetism. In general her mind and views occupied his thoughts almost to the exclusion of her material charms. Women of wide mental outlook and something of individual thought he had met before, but usually these had been of an extremely plain exterior. Of course Joan, his critical faculty assured him, was not perfect by any means. Her nose was certainly not Grecian — in profile it was reminiscent of an Egyptian — her ears on examination were really too big, and her hands too supple and long; but the charm and elusiveness of her personality made any mere physical beauty a secondary matter. She annoyed him — when he was away from her; her views particularly. Sometimes her opinions seemed sound; at others extravagant — until he discovered that she was laughing at him. That always displeased him. Just as he thought that they were both seriously discussing some subject, and that he was hearing her sincere opinions, she would leap into the realm of pure fantasy. Ever she taunted him as a parasite. At first he had believed she had meant it; then that she was joking. That was the crux of all their arguments, he could never determine whether she was serious or not. Often he would attempt, feebly enough, to learn what had happened to her in the past, but always she foiled him.

Several times during the next fortnight a sudden temptation to kiss her seized him. He never yielded, and felt genuinely angry with himself for allowing the wish to sway him for a moment. It was not fair to her, he told himself, and besides — he did not really want to do so. At times the conclusions regarding the natural satisfaction of the mating impulse at which he had arrived on the evening before meeting Joan, occurred to him; but he refused to entertain them.

But one evening when they were watching the moon rise over the sea from the little lighthouse, an uncontrollable impulse came over him to kiss her. Almost before he had realized what was happening he had seized her in his arms and tasted of those taunting, whimsical lips. He saw her eyes flash wrathfully in the soft light and released her. Instantly he received a sharp blow in the face and heard her voice, tremulous with rage, saying:

"If you do that again I'll — I'll never speak to you again as long as I live."

For the moment the influx of passion suddenly loosened by those soft, warm lips swamped reason. The reflex of anger against himself vented itself upon her.

"Well," he began rapidly and thickly. "You belong to me —" and bit down the words.

"You fool!" she exclaimed vibrantly. "You imagine that because of that you have conquered *me*. You *utter* fool. You're just a man, Jim. An utter fool who thinks that when he possesses a woman physically he possesses her very soul. Good God, don't you know yet, will you never learn, that a man may live with a woman for a lifetime and never, *never* really possess her, not even *know* her."

The anger died out of her face. Her eyes gleamed with sudden amusement as she watched him standing before her, pale in the moonlight, battling against a flood of emotions.

"Jim," she said quietly, smiling, "don't be a silly old fool. Be what you decided to be — a platonic friend!"

He winced, and saw the taunting gleam in her eyes and her twitching mouth.

"Damnation!" he ejaculated, and wheeling round, raced away. As he scrambled up the rugged hill face, barking[146] his shins on

---

[146] Barking (informal): to produce a sharp, sudden pain.

knife-edged rocks, he heard her light laugh below, maddening him to spluttering incoherency.

CHAPTER V

As chaos follows recession of a flood, so incoherency is the reflex of any passion. Anger of humiliation, of disgust, of fear, fought for mastery as Jim raced down the cliff path towards the ghostly village in the caressing shadows of the hills. He had never intended to give way; his feelings were purely platonic, he told himself fiercely. Yet — he had. Of course it was the sex impulse which had prompted him to kiss her. That was the worst of having arrived at such a state of introspection: all the motives of one's feelings were laid bare. His wretched mind would no longer permit him to find solace in the glamour of the most handy sophistry; in the pursuit of truth he found that stray portions of it, stragglers on the roadside, would rise up and hit him with unerring accuracy when least expected. Striving to displace emotion and view the episode dispassionately, in accordance with an accepted precept of philosophy, he made his way to "The Three Pilchards" Inn, where in the low-ceilinged room, amid an atmosphere of smoke, cider and Cornish burrs, he endeavored to think things out.

The first conclusion was that he had made a fool of himself. He felt indignant with Joan for misjudging him. He had not thought that because of the episode of years ago that she belonged to him. Yet . . . reluctantly he admitted that in his heart, that is, subconsciously, he *had* entertained that idea. He remembered a favorite dictum that any man who valued a woman solely upon her physical chastity, as the average man does, was therefore a sensualist. Naturally and consistently with this idolization of the material, he wishes, and as the wish is father to the thought, he endows the female whom he deigns to select with all the attributes that his vain and stulted[147] imagination may suggest, of a Goddess in order that she may be meet for him. The whole conception is based on cowardice, the heritage of countless ages of wild life when man was the prey of fiercer beasts. He fears that another stronger, more daring, may take his possession; therefore he seeks to protect himself by constructing a "moral" code whereby any female loses her value in his eyes with her virginity or chastity, and in order to support that doctrine and justify himself, by the belief that a woman is conquered body and soul for always by the man who first possesses her body; or on the other hand as an excuse for discarding her, in the event of any breach of fidelity, resolutely denying that the same law should apply to him. The cream of the jest lies in the fact that this conception of a Goddess is purely material, a physical doll subservient to his pleasure; whereas man is a wondrous creature of intellect as well as physique.

All men's thought tends towards material things; they are obsessed with materialism, dominated by the acquisitive faculty which, grown to a mania, reaches the farcical when, not satisfied with all the things of the world, he must needs be busy laying up a store of treasures in Heaven. The average man entertains the firm conviction that a woman always loves her first lover best through all time, no matter how many other affairs she may have. But Jim knew that the idea was false; that, as usual, it was merely a manifestation of male vanity. Man's colossal self-esteem hypnotizes him into the belief that he is a demigod; although he tacitly acknowledges himself to be a sensualist by placing the material body above all. The old leaven of convention was in Jim still. It is the most difficult feat

---

[147] Stulted (archaic): Deprived of strength and vigor. Similar to the more commonly used *stultified*.

in the world to throw off entirely every ounce of bias drawn up with our mother's milk of convention. Any clear solution of a problem or new point of view, ever flashes through the murk of our understanding as a streak of lightning. The whole difficulty was that he had been brought up and lived in an atmosphere of false values, all the outcome of sensual vanity of the primitive male. Then, if the plane of intellect had advanced at all, as it undoubtedly had, all these values needed readjusting from a sane and clean standpoint. But the evil lay in the fact that to civilized beings, starched and goffered in the swaddling clothes of convention, thought was denied and throttled. We still suffer from the taint of the primitive Oriental who, enslaving women in the time when physical prowess counted most, denied them a soul and held them as chattels, all of which as everything was based upon Vanity. Even, reflected Jim, as an example of the male's vanity overpowering reason, was the fact that we trace our descent through the male; although there may be doubt of paternity, there can obviously be none regarding maternity. There were, as Jim knew and had read, a few intellects in the world who were striving to awaken the people to the world's wrongheaded, obsolete laws and opinions, the fruit of which is an unthinking code of ethics masquerading under the names of honor and love. Another potent example was the law that any woman who from frailty, or strength of character, chose to select her own lover, had to pay for it by becoming a social pariah: whereas a man was free to select a wife, and although forbidden to take a mistress, the act was more honored in the breach. One may read a thousand books, dismiss many as of no import, others as prurient if they dare to leave the superficialities of life and dig beneath the surface to primary motives, things that matter, and, although possibly agreeing in theory with many ideas expounded, be little the wiser until — *life itself rises* up; it is then that truths, read or heard, blaze out like the writing on the wall. Those who are warm wrapped in the cloak of their self-complacency, blinded to the misery they have wreaked, in the name of honor and love, upon those whom they hold most dear, are ever the first to cry out upon anyone who would dare flaunt the truth in their faces. Were Jim still enmeshed in conventional thought or lack of it, he would have considered it his smug duty to insult Joan by offering reparation for the "wrong" he had done her by marriage, oblivious to whether they loved each other or not. He remembered the pangs of futile remorse in the past because he had not married Eve. That both might have turned the glory of life into a hell on earth mattered not one whit to the grinning fetish of convention.

Joan's violent indignation at the unwitting insult he had nearly uttered, had produced an emotional storm which had clarified the mental conception as the atmosphere after rain. He recognized the necessity of preserving his ethical equilibrium from being overbalanced by passion, or by the false teachings of youth.

On a sudden, as he became conscious of the burring chatter about him, he saw the humor of his exploring trip into high ethics amid such environment and laughed; the touch of humor sweetened the mental bath.

Jim did not see Joan again that evening.

Next morning as he made his way past the harbor full of screaming seagulls he was aware that he had progressed further mentally in a few hours than in years; also he felt that she would accept and make easy his apology, whereas with many women the incident would have terminated or at least strained their friendship. Nevertheless the strength to overcome false pride required some effort, and he decided to postpone the moment until they were in the water. Even a woman cannot well preen ruffled vanity feathers with ease while swimming in a choppy sea.

She met and greeted him as usual. As they walked down the narrow footpath in Indian file, Jim entertained a lively gratitude towards her.

Nearing an outlying rock Jim caught her eyes and said:

"Last night — I'm sorry —"

Joan gurgled and swallowed some water.

"I wish you wouldn't make me laugh!" she gasped. "Your choice of a scene for melodrama is indiscreet."

Neither referred to the subject again. In the late afternoon of the same day, after Joan had abandoned work, they were sprawling upon a bed of white and pink sea-thrift on the edge of the cliff near Lake Rock, watching the varied delicate tints of green and violet breathing upon the blue of the sea, through which submerged rocks looked like green puffs of smoke. She had been talking of her past work; of her two pictures, one of which was on the line, the other skied,[148] in the Academy — not that that institution was any criterion of merit — and of her ambitions for the future. Whenever she spoke of her art a peculiar note, caressing, came into her voice, which saddened and annoyed Jim. It was quite a time ere he discovered the cause — jealousy.

"But when you've attained those ambitions?" said Jim. "What then?"

Joan laughed.

"Oh," she said, "I never, never shall! . . . That's where the charm, the glorious happiness lies. Once you attain any ambition the joy is finished. Only in the pursuit of the bluebird is happiness."

---

[148] Skied: when a painting is "skied" in an art exhibit, it's placed so high upon a wall that it remains difficult to see or view properly.

"Oh," said Jim slowly, "it's cruel to believe that." (At one time he would have said, "Oh, rot!") "F'rinstance, supposing one believed one fell in love with a woman —"

"I thought that you didn't believe in love?"

"Well — I believe that it's a very rare and precious thing."

"Which only you could attain?"

Looking at her, Jim saw that her mouth was twitching.

"Oh, I didn't say so. In fact, I should be lucky if ever I could love."

"What do you call love?"

"Good Lord, as well attempt to pin a moonbeam to the floor."

"What were you going to say about yourself in love?"

"Oh — and happiness? Well, if I fell in love, d'you think that I should lose happiness as soon as I attained that woman?"

"But you would never attain her — that is, if she were a fit mate for you!"

"How?"

"Mentally."

"I follow. You mean that many men —"

"And women —"

"And women fall in love with each other's appearance — "

"Are attracted. Don't profane a sacred word."

"And then one finding nothing in the other — only an empty husk — is hopelessly disappointed?"

"Exactly."

"Well, how about the other side? Supposing two intellects fall in love — are attracted, how does happiness come?"

"In the eternal delight and joy at exploring each other's mental world. In the joint appreciation of the subtleties, humor and wonder of life. Can't you imagine two tied to each other, one heartbroken because she — or he — cannot follow the other into higher or other worlds of thought, and he — or she — disgusted, irritated, and disappointed?"

"Good Lord, yes!" exclaimed Jim, and straightway thought of Madge, Eve, Claire and Haiwani. "But everybody isn't blessed or cursed with an intellect. How about the others?"

"Well, everything is comparative. Each mental *and* physical degree should find its mate in the same degree. You don't ask a little horse to run in harness with a big horse, do you?"

"No, but I've heard of cases of a big intellect mated to a little mouse of a woman, and they seemed to get along all right."

"Ah, but were they happy? Wasn't she merely a housekeeper or a doll? Didn't he live in another world to her?"

"Yes, I suppose he must have done. But —"

"But what? We were talking of happiness, the rarest of all things."

"Oh, I never expect it."

"Ah, you may be on the road to it. You don't expect to live on pure joy? Why, you'd be suffocated! The nearest approach to unadulterated happiness, degenerated for want of contrast — you can't have a picture without light and shade, can you? — is the domestic cow. — There are plenty of cows in life, Jim. Look!" — she pointed to a pair of gulls, white streaks in the dying sun. — "They're happy; do you want that? The lower in evolution you go the nearer to content. The higher the type, the greater capacity for suffering and joy. The greater the artist, the greater the pain."

"Good God!" exclaimed Jim, sitting up. "I must be a Shakespeare!"

"Oh, you egotistical parasite!" laughed Joan. "How do you know how great your pain is when you can't know another's agony with which to compare?"

"Goethe must have suffered hell, then!"

"Undoubtedly."

"Do you suffer much, Joan?" said Jim, leaning towards her suddenly.

"Merciful heavens, do you want me to confess that I'm a great artist?" she laughed.

"No, but — do you?"

"Do I look like it?" she demanded, with laughing eyes and dimple-twitching mouth. "Now what do you imagine?"

"Sometimes I think you do — or have, and sometimes — ''

"I haven't, eh?" She laughed. "Well, you see, having three robberies, four murders and arson on my conscience, I —"

"Oh, you're an idiot!"

"Nearer to the truth than you imagine! You remember 'Genius and Insanity' —"

"Oh, rubbish!"

She grew suddenly grave, her mobile lips severe.

"Jim, I want to ask you a question."

"Yes," said Jim earnestly.

"Will you swear to tell me the truth — if you really know it yourself?"

"Yes, I swear," said Jim, startled.

"Why —"

She paused.

"I scarcely dare to ask you."

"Oh, do," implored Jim. "I'll tell you if I know."

"Well, why —"

"Yes?"

"Why is a piece of string?"

She gave a squeal of laughter and leaped to her feet.

"That's the true Riddle of the Universe," she exclaimed, limned on the cliff edge against the darkling twilight. "Come, there's the Stone beginning its nightly wink. It's past suppertime."

CHAPTER VI

So the days wore on for a while upon the platonic plane — or superficially so. Jim was not wholly conscious that his opinion of love had changed until he had found himself expressing unformed thoughts. The more he saw of Joan, the more puzzled and interested he grew. Most of the time the element of sex was obliterated altogether. A semiconscious thought that her lips were tempting to kiss, or that the curve of her neck was beautiful, startled him: at other times she seemed the embodiment of all the women who had ever lived, producing an agony of longing that was exquisite torture. Yet he was loath to admit that he was in love with her. As to her emotions, he could not even make a satisfactory guess. There were moments when her animal magnetism seemed to wrap him in a fierce flame of desire, to change in the moment into a sexless mind. It occurred to him that she influenced and played upon him. He remembered Miêville's boast of playing upon other humans as upon a stringed instrument. Yet he seldom failed to respond. A feeling of gratitude towards her encompassed him. She seemed to understand so easily, and, at times, deliberately to accommodate her mood to suit him — or was it his vanity? Now that he had recognized that the foundation stone of the Temple of Man was vanity he was painfully self-conscious of the fact.

Another phenomenon startled him. He became aware that, although he suffered agony on the physical side which produced insomnia, he had lost all sense of shame. There came to him a sense of exaltation, as joy in something very beautiful. This gave him to think. On the screen of the past he saw other scenes with Eve, Claire, and Virginia, which had awakened a passionate hatred of women, the reflex action of hatred of himself. The solution came to him that the fault was his. He remembered the disgust which had lashed him in the first instance. Unconsciously he had had grafted upon him that all sexual intercourse was a curse from Adam and Eve, the original sin, bestial in any form, but venial if sanctioned and licensed by the Church and State. Jim was merely suffering the agonies of a butterfly emerging into sunlight from the chrysalis, that chrysalis of convention in which mankind is still entombed.

During his relations with Claire he had been amazed because he had not been disgusted; but with Haiwani that emotion had never even suggested itself. It was only after Claire had jilted him that anger against her had arisen; against Haiwani never. With Eve he had always felt a contempt for himself and for her, drugged by a weak yielding to prurient ideas inculcated at school and current among his contemporaries. With Virginia, after he had grown sufficiently sober to realize partially the baseness and true bestiality of the act, he had suffered tortures. Now he wished that he had never known another woman; but quickly he detected the false sentiment, inasmuch that reason pointed out that he could never have obtained a glimpse of the Lamp of Truth save by bitter experience. Out of all tragedy emerges beauty; much as no child is born of woman without pain and labor. Again remorseless reason pointed out that Joan could not have evolved her mental attitude without wide experience. For a moment the old leaven in Jim made him wince, but, with an effort, he dragged himself from the emotional to the intellectual plane. Were she what the world would be pleased to call "pure" (although the mind might be a sewer) she could never have attained her understanding and sympathy. The wider the experience of life, the wider the comprehensive compassion. However, he could only surmise. Her laughing eyes always baffled him.

The more he fought against the suggestion that he was in love, the more every thought cried out upon him, the more every part of his being, physical and mental, longed and desired her with fierce exaltation that would not be denied.

One afternoon of a blazing warm day the two sat upon a bracken and gorse-strewn hillside, watching the lax velvet sails of the fishing fleet drifting through the rocky harbor mouth. Away on the deep sapphire solidity of the sea, gently flecked by fitful cat's-paws, a super-dreadnought,[149] grimly black, stained the cloud-smeared turquoise sky with reeking smoke.

Jim, who had been staring meditatively at the fishing fleet, indigoed against the mirrored glare of the sun, glanced idly at a tall, gray-bearded fisherman slowly passing on the path beneath them. The halting gait spoke eloquently of rheumatism; weak blue eyes were set in a dour lined old face, the whole personality exuding righteous misery.

"Queer, sullen people, some of these Cornishmen," Jim remarked to Joan. "Another old man down the village pointed him out to me as a shining example, as one who had never known the taste of drink or tobacco."

"Yes," said Joan; "he's a leading light in the local Bethel[150] here." She smiled. "I dubbed him St. Peter because he looks so glum and holy."

"Yes," said Jim, laughing; "he looks it. You can almost see the halo. Poor old chap, though; what a waste of life!"

---

[149] Cat's paws: a light air that ruffles the surface of water in irregular patches. Dreadnought: a type of British battleship first launched in 1906, featuring prominent "big-gun" armaments. A more powerful version, the "super-dreadnought," was developed soon afterward and used in both world wars.

[150] Bethel: a chapel.

"Why? Because he doesn't drink or smoke?"

"No — not exactly. I mean — well, by the look of him he seems like so many religious people who think that to be good one must be miserable. I can't understand it. If I were religious I should think I should be joyful and happy. Listen to any of their services on Sunday — moaning, groaning, and whining as if in perpetual fear of the vengeful God of the Old Testament.

Joan looked at Jim lazily.

"Don't you believe in anything, then?"

"No. Do you?"

"Yes. Not perhaps in the orthodox dogma. But surely you have faith in something?"

"No; I haven't," said Jim gloomily. "I can't reconcile modern scientific knowledge and common sense with religion of any sort. I can't consider that we're of so much importance."

"But, at any rate, Jim, religion keeps many people from doing evil."

"Depends upon what you call evil. And anyway, there's not much merit in being kept good by threats of a big stick or the promise of sugar. Hang it, we ought to be above children."

"But that's what we nearly all are — children."

"Good Lord, yes! And as cruel as children. Every sect condemns and persecutes everyone who doesn't believe as they do. And anyone who frankly says he doesn't believe they'd ostracize and put down as a rotter of the first water. Hang it, there ought to be a Society for the Prevention of Cruelty to Agnostics."

Joan laughed.

"Yes, there's some truth in the idea. But it's only human nature. At any rate, religion is needed by many people."

"Merely because they're not grown up?"

"Yes, largely."

"Like children they like to believe in fancies, and be frightened by bogies into being good! But I believe you're right, Joan. Though I think it's far more creditable to a man to 'keep straight,' as they call it, without religion than with it."

"Perhaps. But what's kept you straight, then?"

"Circumstances, probably. Although I don't know. I don't know what it has been. Reason says a sense of equity."

"But don't you believe in *anything*?"

"I don't think I do. Do you?"

"Heavens, yes! I'm certain that there's a grand plan and reason for it all. That we're all tending to something higher — developing, and that it's our duty to foster that. All life is beautiful, wondrously beautiful. We've no right to say there's no solution to a problem because we can't solve it."

"And no right to think we know all about it when we don't," said Jim.

"Exactly."

Jim glanced covertly at her. Her face was serious, her eyes dreamy.

"I think," she went on, "that we're much in the same position as a worker upon a vast and beautiful carpet. We each have our little pattern to work out, and ought to work on that with the best that is in us, realizing the beauty of it, although we cannot hope to see the whole design — until it is finished perhaps."

"Oh, that's emotionalism."

"Oh, no, it's not. It's idealism."

"Well, that's emotionalism."

"It is *not*!" said Joan emphatically, her eyes on infinity.

"Oh, yes, it is. I had — we all had lots of ideals in the past. They all get broken."

"No, they don't; not real ideals, only the sham ones."

"Ah! idols, you mean. I follow. You mean that we take a lump of clay and set it on a pedestal and kid ourselves that it's all we *want* to imagine it is. And that sooner or later we find out that it is clay."

"Yes. I hadn't thought of that concrete expression of it. That's it. Idolism and idealism — the false and the true."

"But idealism — wait. Do you mean that idealism is something that our emotion tends to suggest and which is corroborated, or at any rate not contradicted by, our reason? Is that it?"

"Yes, I think it is. I had the thought, but you defined it. That's where the difficulty always lies, in seizing and reducing a thought to lucid words — or even comprehension."

"Do you know that you often worry me?"

"I worry you!" She looked up at him and laughed as if pleased. "How?"

"Well, I'm older than you are and I've seen more of the world, yet the extraordinary thing is that you teach me such a lot."

Joan pouted with laughter.

"Just a man! You're delicious."

"But joking apart," said he. "I mean it."

Another gust of hilarity shook Joan.

"Of course! Man's vanity is a serious matter — to him. Only women and gods can see the jest."

Jim smiled faintly and pondered.

"I believe you're right," he said. "I thought that I could detect the universal streak when it popped out, but you caught me napping there. Unconsciously I suppose I was apt to consider you merely a woman. That's another strange point — you often make me forget the fact."

"What a compliment!" cried Joan. "All women ought to envy me, for have I not been told that I'm nearly as good as a man!"

"Oh, dam-it-all, I didn't mean that!" he exclaimed, smiling. "I meant that — that — I was astonished that — that —"

"That," she asserted, "that any woman's brain could reach as high a mental plane" — with a dimple-twitching mouth — "as your masculine brain?"

"No, I didn't," denied Jim, suppressing a mutinous thought that she was right. "I merely meant that I've had longer to gain experience in."

"Oh, Jim! Jim!" she exclaimed, laughing. "Really, you're degenerating in thought — and after all the efforts I've taken to improve you!"

Jim looked at her in doubt, uncertain whether she were serious or not, and uncomfortably conscious that she had taught him much.

"I'd love to know what you really do think," he said at last.

"Do you think that it would be worth it?"

"Yes, I do," said Jim, suddenly ardent and conscious that she was a woman. "But worth what?" he added quickly.

Joan laughed and turned away.

"Just exactly what you thought," she said.

Jim opened his lips to speak, but throttled the words, and fell to staring at her profile as she gazed seaward.

"Look; they're coming back!" she said, pointing. "There's not a breath of wind. They're wonderful entering the haven. Makes one think of R. L. S.[151] and pirates with red caps. Listen! I love the sound of distant rowlocks. I wish I could write; don't you?"

"No — I mean yes," said Jim absently.

---

[151] Robert Louis Stevenson (1850 — 1894): widely translated Scottish novelist, travel writer, and author of the celebrated Gothic novella, *Strange Case of Dr Jekyll and Mr Hyde*. One imagines that Stevenson's lively adventure fiction, including popular books such as *Treasure Island* and *Kidnapped*, would have served as rich inspiration for Beadle, who was himself a prolific author of travel and adventure yarns until finally turning to the more somber vision of *Dark Refuge*.

She turned smiling towards him. "What's struck you now?" she demanded. "You look like a Yogi contemplating Buddha."

"Do I? . . . I was just stemming a flood of emotion."

Joan raised her eyebrows.

"Poor Jim! I thought you'd 'given up toys and dollies, And taken to grown-up things'?"

"I was trying to expel all emotion because I've decided on something and wanted to talk about it sanely."

Joan smiled.

"I believe you know," accused Jim, looking at her.

"Know what?" demanded Joan, in round-eyed surprise.

Jim looked doubtful.

"That I want to marry you."

Joan stared at him for a moment, and then went into a peal of laughter.

"Will you?"

"Oh, Jim, what a disappointment! I really thought it was something interesting."

"But will you?" he demanded, coming closer to her.

"Go back!" she cried, laughing. "I'm not going to fall into your arms."

"But will you?"

"Really, Jim, you're very naughty."

Jim started at the phrase, a flash of memory taking him back sixteen years.

"You've been so good," she continued, rising to her feet; "except — well, I won't recall that."

Jim leaped to his feet and confronted her.

"Will you marry me? I want you, and by God I'll have you!"

He gripped her arms fiercely. She flashed a glance which puzzled him.

"No, I won't marry you!" she said. "Let me go, please!"

"Because I said I didn't believe in marriage? I don't. But I'll marry you."

A smile fled across her lips.

"You won't! Let me go; you're hurting me."

"I won't. Will you live with me, then?" he demanded angrily.

"No, I won't. Let me go."

He released her. Her face broke into laughter as she turned and fled down the jagged hillside.

"Damn you!" shouted Jim, and pursued her. Scrambling down, he saw that she meant to take the path to the village and made to cut her off; but she outflanked this move by turning to the left. At length he caught her as she clambered over an iron bedstead-end utilized as a gate to a strawberry patch.

"'And she ran slower and slower,'" she quoted, gasping. "But I didn't!" and collapsed amid the strawberry plants.

Jim leaned on the rickety rail, panting slightly and quizzing[152] her heaving breasts and color-painted face.

"So that's it," he said presently, smiling. "You wanted me to chase you."

"You idiot!" she gasped. "You're too crude for words."

"Well, why did you laugh and run away?" demanded Jim.

"Good heavens! should I stop — and cry?"

"No, but — you were having me on, weren't you?"

"Of course!" She laughed immoderately.

"I don't understand you!" exclaimed Jim, a trifle tetchily.

"Oh, oh, you *are* funny!"

"Perhaps. But it's serious to me."

"I believe you." She checked her hilarity a little. "But can't you see the funny side of it? Where's your sense of humor?"

"Drowned in an idiotic emotion," said Jim savagely.

---

[152] Quizzing: to look at inquisitively.

"Oh, well, if you're going to be so primitive as to lose your temper I'll go on home," she said, rising to her feet. "It's much more peaceful."

"You won't," said Jim.

"Oh, you mean thing!" she exclaimed after glancing round. "I can't scramble through a bramble hedge. What have I got to do?"

"Marry me," commanded Jim.

"But I won't."

"Well, live with me."

"Certainly not."

"But I love you."

"Of course," she said insolently, and smiled. "I know that."

"Damn!"

She brushed back her disordered locks of hair gleaming copper in the sun and bit her lip.

"Don't laugh at me!" he exclaimed angrily.

"Ah, that's better," she said, which Jim imagined referred to her hair. "I'll try to be serious," she assured him, suddenly demure, and leaned upon the rail beside him, watching his anger-furrowed face.

"Well?" sweetly.

"You do love me," he said as one making a statement.

"I didn't say so," she said, her mouth twitching.

"Stop it!" he commanded. "I won't have you laughing at me."

"Excellent!" she murmured, and grew serious.

"What did you say?"

"Oh, nothing, Jim."

"You do!" he said fiercely.

"Do what?" sweetly.

"Love me, damn you."

"Really, Jim!"

She quivered with suppressed laughter. He seized her by the shoulders and shook her roughly.

"Be quiet. I will have a serious answer."

"Of course," she said softly as he released her. "You're not angry, are you, Jim?"

With teeth set he opened his lips; then suddenly laughed. She broke into a peal of laughter. He turned abruptly and strode away.

"Jim!"

He halted and looked over his shoulder.

"Yes?"

"Come here!"

He returned slowly.

"What is it you want to know, Jim?" with great gravity.

"Whether you will come to me — marry or live with me?"

"I've answered you."

"You won't?"

"No."

He looked at her questioningly.

"Why won't you?"

"Ah! Why didn't you ask that before? — I'll tell you why. I do love you —"

"You dar—!" He made to embrace her. She leaped away from the gate.

"Wait." — She came back and leaned over the rail. "I will do neither — now."

"When?" Jim's face lit up eagerly.

"That depends on you." The laughter dimple came and went. "I won't because of many reasons. First of all, because you've got no anchor in life. I mean that your love for me alone won't fill your life. Oh, yes, I know you think it will. Besides, it would irritate me. You're a parasite, Jim. You're not working and glorying in your work upon the little pattern in the Great

Design. You're merely content with existing. You're less than a bullock, Jim, because you produce nothing and you're not even good to eat. That's wrong. Seriously, you've got to justify your existence. You've always been unhappy and discontented, haven't you?"

"Yes. But that's because I'd never met with you. You will complete me."

"No, Jim; you're wrong. All that conception is wrong. Love alone will not justify and fill life. I used to think that someday I should meet someone who could be my other self — that the two halves would make the whole — and all the rest of it."

"Good Lord! so did I. I'm sure of it now."

"You're wrong, Jim. Absolutely. Love is a stimulus to life, *not* the fulfillment — except in some cases with a woman. You've been too self-centered. Thinking only of yourself so much that you've missed the beauty of life. You must have an ideal — not an idol, as you defined it. You must get to work on your pattern and then you'll know real happiness. You'd get tired and discontented with me without it. Oh, yes, you would. Real love is the sunshine of life. I really love you, Jim. . . . No, don't get sentimental. That's not love."

"Well, you mean that you won't have me until I work?" said Jim disconsolately.

"Don't look so glum. You've got a funny conception of work. It is only work to those who have to do something for which they are not suited nor intended: that's horrid, I know. But real work, the thing for which you're made, is a glory."

"But what can I do? There's nothing I know anything particular about — I mean, in the way of work."

"Oh, yes, there is. Everyone is intended for some particular thing. It's your duty to find it out. Often it's like blundering about a dark room looking for the door. But you'll find it if you try."

"I don't understand," said Jim plaintively.

"My ideas?"

"No. I've a hideous idea that you're right. It seems so horribly sane when I don't listen to emotional impulse. No, I meant that you seem to understand life better than I do."

Joan chuckled.

"Oh, man's vanity, Jim!"

"That's all right, but, dam-it-all, your ideas are based on vanity."

"Of course. Everything is. But then there are splendid forms of vanity. And," she continued, answering his expression, "a woman learns quicker, runs through the gamut of emotions sooner than a man. No, your thought is wrong." Jim winced. "And not worthy of you. Still, I understand. — That's why I won't marry you now."

Looking at her, Jim became aware that he had lost all consciousness of sex, yet his eyes told him that she was desirable.

"Well," he said slowly, "I shall go away and try. I can't stay here near you."

"That's what I want you to do. You won't find it here."

"But supposing I never find it?"

"Oh, you will."

"I shall — I shall go tomorrow," he said gloomily, staring seaward.

"Do. . . . Jim!"

He turned. Her lips were held up, her eyes were aflame. He leaped over the gate and took her in his arms.

"Jim, I do love you!" she gasped.

"God!" he whispered. "I won't go. I'll never leave you."

"Emotion, Jim," she whispered, her eyes laughing. "But if I want you to?"

"God, I'd go tonight if I could, but —"

He paused, arrested by something in her eyes. She lowered her eyelids.

"Jim!"

Their lips met. A step sounded as a fisherman passed.

"Damnation!" exclaimed Jim.

CHAPTER VII

ON the railway journey Jim sought to face the other problem which Joan had set him. That she was right he acknowledged. He wondered at his own obtuseness in the past. Yet he *had* set himself an object — the search for the truth; but now he perceived that he had sought with blinded eyes. Truth can never be found while the seeker is living amid a maelstrom of surging emotions; only when one has attained the power of lifting oneself above the seethe and turmoil can a clear, if momentary, glimpse be obtained.

Yet what could he do? No profession nor special qualification had he. The elementary and subsidiary question of earning bread and butter was removed. All his energies were free — to what end? Questions such as these are not solved in five minutes. Many are they who live a futile life by responding to a "call" based upon emotional impulse, without pausing to examine and test in the light of reason. He might devote his life to the poor in the East End of London or to the advancement of Eugenics. The point was, in what way could he use himself to the best advantage?

He took up his quarters in London fully intent upon solving the problem. The first mental trouble was the fact that he had lost the power of concentration. Strive as he would to banish Joan, her image or her personality ever thrust itself into his mind. Physically, too, his body cried out upon him, more powerfully and insistently than ever before. Yet he knew that he would be true to Joan. There would be no temptation, as the physical impulse, dominated by the mind, was concentrated upon the one object. Nevertheless, he suffered mental and physical agony continuously, as intense lovers do, although they may not recognize the cause.

One wet forenoon Jim entered the tube at Knightsbridge to go to Piccadilly Circus. He found the smoking carriage full with straphangers and turned through the gangway to the next compartment. Staring idly around, he became aware of the vacuity of expression in the people about him: that certain animalism characteristic of faces in a crowd. They had the solemn, ruminating appearance of cows chewing the cud. That was what most of them were, he reflected, types of the human ruminant ever chewing the cud of petty events. At Down Street two passengers entered the compartment. One, a fair, portly man in a morning coat and bowler hat, with heavy yellow moustaches, took the seat opposite him. As he sat down there seemed something familiar about his manner. He stared at Jim curiously. Jim returned the stare for a moment; then they recognized each other.

"Gee-gee!"

"Jim!"

"Well, I'll be damned!" shouted Jim above the roar of the tube. "Why, this is good, old man. I've been wondering where you'd got to for years. Wrote you ages ago, but you didn't reply. Gad! I didn't know you, you're so fat."

"What?"

"Fat — too fat!" roared Jim.

"You've altered a bit, too," yelled Graham. "Face harder and cynical."

"Have I?" with a droop of the mouth. "So have you. And you look sad and weary. You always used to be cheery. — No, cheery! — Get out here. — Have lunch. — Can't talk here. Yes, come along!"

They alighted at Dover Street and took a taxi.

As they sat down to lunch Jim noticed with a shock that Graham was bald. After a rapid fire of questions Jim mentioned the episode of his flight from England, and they discussed Eve in the light of their respective experiences. Graham was the more merciless, flippant, and cynical. Being in a talkative mood, Jim launched into his subsequent experiences over coffee, liqueurs and cigarettes. He concluded the narrative without reference to Joan, dimly sensitive lest Graham would smile.

"So you've not met *the* woman yet?" said Graham, staring at Jim meditatively.

Jim hesitated, hating himself for his irresolution.

"Well, I have," he said slowly. "But that's different." He paused again, conscious that he was not conforming to his principles. "She's a girl I met — years ago, but —" He found that he could not give his confidence, fearful that Graham would not understand.

"You're not married, are you?" inquired Graham, suspiciously.

"Good Lord, no!" denied Jim, and was surprised at his own indignation.

"For God's sake, don't!" exclaimed Graham vehemently. "Are you going to?"

"No — yes; that is, I don't know. But leave that. Perhaps I'll tell you some other time. Now, George, old man, step in. — You seem to have lost your virginal optimism!"

"I never had much," said Graham. "You've had some severe knocks — but you've avoided coming a matrimonial mucker[153] — as yet —"

"Yes," interposed Jim hastily.

---

[153] Mucker (in mining and quarrying jargon): a person who shifts broken rock or waste. In old-fashioned slang: (a) a friend; mate; (b) a coarse, vulgar, ill-bred person.

"At any rate, you've had a lesson in the first instance. I saved
—"

"Yes, yes, I know. Thanks, old boy. But, George," he added
quickly, struck by a sudden thought, "was that true?"

"What?"

"Why — well, you remember — when I wanted to marry her
— Eve. You said —"

He paused for Graham to help him out, conscious of a
shadow of the emotions of that past time. Graham feigned
perplexity, chewing his moustache ends.

"Oh, dam-it-all, the things you said about Eve which stopped
me marrying her."

"Well, what about it?"

"Oh, I want to know whether they were true after all. I've
often wondered since."

"Why?"

"I don't know. I have. Were they true?"

Graham seized an opportunity to help himself to the sweets.

"Then," said Jim persistently, "they were not true?"

Graham finished a mouthful, slowly pondering. "Well," he
said at length, "you may as well know now. They were *not* true.
I saw that nothing else would stop you and it seemed the only
way out."

"And the story about Greener?"

"Don't know — he knew her," said Graham slowly. "I did it to
save you, Jim."

"Good God! — but —"

"Well, you would have married her if I hadn't, wouldn't
you?"

"Yes, I suppose I would have."

"And if you had?"

The sense of growing indignation passed. Jim looked at
Graham and dropped his eyes.

"Thank you again, George," he said slowly. "I didn't realize — until now. My God, you were a pal!"

Both strove to avoid any sign of emotion, yet Jim knew that Graham must have loved him well.

"Do you know — did you ever hear what — what became of her?" inquired Jim after a pause.

"Yes, I heard she went to South Africa — married some fellow who took her out."

Jim said nothing, but looked relieved.

"You always were such a simple youth," observed Graham at length, breaking the munching, clattering silence.

"Was I?" said Jim. He looked up for a moment, thinking that the remark threw a new light on other people's view of himself as a youth.

"Yes, I was able to save you," continued Graham, with the air of one taking up the thread of a story after an untoward interruption. "And that's the strangest touch in our joint stories. I saved you, but couldn't save myself."

"What on earth do you mean? Are *you* married?"

"Yes, I'm married!"

"Good God! — Poor old boy! I think I understand. I *am* sorry, George."

"A few months after your affair, I finished my course and went down to Cornwall."

"Damn!"

"What's the matter?"

"Nothing. Go on."

"Well, I met a girl there. She was sweetly pretty, barely seventeen. I knew her for some months, and — well, the usual happened." Graham paused. "Strange, I can't excuse myself.

Since I've tried to remember what I really thought then.[154] I was very wise to you, Jim, but — I couldn't advise myself. I thought that I was genuinely in love, but from any reasonable point of view I had no right to think of marriage or any girl. You know I have no people to help me, no money. After my course was over I had to struggle to provide for myself. I could not expect to afford to support a wife for years to come. Well, I was to blame, but I loved her. Her father was a Methodist clergyman — the hard, puritanical type. He disowned her. I married her at once. I couldn't do less. We had to live on what I could earn — which wasn't much, so you can imagine we had a rough time. After the birth of the child, a change seemed to come over her. She grew more fretful — peevish and dissatisfied. By nature she was intended for a butterfly — to live in pretty frocks, and that sort of thing. Poor girl, it must have been hard for her — it was hell to me. She loved me in those early days — in her way. Well, it all developed slowly into a tragedy. Her whole nature seemed changed. . . . Oh, God, what is the use of life?" Graham paused and stared at his wine glass. "I tried to reason with her. Useless. I wrote to her people and implored them to either help for her sake, or to let her go home for a while. They ignored my letters. I *slaved* to make money, but — well, you know what chance I had in my profession. She would have fine clothes — at any cost. I did my best, God knows, but it all dragged me down. She used to work herself up into an hysterical rage against me. It was awful — awful! At last I knew that I couldn't trust her. My God! I nearly went mad. Then — one day she disappeared. She left the child. Poor little wretch! I wished he'd never been born. For a long time I couldn't trace her. Then I found that she'd been living with another man. I saw her and — offered to take her

---

[154] The colloquial use of the term "since," which is meant to convey "Ever since." Thus, "Ever since, I've tried to remember what I really thought then."

back — for the child's sake. She wouldn't. I haven't seen her since. No, I cannot divorce her — it's too expensive for a poor man. Besides, I love her more than ever I did. That's the extraordinary part. I *can't* hate her. Ah, well, what does it matter? That's why I didn't write in answer to your letter. — Well, shall we go?"

"Poor old boy!" said Jim. "Look here, we'll dine somewhere and go to a show afterwards. You want cheering up."

"I can't, Jim. I really came up on business for the day — which I haven't done, by the way."

"Yes, you must, old boy," insisted Jim. "You can't refuse after so many years."

During dinner Jim became sadly conscious that they had drifted into planes even further apart than of yore. He found difficulty in finding mutual topics. Graham stared perplexedly when Jim began to air some of his views — and Joan's. Jim became nervous and uncomfortable. The only topics which seemed to interest Graham were football and women. Of the former Jim knew nothing. They discussed the latter, or rather Graham did, irritating Jim to boredom. Graham, lapsing from the sentimentality in which he enveloped his wife, related numerous petty and sordid intrigues. They discussed women generally, mainly of the street. Jim remarked that such were more to be pitied than condemned, that civilized man was to blame. Graham thought the statement absurd, said so, and taxed Jim with being no better than most men. Jim admitted the one and only case. Graham smiled disbelief. Jim retired into his shell. Later on, referring to his wife, Graham talked more sentiment, commiserating himself and protesting undying pure love for her. Opinions were loosened by wine. Jim remarked that he could not understand Graham's attitude to other women if he loved his wife. Graham indignantly replied "that was different; she's my wife." Puzzled and irritated, Jim was grieved because of the gulf that yawned between him and this man who had been as true a friend as he knew how, and to whom Jim certainly owed a debt. He was glad when the dinner was over.

Whilst driving from the theater to Romano's for supper,[155] their taxi was held up in the traffic at the corner of a street. A woman emerged from a restaurant escorted by an overdressed young man of the undergraduate type. She was laughing gaily. In the flood of electric light her flashing eyes and pouting red lips looked wild and tempting. Jim recognized her.

"Look," he said, drawing Graham's attention. "That's the poor devil of a girl I met at the Empire."

Graham leaned forward as she entered a hansom; the lights flashed full upon her features.

"My God!" he exclaimed.

---

[155] The narrative sequence of dining first at Romano's and then attending a show seems to be reversed here (i.e., one would expect to read: "Whilst driving from Romano's to the theater"). Romano's was a celebrated restaurant on the Strand known for serving champagne and caviar, where young men actually did sip the bubbly from the fashionable shoes of their alluring female companions. Romano's maintained a special relationship with the Gaiety Theatre, which was located nearby, at the eastern end of the Strand. In the 1890s, the Gaiety hosted Edwardian musical comedies featuring dancers known as the Gaiety Girls, who were renowned for their refined elegance and youthful beauty. The Gaiety made an arrangement with Romano's for the "girls" to dine there at half-price, which further increased the enormous popularity of the restaurant. "To Romano's flocked the Bohemians, men and women of the greasepaint, authors, journalists, artists of all kinds, soldiers, sailors … men of the law, of finance, of the race-course and the prize rings – and crooks as well. The place was really an informal club of which they were all members." See W. MacQueen-Pope, *Ghosts and Greasepaint*, London: Robert Hale, 1951, as cited online at arthurlloyd.co.uk. The Gaiety's unique brand of music hall entertainment and burlesque exerted a powerful influence on the evolution of contemporary musical comedy. It's quite probable that the show Jim is about to attend was featured at the Gaiety, especially since Beadle had a knack for being at the right place at the right time.

"What's the matter?"
"That's Virginia — my wife!"

CHAPTER VIII

ALTHOUGH all things may be roughly divided into types, there are many which, standing midway, defy classification, as the platypus; so that to label anything — or anyone — arbitrarily, is tacitly acknowledging careless thought. Thus between the animate and the inanimate are many phenomena upon whose position in the scale science cannot agree. Among the animate manifestation mankind is most distinctly marked by consciousness of self, the Ego, in contrast to the merely conscious animal. From the self-conscious there is arising a super-type which will in the distant future be as distinct from the ego-bound mankind as man is from the animal. Undoubtedly he will bear characteristics of the ordinary man, as man strongly exhibits many characteristics of the brute. The argument that man has not improved since, say, Babylonian days is beside the point. We cannot judge. What is a mere four or five thousand years in the millions of the world's development? As even the most intelligent ape cannot conceive the meaning and the power of the written word, neither can the average man, swaddled in the baby clothes of limited self-consciousness, fully comprehend the portent of cosmic consciousness. Animals act from instinct without reason or knowledge; man acts with limited knowledge and reason. So surely one who acts with a full and complete knowledge of the cause and effect of each emotion, of a comprehension of the Cosmos, is obviously of a higher development.

All through the recorded ages there have been flashes in the pan, from Lucretius to the present day. They have had the Cosmic sense and extolled the wondrous beauty and glory of life. One of the immutable laws is change. Man, as all things, is in a transitory stage. There is a vast army of Jims and Joans, slowly and painfully sloughing off pieces of the skin of ego-bound convention; refusing to worship the idols built upon a basis of egotism; passionately seeking and demanding to know the truth; becoming conscious of the sweetness of doing good without material reward in this or any other world, of the glory of life for life's sake. Ever and again their voices, Artists, Poets, Writers, Thinkers, ring across the world hailing each other, like buck approaching the forest fringe, rejoicing in the glow of the sunlit plains beyond. Art is the awakening of the cosmic consciousness, of the wondrous beauty and grandeur of the Universe and all that therein is.

Dimly Jim began to perceive. For years the strain of the artist had struggled within him blindly seeking light. The touch of the universal artist which is in all of us, often atrophied perhaps, had kept him "straight," as he termed it: and even the good influence which Madge as his Fylgja had exercised over his boyhood was due to that trait, inasmuch as she, or his conception of her, had only existed in his own imagination. The temptation to do a wicked act had been crushed or retarded, because it was ugly; it offended the artistic sense. It is that sense, struggling for expression, which makes martyrs and monks of us: thus it is that in ourselves lies our own salvation or damnation. Many of us grope and suffer all through life: to others a chance act or word gives the clue which leads to happiness. Passing the love of women is the love of an artist for his work, whether he — or she — be a charwoman or a painter. And on that great happiness may come the sunshine of true love, like the sun revealing the sapphire beauty of the sea.

Jim dreamed these thoughts, amazed and aweful[156] at the strange sense of happiness they gave him. Yet as he realized the deeper grew the pain, because as yet he had not found his métier.

To Jim the meeting with Joan had appeared as a flash of lightning, illuminating the darkness of his understanding. After he had left her and had retired within himself to the Olympian heights where the tides of emotion could not reach, he experienced that rare cold joy in the knowledge that his reason approved of his love. Many are the lovers who are driven frantically from any attempt to explore the upper altitudes of their mind lest reason grimly point to hideous truths. He realized that she stimulated thought, not cloyed it, as the loves of most men do; and, moreover, that her mind would grow and respond with his mind. An uncomfortable idea confronted him that she was of a higher mental development. Immediately an impulse bade him flee from the rarefied atmosphere toward the lower depths where the sweet waters of vanity might lave him. But resolutely he faced the problem. Reason pointed out that he could not know — yet. Much might be secondhand thought from others. The momentary suspicion that the idea was lacking in generosity, was wiped out by the reflection that the greatest minds must necessarily use other men's thoughts. The great majority were merely human gramophones churning out the medley of platitudes brayed into their ears without discrimination. In the thinking man, above the level of the herd, was the power to select and examine the grains of thought amid the chaff of the mental world; still higher came the real thinker

---

[156] Beadle's idiosyncratic spelling of *awful* is probably intentional here, signaling to the reader that the term is used in the sense of "filled with awe; "displaying great reverence." (Cf. Herman Melville: "this sea, whose gently awful stirrings seem to speak of some hidden soul beneath.")

who, from data collated, deduced, and contributed to the world something original.

On the physical side he had no doubts whatever: all his senses delighted in her. Both sentiment and reason told him that he had found a fitting mate. The higher the type the more difficult it is to find a mate, inasmuch that the larger the mental world the more difficult to find another to match it. Where true love is, both mental and physical planes are equal: that, and that alone, is the true marriage, worthy of the solemnity and sanctity of Church and State. And yet the ceremony, that Symbol of the most difficult state that humans may attain, is within the reach of any couple to mock and desecrate.

Two or three times a week he received long letters from Joan, urging, helping, chaffing, loving. He felt the need, the imperative desire to help on others towards the goal. Only the method was to be chosen. Yet all the while coexistent with the growing need for active work, was the call of the mate. In one letter he read, or fancied that he read, between the lines a suggestion that he need not wait. He wrote to that effect and received an indignant denial. His spirits sank as he read. Then suddenly a flash of inconsistent memory brought a phrase of Joan's to his mind. He remembered a queer, quick glance she had given him; then she had laughed, apparently at nothing. . . . He began to think that he was apt to be dense sometimes; but to make amends he packed his bag and went to Cornwall by the night train.

All day rain had been falling, but as the locked wheels of the morning 'bus slid down the steep hill into Crumplehorn,[157] the sun burst out, scattering diamonds on the dripping world.

He found her in the studio. She looked up in surprise from scraping her palette.

---

[157] Crumplehorn: a hamlet in Cornwall, at the northern end of Polperro.

"Jim!"

"Yes," he said, and closed the door.

"Why, what's the matter?" she inquired. "You look so happy."

"I am," he said, looking at her, smiling.

"What's the matter, then? What have you come down here for?"

"You."

"Me!"

Palette and knife in hand, she burst into laughter. He waited, still smiling in a nervous, fixed way, until she had finished.

"Well?"

"I want you, Joan, and I've come for you. We'll be married next week."

"Oh, will we? Have you forgotten what I said?"

"No, nothing that you've said. I've proved it. So now I'm going to take my reward."

"You're not."

"I am."

He stuck out his underlip as he looked at her. She smiled and shook her head.

"That's not what I said."

"You told me once that I wasn't to wait for happiness. I'm not going to. You said that I was to seek it. I've found it. And you told me to seize it firmly, quickly. And I'm going to! But I want some sunshine, too."

On the word he took the knife out of one hand, the palette out of her other, and then threw them on the floor.

"Now," he said, and took her in his arms. . . .

"Jim," she said softly, "I believe you know."

"What?"

"What a woman wants!"

He smiled, a little doubtfully.

"I know," he said, "that we love each other, that life is very sweet and all the world is very beautiful."

"Oh, Jim," she said, smiling up at him. "You know such a lot now, don't you? You know —"

But he smothered the words on her lips.[158]

FINIS

---

[158] Beadle's marriage to Sylvia Hornsby was officiated at the British Consulate General in Paris on 14 March 1914 (just four months before the outbreak of WWI). On the marriage certificate Sylvia is registered as "artist"; Charles as "novelist." They were residing at 4, rue de la Grande Chaumière, a few doors away from the famous Académie de la Grande Chaumière (located at #14), where Modigliani, Gauguin, and many other artists drew from the nude. As noted in Beadle's *Artist Quarter*, Modigliani would later live at #8.

Afterword

Charles Beadle's Pilgrimage of Passion,
by Rob Couteau

True to its title, *A Passionate Pilgrimage* opens on a scene depicting Jim's obsession with Madge, a prim and proper young lady whom he's placed upon an impossibly high pedestal. He pines but dares not kiss her lips or cheeks, instead settling for a polite peck on her fingertips. This obsequiousness toward the feminine form and all it represents foreshadows some of the novel's major themes:

What lies behind a man's deification of the feminine? What is the difference between an "ideal" and an "idol"? What happens when an idol is shattered to expose a hollow inner core: one incapable of triggering further idealization? What dangers lie in store when society promotes both a deification and a denigration of the feminine principle? And how can a young man maintain a proper, heartfelt rapport with a woman if she triggers such powerful reactions and projections? These questions concern not only the protagonist's personal preoccupations; they also represent some of the unresolved dilemmas of the Victorian era.

The next key signpost arrives when Jim is preparing to relocate to London, to commence his life's journey, and father and son sit down to have a heart-to-heart talk. This is where Beadle's personal biography is masterfully intertwined with fictional narrative. Like the actual Charlie Beadle, Jim has lost his mother at a very early age: he cannot even remember her. And in Jim's case, we sense the personal mother has been replaced by a looming, archetypal image of purity and perfection: one that defies the limitations of human existence. In the absence of a maternal figure who can serve as a particularized model of the "feminine," Jim is left to imagine a more boundless, universal, idealized form.

Jim's father also promotes this notion of wife and mother as unblemished saint, and he encourages his son to do the same:

> "There's another thing, Jim, my boy," he said abruptly. "Women — always be chivalrous to women. Remember that your mother was a woman — the dearest little woman that ever lived. Remember that I trust you to behave as my son."

It's a significant symbolic signpost, because Mr. Litham is unwittingly setting Jim up for failure. Yes, the love of a good woman can nourish, support, and inspire a man in so many unspeakably wonderful ways. But Henry Litham fails to warn his son that not every woman is as magnanimous, trustworthy, or compassionate as dear old Mum; and that women as a whole are no better than men – as he will soon discover. After absorbing "pater's" pep talk about setting out on a "Great Adventure," Jim is fated to remain oblivious behind a figurative pair of rosy-tinted spectacles. One can easily imagine the floodlights beaming from his widening eyes whenever he's approached by a wily, rapacious female, hot on the scent of boyish gullibility.[159]

---

[159] In portraying this state of idealization that can only come crashing down, one wonders to what extent Beadle borrowed from his own coming-of-age experience. Similar clues appear in *Dark Refuge*. From the inception of his writing career, the author never hesitated to explore the psychological mechanisms that trigger a character's behavior, and he maintains this same approach when shaping his autobiographical protagonists.

Added to this disastrous formula is another element guaranteed to make things more interesting; for this is England, where considerations of class remain primary, especially during this period. Behavior dictated by hierarchy may help to maintain social cohesiveness, especially in an island community, but in the long run such regimentation can easily morph into an institutional form of power play. We get a peek into this dynamic on Madge's birthday, when Jim offers her his deceased mother's locket, "which had a large pearl set in the center." He surrenders the heirloom only because he cannot afford to purchase something befitting her class. "'Madge, I — I couldn't get you what I wanted to,' he said, flushing, ashamed of his comparative poverty; 'but I'd rather you had this. Will you? It was the mater's, you know.'"

Another thing that separates the two childhood friends is their age difference. It's Madge's twenty-second birthday, while Jim is only nineteen. In Jim's mind, besides reducing his stature as a suitable mate, Madge's seniority augments his perception of her as being "above": a woman who naturally assumes a superior position on a glittering throne.

As he prepares to take leave of Madge and of the comfortable, bucolic setting at Abbey Lodge (with its sloping hillside, undulating moor, and "leaf-carpeted carriage drive"), he's poised for failure. "For a moment Jim's eager lips seemed about to make further demands on futurity; but he hesitated, and that moment fled forever." As so often happens with the adolescent mind, a single action – or lack thereof – leaves an indelible impression that will forever affect the subject's future destiny.

When he gallops away ("without daring to look at her again"), Jim more or less surrenders to the inevitability of losing an "ideal" mate. Yet, he continues to maintain this vision of Madge as a guiding light: a personified *anima* or, as the narrator has it, a *fylgja*: a guardian spirit (from Norse myth) that accompanies one throughout life.

At the close of this first section, Beadle completes the portrait:

> Madge to him represented the ideal of womankind —
> a curious combination of his mother, whom he could
> not remember, ideas vaguely absorbed from reading,
> and what he thought he wished....

> To Jim she had been that ludicrously impossible,
> ineffably sweet image that adolescence ever fashions
> out of a strange alloy of clay and idealism.

Yet, in contrast to our passionate pilgrim – who's so readily consumed by burning desire – Madge remains remarkably detached. "Perhaps," Jim wonders, "Madge's phlegmatic temperament forbade any exhibition of emotion."

And perhaps this doesn't bode well for such an impulsive, desire-driven lad.

Jim will continue to judge the women he meets by comparing them to this glorified image (always wondering if, against all odds, he might one day return and take her as his wife). But Madge simply appears to be toying with him: enjoying the adoration she receives, but masking her true intentions. For she's already set her sights upon another man. At best, she behaves like an older sister who guides Jim while never swerving from a platonic path. But there's little indication this "being of ineffable superiority" wants anything more serious than that. And so, Madge becomes the first of several dominant females who will trigger his obsessions.

Jim's fearlessness in involving himself with such strong-willed creatures represents one of the more modern aspects of the story, and this despite his belief in a man's intellectual superiority over a woman. But even that presupposition is challenged and gradually transformed as he undergoes a final metamorphosis, resulting in a portrait that's far from typical in the Anglo-Saxon literature of 1915.

* * *

After our country bumpkin arrives in London, it doesn't take long for him to fall into a trap.

One of the novel's most devious but delightfully rendered figures is Eve. It's a fitting moniker because not only will she take Jim's virginity in a literal sense; she'll also cast him from the garden of his own naivete, especially regarding the complex nature of women, and set him on an authentic journey. Not a path chosen by his father, but one that he selects on his own, largely as a result of youthful folly.

Eve's appearance is brief but she's vividly portrayed, and her presence resonates throughout the chronicle. They meet at a crucial moment, after a disconsolate Jim has become bored with his architectural training: a profession unsuited to his more romantic, adventurous spirit. Blame it on the "advent of spring," when suppressed emotions begin to well up and tug – pulling him from his desk.

Stepping into Green Park, "he had never noticed how many pretty women there were in London. Ripe lips and sparkling eyes seemed hastening on all sides to bus or train. He felt unusually happy, suppressing, with an effort, a wild inclination to dance and sing." That's when Eve shows up.

"She wore a small black hat with a scarlet feather, a loose dark jacket and full skirt, and walked with a jaunty swing. Obeying a sudden impulse, he quickened his stride to overtake her, wishing to see whether the face was as alluring as the figure." Scurrying down a flight of steps at an outdoor monument and taking them two at a time, Jim glanced sideways as he bounded past her. A glimpse of a pair of demure eyes made him miscalculate the next step; he stumbled, and jumped to save himself. There was a faint squeak behind him as he managed to recover his balance. Turning in time to field her parcel bouncing down the bottom steps, he was dimly aware of a rapid, appraising glance, quickly veiled in an expression of startled shyness.

Here the narrator offers some essential hints whose meaning will grow apparent later on. For Eve is indeed "demure" in the sense of being *affectedly* modest. Her coyness is coquettish and, while she appears to be ingenuous, she's actually a master of artful playfulness, of seduction camouflaged as innocent repartee. And note the "appraising gaze" – the ardent female gaze – of which Jim remains only "dimly aware" before it's "quickly veiled," then altered to an "expression of startled shyness." Rapidly sizing him up, Eve activates her feminine wiles, deftly nurturing the seeds of Jim's infatuation. Her gaze penetrates its target. [160]

---

[160] The French term *amour fou* might better encapsulate Jim's reaction, but during this period London's "man about town" used a far more evocative term. While the venerable Oxford English Dictionary defines *cunt-struck* as "Sexually infatuated with a woman or women," a meatier rendition is provided by *A Dictionary of Sexual Language and Imagery in Shakespearean and Stuart Literature*: "Enamored of women: who may, in turn, be either *cock-smitten* or *prick-struck*." (But in Eve's case, rather than being smitten, her attention is pinned – like a Victorian bill spike – to the money trail.) Such vivid subterranean slang, preserved in privately printed erotica, represents one of the richest, most subversive undercurrents to the Victorian sensibility.

An infamous eleven-volume erotic chronicle known as *My Secret Life*, pseudonymously authored by a gentleman named "Walter," contains a chapter subtitle reminiscent of Jim's "Eve" encounter: "A street meeting. Beauty struck. And cunt struck." The narrative reads: "In a moment I was struck with her beauty, in the next minute cunt struck." (Volume 9, chapter 3.)

An edition of twenty-five copies of *My Secret Life* was privately printed during a seven-year period, beginning in 1888. These and subsequent printings (many of them pirated) were subject to obscenity prosecution in the U.S. and UK until Barney Rosset's Grove Press issued an unexpurgated American edition in 1966. By then, the British definition of obscenity remained more stringent than its American counterpart. As late as 1969, an English printer named Arthur Dobson was handed a two-year prison sentence for daring to produce a new edition of Walter's obsessively elaborate chronicle – running 4,000 pages and composed of over a million words.

But *My Secret Life* is more than just your run-of-the-mill diary of erotic exploits; it's also sprinkled with lucid observations that counterbalance its repetitiveness. One such reflection is this critique of censorship itself: "The absurdity of calling anything indecent or improper, which men and women may like to say or do together when in private, had not occurred to me. I now believe that it matters not whether what they do be called unnatural, or beastly, or not. So long as both like it and enjoy it, it is natural to them, concerns no one else, is in the instincts of their nature, and is to them proper." A more educated conclusion than anything produced by the Circulating Libraries Association! Commenting on this passage in 2003, Professor Ellen Rosenman writes: "Repeated throughout his expansive memoir, this libertarian creed seeks a realm of sexuality requiring only the body's raptures for its justification. Walter imagines sexual pleasure as escaping the deformation of conventional morality: it is, as he says, private, instinctive, and – in a word whose variance occur three times in this short passage – natural." Ellen Bayuk Rosenman, *Unauthorized Pleasures: Accounts of Victorian Erotic Experience*, London: Cornell University Press, 2003, p. 1.

"Cunt-struck" was briefly revived in *Tropic of Cancer* (1934) when Henry Miller's autobiographical narrator remarks: "I like Van Norden but I do not share his opinion of himself. I do not agree, for instance, that he is a philosopher, or a thinker. He is cunt-struck, that's all. And he will never be a writer." Four years later, in *Dark Refuge*, Beadle has Cecci, a character based on Modigliani, complain about one of the women in his life: "No wonder my stuff is rotten with a model like that! I must have been cuntstruck, that's all, because her body pleased me in bed, and she looks like a Tintoretto angel." By 1938 the "proper" boundaries of high art had been considerably extended, at least in Paris.

When Jim falls for her coy facade and asks "You don't mind me talking to you, do you?" she replies "You know you oughtn't to" – all the while maintaining a poker face. Until adding, with a pout, "I *am* naughty!" After Jim learns her name and suggests, with a rosy blush, "Let's come and have some apples!" Eve doesn't miss a beat: "'Oh,' she said ingenuously, 'I love apples.'"

Perhaps most telling, when Jim informs her that he's "nearly twenty, "Eve pouted and said, a trifle mendaciously, that that was her age. He felt in closer sympathy with her over this strange coincidence."

We later learn from a slip of the tongue that Eve was indeed being mendacious; her real age is twenty-four, although the slip sails past Jim's attention. The incident marks a nicely shaped contrast to that earlier encounter between Jim and Madge, when their age difference posed an obstacle. But here, without hesitation, Eve deals with the problem simply by lying. Her goal is not union based on truth but the cultivation of an illusion that will serve her endgame: escaping from a dreary, working-class job in a hat shop by forcing Jim into marriage.

Jim is so divorced from his authentic feelings that he convinces himself that his interaction with Eve will remain platonic. For the specter of Madge – ever shining on a gilded pedestal – still looms. To involve himself with a woman like Eve, who's clearly beneath his station, would be an act of blasphemy against his sacred *fylgja*. But when feeling is eclipsed by reason, it can revolt by reshaping itself into an "idea" whose secret purpose is to liberate a suppressed emotion.

In Jim's case, he contrives a "valiant" action: he'll offer Eve some superficial entertainment as a diversion from her tedious labor. After she informs him of the long hours, "he decided that it was his duty to make her lot happier in any way he could…. He had eagerly seized upon her hard condition in life to play the Good Samaritan." But along with this comes an "ardent desire to kiss her": the emotion that's been secretly stowed away, hidden in a Good Samaritan conceit. Like the wheels of a Trojan horse, such enlivening impulses glide smoothly into place. For indeed, life is a feeling. But when he summons the courage to act on his desire, Eve feigns shock and dismay:

> "Oh, Jim, *why* did you kiss me?"
> "I tried not to," he said truthfully. "Really I did."
> "Oh, why did you!" she cried in distress. "No man has ever kissed me before."
> For the fraction of a second a sense of proportion hovered in his mind, but it was drowned as he looked into her eyes, earnest and steady. She plucked at his arm as if compelling faith.
> "You *do* believe me, don't you, Jim?"
> "Yes," he said solemnly. "I do, Eve."

His kisses are soon reciprocated, however, leading to ever-more urgent passions, until he's "drunk in his worship at the shrine of Eros." One assumes this is the place where ripe young women become pregnant:

> "I say, ole boy, I've got some news for you," she said suddenly. "Can't you guess?" as he looked enquiringly.
> "Why, you soppy ole thing!
> Gimme a kiss and I'll tell you!"

Particularly amusing is the "I say, ole boy," spoken in that delightfully blithe British fashion.

In a cleverly contrived twist, when chivalrous Jim decides to do the right thing and secure a marriage license, he's informed by a functionary that, since they're only nineteen years old, they cannot marry without parental consent. Jim returns to tell Eve the bad news, but then the veil drops – for a split second – and we grow privy to her true nature:

In the evening Jim diffidently informed Eve of his experience.

"You *are* a fool!" she retorted, with a greater display of temper than he had ever seen before. "I'm twenty-fo— I mean, why didn't you say you were twenty-one — and me, too?"

Thanks to Beadle's compelling storytelling, there are actually four characters at work here:

First, the charmingly duplicitous Eve, who, despite her chicanery, remains one of the most engagingly drawn figures in the text.

Second, there's our gullible untested pilgrim, a green knight marching without suitable psychic armor through the appropriately named Green Park. Ironically, Eve's lies will force him to seek his own truth.

Third, the wry narrator, who offers a sly wink or witty hint at every chance he gets. To the extent that the tale reflects the author's biography, Beadle as seasoned raconteur is now looking back with amused insight at his former folly, or at what he terms (in *Dark Refuge*) his "quondam self." In this way, the *narrative gaze* attempts to seduce us through a multifaceted combine of creative reminiscence.

A fourth and final figure is "the reader" – object of the narrational gaze – who partakes in the narrator's limited omniscience and vicariously lives through each character while simultaneously attempting to plumb their mystery and depth.

In any case, how ironic that Eve's prevarication returns like a boomerang to create such havoc! For the delay provides Jim with an opening: his friend Graham informs him that this dear young woman is not all that she's cracked up to be: "Eve has tried this game before," he says, and the ploy turned out to be an "Arabella trick."

It takes a moment for this to properly sink in. Jim's initial reaction is to doubt Graham; then he comes to believe him but remains adamant that eloping is still the right thing to do. But with unflagging determination and fraternal compassion, Graham steers his friend away from Eve and from the *mariage de réparation*, thus safeguarding his freedom.

From this point on, Jim swings pendulum-like between the poles of "woman as a being of ineffable superiority" to "woman as the devil" – as the old blues song has it. But he gradually comes to realize (thanks to being mentored by his Irish friend, Biddy) that such devilish impulses incarnate just as easily in a masculine form.

* * *

In her initial appearance in the novel as an emotionally independent, bratty young narcissist, Joan is well aware of how pretty she is, and she doesn't hesitate to flaunt her beauty to torment her prey. Perhaps, Jim as self-styled "misogynist" (as he will later identify himself, before undergoing a life-changing transformation) has finally met his misandrist match. ("You're only a man. All men fall in love with a pretty girl. Yes, I know I'm pretty." And later on: "You're just a man, Jim. An utter fool …") Pulling the strings of his desire, Joan plays him like a puppet, impelling Jim to dance to her every tune. Being closer to his station in life, she possesses a more sophisticated manner and bearing than Eve, which only makes her that much more desirable.

Since most of the action during this close encounter occurs in the narrow confines of a railway compartment, the tension builds with compressed intensity. The author's creative power really comes to the fore here, as images unfold like a cinéma vérité composition while the train jolts and Joan fends off Jim's advances; all the while egging him on, mercilessly teasing, seducing, and overwhelming him with her sensuality and skillful coquetry. She lets her hair fall "accidentally" across his burning cheeks, pushing him away while simultaneously luring him to the brink – just before banishing Jim from the compartment when he dares to steal an unauthorized kiss. Until finally, when the train shudders, he loses his balance and Joan, with arm extended, accidentally pokes him in the eye.

> A violent jolt of the carriage threw him off his balance. Thrusting out her hands to fend him off, she caught him in the left eye with her finger. The pain was momentary, but intense.
>
> "God!" he exclaimed, and fiercely caught her up in his arms and held her, raining kisses on her face and neck.

The action is replete with cinematic close-ups, literary jump cuts, rapid dramatic shifts, and plenty of amusing repartee.

The dialogue also provides a unique snapshot of how this particular generation secretly conducted themselves behind curtains of convention. The sexual electricity crackling within this crucible is generated as a result of two opposing tendencies: the protagonists are each programmed to preserve a certain amount of Victorian decorum; but this is counterpointed by the budding passions of a new generation ready to claim its post-Victorian freedoms. Regarding the latter, we can only surmise how the scene actually ends by observing what transpires the following morning:

> Jim, looking very grave and preoccupied, made his way along to the dining car. Erewhile Joan joined him. She appeared nervous, and her eyes were slightly red. Neither looked at each other as they exchanged greetings.

We eventually learn that Joan has been weeping, ashamed over betraying her future husband. For she's lost her virginity to Jim, who will now go his separate way.

Shortly afterward, the railway journey across Africa culminates with Joan's prearranged meeting with her fiancé. Just before they arrive at the station, Joan extracts from Jim a promise: when the train pulls into Bulawayo, he must disappear and cease to acknowledge her existence. But then, in a rare display of affection, she bursts into tears and showers him with kisses.

As a final humiliation, Jim is forced to walk past Joan and Harry as they embrace on the platform. Equally demeaning, just as he's within earshot, Joan complains that she felt lonely amidst the "grumpy men" who were traveling on a "mostly empty" train. Flabbergasted at her suave duplicity, Jim wonders what to think of a woman who could so blithely deceive her future husband. The incident provides yet another reason for Jim to stoke his hatred of the opposite sex. Soon, he will identify himself as a misogynist and refuse to engage in romantic relationships.

Part of the solution to Jim's problem arrives when he begins to realize that his contempt is related to "an unacknowledged fear of the opposite sex." In this sense, the novel fits neatly into what was then known as the "sex-problem" genre,[161] although it lacks the fulsome purple prose that normally encumbers such tales.

* * *

Jim's cathartic metamorphosis occurs after he travels "up country," to engage in an expedition. (Most likely, based upon Beadle's actual experiences in Africa circa 1898 – 1911.) The

---

[161] A euphemism for stories that explored sensitive moral issues, especially those relating to sexual conduct.

narrative suddenly shifts gears, now assuming a tone more reminiscent of genre fiction. It's as if the author can't make up his mind whether to pursue a work of high literature or a mixed-genre adventure tale.[162] Among the melodramatic highlights:

---

[162] Beadle continued to develop this cross-genre form in his next full-length novel, *Witch-Doctors*: his most commercially successful, widely reviewed fictional work. First appearing as a four-part *Adventure* serial in 1919, it was later published in 1922 by Jonathan Cape in the UK and by Houghton Mifflin in the U.S. Regarding motifs, imagery, and dramatic development *Witch-Doctors* is clearly a work of genre fiction, but one that also reflects a refined literary craftsmanship and willingness to explore sophisticated sociological themes that don't ordinarily make an appearance in the adventure fiction from this period.

UCLA Professor Michael North, author of *Reading 1922*, favorably compares *Witch-Doctors* with the work of British anthropologist-ethnologist Bronisław Malinowski. While dissecting the implicit problems in Malinowski's participant-observer model, in which an ethnologist "must 'join in' so as to share the point of view of the society under investigation and yet also remain outside so as to grasp it in a way that a participant never can," North concludes: "It did not take long for the contradictions in this project to appear. In fact, Malinowski might have read before the year was out a vulgarized version of his program and its contradictions in a popular novel, Charles Beadle's *Witch-Doctors*. Beadle's anthropologist, an American named Bernier ... does such a good job of entering into the point of view of his subjects that he becomes their new King-God.... With his notebook at the ready even as he is elevated to godhead, Bernier represents a complete, if very early, satire on the celebrated contradiction between the two roles of the participant-observer, between experience and interpretation as sources of ethnographic authority. But Beadle's novel also demonstrates that there is a deep contradiction within the contemporary notion of ethnographic experience itself. For the more completely the anthropologist experiences a society as its members do, the less there actually is to experience. The events of life come to be constituted *as* experiences only through the intervention of the outsider; they appear only against the background of his incomprehension. And this contradiction appears just as vividly in *Argonauts of the Western Pacific*, perhaps because Malinowski tried so hard to give his ethnography the experiential vividness

After Jim's party is ambushed by King Sepopa's Marutse-Mabunda natives, most of his men are butchered and killed. While suffering from malaria-induced delirium, he's taken prisoner. His friend Miêville is horribly tortured in a ritualized execution, witnessed by a heartbroken Jim. The latter's life is spared only because the king's sister, Haiwani – a bronzed-skinned beauty with dark, quasi-Arabic features – has taken a fancy to Jim. Her dominance is seated in the fact that, at any moment, she can order her lover's death.[163]

Regardless of the genre fiction elements that creep into the narrative at this juncture (including the use of archaic English in dialogue, e.g., "Thou hast two tongues"), the portrait of Jim's native wife, Haiwani, remains one of the most memorable. Of course, a modern reader will have to exercise forbearance over the appearance of racial epitaphs and other dated characterizations. There's also plenty of romanticized exoticism, as will inevitably be found in tales born at the beginning of the century. But if we look carefully beneath the surface, what emerges is a genuine love affair between two people of vastly different cultures, who each grow to cherish and respect their differences and to construct uniquely fashioned bridges to ameliorate a sense of separation. (Utilizing a playful touch of symbolism, the narrator describes how "Jim now endeavored to

---

of a novel." See Michael North, *Reading 1922: A Return to the Scene of the Modern*, New York: Oxford University Press, 2001, pp. 50-51, 56.

[163] Cf. Beadle's essay "Our Trip Down the Zambezi," published in the *Wide World Magazine* in May 1907. There he recounts a 1904 meeting with the Queen of Nalolo (in modern-day Zambia), who develops a grisly reputation after slaughtering one of her councillors with a battleaxe. This 250-pound royal was accompanied by "her present husband – nobody of importance, according to Barotseland law. If the Queen tired of him, under the old *régime*, she either divorced him or had him strangled, the latter being quite a convenient and inexpensive method, but stopped of late years by British influence."

solace himself with native tobacco, adapting leaves of a Gibbon's 'Rome' as cigarette papers.")

At first, Jim wishes only to escape. But by the end, he grows increasingly content with his playful, affectionate, remarkably empathic mate. Solely through the vehicle of her heart, Haiwani can "read" Jim with profound emotional clarity, despite having little grasp of the Queen's English. And when, heartbroken, she sacrifices her life in the belief that her absence will lead to Jim's spiritual freedom, only then does he come to realize who and what Haiwani really is: a figure of exceptional virtue and self-abnegation. Although at first he frets over their intellectual differences, in many ways Haiwani remains a cut above Jim – and above the other women in this chronicle – when it comes to her bountiful emotional intelligence and her physical and spiritual fidelity.

Unfortunately, the wisdom of the heart is a quality that many young pilgrims – in particular, the hyper-rational types – fail to appreciate until it's too late. And sadly, Jim is no exception. In his quest to find "the" woman – his perfect spiritual and intellectual match – he remains blind to some of these more essential matters. But reading between the lines, it's clear that Haiwani has opened his heart, paving the way for his later transformation with Joan (who will return at the novel's end, as a widow). Following an incident that illustrates the remarkable depth of Haiwani's love, we witness a "turning point in Jim's mental position":

> although there was Promethean fire in her passion, her
> delicacy was vestal in natural simplicity. In hours of
> passion he was sure he loved her and was happy.

Jim continues to view the other women in his life with a mixture of admiration and disappointment (both evaluations being in constant flux), but for Haiwani he always maintains nothing but the highest regard. He eulogizes her thus:

> The Bronze Goddess! She, the savage, had been the finest and best of all. If she were not dead he would return straight to her....

> If only Haiwani were alive, by God, he'd go back to her. A great loneliness laid hold upon him. All civilization was false and rotten. He would return to the veld, where things were close to nature, passionate and true. A house seemed like a suffocating trap. He must get away from the dreary wilderness of bricks and mortar, away to the freedom, the masterfulness of the wilds.

Especially when considered in a broader historical context, what Beadle has attempted here is something rather subversive, because he portrays a turn-of-the-century interracial couple in an exceedingly positive light. The affair directly challenges the notion that one mustn't marry outside one's social class, never mind outside of one's racial categorization. For British colonialists of the early 1900s, sex with a "savage" was regarded as an acceptable diversion as long as it wasn't discussed in polite company. (There was even a slang term for it: "black velvet.")[164] But a more serious relationship would have been

---

[164] Beadle's short story "Black Velvet" appeared in the March 1932 issue of *This Quarter*, a respected literary journal edited by Edward Titus (the husband of Helena Rubenstein) under his Black Manikin imprint in Paris. Set in a vividly painted African landscape, it's the story of a white colonialist who selects a beautiful young Black woman to serve as erotic playmate. At the end of the tale, when he prepares to repatriate to his proper British household, he passes her on to his incoming colonialist colleague – like a gift to be shared among an elite class of men. The ending of "Black Velvet" is

laughed at or severely frowned upon. Yet the narrator tells us that Jim "was sure he loved her and was happy."

Was this the sort of thing that tipped the censors' scales when they labeled the novel as "objectionable"? One wonders: "Objectionable to whom?" If only the prudes in charge of banning books had displayed the same level of sensitivity when it came to the stereotypical manner in which Blacks were almost invariably portrayed!

* * *

When Jim reunites with Joan near the novel's end, besides lambasting him with captious taunts and enervating critiques, she also attempts to counter his cynical worldview with what she believes to be a more holistic approach. After he asks "Supposing two intellects fall in love — are attracted, how does happiness come?" she replies:

> "In the eternal delight and joy at exploring each other's mental world. In the joint appreciation of the subtleties, humor and wonder of life. Can't you imagine two tied to each other, one heartbroken because she — or he — cannot follow the other into higher or other worlds of thought, and he — or she — disgusted, irritated, and disappointed?"

> "Each mental *and* physical degree should find its mate in the same degree."

> "The nearest approach to unadulterated happiness, degenerated for want of contrast — you can't have a picture without light and shade, can you? — is the

> domestic cow. — There are plenty of cows in life, Jim. Look!" — she pointed to a pair of gulls, white streaks in the dying sun. — "They're happy; do you want that? The lower in evolution you go the nearer to content[ment]. The higher the type, the greater capacity for suffering and joy. The greater the artist, the greater the pain."

These are a few of the platitudinous effusions that fall from Joan's (often smirking) lips. While they may contain a grain of truth, her remarks about art and spirituality often seem pat and dated; others resemble a cross between New Age aphorism and a call for the Übermensch.

A bildungsroman traditionally ends on a philosophically broadening, psychologically enlightening note. But what we're left with here more resembles a superficial pop music lyric rather than a sophisticated literary symphony. The sentiment may be noble, but the tone rings didactic. While some of these ideas may have been revelatory for a certain mass audience at that time, today they fail to astonish. The preachy dialogue also serves to remove any sense of mystery or allure surrounding Joan's persona.

All this occurs at the most sensitive point in a novel's spine – its conclusion. Instead of being swept into a climactic finale, the reader's attention drifts into a seagull-festooned breeze. Moreover, as a result of such trite clichés, we're left with a sense of disappointment when it's revealed that Joan is "the" woman who will inspire Jim's soul. Rather a shallow muse!

Nonetheless, a certain symmetry exists between these two characters; for Joan closely mirrors Jim's disdainful, haughty remove from the hoi polloi. Like Joan, he places himself on an ethical pedestal as he gazes down with blatant condescension upon the shortcomings of the masses and their rigid, myopic conventionalism. (Indeed, there's much pedestal hopping to be found in this pilgrimage!)

What's sorely lacking in Joan's formula of union based on intellectual compatibility is the equally important ballast of emotional connection, triggered by the desire-driven god, Eros. Whereas passion can lead to <u>com</u>passion (think of Jim and Haiwani), alienation and estrangement result when the intellect usurps the role of the feeling function. Therefore, the "heroic" resolve of this couple to transcend mere "emotionalism" may eventually founder, imperiling Eros and its potentially unifying bonds.[165] Taking a step back into Beadle's actual life, one wonders if this was the sort of shortcoming that led to the catastrophic marital discord described in the autobiographical *Dark Refuge*.

Though the characters may be overreaching here, it's important to note that, with Joan's help, Jim is able to rectify a previously destructive life pattern. Until now, he's been victimized by unrestrained passion, which has led him astray. He gradually comes to realize that passion must be tempered with conscious purpose. Rather than blindly following its lead, it should be given and received through vessels that make for

---

[165] Though even Eros can be taken too far. In the immortal words of Denis de Rougemont: "Eros is complete Desire, luminous Aspiration, the primitive religious soaring carried to its loftiest pitch, to the extreme exigency of purity which is also the extreme exigency of Unity. But absolute unity must be the negation of the present human being in his suffering multiplicity. The supreme soaring of desire ends in non-desire. The erotic process introduces into life an element foreign to the diastole and systole of sexual attraction – a desire that never relapses, that nothing can satisfy, that even rejects and flees the temptation to obtain its fulfillment in the world, because its demand is to embrace no less than the All. It is infinite transcendence, man's rise into his god. And this rise is without return." Denis de Rougemont, trans. Montgomery Belgion, *Love in the Western World*, Greenwich, CT: Fawcett, 1966, p. 64.

fitting containers. In other words, unconsciously driven emotion must evolve into a more sophisticated expression of feeling. I believe this is what really lies at the core of a larger, more holistic message that begins to emerge here.

By mulling over such matters during a period of self-imposed exile, Jim overcomes his limitations and connects to a more transcendental purpose in life. And it's thanks to Joan that he engages in this introspection, from which he will emerge as a more mature, self-confident man.

* * *

While *A Passionate Pilgrimage* contains a traditional happy ending – perhaps required by publishers of "sex-problem" fiction, since the genre targeted a mass-market, "six-shilling novel" crowd – *Dark Refuge* was burdened by no such constraint. For publisher Jack Kahane, the only proviso was that a novel be thoroughly unconventional, unabashedly anti-conformist, and morally or sexually provocative down to its roots.

Instead of a "boy meets and romantically conquers a reluctant girl" motif, *Dark Refuge* ends with a twisted vision of the cosmos satirizing its own spiritual emptiness. The latter is personified by the narrator's dismemberment as he whirls through galaxies and shuttles into mysterious folds of time and space. After his eyeballs are wrenched out, they spin away – "sporting like butterflies" – yet he continues to chronicle his own atomization:

> Through the empty sockets cascaded jewels which were, I knew, my virtues and my vices; and much I wondered that each gem was more beautiful than the other.
>
> Then my genitals sloughed; my penis chased an amorous star with the ardor of a stag after a rutting

doe; my testicles became the moons of a lonely planet. My belly split; my guts convolving their length, resembled a sea serpent frolicking in an indigo sea.

He's even informed that the "Only God," the "Last Delusion, The Unique One," is named "YT-IL-IT-UF," which a discerning reader will unravel as FUTILITY spelled backward.

Then we arrive back home, at the narrator's flat, where he's seated before a triocular "alabaster idol, Ganesha, in the flickering light of the guttering candle stub."

Was it all a hashish-induced hallucination? We don't know, and Beadle refuses to tell us.

Compare this to a passage from the concluding chapter of *A Passionate Pilgrimage*: one that's atypical for the author not only because of its message but also because of its incongruous tenor and tone:

> All through the recorded ages there have been flashes in the pan, from Lucretius to the present day. They have had the Cosmic sense and extolled the wondrous beauty and glory of life. One of the immutable laws is change. Man, as all things, is in a transitory stage. There is a vast army of Jims and Joans, slowly and painfully sloughing off pieces of the skin of ego-bound convention; refusing to worship the idols built upon a basis of egotism; passionately seeking and demanding to know the truth; becoming conscious of the sweetness of doing good without material reward in this or any other world, of the glory of life for life's sake. Ever and again their voices, Artists, Poets, Writers, Thinkers, ring across the world hailing each other, like buck approaching the forest fringe, rejoicing in the glow of the sunlit plains beyond. Art is the awakening of the cosmic consciousness, of the

> wondrous beauty and grandeur of the Universe and all
> that therein is.

It's as if the setting sun of Victorian idealism has cast a final ray of golden light.

Conversely, the lurid horror described at the end of *Dark Refuge* may be viewed as a prophetic vision of what's soon to come. For, in 1938 – the year of its publication – the cynic in Beadle had every right to acknowledge the nihilistic presence of "Futility" occupying a divine throne. Yet, he continued to create, even in the face of all that … and even while *face à face* with the mocking, garish grin of Ganesha, whose dilating third eye symbolizes cosmic consciousness and the ability to peer beyond a veil of illusion. Ironic, because, for Beadle, upon lifting the veil we encounter merely an empty void – perhaps one echoing with sardonic laughter.[166]

While the Beadle of *Dark Refuge* is a more mature author, he's also a more pessimistic one. By then, the aspiration for a sacred, spiritual marriage had been obliterated, to be replaced by the signature of Futility scrawled across a cosmogonic canvas. Both Madge and Joan have been succeeded and supplanted by the absurd. The world was about to be engulfed in flames and befouled by the stink of gas chambers, so perhaps the characters who scurry about *Dark Refuge* seeking cheap thrills and a momentary fix cannot be gainsaid. Echoing this view, we have a brief but revealing contemporaneous testimony:

Shortly after Jack Kahane died, his son Maurice Girodias was seated inside the Obelisk office, staring at a display of authors' photos. Among the intriguing facades "pinned to the gray burlap that covers the wall," says Maurice, was "the satanic face

---

[166] In one of his letters to his niece composed during the Great Depression, Beadle writes: "God's a humorist such as the Jews never suspected." And the reference is clearly to a black humor.

of Charles Beadle, the author of *Dark Refuge* – who knows, perhaps one of the true prophets of the future?"[167]

* * *

A handful of clues provide us with a faint outline of Beadle's final decades.

The same year that Kahane passed away, Beadle returned to his unwelcoming native soil, at least temporarily. On 29 September 1939 his name appears in the England and Wales Register,[168] recording his residence in St. Albans, Hertfordshire. It's likely that he repatriated because war with Germany seemed imminent, and events were unfolding with the rapidity of a Gatling gun. 1 September 1939: Germany invades Poland. 2 September: the tubercular Jack Kahane dies from heart failure, probably self-induced from excessive alcohol consumption.[169] 3 September: France and England declare war on Germany.

According to the diaries of the occultist Aleister Crowley, between June and October of 1939 the two men dined together on five separate occasions at Crowley's residence in Chiswick. It wasn't until October that the so-called *voyant* finally figured out Beadle's ulterior motive: "Here to pick my brains regarding Montparno," i.e., Montparnasse, Crowley's former hunting ground, where the two once rubbed shoulders. Beadle was

---

[167] Maurice Girodias, *The Frog Prince*, New York: Crown Publishers, 1980, augmented English translation, p. 350.

[168] "The 1939 Register was taken on 29 September 1939. The information was used to produce identity cards and, once rationing was introduced in January 1940, to issue ration books. Information in the Register was also used to administer conscription and the direction of labour, and to monitor and control the movement of the population caused by military mobilisation and mass evacuation." See NationalArchives.gov.uk.

[169] This according to his son, Maurice, who regarded his father's death as a suicide.

collecting material for a chronicle that would appear in June 1941, when Faber and Faber published *Artist Quarter*, a nonfiction work about Modigliani and the Parisian artist scene that Beadle pseudonymously coauthored with Douglas Goldring. Among other things, it contains material culled from interviews Beadle conducted in France during the late 1930s.

In October 1943, Beadle's friend and former Montmartre neighbor, Beatrice Hastings, committed suicide in Worthing, Sussex. (Suffering from gastroenteritis pain, she was convinced that she had cancer.) Shortly afterward, Beadle and Goldring received a manuscript from her estate: a surrealist novella entitled "Minnie Pinnikin," written by Hastings in French, which dramatizes her relationship with Modigliani.

From this point on, attempting to track Beadle's footfalls through the literary veld is a task that yields diminishing returns. His genre fiction appears in only four issues of *Short Stories* magazine between December 1945 and June 1947, with this final issue hosting his last original story, "Nameless Spy." Thanks to Modigliani scholar Kenneth Wayne, we also know that William Lieberman, curator of the Museum of Modern Art, was preparing for a 1951 exhibit of Modigliani's work "when he was put into contact with Goldring and Charles Beadle by the art historian Douglas Cooper," and through them Lieberman "obtained a copy of Minnie Pinnikin."[170] Wayne doesn't mention the year that Lieberman contacted the authors, but since the exhibit opened in April 1951 a safe guess would be circa 1949 – 1950.

In February 1952 one last Beadle tale appeared in *Short Stories* ("The Idol," reprinted from a 1933 issue of the magazine). But then, the footprints vanish. The time, place, and circumstances of Charles Beadle's death still remain a mystery.

---

[170] Kenneth Wayne, *Modigliani and the Artists of Montparnasse*, New York: Harry S. Abrams, 2002, p. 205.

The Two Beadles:
A Postscript by John Locke

Rob Couteau and I met through our mutual interest in Charles Beadle, though we came at him from different directions. I produced two books of Beadle's African adventure fiction originally published in magazines from 1918-25: *The City of Baal* (2007), a story collection, and *The Land of Ophir* (2012), a short novel. The majority of the material came from *Adventure*, which specialized in authentic and historically grounded adventure fiction. Rob's interest was in the post-WWI Parisian artistic scene where Beadle mingled with Bohemians and wrote novels based on his experiences. Rob has been reprinting these novels, a boon for Beadlemaniacs.

Our two Beadles were seemingly different people, though both were writers. They are, of course, the same person, with two writing souls. The adventure writer used his African experiences to make money, of which there is never enough; and the Bohemian poured his literary ambitions into his novels while living a marginal existence. Both souls are well worth reading today.

Beadle never wrote an autobiography but, bit by bit, his story has been coming together, joining the two souls, to give us an intelligible picture of the whole person. In particular, *A Passionate Pilgrimage* possesses strong autobiographical elements, offering powerful insights.

It is, perhaps, Beadle's most revealing autobiographical fiction. Its protagonist, timeline, and settings correspond closely to his own life.

When using autobiographical fiction to flesh out an actual biography, we always bump into the question: where is the line between life and fiction? The author could adopt the framework of his real life while coloring in the spaces with fictional episodes – to make points that his real life can't, to create composite characters, or just to make a better, or more balanced, story. Our approach is to corroborate as much as possible, painting the unknowns into a shrinking corner. Rob's well-researched footnotes to *A Passionate Pilgrimage* contribute a lot to this effort. In addition to validating the native African elements – a challenging task – he has identified confessions in letters, sometimes from *Adventure's* column *The Camp-Fire*, wherein authors discussed the real-life bases to their stories. Here and there, Beadle dropped bits and pieces of his life, like his experiences hawking jewelry in Johannesburg, part of the plot of *A Passionate Pilgrimage*.

An intriguing aspect of the novel is that it addresses two fundamental questions about Beadle, which may not be addressed elsewhere. Why did he go to Africa? And why did he become a writer?

The Africa question is the most straightforward. In the novel, the protagonist, Jim, is obsessed with resolving the role that women will play in his life. Thus, it's a double blow to his ego when his childhood friend Madge becomes interested in another man at the same time his girlfriend Eve tries to manipulate him into marriage with a false claim of pregnancy. Feeling his prospects hopeless, he books passage to South Africa and joins the British South Africa Police, which polices Rhodesia. This draws him into the Second Boer War. The Africa adventures dovetail precisely with Beadle's actual experiences, though the novel takes a five-year leap over them.

In the end, the question leaves us with two possibilities, either that *A Passionate Pilgrimage* identified Beadle's true motivations in going to Africa; or that Beadle was uncomplicated by romance and simply another young man looking for adventure.

The second question – why he became a writer – zeroes in on a weakness in the novel. The closing chapter provides a plausible answer to the question, but it feels tacked on. Through the majority of the narrative, Jim grapples with his views on women. Other than this pondering – which many nonwriters dwell upon – there is little to connect him to writing.

There is a suggestion, early on, when Jim leaves the countryside for London to study architecture that he may have a mind for complex problems, something that could indicate potential for writing fiction. Designing a building and planning a novel both require cohesively integrating an elaborate structure with a myriad of detail. But any possibility that this analysis applies to Jim is quickly dispelled. We discover that "[my father] thinks because I was keen on drawing that I'd make a good architect. So I suppose it's got to be that. But I do hate it." Later, his relationship with Eve is far more compelling than his studies: "more joy was there in the house of Jim over one lingering kiss than in the solving of ninety and nine architectural problems." That's about as far as we get.

In the last chapters of the novel, Jim runs into Joan by chance in Cornwall. He'd met her years before on a train to Rhodesia. Now *she* is an artist, one of the numerous landscape painters in the region. Their awkward friendship hangs up on Jim's ceaseless desire to find the woman who can complete his life.

Joan idly asks him: "I wish I could write; don't you?"

"No – I mean yes," says Jim absently.

Joan has planted a seed which begins to grow.

Jim wants to marry her, but she identifies a major impediment:

"You've got no anchor in life. I mean that your love for me alone won't fill your life. Oh, yes, I know you think it will. Besides, it would irritate me. You're a parasite, Jim. You're not working and glorying in your work upon the little pattern in the Great Design. You're merely content with existing. You're less than a bullock, Jim, because you produce nothing and you're not even good to eat. That's wrong. Seriously, you've got to justify your existence."

Jim can't disagree once the problem is identified. Slowly, his artistic soul blossoms. He senses the artist within. We discover that the seed has been dormant: "For years the strain of the artist had struggled within him blindly seeking light." Though, again, this latent yearning for art is invisible before the end of the narrative. Jim's contemplation of the artist within reaches grandiose heights: "Art is the awakening of the cosmic consciousness, of the wondrous beauty and grandeur of the Universe and all that therein is." But what kind of artist should he be? "Jim dreamed these thoughts, amazed and aweful at the strange sense of happiness they gave him. Yet as he realized the deeper grew the pain, because as yet he had not found his metier." Indeed, that secondary awakening does not occur in the narrative, as if Beadle was reluctant to make Jim a writer, alerting the reader to the autobiographical content.

At any rate, the need for Jim to create his own life before sharing it with a woman, and for that life to be an artist's, is very plausible as Beadle's explanation of his own evolution.

The two questions, Africa and writing, receive satisfying answers in *A Passionate Pilgrimage*. But how much is Beadle's life and how much his imagination?

He leaves one last clue in the narrative – in the narrator's voice:

"There is a vast army of Jims and Joans, slowly and painfully sloughing off pieces of the skin of ego-bound convention; refusing to worship the idols built upon a basis of egotism; passionately seeking and demanding to know the truth; becoming conscious of the sweetness of doing good without material reward in this or any other world, of the glory of life for life's sake."

That passionate seeking of truth, which Beadle so clearly believed in, could hardly take form, in his autobiographical novel, as a figment of someone else's imagination. It's most convincing as Beadle's own philosophy.

John Locke has been interested in the pulp magazine era and its fiction, particularly in the 1920s and 1930s, for many decades. In the 1990s he started collecting information on the era, which led to writing historical treatments about the publishers, editors, and most of all the authors. Many of his findings have been published in his Off-Trail Publications books. In 2018, he jumped up to book-length histories with *The Thing's Incredible! The Secret Origins of Weird Tales*. He's currently completing a book about writers behaving badly in the 1920s.

Bibliography

Beadle, Charles. *A Passionate Pilgrimage*. London: Heath, Cranton, and Ouseley, 1915.

— *Dark Refuge. Edited with Annotations and an Afterword by Rob Couteau*. New York: Dominantstar, 2023.

— *The City of Baal*. Castroville, CA: Off-Trail Publications, 2007.

— *The Land of Ophir*. Elkhorn, CA: Off-Trail Publications, 2012.

— *Witch-Doctors*. London: Jonathan Cape, 1922. Boston: Houghton Mifflin, 1922.

Bradshaw, David; Rachel Potter, eds. *Prudes on the Prowl: Fiction and Obscenity in England, 1850 to the Present Day*. Oxford: Oxford University Press, 2013.

Churchill, Allen. *The Literary Decade*. Englewood Cliffs, NJ: Prentice-Hall, 1971.

de Grazia, Edward. *Girls Lean Back Everywhere. The Law of Obscenity and the Assault on Genius*. New York: Random House, 1992.

de Rougemont, Denis. *Love in the Western World*. Translated by Montgomery Belgion. Greenwich, CT: Fawcett, 1966.

Douglas, Charles. *Artist Quarter: Reminiscences of Montmartre and Montparnasse in the first two decades of the twentieth century*, London: Pallas Athene, 2021. ("Charles Douglas" is the portmanteau pseudonym of Charles Beadle and Douglas Goldring.)

Girodias, Maurice. *The Frog Prince*. New York: Crown, 1980.

Hoffman, Arthur, ed. *The Camp-Fire. The Complete Correspondence From the Pages of Adventure, 1918-1920*. Norwood, MA: Steeger Books, 2023.

North, Michael. *Reading 1922: A Return to the Scene of the Modern*. New York: Oxford University Press, 2001.

Pearson, Neil. *Obelisk: A History of Jack Kahane and the Obelisk Press*. Liverpool: Liverpool University Press, 2007.

Rosenman, Ellen Bayuk. *Unauthorized Pleasures: Accounts of Victorian Erotic Experience*. London: Cornell University Press, 2003.

Illustrations

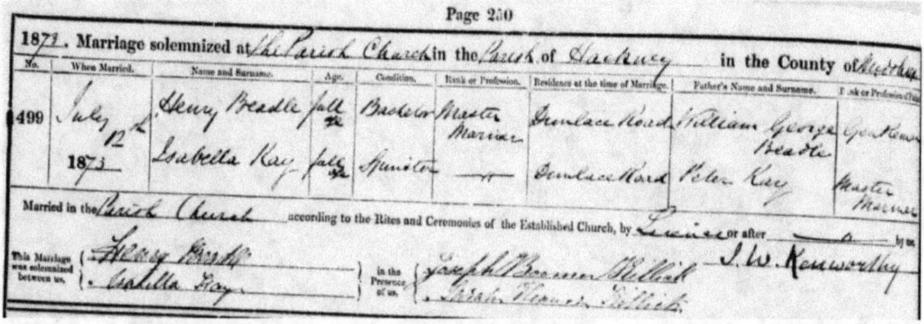

Page 250

1873. Marriage solemnized at the Parish Church in the Parish of Hackney in the County of Middlesex

No.	When Married.	Name and Surname.	Age.	Condition.	Rank or Profession.	Residence at the time of Marriage.	Father's Name and Surname.	Rank or Profession of Father.
499	July 12th 1873	Henry Beadle	full age	Bachelor	Master Mariner	Isenlace Road	William George Beadle	Gentleman
		Isabella Kay	full age	Spinster	—	Isenlace Road	Peter Kay	Master Mariner

Married in the Parish Church according to the Rites and Ceremonies of the Established Church, by Licence or after ——— by me, J. W. Kenworthy

This Marriage was solemnized between us, Henry Beadle, Isabella Kay

in the Presence of us, Joseph ... Pillick, Sarah ... Pillick

12 July 1873: Marriage of Henry Beadle and Isabella Kay at St. John's, Hackney, London. Both Henry and Isabella's father, Peter Kay, were master mariners. Henry's father, William, is listed as a "gentleman."

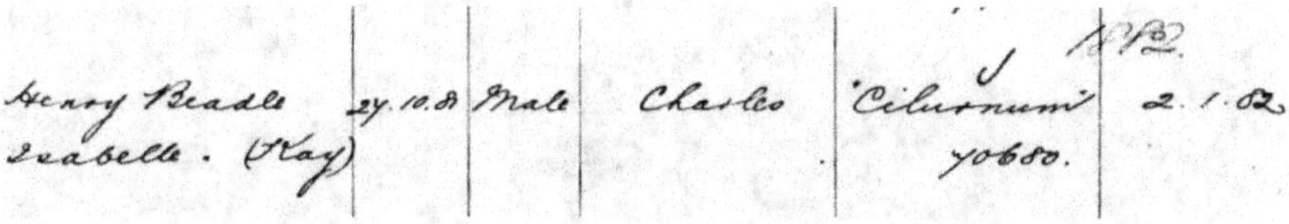

Henry Beadle Isabelle (Kay)	27.10.81	Male	Charles	"Cilurnum" 70680.	1882 2.1.82

27 October 1881: Record of Beadle's birth aboard the SS *Cilurnum*, from "UK Registers of Births, Marriages and Deaths at Sea, 1844-1890." Other documents, such as his draft registration card, indicate he was born the day before, on 26 October 1881.

(Above:) The brothers Henry, Charles, and William Beadle. (Below:) Various portraits of Beadle from a family album. Courtesy of Beadle's great-niece Patricia and her daughter Liz.

Circa fall 1900 or 1901: Beadle in Mashonaland, South Africa. Courtesy archive of Patricia and Liz.

During this period Beadle received various decorations and service awards. The "Roll of individuals entitled to the South Africa Medal and Clasps, April 1901" includes trooper Charles "Marmaduke" Beadle, who served in the National (Waldon's) Scouts and Orange River Colony Volunteers, Nesbitt´s Horse, Regiment Number 1014. Beadle may have fictionalized his middle name in order to enlist a second time.

Undated photo of Henry Beadle (1844 – 1906), father of Charles. Courtesy of Patricia and Liz.

Another photo of Henry Beadle, courtesy of Patricia and Liz.

Photo of Charles Beadle featured in *The Wide World Magazine*, May 1907.

Ship's Name.	Official Number.	Steamship Line.	Master's Name.	Registered Tonnage.
S. S. AGADIR.	124092	THE MERSEY STEAMSHIP C⁰ L^D.	J. B. Mansfield	1642

I hereby Certify that the Provisions actually laden on board this Ship are sufficient, according to the requirements of the Merchant Shippi...

Date 25ᵗʰ April 1908

NAMES AND DESCRIPTIONS OF **BRITISH** P...

Port of Embarkation.	Contract Ticket Number.	NAMES OF PASSENGERS	Class.	Profession, Occupation, or Calling of Passengers.	ENGLISH.				WELSH.			
London		Mr Charles Beadle	1				1					

Passenger list of the SS *Agadir*, 23 April 1908, with Beadle on his way to Morocco, where he would interview Sultan Mulai-El-Hafid.

Beadle disguised as a dancing girl or, alternately, a holy man, during his June 1908 expedition to Fez, published in the photo essay "A Talk with the New Sultan of Morocco," *The Pall Mall Magazine*, October 1908.

"Your [affectionate] nephew Charlie." Courtesy of Patricia and Liz. "I might have had reason to view some of these encounters with even more miscellaneous feelings, had I known that my guide accounted for my complete disguise by confiding to our assistants that I was a dancing girl bound for the household of a distinguished native official. At other times I was, it seemed, a holy man." ("A Talk with the New Sultan of Morocco.")

(Sideways view:) Rare dust jacket of Beadle's first novel, *The City of Shadows: A Romance of Morocco*, published in the spring of 1911.

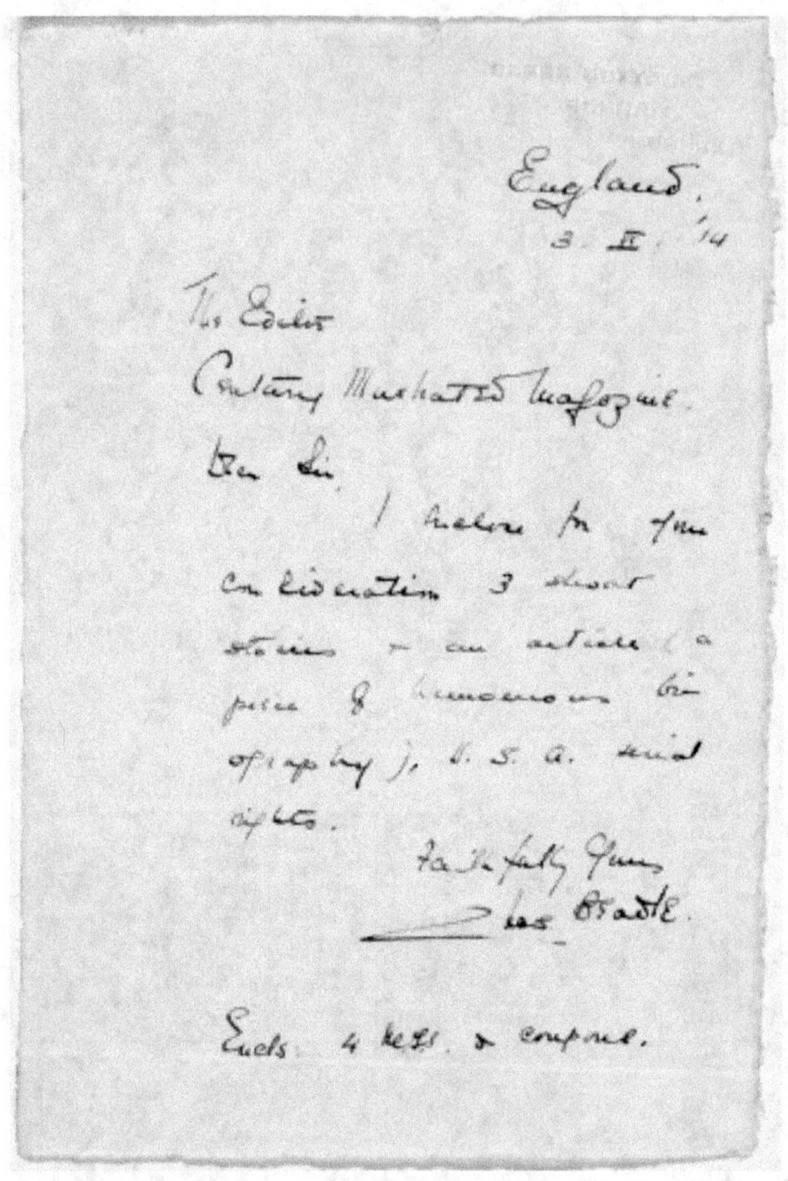

3 June 1914: A letter to the editor of *Century Illustrated*: "England. / 3 VI 1914 / The Editor / Century Magazine / Dear Sir, I enclose for your consideration 3 short stories & an article (a piece of humorous biography) for USA serial rights. Faithfully Yours Charles Beadle Encl. 4 Ms. & coupons." A watermark on top reads: "Creek Cottage, Bosham, Sussex." Courtesy of New York Public Library, Century Company records, Series I.

A PASSIONATE PILGRIMAGE

By CHARLES BEADLE

September 1915: Publication of *A Passionate Pilgrimage*. Hardcover edition, embossed with an image of Beadle's handwriting in red ink.

12 September 1918: A month short of his thirty-eighth birthday, Beadle registers for the military draft in San Francisco, just before relocating to Sausalito. Under the heading "Description of Registrant" it notes that he's of medium height, with a slender build, blue eyes, and gray hair. His occupation is "Novelist." Under "nearest relative" he lists his daughter (then living in Boscombe, Bournemouth, England).

MAIRIE DE CANNES
Alpes-Maritimes

Acte de décès - Copie Intégrale

N° 63

Hornsby
Sylvia Grace Ellen

Le *neuf Septembre* mil neuf cent quinze à dix neuf heures trente, *Sylvia Grace Ellen Hornsby* née à *Londres (Angleterre) le vingt huit Octobre mil huit cent quatre vingt onze*, sans profession, fille de *Edmond William* et de *Teresa Isabelle Hornsby*, épouse de *Charles Beadle*, domiciliée à *Cagnes (Alpes Maritimes)* est décédée à Cannes, *Hôtel Beau Rivage*. Dressé le *quatorze Septembre* mil neuf cent quinze, à *quinze* heures du *[...]*, sur la déclaration de *Joseph Jallier*, Cinquante deux ans, Comptable et de *Antoine Aragon*, Soixante quatre ans, retraité, tous deux domiciliés à Cannes, qui, lecture faite, ont signé avec Nous *Marcellin Bella, Chevalier de la Légion d'Honneur, Adjoint au Maire de Cannes, Officier de l'Etat civil par délégation.*

Copie délivrée selon procédé informatisé.
A Cannes, le 28 juin 2022

Pour le Maire,
L'officier de l'état civil par délégation

Copy of Sylvia Hornsby's death certificate, retrieved by Céline Cardon on 30 June 2022. The French vital statistics bureau had misspelled her surname (it appears in their index as "Homsby"), making its retrieval a particularly tricky task. From this document we learn that Sylvia died at the Hotel Beau Rivage (now known as the Hotel Majestic). This was during a period in which the villas and hotels of Cannes were used as hospitals, especially for the soldiers of WWI. So she essentially died "in hospital" on 13 September 1915.

FACING PAGE:

Circa 1915: A Modigliani portrait of Charles Beadle, titled *Le Pèlerin* ("The Pilgrim"), pencil on paper, 42.5 x 24.5 cm., featured in a Sotheby's catalog for Sale 6019, held in New York on 17 May 1990. The estimated value was set at $40,000 – $50,000.

The catalog caption quotes a passage from *Artist Quarter* in which the narrator says that Modi represented him with "the head of a hunting dog protruding between my thighs." The catalog adds: "There are three similar drawings of young pilgrims in private collections, but none include the dog…. [Modigliani biographer Pierre Sichel] "ascribes much of the [*Artist Quarter*] biography … to Charles Beadle … He attributes the anecdote concerning *Le Pèlerin* to Beadle rather than Douglas."

The anecdote in *Artist Quarter* includes Beadle's statement that the drawing was stolen: "Some years after Modi's death the drawing was on show at Zborowski's gallery – just before the latter's death – and was stolen." (*Artist Quarter*, page 227.) Léopold Zborowski died in Paris on 24 March 1932. Therefore, the portrait was still in circulation in 1930, the year that *Expatriates at Large* was released.

Sotheby's dates it from 1916 to 1917, but by November 1916 Beadle was in New York. A more likely time frame is 1914 to 1916, when Beadle's friend and neighbor Beatrice Hastings was involved with Modigliani. (Note how the date corresponds to the 1915 publication of *A Passionate Pilgrimage*.) Regarding the related "Pilgrim" drawings mentioned above, the Sotheby's catalog cites the authoritative J. Lanthemann, *Modigliani, Catalogue Raisonné*, Barcelona, 1970, pp. 345-346, illustration nos. 774, 778, 779. One of these drawings, titled *Le jeune Pèlerin* ("The Young Pilgrim"), was sold at a Christie's auction on 18 June 2007 for $55,636.20. On page 209 of Beadle's novel *The Esquimau of Montparnasse* (1928), the Esquimau protagonist remarks: "I'm merely a pilgrim, I seek and never find."

Charles Beadle

Collectors are searching all over the world for pictures by Modigliani, the artist who died in obscurity, who has now become a sensation in the world of art. A new Modigliani has just come to light, a portrait of the novelist, Charles Beadle (above), whose new book, "Expatriates at Large," is soon to be published by Macaulay.

From the *Omaha World-Herald*, 23 February 1930, p. 57. On 9 November 2024, John Locke discovered a fifth Modigliani "Pilgrim," and one that includes a hunting dog. Note Modigliani's signature at the top left and the words "Le Pèlerin" at bottom left. If this was the portrait that was stolen and never recovered, its disappearance could explain why it doesn't appear in any catalogs and has, until now, been lost to history. As noted above, Lanthemann's *Catalogue Raisonné* includes three other "Pilgrim" portraits "but none include the dog." The newspaper caption unequivocally identifies it as Modigliani's "portrait of the artist Charles Beadle," which we know was still in circulation in 1930, when *Expatriates at Large* was first published. So, it appears that Modigliani made at least *two* portraits of Beadle as the "Pilgrim."

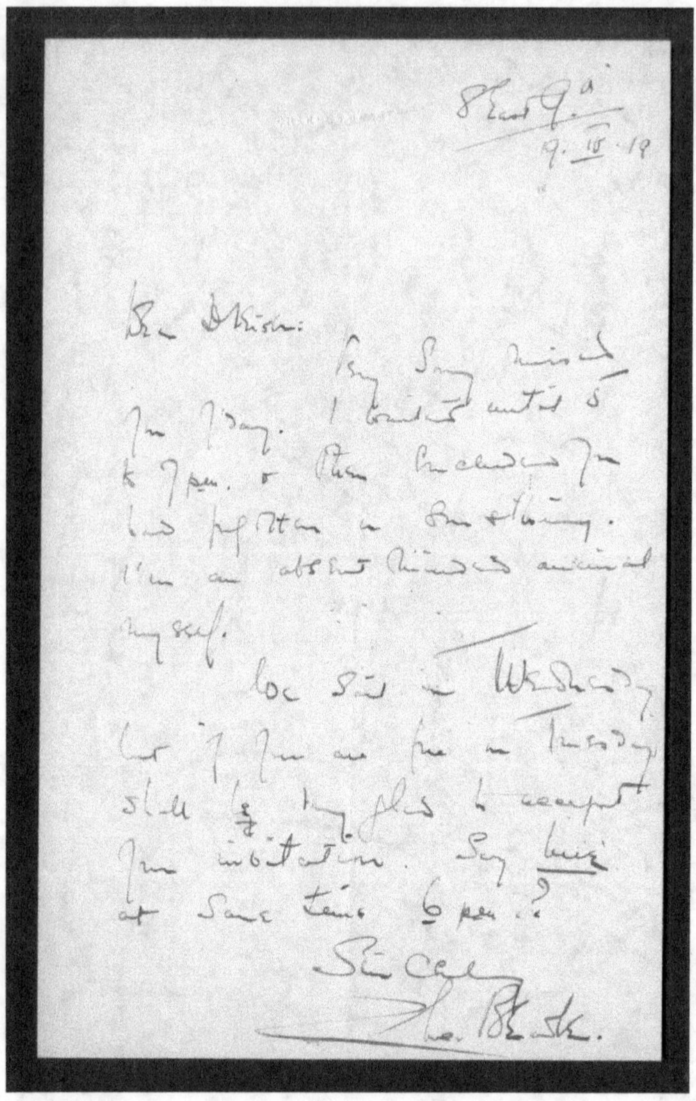

19 October 1919: Letter to author Theodore Dreiser: "8 East 9th / 19.10.19 / Dear Dreiser: Very sorry missed you y'day. I waited until 5 to 7 p.m. and then concluded you had forgotten or something. I'm an absent minded animal myself. We said on Wednesday but if you are free on Tuesday shall be very glad to accept your invitation. Say here at same time 6 p.m.? Sincerely Chas. Beadle." Beadle's flat was located between University Place and Broadway, three blocks north of Washington Square Park. Dreiser lived at 165 West 10th, a half mile west of Beadle. (Courtesy of the University of Pennsylvania, Kislak Center for Special Collections.)

An artistically enhanced photo of Beadle from the 6 April 1930 edition of the *Buffalo Times*, featured in their "Important Books of the Week in Review" column. Reviewer Kate Burr writes: "'Expatriates at Large' is a novel of genuine power. But the power is impaired by a splurge at brilliancy. Too often the cynicism is forced. The dialogue oscillates too sharply between wit and vapidity. Why ignore the intervening gamut?" Thanks to John Locke for uncovering this rare image.

On 18 May 1930 the *Sioux City Journal* published a copy of the same publicity photo but without any enhancement. Writing about *Expatriates at Large*, reviewer Vera Edwards opens her piece ("Paris Quartier Latin Sans Romantic Gloss") with the sentence: "A portrait of Charles Beadle has just come to light, by Modigliani, the artist who died practically unknown and has now become a sensation in the world of art."

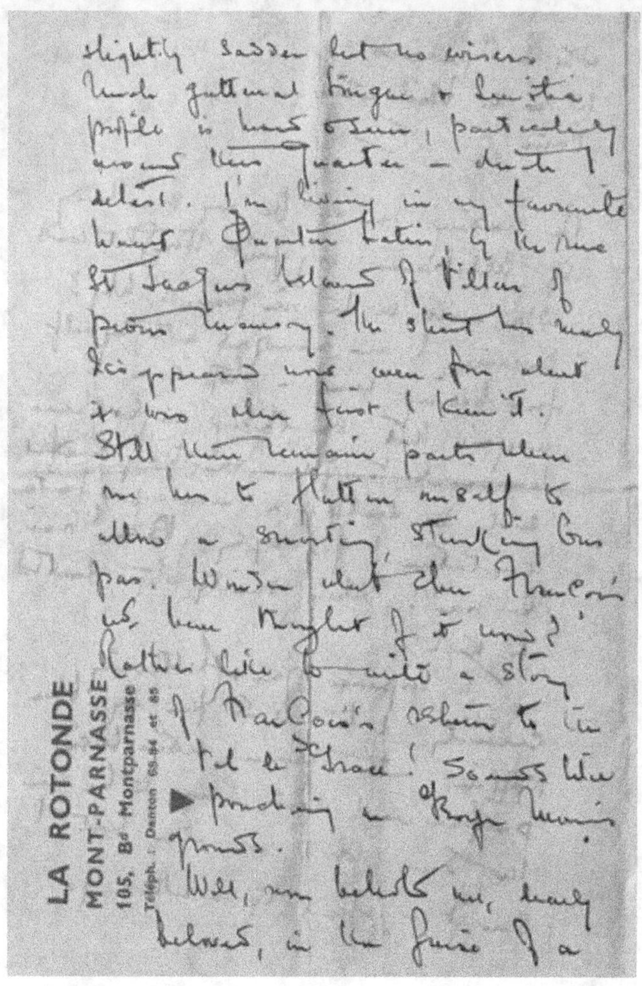

Circa spring 1933: Second page of a letter composed by Beadle and sent to his niece Isabel, with the return address of "Hôtel des Capucines, 13, rue des Feuillantines, Paris." The letter is written on stationery from the Café de la Rotonde, which was located just a few blocks from the Hôtel des Capucines. Courtesy of Patricia and Liz.

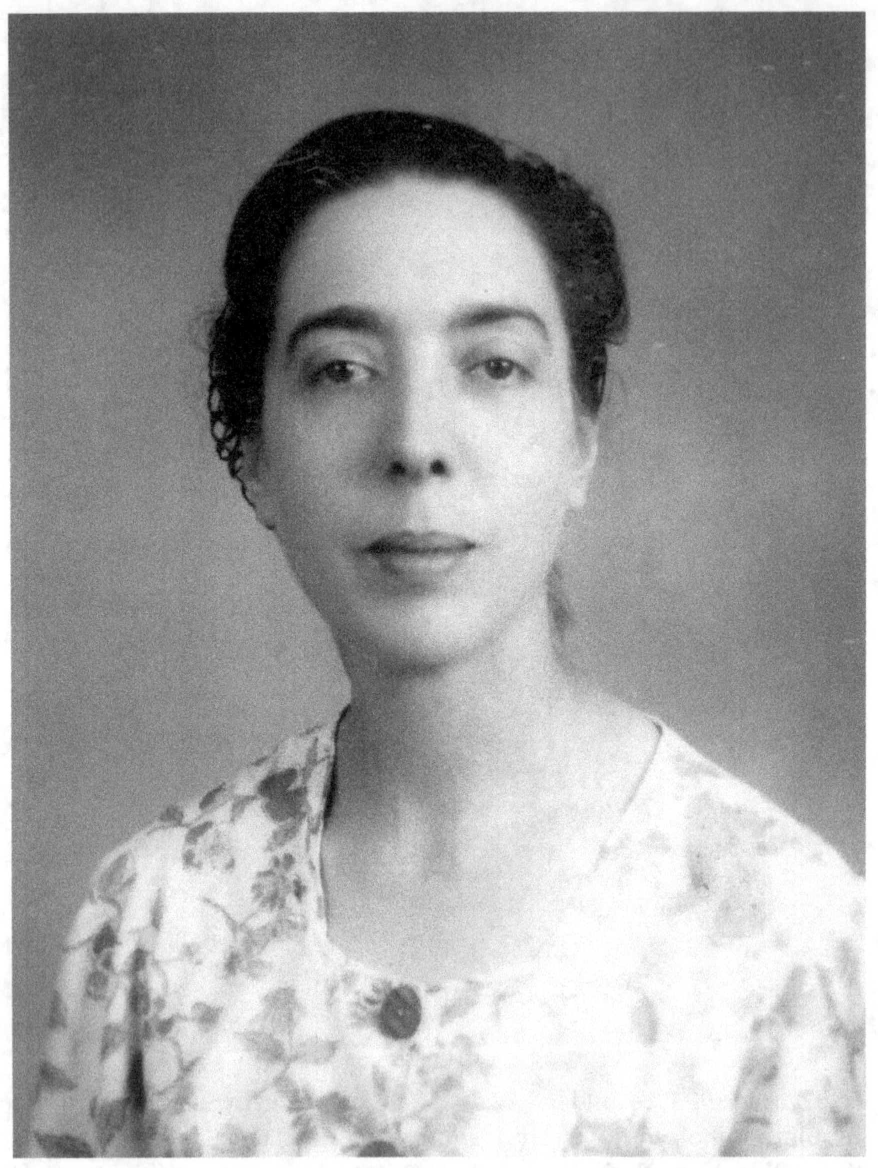

Passport-sized snapshot of Isabel Hettie Beadle (1904 – 1999), daughter of Charles' older brother William. If Isabel is thirty years old here, the photo would date from 1934, when she was corresponding with her uncle. Charles severed contact with the rest of his family, but he conducted a lengthy correspondence with his niece, writing from various locations in France. Courtesy of Patricia and Liz.

When and where born	Name, if any	Sex	Name and surname of father	Name, surname and maiden surname of mother	Occupation of father	Signature, description and residence of informant
Seventh August 1946. 9 Saxonbury Road U.D.	Elizabeth Owen	Girl	Igor Bely	Jane Owen Bely formerly Beadle at 14 Dean Park Road. Bournemouth. U.D.	Chemical Engineer of 29 Rue Assalit. Nice France.	Jane Owen Bely mother 14 Dean Park Road. Bournemouth.

7 August 1946: Birth of Elizabeth Owen Bely, daughter of Jane Beadle and Igor Bely, at 9 Saxonbury Road (about four miles east of Jane's residence at 14 Dean Park Road, Bournemouth, England). Igor is identified as a "Chemical engineer of 29, rue Assalit, Nice, France."

Le _Vingt trois Août_ mil neuf cent soixante deux, _trois_ heures _trente minute_ est décédé _en son domicile 99 avenue Cyrille Besset_ _Elisabeth Owen_ BELY née à _Bournemouth (Grande Bretagne)_ le _sept Août_ mil neuf cent _quarante six_ sans profession fille de _Igor Bely_ quarante six ans _traducteur_ et de _Jane_ BEADLE _son épouse interprète domiciliée à Nice 20 rue Parmentier_ célibataire Dressé le _vingt cinq Août_ mil neuf cent soixante deux, _dix_ heures, sur la déclaration de _et fils de la défunte_

qui, lecture faite a été invité à prendre directement connaissance de l'acte et à le signer avec Nous _____ Auguste VEROLA, Chevalier de la Légion d'Honneur

Adjoint au Maire de Nice, Officier de l'Etat Civil par délégation

Elizabeth Bely died at the age of sixteen on 23 August 1962 at her home at 99, Avenue Cyrille Besset, Nice. Her death certificate identifies her as the daughter of Igor Bely, "translator," and his wife Jane Beadle, "interpreter." Jane's address is listed as 20, rue Parmentier, Nice.

VILLE DE NICE

ACTE DE DECES
COPIE INTEGRALE

N° 005012 / 2002 Jane BEADLE

Le vingt six novembre deux mil deux à une heure treize minutes, est*****
décédée avenue des Roses "Rimiez", Jane BEADLE, née à Saint-Tropez (Var)
le 8 juillet 1915, en retraite, domiciliée à Nice (Alpes-Maritimes) 8,**
avenue Georges Clémenceau, fille de Charles BEADLE, et de Sylvia Grace**
Ellen HOMSBY, décédés ; veuve de Igor BELY.****************************
Dressé le 28 novembre 2002 à 9 heures 28 minutes sur la déclaration de**
COPPOLANI Tony, 39 ans, Chef de Bureau à Nice (06), 3 rue Alexandre*****
Mari, qui, lecture faite et invité à lire l'acte, a signé avec Nous,****
Andrée GUILLAUMIN, fonctionnaire de la Mairie de Nice, Officier de******
l'Etat-Civil par délégation du Maire.********************************

Nice,
le 7 juin 2022,
Pour copie conforme,
L'Officier de l'Etat Civil délégué,

Aurélie FAREY

Jane Beadle's death record, retrieved by Céline Cardon on 13 June 2022. (The surname of Jane's mother is misspelled, and it appears as "Homsby" instead of Hornsby.) Jane lived at 8, Avenue George Clémenceau, but at the time of her death on 26 November 2002 she was at the Avenue des Roses, in the Rimiez quarter of Nice. This quarter also hosts the Hôpital Les Sources, a geriatric institution. The record also includes the name of Jane's husband, Igor Bely (1916 – 1978).

Timeline

2 January 1844. Birth of Charles' father, Henry Beadle, in Barking, Essex, England.

23 May 1849. Birth of Charles' mother, Isabella Kay, in Liverpool.

12 July 1873. Marriage of Henry Beadle to Isabella Kay at St. John's, the parish church in West Hackney, London. According to the marriage certificate, Henry Beadle and Isabella's father, Peter Kay, were both master mariners. Henry's father, William, was a "gentleman." The newlyweds live on Dunlace Road.

12 July 1876. Birth of poet Max Jacob in Quimper, France. Max will later play a major role in Beadle's novel, *Dark Refuge* (1938), portrayed as the character "Isidore 'Izzy' Ginsberg."

27 January 1879. Birth of Beatrice Hastings (née Emily Haigh) in Hackney. Hastings was romantically involved with Amedeo Modigliani while she was Beadle's neighbor in Montmartre and is portrayed in both Beadle's fiction and nonfiction. She also produced the first English translations of Max Jacob's poetry.

25 October 1881. Birth of Pablo Picasso in Malaga, Spain. Born just days apart, Beadle and Picasso will move in similar circles in both Montmartre and Montparnasse.

26 or 27 October 1881. Birth of Charles Beadle at sea, aboard a Merchant Marine vessel, the SS *Cilurnum*, to Isabella and Henry, the ship's captain. Charles is the youngest of four children. (Henry junior, born in 1874, is the oldest, followed by William, and then Catherine, who died after less than nine months.) The family resides in West Hackney, where Charles is raised.

[Age 2] 2 July 1884. Death of mother from "consumption" (i.e., tuberculosis) at sea, while aboard the SS *Cilurnum*.

[Age 2] 12 July 1884. Birth of Modigliani in Livorno, Italy. In *Dark Refuge*, Modi is portrayed as "Ceccilini" (or "Cecci"), and his biography forms a major part of Beadle's *Artist Quarter* (1941). Modigliani composed a pencil sketch of Beadle circa 1915, a reproduction of which was recently rediscovered by John Locke and included in our new edition of *A Passionate Pilgrimage* (Dominantstar, 2025).

[Age 3] 22 October 1885. Sixteen months after the death of Beadle's mother on the SS *Cilurnum*, the ship is destroyed by fire. A court rules "the explosion and the subsequent loss of the said ship was due to the fire generated by spontaneous combustion in the coal which she had on board, and that the master, officers, and crew used all proper measures ... to save the vessel." Source: Merchant Shipping Acts, 1854 to 1876.

[Age 9] 5 April 1891. English census records that the Beadle family is still residing at 80 Benthal Road, West Hackney.

[Age 9] July 1890. Death of maternal grandmother Catherine Owens, who raised Charles while his father was at sea. Perhaps as a tribute of his enduring affection for her, he will later give his daughter, Jane, the middle name of "Owen." (And Jane will give her daughter, Elizabeth, the same middle name.) On 8 March 2009, Beadle's great-niece Patricia wrote to biographer Neil Pearson and said that Charles "had an odd upbringing." When I spoke with Patricia on 6 October 2022 and asked what she meant by this, she said Beadle's father Henry and his second wife, Sarah Killick, "were frequently away at sea on long voyages, so we think the children were cared for by Henry's sister Sarah Beadle, and by Catherine Owens, Charles' grandmother, who lived with them. Catherine was wealthy and blind."

[Age 17] 6 November 1898. Enlists in the British South African Police (BSAP) as Charles "Marmaduke" Beadle, Regimental No. 1019, Matabeleland Division. (Stationed in southwestern Zimbabwe.) According to Beadle's great-niece Patricia, "Charles and his brother joined the South African Police to fight in the Boer War. London was rife with recruiting posters back then. Henry later went missing. He was possibly killed in the war, although there's no military record of his death. I also heard that Henry may have died in a bicycle accident." Source: Conversation with Beadle's great-niece Patricia on 6 October 2022.

[Age 18-21] Abt. 1899 – 1901. Transvaal, South Africa. Serves in the Second Boer War (BSAP), in Morley's Scouts, Stock and Recovery Department. (Source: autobiographical sketch in "The Camp-Fire" column, *Adventure* magazine, 3 July 1918.) During this period Beadle receives various service awards.

[Age 18] September 1900. At age sixteen, Modigliani contracts pleurisy, which develops into tuberculosis.

[Age 18] Fall 1900. Mashonaland, South Africa. Guest of an Englishman named Mason, who owns a large farm. Beadle is nearly killed by a lioness during a hunt organized there on his behalf. (Source: "My Narrow Escape From a Lioness." *The Brooklyn Daily Eagle*, 7 August 1910.) Historian Geoffrey Pocock informed me that "the only Mason who is listed as a Founder-member of the Legion of Frontiersmen in London is Charles "Chinese" Mason, whom Beadle would have known and have met at early meetings." Source: email from Geoffrey, 18 August 2022.

[Age 19] 18 July 1901. Discharged from British South African Police.

[Age 21] Abt. 1902. Transvaal, South Africa. Employed by Transvaal Customs as Assistant Compound Manager, Witwatersrand Native Labor Association. Source: *Adventure*, 3 July 1918.

[Age 22] August 1904. Travels along the Zambezi River, Chikoti, Zambia. The expedition is chronicled in Beadle's essay, "Our Trip Down the Zambezi," published in the *Wide World Magazine* in 1907.

[Age 23] 1905. Henry Roger Pocock forms the Legion of Frontiersmen; Beadle is a founding member.

[Age 23] December 1905. Government House, Fort Portal, Uganda. "Engaged in recruiting and registering fresh porters" for an expedition into the Congo. (Fort Portal: aka Kabarole, formerly of the Toro Kingdom.) Source: Beadle's essay "Two Close Calls" in *The Captain: A Magazine for Boys and "old Boys,"* June 1910.

[Age 23] 5 January 1906. Beadle's expedition embarks from Fort Portal and enters the Congo, where he's attacked by a buffalo and almost killed by stampeding elephants.

[Age 24] Abt. January 1906. Modigliani expatriates from Italy to Paris.

[Age 24] 19 March 1906. Death of father in Buenos Aires. Charles receives a substantial inheritance, including assets that would normally have gone to his brother Henry, who disappeared in South Africa. This allows Charles to finance future expeditions. Source: conversation with Patricia, 6 November 2022.

[Age 24] Abt. 1906. London. Elected as a Fellow of the Royal Geographical Society (FRGS).

[Age 25] January 1907. Residing at 98 Cazenove Road, Stoke Newington, near the street where he grew up. Source: Masonic registry, listed below.

[Age 25] 11 January 1907. London. Initiated into the Masonic Commemoration Lodge No. 2663. Source: United Grand Lodge of England Freemason Membership Registers, 1751-1921; Folio Number 153.

[Age 25] February 1907. Northumberland Avenue, London. Elected to the Royal Colonial Institute. Source: *Journal of the Royal Colonial Institute*, February 1907, p. 138.

[Age 25] May 1907. Publishes photo-essay, "Our Trip Down the Zambezi," in *The Wide World Magazine*. One photo portrays Beadle with his back to the camera, sporting a pith helmet.

[Age 26] June – July 1907. Picasso paints *Les Demoiselles d'Avignon*. Modigliani visits his studio and sees the painting. In the first volume of *A Life of Picasso* (1991), John Richardson calls it a work that "established a new pictorial syntax" and "the first unequivocally twentieth-century masterpiece, a principal detonator of the modern movement, the cornerstone of twentieth-century art."

[Age 26] September 1907. Resigns from the Masonic Commemoration Lodge.

[Age 26] Abt. February 1908. Travels to Borneo. (Source: diary of Roger Pocock, housed at the Bruce Peel Collection, University of Alberta.) In his autobiographical "Camp-Fire" sketch from 3 July 1918, Beadle notes: "Went to Dutch Borneo, rubber planting. Afterward returned to go to Morocco."

[Age 26] 23 April 1908. Embarks from the Port of London aboard the SS *Agadir*, heading for Morocco.

[Age 26] 4 May 1908. Arrives in El Jadida (originally known as Mazagan), a port city on the Atlantic coast. There he secures the services of William Redman, a British merchant and mercenary versed in the local language and customs. Together they travel seventeen km (about ten miles) north along the coast, to the nearby town of Azemmour.

[Age 26] 19 May 1908. Beadle and Redman embark on a steamer, the *Gibel Kebir*, heading further north to Tangier, where they will join Andrew Belton.

[Age 26] June 1908. A confidential memo penned at the British Foreign Office notes that, after departing from Tangier for a fortnight, Beadle will return around 17 June, to reside at the Hotel Cavilla. Source: letter from Lord Mountmorres to Hubert White, Chargé d'Affaires, Tangier, archived at the British Foreign Office. (Appended to 21 June 1908 memo, as noted in Timeline below.)

[Age 26] 8 June 1908. Prevented from traveling from Tangier to Fes due to civil war. Beadle then boards the *Quetzil*, a steamer headed south, to the coastal city of Larache.

[Age 26] 9 June 1908. Arrives in Larache, where he's joined by Redman and Bolton, who had arrived earlier on another vessel.

[Age 26] 10 June 1908. Redman, Bolton, and Beadle travel inland to Ksar el-Kebir, about thirty km southeast of Larache.

[Age 26] 14 June 1908. After a "wretched journey" during which Beadle is disguised as a dancing girl, the expedition arrives in Fes. Source: Beadle's interview with Moulay Hafid, published in *Pall Mall Magazine*.

[Age 26] 21 June 1908. Following Beadle's successful interview with the Pretender Sultan, Hafid, a memo from the British Foreign Office expresses concern that Beadle, Redman, and a third man (presumably Andrew Belton) "are being treated as if on [a] mission from His Majesty's Government. Steps taken to counteract this impression." The memo adds that Beadle and Redman "arrived from Gibraltar via Larache."

[Age 26] 19 August 1908. According to a contemporaneous newspaper report, Beadle and Redman remain in Fes during the Battle of Marrakech: a decisive encounter between opposing sultans that results in the forces of Moulay Hafid defeating the army of Sultan Aziz. (Source: "Swindon Doctor in Fez," *Swindon Advertiser and North Wilts Chronicle*, 5 May 1911.) Beadle later portrays this conflict in his novel, *The City of Shadows*.

[Age 26] Early October 1908. Publishes photo-essay, "A Talk with the New Sultan of Morocco," in *Pall Mall Magazine*. It includes a picture of Beadle in disguise, his face obscured by veils.

[Age 27] 17 November 1908. Camping in South Africa with fellow members of the Legion of Frontiersmen. Source: Roger Pocock's diary, which notes: "Beadle to camp."

[Age 27] January 1909. Socialite Natalie Barney moves from Neuilly to 20, rue Jacob, Paris, where she hosts a famous salon for the next sixty years. Beadle uses her as the model for his character, "Theodosia" (a wealthy sybarite, poetess, and self-identified "androgyne") in the novel *Dark Refuge*.

[Age 27] Circa early 1909 – June 1909. Morocco. Begins to write fiction. Source: Beadle's contribution to the forum "Contemporary Writers and Their Work," published in *The Editor*, 25 February 1920.

[Age 27] Circa May – June 1909. Repatriates to London from Morocco. Source: "What Has Happened to Muley Hafid," *The Sphere*, 3 July 1909.

[Age 28] 9 December 1909. Henry Roger Pocock's diary notes that Beadle was one of several friends who "visited Pocock the day after an operation on his foot," but their whereabouts are not recorded.

[Age 29] October 1910. The first issue of *Adventure* (dated November 1910) appears on newsstands. Beadle will become one of its major contributors.

[Age 29] abt. February 1911. Publication of *The City of Shadows: A Romance of Morocco* (London: Everett and Co.). According to historian Geoffrey Pocock, Beadle's novel offers the "best account" of the Battle of Marrakech. Source: private communication with Pocock, 12 September 2022.

[Age 29] 2 April 1911. Resides at 69 Antrim Mansions, Hampstead, London. Source: 1911 English census, which identifies Beadle as "author."

[Age 29] July 1911. Café La Rotonde opens at 105, Boulevard Montparnasse. (Source: Luc Bihl-Willette, *Des tavernes aux bistrots: Une histoire des cafés*, Paris: L'Age d'Homme, 1997, p. 174.) The Rotonde is prominently featured in Beadle's novels, *The Esquimau of Montparnasse* and *Dark Refuge*.

[Age 30] 23 September 1912. Picasso leaves Montmartre to rent a flat in Montparnasse, at 242, Boulevard Raspail. His studio is a ten-minute walk from La Rotonde, which he patronizes along with Modigliani, Max Jacob, André Salmon, and many other artists and writers, including Beadle.

[Age 31] October 1912. Publication of Beadle's second novel, *A Whiteman's Burden* (London: Stephen Swift and Co.).

[Age 32] 1914. London. Elected as Fellow of the Royal Geographical Society.

[Age 32] 14 March 1914. British Consulate General, Paris. Marries Sylvia Hornsby (1891 – 1915), daughter of Edmund Hornsby (1861 – 1908) and Teresa Ashwell (1866 – 1940). The couple resides at 4, rue de la Grande Chaumière, a few doors away from the famous Académie de la Grande Chaumière (located at 14, rue de la Grande Chaumière), where Modigliani, Gauguin, and many other artists drew from the model. Source: certified copy of marriage certificate, in possession of Beadle's great-niece Patricia, who recalls having a Picasso print in the house, "for which Sylvia probably modeled."

[Age 32] 3 June 1914. Posts a letter from Sussex to New York's *Century Illustrated* magazine, submitting "3 short stories & an article (a piece of humorous biography)." A watermark at the top-right corner of the stationery reads: "Creek Cottage, Bosham, Sussex." Source: New York Public Library, Century Company records, Series I.

[Age 32] 28 July 1914. Austria-Hungary declares war on Serbia.

[Age 32] 1 August 1914. Germany declares war on Russia. The French General Staff issues the Order for Mobilization.

[Age 32] August 3, 1914. Germany declares war on France. The following day, Britain declares war on Germany.

[Age 33] c. 1915. Modigliani creates a pencil drawing of Beadle, composed in Beadle's flat at Place du Tertre. Titled *The Pilgrim*, the portrait is described in detail in Beadle's Modigliani biography, *Artist Quarter*. (See Illustrations, above.)

[Age 33] January 1915. The hallucinatory drink absinthe is banned in France by presidential decree.

[Age 33] 8 Jul 1915. Birth of daughter, Jane Owen Beadle (1915 – 2002), in Saint-Tropez.

[Age 33] 20 August 1915. Letter from former U.S. President Theodore Roosevelt to Charles Beadle, addressed to Beadle's residence at Villa Robinson in St. Tropez, thanking him for sending his book (probably the forthcoming *A Passionate Pilgrimage*).

[Age 33] September 1915. Publication of Beadle's third novel, *A Passionate Pilgrimage* (London: Heath, Cranton, and Ouseley), while Beadle resides at Villa Robinson, St. Tropez. Source: Last Will and Testament of Sylvia Beadle.

[Age 33] 13 September 1915. Death of Sylvia Beadle, in Cannes. According to her death certificate, she died at the Hotel Beau Rivage (now known as the Hotel Majestic) during a period in which the villas and hotels of Cannes were requisitioned as hospitals, especially for the soldiers of WWI.

[Age 34] 13 November 1915. D. H. Lawrence's novel, *The Rainbow*, is banned in Britain. Censors burn over 1,000 copies.

[Age 35] 30 October 1916. Embarks from Cadiz, Spain aboard the SS *Montserrat*, heading to New York. On the ship's manifest Beadle lists Beatrice Hastings as his "closest friend living in country of departure," noting her address at 13, rue Norvins, Paris (Montmartre). His contact information in Manhattan is Paul Tausig, 104 East 14th Street. An ad for the company Paul Tausig & Son appears in the 28 July 1910 issue of New York's *The Call* newspaper, advertising "Steamship tickets to all parts of the world. Railroad tickets to all parts of the United States and Canada. Money orders and drafts sent to all parts of the world. Foreign money bought and sold. Located in the German Savings Bank Building." The manifest indicates that it's Beadle's first trip to America.

[Age 35] 14 November 1916. Arrives in New York City.

[Age 36] March 1918. Outbreak of the Great Influenza Pandemic, with the first documented case occurring in Kansas. By the end of the pandemic in 1920 about 500 million will be infected worldwide, resulting in fifty million to one-hundred million deaths, with 675,000 fatalities occurring in the United States.

[Age 36] 3 April 1918; 3 May 1918. *Adventure* lists Beadle as a travel expert in its "Ask *Adventure*" column. ("A Free Question and Answer Service Bureau on Information on Outdoor Life and

Activities Everywhere and Upon the Various Commodities Required Therein." His area of expertise is Africa: "Transvaal, N. W. and Southern Rhodesia, British East Africa, Uganda and the Upper Congo ... Covering geography, hunting, equipment, trading, climate, mining, transport, customs, living conditions, witchcraft, opportunities for adventure and sport." Beadle's contact info is still c/o Paul Tausig & Son. This is the first of many mail-drop locations that the peripatetic author will provide to *Adventure*: a useful resource for tracking his whereabouts.

[Age 36] 18 May 1918. Publishes "The Christman," the first of twenty-six stories that Beadle will publish in *Adventure*. His contact info is still c/o Paul Tausig & Son.

[Age 36] August 1918. Residing in, or traveling through, Grand Isle, Jefferson, Louisiana. (Source: announcement in *Adventure*, 18 August 1918.) Around this same time Beadle may have visited nearby Mexico.

[Age 36] 12 September 1918. A draft registration card in San Francisco notes that Beadle was living at the King George Hotel on 334 Mason Street, and that he would soon be moving to 119 Central Avenue, in nearby Sausalito. Under "Description of Registrant" it says that he's of medium height with a slender build, blue eyes, and gray hair. His occupation is "Novelist."

[Age 36] 3 October 1918. Contact info in *Adventure* is still Authors' League of America, New York. (Repeated in issues 3 January – 3 February 1919.)

[Age 37] 11 November 1918. Armistice. End of World War I.

[Age 37] 23 April 1919. Departs from New York aboard the SS *Rotterdam*, traveling second class, headed for Paris. His address is registered as 7, Place de Tertre, Paris. Source: Rotterdam, Netherlands, Passenger Lists of the Holland-America Line, 1900-1969.

[Age 37] Late April or early May 1919. Arrives in Paris and resides at the Grand Hotel. Source: Rotterdam, Netherlands, Passenger Lists, etc.

[Age 37] 15 March 1919. *Adventure* publishes the first installment of Beadle's *Witch-Doctors* (a four-part serial appearing between March 15 and May 1, 1919). Published in book form in 1922 by Jonathan Cape (UK) and Houghton Mifflin (U.S.).

[Age 37] 3 April – 3 May 1919. Contact info in *Adventure* is still Authors' League of America, New York.

[Age 37] 18 August – 18 September 1919. Contact info in *Adventure* changes to 7, Place de Tertre, Paris. Repeated in the 3 December 1919 and 3 March 1920 issues.

[Age 37] 19 October 1919. Corresponds with novelist Theodore Dreiser while residing at 8 East 9th Street in Manhattan. Source: University of Pennsylvania, Kislak Center for Special Collections, Rare Books and Manuscripts.

[Age 38] 8 January 1920. Spotted in Paris by occultist Aleister Crowley: "I ran around Paris, and walked into Lapérouse for lunch to find Beadle and Willy!" (The latter was the Pulitzer Prize-winning journalist Walter Duranty.) Source: Aleister Crowley, *The Magical Record of the Beast 666. The Diaries of Aleister Crowley, 1914 – 1920* (London: Duckworth, 1972), p. 90.

[Age 38] 17 January 1920. Volstead Act goes into effect in the United States, prohibiting manufacture and sale of alcohol. Prohibition Era continues until 1933.

[Age 38] 18 January 1920. *Adventure*'s "Camp-Fire" column publishes a letter from Beadle postmarked from Paris.

[Age 38] 24 January 1920. Death of Modigliani.

[Age 38] 25 January 1920. Death of Modigliani's companion, Jeanne Hébuterne, by suicide.

[Age 38] 3 August 1920. Residing in Westminster. Source: announcement in *Adventure*, August 3, 1920: "Care Society of Authors and Composers, Central Buildings, Tothill St., Westminster, London." This same info is repeated in the 18 October 1920 and 16 March 1921 issues.

[Age 38] 3 October 1920. The "Camp-Fire" column publishes a letter from Beadle, postmarked from Paris.

[Age 39] 6 October 1920. Hôpital Cochin, Paris. Death of Modigliani's lover, Simone Thiroux, from tuberculosis.

[Age 39] 18 January 1921. *Adventure*'s "Camp-Fire" column publishes a letter from Beadle, postmarked from Paris.

[Age 39] 21 February 1921. After *The Little Review* publishes excerpts from James Joyce's *Ulysses* in its 1920 issue, the magazine is successfully prosecuted for obscenity, effectively banning *Ulysses* from publication in the U.S.

[Age 39] 3 May 1921. "Camp-Fire" column publishes a letter from Beadle, postmarked from Paris.

[Age 39] 1921. Max Jacob is portrayed by Picasso as a monk in his two large paintings of the *Three Musicians*.

[Age 40] 2 Feb 1922. Sylvia Beach publishes Joyce's *Ulysses* in Paris.

[Age 40] June 1922. After serialization in *Adventure* in 1919, *Witch-Doctors* is issued as a book by Jonathan Cape in London and by Houghton Mifflin in Boston.

[Age 40] 20 June 1922. Beadle's contact information in *Adventure* is now "Île de Lerne," a small island off the northwest coast of France, in the Gulf of Morbihan.

[Age 41] 1923. The Dingo Bar opens at 10, rue Delambre in Montparnasse: the site where Hemingway will meet Fitzgerald, two years later. One of the only all-night pubs in Paris, it will eventually become one of Beadle's favorites. Frequented by artists and writers during the 1920s and Thirties, the clientele includes Pablo Picasso, Aleister Crowley, Nancy Cunard, and Isadora Duncan, who lived in a flat across the street.

[Age 45] April 1927. Publication of Beadle's fifth novel, *The Blue Rib: A Romance of the Riviera* (London: Philip Allan and Co.).

[Age 45] August 1927. Residing in the vicinity of Nice. Source: Beadle's letter to his niece Isabel.

[Age 46] July 1928. An unexpurgated edition of D. H. Lawrence's *Lady Chatterley's Lover* is privately published in Florence. The novel is subsequently declared "obscene" and banned in Britain until 2 November 1960; and in the States until 21 July 1959.

[Age 47] Fall 1928. Publication of Beadle's sixth novel, *The Esquimau of Montparnasse* (London: John Hamilton). A quasi-autobiographical satire about Parisian expatriates, it includes characters based on Modigliani, Beatrice Hastings, Simone Thiroux, and Beadle (as the "Esquimau").

[Age 48] 29 October 1929. A stock market crash ushers in the Great Depression.

[Age 48] February or March 1930. *The Esquimau of Montparnasse* is republished as *Expatriates at Large* (New York: Macauley).

[Age 48] 18 May 1930. The *Sioux City Journal* features a fuzzy image of Beadle, standing in profile, which accompanies a review of *The*

Esquimau of Montparnasse, "Paris Quartier Latin Sans Romantic Gloss."

[Age 49] Circa 1930. Teaching English as a second language at the International School, located at 1, Avenue St-Hilaire, Grasse, Côte d'Azur, France. Source: letter to Isabel.

[Age 49] 19 February 1931. Residing in the vicinity of Nice. Source: letter to Isabel.

[Age 50] Circa October 1931. Visits Paris but doesn't return again until circa May 1933. Source: letter to Isabel, circa spring 1933.

[Age 50] 1 January 1932. Breaks his ankle. After recovering, works as "a cabin boy on a yacht." Source: letter to Isabel, circa spring 1933.

[Age 51] Circa May 1933. Returns to Paris after an absence of "about 18 months." Source: letter to Isabel, circa spring 1933.

[Age 51] May 1933. Paris. The Palais-Royal Press publishes Beadle's seventh novel, *The White Gambit*.

[Age 52] 5 December 1933. End of Prohibition in America.

[Age 52] May 1934. The Dingo's charismatic barman, James "Jimmie" Charters, publishes *This Must Be the Place; Memoirs of Montparnasse*, edited by Morrill Cody, with an Introduction by Ernest Hemingway. Beadle is included in a list of notable patrons mentioned at the back of the book; his favorite drink is said to be a glass of white wine.

[Age 52] 1 September 1934. Jack Kahane's Obelisk Press publishes Henry Miller's novel, *Tropic of Cancer*, which is banned in the U.S. until 1964.

[Age 53] October 1934. Beadle writes a letter to Isabel addressed from the Promenade des Anglais, Nice, which includes the remark:

"The few friends I have are as broke almost as I am. Others don't know me ..."

[Age 56] June 1938. Jack Kahane publishes Beadle's eighth and final novel, *Dark Refuge*. It features thinly disguised portraits of Modigliani, the art dealer Léopold Zborowski, Max Jacob, Beatrice Hastings, and others from the Parisian demimonde.

[Age 57] 6 June 1939. Beadle visits Aleister Crowley at Crowley's home in Chiswick, England: the first of five dinner engagements there, lasting through 23 October (see below).

[Age 57] 1 September 1939. Germany invades Poland.

[Age 57] 2 September 1939. Publisher Jack Kahane dies from heart failure, possibly induced by a suicidal consumption of alcohol.

[Age 57] 3 September 1939. Two days after Germany invades Poland, both France and England declare war on Germany.

[Age 57] 29 September 1939. Beadle is residing at 331 Homewood Road, St. Albans, Hertfordshire. Source: 1939 England and Wales Register. The National Archives; Kew, London; 1939 Register; Reference: RG 101/16681.

[Age 57] 23 October 1939. Chiswick, England. After Beadle's fifth dinner engagement chez Crowley, the occultist notes in his dairy: "Here to pick my brains regarding Montparno" (Montparnasse). Beadle is gathering material for his only nonfiction book, later published as *Artist Quarter*.

[Age 58] 14 June 1940. German troops enter Paris and march on the Champs-Élysées as Nazi tanks rumble around the Arc de Triomphe.

[Age 58] 20 June 1940. Death of Beadle's mother-in-law, Teresa Ashwell, at La Maison Jaune, Chemin de St. Claude, Antibes. She leaves behind an estate worth £113, 17s, 1d. Source: England and Wales, National Probate Calendar (Index of Wills and Administrations), 1858-1995.

[Age 59] June 1941. Faber and Faber publishes *Artist Quarter: Reminiscences of Montmartre and Montparnasse in the First Two Decades of the Twentieth Century*. Coauthored by Charles Beadle and Douglas Goldring under the portmanteau pseudonym "Charles Douglas," the chronicle will eventually be recognized as a seminal work on the life of Modigliani.

[Age 62] October 30 or 31, 1943. Convinced that she's suffering from a terminal illness, Beatrice Hastings commits suicide in Worthing, Sussex. Shortly afterward, Beadle and Goldring receive a manuscript from her estate: a surrealist novella titled "Minnie Pinnikin," written by Hastings in French, which dramatizes her relationship with Modigliani. According to Modigliani scholar Kenneth Wayne, the curator of the Museum of Modern Art, William Lieberman, was preparing for a 1951 exhibit of Modigliani's work "when he was put into contact with Goldring and Charles Beadle by the art historian Douglas Cooper," and "through them he obtained a copy of Minnie Pinnikin." Source: Kenneth Wayne, *Modigliani and the Artists of Montparnasse*, New York: Harry S. Abrams, 2002, p. 205; and private communication with Wayne.

[Age 62] 24 February 1944. The Gestapo arrest Max Jacob in France.

[Age 62] 5 March 1944. Two days before being shipped to Auschwitz, Jacob dies at the Drancy internment camp.

[Age 63] 2 September 1945. End of World War II.

[Age 64] 7 August 1946. Birth of Beadle's granddaughter, Elizabeth Owen Bely, daughter of Jane Owen Beadle and Igor Bely, in Bournemouth, England.

[Age 65] 10 June 1947. *Short Stories* magazine publishes "Nameless Spy," Beadle's last known original publication.

[Age 70] February 1952. *Short Stories* republishes Beadle's "The Idol," a tale that first appeared in their 10 October 1933 issue.

Charles Beadle Publications

<u>Literary and genre fiction novels:</u>

— *The City of Shadows: A Romance of Morocco.* London: Everett and Co., 1911.

— *A Whiteman's Burden.* London: Stephen Swift and Co., 1912.

— *A Passionate Pilgrimage.* London: Heath, Cranton and Ouseley: 1915.

— *Witch-Doctors.* London: Jonathan Cape, 1922. Boston: Houghton Mifflin, 1922.

— *The Blue Rib: A Romance of the Riviera.* London: Philip Allan and Co., 1927.

— *The Esquimau of Montparnasse.* London: John Hamilton, 1928. Later republished as *Expatriates at Large.* New York: Macauley Company, 1930.

— *The White Gambit.* Paris: Palais-Royal Press, 1933.

— *Dark Refuge.* Paris, Obelisk Press, 1938.

<u>Nonfiction:</u>

— *Artist Quarter: Reminiscences of Montmartre and Montparnasse in the First Two Decades of the Twentieth Century* (with Douglas Goldring). London: Faber and Faber, 1941. Published under the pseudonym "Charles Douglas." Later republished as *Artist Quarter: Modigliani, Montmartre and Montparnasse*. London: Pallas Athene Arts, 2018.

<u>Short works of fiction and nonfiction in journals and periodicals:</u>

— "Our Trip Down the Zambezi" (nonfiction). *The Wide World Magazine: An Illustrated Monthly of True Narrative, Adventure, Travel, Customs and Sport*, May 1907.

— "A Talk with the New Sultan of Morocco" (nonfiction). *Pall Mall Magazine*, October 1908.

— "What Has Happened to Muley Hafid" (nonfiction). *The Sphere*, 3 July 1909.

— "Two Close Calls" (nonfiction). *The Captain: A Magazine for Boys and "old Boys,"* June 1910.

— "My Narrow Escape From a Lioness." *The Brooklyn Daily Eagle*, "Junior Eagle" section (nonfiction), 7 August 1910.

— "In the Heart of the Kopje. A Story of the Mashonaland Rebellion." *The Wide World Magazine* (nonfiction), June 1912.

— "The Triumph of Tony." *Windsor Magazine*, July 1912.

— "The Better Man." *The London Magazine*, March 1913.

— "Romance for Sylvia." *Cassell's Magazine of Fiction*, March 1913.

— "A Decade of Christmas Dinners." *The Badminton Magazine of Sports and Pastimes* (nonfiction), December 1914.

— "A Pinch of Fever." *The Badminton Magazine*, June 1915.

— "An African Love Song." *The International*, October 1917. This piece appears to be a translation into English of a traditional African poem. (The same issue of the *International* features a lead story by Aleister Crowley titled "Cocaine.")

— "NQO," *The International*. December 1917.

— "The Palm Tree and the Window." Originally slated to appear in the March 1918 *International*. (In the February issue, under the feature "Jugging the March Hare," Aleister Crowley remarked: "Mr. Charles Beadle brought out his Eastern comedy, "The Palm Tree and the Window.") However the story never made it into print.

— "A Doctor of Men. *The International*. April 1918. (In the March issue, under the title "April Showers of Amusement," Crowley writes: "Charles Beadle contributes a delightful sketch of life in the Latin Quarter of Paris with its curious mixture of religious fervor and debauchery."

— "The Christman." *Adventure*, 18 May 1918.

— "The Autocrat." *Everybody's*, June 1918.

— "The Idol of 'It.'" *Adventure*, 3 July 1918.

— "John O'Damn." *Adventure*, 3 August 1918.

— "The Double Scoop." *Adventure*, 18 August 1918.

— "The Cave." *Adventure*, 3 October 1918.

— "The Winged Avenger." *Adventure*, 18 October 1918.

— "The Black Lure." *Adventure*, 18 November 1918.

— A story in *The International*. December 1918. (In the November issue, in a feature titled "The Editor Boosts the Next Number, Aleister Crowley writes: "A story of African magic by Charles Beadle is really better than any of Kipling's African tales. That's going some, but it is true."

— "Rabbit: Philosopher" (novelette). *Adventure*, 18 January 1919.

— "Witch-Doctors" (novella). *Adventure*, 18 March 1919 (part one); 3 April 1919 (part two); 18 April 1919 (part three); 3 May 1919 (part four).

— "Uncle." *Ainslee's*, April 1919.

— "The Breaker of Idols." *Ainslee's*, May 1919.

— "Red Infidel" (novelette). *Adventure*, 18 May 1919.

— "Through Rabat's Eyes." *Argosy*, 2, 16, 19 August 1919.

— "The Tree of Life" (novella). *Adventure*, 3 August 1919.

— "The White Frog." *Adventure*, 18 August 1919.

— "Through Rabat's Eyes" (3-part serial). *Argosy*, 2, 9, 16 August 1919.

— "Captain Tristtam's Miracle." *Adventure*, 18 October 1919.

— "The Inner Hero." *Romance*, November 1919.

— "The Brothers." *Romance*, December 1919.

— "The Woman Courageous." *Ainslee's*, January 1920.

— "The Alabaster Goddess." *Adventure*, 3 January 1920.

— "Technique." *The Blue Magazine*), February 1920.

— "The Spell." *Adventure*, 18 February 1920.

— Untitled. *The Editor: The Journal of Information for Literary Workers* (nonfiction contribution to the forum "Contemporary Writers and Their Work." A discussion of Beadle's writing process), 25 February 1920.

— "An African Love Song." *Coterie* No. 4, 1920. (Reprinted from *The International*, October 1917.) The *Coterie* journal, a quarterly of art, prose, and poetry, boasted an impressive editorial board, including Conrad Aiken, T. S. Eliot, Richard Aldington, and Aldous Huxley. This particular issue features a poem by Douglas Goldring, who would later coauthor the book *Artist Quarter* with Beadle. It also hosts work by several of these contributing editors, poetry by Amy Lowell, and drawings by Zadkine and André Derain.

— "The Singing Monkey" (novella). *Adventure*, 3 March 1920.

— "The Picture." *The Blue Magazine*, June 1920.

— "The King's Sword." *Adventure*, 3 August 1920.

— "The McIntosh" (novella). *Adventure*, 3 October 1920.

— "The Bowl of Alabaster." *Adventure*, 18 September 1920. (A sequel to "Alabaster Goddess.")

— "The City of Baal." *Adventure*, 18 January 1921.

— "Buried Gods," (novella). *Adventure*, 3 September 1921.

— "The Land of Ophir" (3-part serial). *Adventure*, 10, 20, 30 March 1922.

— "Gifts of Diamonds." *Adventure*, 20 June 1922.

— "The Lost Cure" (novella). *Adventure*, 30 January 1923.

— "Sparklers and the Rascals" (novella). *Top-Notch Magazine*, 1 March 1923.

— "The Ghost of Fat Lung." *Argosy Allstory Weekly*, 4 August 1923.

— "Toll of the Jungle." *Tip Top Stories of Adventure and Mystery*, January 1924.

— "The Alabaster Goddess." *The Regent Magazine*, June 1924. (Reprinted from *Adventure*, 3 January 1920 or 1921.)

— "The Philanthropist" (novella). *Short Stories*. 10 June 1924.

— "White Medicine." *Short Stories*, 10 August 1924.

— "The Blond Spiders" (novella). *Adventure*, 20 December 1924.

— "The Wild Man." *Short Stories*, 25 February 1925.

— "White Magic." *The Frontier*, March 1925.

— "Romance," *Adventure*, 20 April 1925.

— "The Mark of the Leopard." *Short Stories*, 10 May 1926.

— "Hashish," "Voyage," and "Small Body." Bob Brown. *Readies for Bob Brown's Machine*. (Cagnes-sur-Mer: Roving Eye Press, 1931), p. 105.

— "Black Velvet." *This Quarter*. March 1932.

— "The Idol." *Short Stories*, 10 October 1933.

— "Mr. Burnjack's Crime." *The 20-Story Magazine*, January 1935.

— "Magic Head." *Short Stories*, 25 October 1938.

— "The King of Many Voices." *Short Stories*, 10 November 1939.

— "The Explorer's Graveyard." *Short Stories*, 25 April 1941.

— "The Baboon's Paw." *Short Stories*, 10 December 1945.

— "Ant Island." *Short Stories*, 10 October 1946.

— "Lost Heritage." *Short Stories*, 25 December 1946.

— "Nameless Spy." *Short Stories*, 10 June 1947.

<u>Posthumously reprinted stories and collections:</u>

— *The City of Baal*. Introduction by John Locke. Castroville, CA: Off-Trail Publications, 2007.

— *The Land of Ophir*. Introduction by John Locke. Castroville, CA: Off-Trail Publications, 2012.

— *The Blond Spiders* (e-book). Good Press, 2020.

— *The Double Scoop* (e-book). DigiCat, 2022.

<u>Commentary in *Adventure*'s "The Camp-Fire" column:</u>

— 3 July 1918. A detailed five-paragraph autobiographical sketch, from which we can draw various threads from Beadle's early life, including childhood trips into Asia and various titles of employment later in Africa. (The letter was composed circa May 1918. See John Locke's "Introduction" to *The City of Baal*, p. 13.)

— 18 January 1920: A commentary on the walled cities of Zululand (with a passing reference to Sir Richard Burton).

— 3 October 1920. Describes the events that inspired "The McIntosh."

— 18 January 1921. Some remarks about "The City of Baal."

— 20 June 1922. Provides biographical background to "Gifts of Diamonds."

Commentary in *Adventure*'s "Ask Adventure" column:

— "Diseases of East Central Africa." 18 September 1918.

— "The Rhodesian Mounted Police." 18 September 1919.

Letter to *Romance* magazine's "Meeting-Place" forum:

— January 1920. Beadle remarks that "Personally I have a theory that a writer should only use material which he has more or less actually lived. Anyway, I work on that principle." And he adds: "That is all writing is (to me); a mania to tell other folk what I see in my walks abroad."

Reviews of Beadle's Novels

<u>*The City of Shadows* (1911):</u>

— *The Times* (London).

— *Manchester Courier*.

— *Daily Mirror* (London).

— *Westminster Gazette* (London), 11 March 1911, p. 1.

— *Croydon Chronicle and East Surrey* (London), 18 March 1911, p. 20.

— *Globe* (London), 7 April 1911, p. 6.

— *The Academy and Literature* (London), 6 May 1911, p. 555.

<u>*A Whiteman's Burden* (1912):</u>

— *The Athenaeum: Journal of Literature, Science, the Fine Arts, Music and the Drama* (London), 26 October 1912, p. 477.

— *The Scotsman* (Midlothian, Scotland), 4 November 1912, p. 2.

— *The Review of Reviews* (London), 1912, vol. 46, p. 696.

A Passionate Pilgrimage (1915):

— _Freeman's Journal_ (Dublin), 2 October 1915, p. 8.

— _The Devon and Exeter Gazette_, 2 November 1915, p. 6.

— "Echoes from Everywhere: What Men and Women are Talking of." _Liverpool Echo_, 11 November 1915, p. 4. (A list of quotations from various books, including three from _A Passionate Pilgrimage_.)

Witch-Doctors (1922):

— _The Scotsman_ (Midlothian, Scotland), 13 July 1922, p. 2.

— _The Times_ (London), 28 July 1922, p. 13.

— _Punch_ (London), 16 August, 1922, p. 168.

— "An American God." _Westminster Gazette_ (London), 29 August 1922, p. 12.

— _The Province_ (Vancouver), 30 August 1922, p. 6.

— _The Kingston Whig-Standard_ (Kingston, Ontario), 2 September 1922, p. 4.

— _Calgary Herald_ (Calgary, Alberta), 2 September 1922, p. 2.

— _The Topeka State Journal_ (Topeka, Kansas), 9 September 1922, p. 8.

— _The News Journal_ (Wilmington, Delaware), 9 September 1922, p. 8.

— *The Kansas City Star* (Kansas City, Missouri), 9 September 1922, p. 6.

— *Evening Public Ledger* (Philadelphia), 12 September 1922, p. 18.

— *Liverpool Post and Mercury*, 13 September 1922, p. 9.

— *New York Herald*, 17 September 1922, p. 19.

— *Buffalo Morning Express and Illustrated Buffalo Express* (Buffalo, New York), 17 September 1922, section 7, p. 4.

— "Fiction Snapshots," *New York Times Book Review and Magazine*, 17 September 1922, p. 7.

— *Buffalo Courier* (Buffalo, New York), 24 September 1922, p. 15.

— *New York Tribune*, 24 September 1922, section 5, p. 7.

— "Charles Beadle Tells Something about Himself." *Deseret News* (Salt Lake City), 30 September 1922, section 5, p. 3.

— *Detroit Free Press*, 15 October 1922, p. 12.

— *Daily Arkansas Gazette* (Little Rock, Arkansas), 15 October 1922, p. 4.

— *Hartford Courant*, 15 October 1922, p. 13.

— *Democrat and Chronicle Rochester* (Rochester, New York), 15 October 1922, unpaginated, section B.

— "The Witch Doctors." *Oakland Tribune* 15 October 1922, section S, p. 8.

— *The Chattanooga News*, 28 October 1922, p. 8.

— *Omaha Daily Bee*, 5 November 1922, p. 8.

— *The Buffalo Times*, 26 November 1922, p. 45.

The Blue Rib: A Romance of the Riviera (1927):

— *Aberdeen Press and Journal*, 21 April 1927, p. 3.

— *Montrose Standard* (Angus, Scotland), 22 April 1927, p. 6.

— *Birmingham Post* (West Midlands, England).

— *The Observer* (London), 15 May 1927, p. 8.

— *Sheffield Daily Telegraph* (Yorkshire, England), 11 June 1927, p. 10.

The Esquimau of Montparnasse (1928):

— *Sheffield Independent* (Yorkshire, England), 12 November 1928, p. 3.

— *Birmingham Daily Gazette* (Warwickshire), 22 November 1928, p. 3.

— *Northern Whig* (Antrim, Northern Ireland), 24 November 1928, p. 11.

<u>*Expatriates at Large* (1930):</u>

— *Argus-Leader* (Sioux Falls, South Dakota), 9 March 1930, p. 14.

— *Saturday Review of Literature*, April 1930).

— *Buffalo Times* (Buffalo, New York), 6 April 1930, p. 6-B.

— *Buffalo Evening News* (Buffalo, New York), 19 April 1930, p. 4.

— *Kansas City Star*, 19 April 1930, p. 8.

— *San Francisco Examiner*, 20 April 1930, p. 10 E.

— *Boston Globe*, 26 April 1930, p. 13.

— *Sioux City Journal* (Sioux City, Iowa), 18 May 1930, unpaginated. Features a photo of Beadle standing in profile.

— *The Minneapolis Star*, 3 June 1930, p. 15.

— *Birmingham News*, 8 June 1930, p. 4.

— *The Gazette* (Cedar Rapids, Iowa), 22 June 1930, p. 5 A.

— *New York Times Saturday Review of Books and Art*, 22 June 1930, p. 9.

— *St. Louis Post-Dispatch* (St. Louis, Missouri), 2 July 1930, p. 3 C.

— *Atlanta Constitution*, 3 August 1930, p. 8.

— *Detroit Free Press*, 17 August 1930, part four, p. 4.

— *Los Angeles Evening Post-Record*, 19 August 1930, p. 2.

— *Brooklyn Daily Eagle*, 10 September 1930, p. 18.

— *Book Review Digest*, 1931, volume 26, p. 62.

<u>*The White Gambit* (1933)</u>:

— *The Daily Times-News* (Burlington, North Carolina), 10 June 1933, p. 2.

<u>*Artist Quarter: Reminiscences of Montmartre and Montparnasse in the First Two Decades of the Twentieth Century* (1941)</u>:

— *The Observer* (London), 13 July 1941, p. 3.

— *Birmingham Post* (Birmingham, West Midlands, England), 22 July 1941, p. 2.

— *News Chronicle* (London), 1941.

— *Western Mail* (Cardiff, South Glamorgan, Wales), 5 August 1941, p. 2.

— *Time and Tide* magazine (London), 1941.

— *The Gazette* (Montreal), 29 November 1941, p. 21.

Appendix A:

Additional Materials

"Two Close Calls," *The Captain: A Magazine for Boys and "old Boys"*, **June 1910**

I LEFT Toro (Fort Portal), my diary tells me, on the early morning of the fifth day of the New Year, 1906. I had been held up at this Government station for some three weeks, engaged in recruiting and registering fresh porters before crossing the border into the Congo. The Waganda men whom I had brought with me from Entebbe refused point-blank to entertain any idea of entering the country of the Bulamatadi, listening with ready ears to exaggerated tales of the horrors and distances. The Wunyoro, too, were averse to volunteering except at exorbitant rates, usually contenting themselves with doggedly shaking their heads and pretending not to know where such a country was. In many cases they were not lying, as few of them knew aught of any country outside their own districts; the country of the Bulamatadi, the Sudan, and Ulayi (Europe) being all vaguely classified together. At length, by means of judicious baksheesh to Kasagama, the "King," and the Kati-Kiro (prime minister), who would insist upon sitting on my bed in my tent whilst negotiating, succeeded in gathering a bunch of "volunteers." Then came the registering with the Government, at which chance they developed all manner of diseases and divers fantastic reasons why they should be excused.

At last tents were down, and the long line of the "Safari" streamed out past the small Indian bazaar towards the Crater camp, where it is usual to halt; but, considering that this place was in unhealthy proximity to Toro and my men's homes, I pushed them on to the escarpment, a good twelve miles.

Late in the afternoon, I sat upon a convenient rock to enjoy one of the most magnificent sunsets to be seen the wide world over.

By noon next day we reached the Semliki River, and pitched camp upon the opposite bank. Ferrying the loads across occupied the rest of the day. 1 took my rifle and went off to shoot Pookoo – Uganda cob – and a few crocodiles. There was a good deal of buffalo about, so the natives told me; mostly in the foothills and to the southwest. They spoke true words, I discovered.

At two next morning I awoke the camp, and by dint of much blackguarding and calling of names, we got on the move by three. There was no moon, so I had lanterns carried at the head and tail and in the middle of the caravan. We swung along across the plain quite gaily for an hour and a half and were well amongst park bush and cactus. I glanced at my wristwatch, with a thought of calling a halt for the usual spell, when I heard a sudden commotion at the head of the line and noticed the headlight flying across an open space at right angles to the line of march. The middle light went out amid a chorus of yells, and I heard the thump of loads going down and the rustling of flying figures in the grass on both sides of me. The light near me also disappeared, while its bearer fled with an inarticulate yell. At the same moment I heard the sound of furious galloping. I dropped to the ground to get the objects against the skyline. Trees, bushes, and the flying head of a man were silhouetted against the stars; then a grayish mass with a glint of eyes appeared.

It was a charging buffalo!

For a moment I hesitated whether to shoot, fearing to hit any of the men in the darkness. The animal was almost on top of me when I fired hurriedly from the hip and fled away at right angles, as with a snort the beast thundered past behind me. Running through the grass I kicked something soft, which grunted, as I fell head foremost into a bush. I scrambled out, scratched and torn, and sat still watching and listening. The cause of my fall was one of the porters in hiding. I whispered "Obani?" He mumbled something in Lunyoro which I could not understand.

Shouting was still going on some distance up the trail. The buffalo had apparently disappeared, but I knew of old that the animal in question has an inveterate habit of waiting quietly behind a bush and then suddenly charging, usually with disastrous effect to the unwary. Some bushes crackled near[by]. I jumped and peered, but could see nothing. I knew from the thud and snort after firing that I had wounded him, and wished that I had not been so hasty, as otherwise Mr. Buffalo might have gone peacefully on his way, while he would now be probably hanging about minus some blood and very angry.

The men kept shouting to one another at intervals. I heard Kagswa, my headman, asking where I was. I replied, and inquired where the buffalo was, but he did not know and said it was not safe to move in the dark. I asked him where *he* was. He replied, "Up a tree." As I laughed I heard a shriek close by, a snort and pad of hoofs, then a renewed outburst of shouts and inquiries. I felt very uncomfortable, every moment expecting the buffalo to wind me and charge.

I started out to crawl towards the nearest large tree. I dared not stand erect. I climbed up the tree and made myself as comfortable as possible. I could not see any signs of the buffalo; in the next tree was the dark shape of another porter. I tried to see the time, but could not. I shouted to Kagswa, and gradually picked up the voices of several others. A dismal voice came from away on my left. It was the cook; whilst telling his tale of woe his voice ceased abruptly in a stifled yell. The noise of pots and pans clashing sounded. I shouted to the cook again, but could get no answer, and wondered if the beast had got him.

Hanging on to the tree, my limbs got stiff, but it did not seem healthy to wander about in the dark; moreover, I could do no good. I seemed to have been there hours, listening eagerly to an occasional shout of the carriers and the usual voices of the forest, when a faint flush began to appear in the east.

Gradually trees and things grew out of the gloom; in twenty minutes it was broad daylight. I laughed as I took stock of my immediate surroundings. Seven trees were fully occupied with human tenants, three or four in each tree; on the ground, huddled in impossible attitudes and peering about like scared apes, were five more men, one of whom was the cook, unhurt. Round and about, amongst the grass, were bales and boxes.

I climbed out of my perch, and inquired for the buffalo. Nobody knew exactly, but everyone was certain that he was not far away. Then rose a chorus of lament and fearful hairbreadth escapes. One man swore the buffalo had trodden upon him; another had been tossed; yet another declared that the beast had walked up, eyes glaring, and *smelt* him! By degrees the men began to drift in from all quarters of the compass, in various stages of blue funk. I walked round, keeping a wary eye open, I must confess, chaffing those who still clung to points of vantage.

After a while I began to grow confident that the beast had departed. I examined his spoor and searched for traces of blood, intending to follow him up, warily, and try my best to bag him. Under Kagswa's superintendence the men were collecting the discarded loads, and I started off with M'tandwa, my gun bearer, when suddenly a hubbub, preceded by a bloodcurdling yell, arose, and the men hurriedly began to select available trees.

I hesitated for a moment, threatened M'tandwa with unutterable penalties if he bolted with my reserve gun, and advanced cautiously towards the sound of the first yell. We had passed through the next small glade when a man in a tree gesticulated, pointing beyond him. I gave a final glance at my gun breech and, motioning to the gun bearer to keep close in behind me, crept forward. Another man in a tree directed me, and, turning through a patch of bush, half expecting to be rushed at close quarters, I peered through the foliage. The man above got excited, and commenced to chatter. I turned to quiet him, when the rapid "s-s-s!" and pointing finger of M'tandwa drew my attention.

As I looked, I caught sight of the top of the buffalo's head over a clump of bush.

The idiot in the tree broke out again. Like lightning the buffalo whipped round through the intervening bush and, head down and eyes shining wickedly, charged. He had been standing at about forty paces.

I heard the sharp intake of breath of my gun bearer behind me as I brought my gun to my shoulder and felt for a firm stand. I half lowered the rifle, preferring to wait until the beast was clear of the bushes and their shadows. The rising sun behind me shone straight in his wicked eyes as he plunged across the open, lit up the points of my sights, and when within fifteen paces nearer than I had intended, I fired full above the eyes, just under the ruffle of his crest, and leapt aside. keeping my eyes upon him, I shouted for my second gun. There was no need. He crumpled up, shot through the brain, although the impetus of his charge carried him just beyond where I had stood to fire. M'tandwa stood well, putting the fresh gun in my outstretched hand as I watched the last convulsive twitches.

Soon there was much whooping and chanting as the natives gathered round the fallen beast. My cook was early on the scene, keen upon securing the tidbits for me – and himself. I had coffee made and proceeded to breakfast on fresh kidneys, whilst the bearers sliced up the meat amongst them. Kagswa reported five loads missing. The delinquents were named and dispatched, with a headman, to find them on pain of forfeiting their share of meat plus the usual penalties. They found them.

II.

It was nine o'clock before the caravan got under way again, and only by the use of much breath, chaffing, bullying, and jeering did I succeed in persuading them to reach the village on the top of the Congo plateau. On the next hill to the east was the site of one of Stanley's famous camps, overlooking Lake Albert.

Many of Emin Pasha's old soldiers had settled down in this region; one of them was a titular chief of this village. I arrived there about four in the afternoon. It had been a stiff uphill climb in the broiling noonday sun all the way from the place of the buffalo episode.

During the rest of the afternoon the carriers arrived in twos and threes. For the last half mile the track wound round and up the side of a hill nearly as steep as the escarpment on the Uganda side, and I was deeply thankful to loll in the shade of a deserted mission house just outside the village stockade.

Some minutes elapsed ere the chief appeared, during which a considerable commotion ensued inside the village. At length he showed up, bearing a bowl of fresh milk, for which I blessed him, in kind as well as words. He had at first thought that I was a Belgian; later he diffidently explained that my approach had been noticed and that he had been busy sending off his flocks and herds to a safe health resort in the hills, but now it was all right. He didn't seem to like the Belgians somehow. He had just begun to explain that there was another white man there, when a voice said:

"Hullo! it's an Englishman!" and a tanned, stalwart figure, clad in shirt and khaki slacks, advanced and shook hands.

We dined together sumptuously on buffalo steaks, and

chatted far into the night, after the manner of the exile. He was engaged in trading and elephant shooting, and invited me to join in a hunt on the morrow. I accepted with alacrity. Kagswa was summoned and instructed to tell the men that we would not march in the morning. Kagswa delightedly bawled the news to the gorging savages spread in numerous rings around their respective fires.

About two in the morning we lay down to snatch a brief sleep. At four-thirty Kagswa awakened us, bringing coffee and biscuits, and, together with our friend the chief and three of his men, we left camp, and struck downhill to the west. A steady tramp of nearly an hour, mainly through dense forest – the fringe of the famous Ituri forests – and we came hot upon the spoor of our quarry. Several times as we marched we heard the crash of bushes and saplings, indicating their proximity. It was close upon sunrise when, from the top of a small hill, covered with eight-foot elephant grass, we saw vistas of herds and herds of elephants. The greatest danger in such a stiff country is when the herds, other than the one under consideration, take into their vast noodles to stampede. Several and distinct herds of elephants rushing excitedly about, in different directions, through stuff which is only as grass to them but like a Hampton Court maze to a human being, has sufficient potential sensations to titillate the most jaded of palates. An African elephant is as blind as a bat and as deaf as a post, figuratively speaking; so the obvious safety zone is not necessarily distance, but up wind.

To obtain this strategic position we maneuvered successfully, as regards our own particular herd; but the others interfered. Numerous avenues had been made by the passage of the brutes, the elephant grass standing like a wall on either side, criss-crossed in every direction. We walked openly – that is, upright – in single file, and our guides led us to within two hundred yards of the selected herd. After a whispered consultation we crept forward cautiously, with M'tandwa and the chief in attendance, through a small belt of dense forest.

From the edge we could see about ten elephants, one quite close and apart from the others. All were standing up to their knees in swamp. Some, filling their trunks, spouted the water over their own broad backs; others tore off bunches of twigs; all were making a vast amount of noise, snorting and squelching about amid the crackling of young timber.

M'tandwa, who had left our side, suddenly reappeared to the right, signaling. We followed up a track, crouching. "Hiya," said the native, indicating the lonely one, "obaya sana" (She no good). "The King of elephants is quite close. Come!" We followed, plunging back into the forest. Presently there came a sibilant "s-s-s."

Peering through the interstices, we saw the heads and shoulders of several elephants. Lying flat in the grass we wriggled closer, dragging our guns along the ground. Another forty paces, and M'tandwa stopped, finger on lips, and slowly stood up under cover of a bush. Presently he signaled dumbly to my friend and Kagswa to go to the left, motioning myself to follow him. I did so. Then came another wriggle for sixty paces at right angles ere M'tandwa halted, peeped through the top of the grass, and grinned, opening wide his hands to indicate huge tusks.

I had placed wads in the muzzles of the rifles to protect them during the crawl through the swamp. I withdrew them and looked to the breeches of both. I was soaked to the skin, very muddy and scratched all over. Rising cautiously, I located the elephant indicated by M'tandwa. He was standing motionless, his huge tusks gleaming, about sixty paces away, and three-quarters on; I dropped down and crawled around a little to improve my position.

I wondered how the others were progressing. I dared not delay my shot for fear he might move or go away. Drawing a very careful site on almost the rim of his huge ear, and low down, I fired. I heard the dull thud of the impact. Simultaneously another shot rang out not far away, and then came shrill trumpetings and a crashing of saplings and bushes. My beast had disappeared, apparently swallowed up by the earth.

I started forward to explore when M'tandwa, his face a dirty ash color, caught my arm.

"Listen! Said he, indicating the rear of our position. I did so; and suddenly became conscious that the trumpeting and crashing had increased to a pandemonium which came from all around us. *All the elephants in the valley had stampeded in different directions, and we were in the center!*

I did not know what to do and felt myself go icy cold.

"Upesi! Miti! Upesi!" (Quick! The trees!) cried M'tandwa. We ran back, slipping and stumbling in the elephant tracks, to the nearest trees. Halfway there, the screaming and the crashing increased in volume right ahead of us. Then out of the gloom of the forest charged a herd of elephants, trunks up, shrieking in blind fright, young trees and bushes bowing down before them like an asparagus bed before a lawn roller. It was worse than useless to fire; one might as well have attempted to stop an avalanche. M'tandwa yelled, flung down my spare rifle and fled to the right. I hesitated; then followed suit in the opposite direction.

No sooner had I commenced to run, or flounder, than I lost my nerve completely. I believe I yelled, too, in my agony of fright. The whole universe seemed full of leviathans intent upon stamping me to death. I imagined the black stinking ooze being forced into my mouth and ears. I saw myself after, a mere indistinct jumble of mud, blood and grass. I fell several times in the huge footprints. I lost the perspective of things; I seemed to have been racing for miles and miles; I became horribly conscious that one of my leggings was undone; then the vast, thundering army behind seemed to loom over me, and I shrieked with terror.

A sudden stumble; a vision of black-brown hides, trees, sky; a splash, and cold water closed over my head. I had fallen into a pool or elephant wallow. I crawled out, gasping, and lay in a tumbled, panting heap half out of the pool of mud and water, trembling with fright and shock, whilst the crashing of bushes all about me sounded like thunder in my ears.

At length the hubbub subsided. I lay where I was, too scared to move. My nerves had completely gone for the time being. I literally jumped at every sound. After a while I started to shout, and at length was answered by Kagswa.

The elephant I had fired at lay dead some distance away. My friend and Kagswa had had ample time to climb into a large tree, from the branches of which they shot two more. As for M'tandwa – alas! the elephants who missed the master did not miss the man.

Review of *A Passionate Pilgrimage* from the *Devon and Exeter Gazette*, 2 November 1915, p. 6

'A Passionate Pilgrimage,' by Charles Beadle, author of 'The City of Shadows,' 'A White Man's Burden,' etc. (Heath, Cranton, & Ouseley, Ltd., Fleet-lane, E.C.), is a book which is fated to meet with a varied reception. Some libraries have banned it, others have it in circulation, so that, in view of the conflicting attitudes assumed, the author and publishers would be interested to know the opinions of readers. Those opinions will be influenced by the point of view from which the perspective is taken. The man about town may see nothing in the book to object to; there are, on the other hand, many who will fail to see what benefit is conferred upon the public by writing such a work. As a literary effort the book is decidedly good; there are descriptions of bush life, manners, and scenery which are admirably detailed and intensely interesting. Wit, humor, and philosophy are found in abundance, and the story is one which is by no means overdrawn. Lads fresh from the country on going to London fall into temptation. They fancy themselves in love with some country miss, but their constancy disappears as they are drawn into the vortex of London life. And so Jim forgets Madge, and fancies himself in love with Eve, a seemingly pensive miss who soon throws off her cloak of reserve. They dine together, meet frequently, and, what is not at all an uncommon thing, end up by living together. Then Jim runs away to South Africa to rid himself of responsibilities. But he is ever susceptible to the charms of women, becomes entangled again and again, but fails to reach the heights of happiness until he lands in Cornwall. Few obtain a glimpse of the Lamp of Truth, save by bitter experience, and this Jim has to swallow to the full. Does the relating of such bitter experience enable men and women, youths and girls who are in pursuit of the Blue Bird, to avoid pitfalls and hidden dangers? In some cases, yes; in others, no. It is questionable whether the policy of keeping young people in ignorance of the results of sex impulse is the wisest course to adopt, but there is, again, the question whether or not the discussion of so important a question is matter for wide publication or should not be a more sacred duty imposed upon parents. We object strongly to literature of a pornographic character, but there are dangers associated with hiding the truth. There should be, and is, a happy medium in giving warnings and instructions. The "Passionate Pilgrimage" has, perhaps, not quite found that medium, and, as we have said, it will not suit all tastes. It is clearly not a volume for the family circle.

———————————

Commentary in *Adventure*'s "Camp-Fire" column, 3 July 1918

Charles Beadle's story in this issue is not his first in our magazine but, though he followed our established custom and sent in his self-introductory talk to the Camp-Fire, the mails brought it too late to appear along with his former story, the Christ man, so here it is in the issue with "The Idol of It":

My native heath is somewhere in mid-Atlantic. I was born rolling and have been ever since. No moss. My infancy was spent around Siam and the farther East: early memories, fire-flies mosquitoes and ayahs. ["Ayah": a nurse or maid native to India.] Educated at boarding schools in England; hence no home life and consequent atrophy of the sentimentalities. Parental Government required me to become a consulting marine engineer; but a congenital dislike of work and a gaudy poster persuaded me to learn poker, to starve in Cape Town where I held down a waiter's job for four hours and to join the British South African Police.

Too late for big rebellion but kindly chief got up a small one to console me; saw Boer War in B. S. A. P. [British South African Police], Morley's Scouts (unpaid Looting Corps) (if any of the Scouts should read this should be glad to hear from them) and Stock Recovery Dept. After Peace held various jobs from three days to a week – in a news office, a bar, hawker, insurance agent – and peddled cheap jewelry for three months (and made money!); served in Transvaal Customs and became Asst. Compound Manager to the Witwatersrand Native Labor Association.

Then I raised a syndicate to support me for an exploring-trip on the headwaters of the Zambezi. Returned to London to promote a company; failed – of course. A head on a coin sent me to British East Africa and Uganda; native trading, running transport from Victoria Nyanza to the Kilo Mines, Congo; shooting and various ventures. England again, company promoting; and failed again.

Went to Dutch Borneo, rubber planting. Afterward returned to go to Morocco; penetrated into interior in disguise during rebellion; met Pretender Sultan, Mulai Hafid; instead of cutting my throat or crucifying me as predicted he gave me a palace and an escort and treated me as an ambassador; eventually I failed and Hafid lost his throne. We both had a royal time, anyway.

Until I came to America last year I have lived in France.

The material of the "The Idol of It" was gathered in the forests of the Upper Ituri district of the Congo when I was running caravan from Entebbe to Kilo. As brothers of the solitude know, many strange things happen and stranger states of mind come to pass. The trick of chatting to a photo or a magazine cutting for the sake of companionship and hearing your own white voice is not uncommon. I've done it myself. In the Police I had a mate on an outstation who did go crazy. He was given his discharge later, started off to walk (!) to Umtali and encountered a lion. Apparently the lion was not dying for social companionship as poor old Denham was!

The scene of "The Christman" is laid on the upper waters of the Zambezi: in fact, the exact village is indicated. The story was founded – or rather suggested – by an incident which happened on my trip. A bearded gentleman – as described in the story – arrived at Livingstone from nowhere in particular with a wonderful tale of hidden jewels and buried Ivory in the southern Congo. A prospector named Poindextre fell for it and financed the safari. Just after they had gone we heard that our bearded friend was wanted for murder and robbery in Cape

Town. The next thing was that Poindextre was found nearly dead with blackwater fever in a native kraal. His charming partner had abandoned him in the bush, taking guns and outfit. Natives had found him. He recovered, came down to Livingstone, had a relapse and died. "Miêville" was never heard of again.

From "Ask *Adventure*," 18 September 1918

"Diseases of East Central Africa"

Question: – "I have knocked about considerably in various countries and it has long been my desire to visit the "dark continent." I have roughed it a great deal, am a good shot, etc., etc.

(1) "What are health conditions around and between Lakes Tanganyika and Victoria? That is, is it a healthy region?

(2) From an African point of view is it heavily forested?

(3) Is game more or less abundant there than in other parts of the interior? Especially large game, *i.e.*, of cat and herb-eating species?

(4) Can one live off the country outside medicinal and other necessities not furnished by nature?" – W.E.C., Belmore, Ohio.

Answer, by Mr. Beadle: – (1) Health conditions between Lakes Tanganyika and Victoria are fairly bad. Malaria, spirillum, blackwater, and sleeping sickness are the principal diseases. In case you are not familiar with these I will explain briefly, taking it for granted that you know what malaria is.

Spirulam is given to man by the bite of a tick and produces a fever very like malaria, but quinine has no effect; it lasts some time and knocks you out, leaving the patient usually very weak, but never have I heard of it being fatal.

Blackwater is violent inflammation of the kidneys (it is a matter of dispute whether blackwater is the result of excessive malaria or not) resulting in the urination of blood (hence the name). Very often fatal as the patient dies of heart failure. Medicines are calomel and purge thoroughly (stop quinine), and as much champagne and brandy as the patient will take with the object of keeping up the heart's action, on which everything depends. If you get blackwater once and get over it my advice is to clear out of the country.

Sleeping sickness is given by the bite of the tsetse fly (rather like a horsefly with the wings crossed). First produces a slight fever, headaches, etc., and perhaps vomiting, afterward affects the nervous system with the result that patient becomes restless, irritable and indifferent by turns until finally he lapses into a coma – sleep – attendant with anemia and a general wasting away. There is no cure yet discovered. The percentage of these flies with the germ in them ready for business is reckoned to be about two per cent.

But still don't run away with the idea that the country is fatal. I've lived there and the only thing I collected was malaria and not much of that.

(2) From a general African point of view it is fairly wooded. That is[,] compared to the Congo forests the forest there is slight and variable. There are uplands with open rolling country and scrub.

(3) Game (large) is fairly abundant but varies greatly. Stretches without game at all and in other parts extremely thick – of both sorts.

(4) No, you cannot reckon on living off the country. Chickens, eggs, and sometimes goats and milk are obtainable at villages by trading – if the natives happen to be friendly and they usually are if you know the way to go about it. Game is too

erratic to rely upon. One week you may have enough to feed a caravan to gorging and the next not enough for a dog, and as for said villages there are large tracts uninhabited. Sometimes you can get sweet potatoes, but rarely in my experience. And Nature's supply of food for man, white men particularly, is conspicuous by its absence in most of Africa.

From "Ask *Adventure*," 3 November 1918

"Travel in Upper Congo"

THIS inquirer puts thirteen questions to our expert with regards to people and things in that region of Africa made famous by Stanley and Livingstone. Here's hoping the number of his queries won't hoodoo his expedition:

Question: – "I am a young man interested in taking a trip to the Upper Congo in Africa, and would like the following information –
   "1. – What are the opportunities for adventure?
   "2. – How are the customs and living conditions?
   "3. – What are the chances for big-game hunting?
   "4. – What kind of an outfit should be taken?
   "5. – Are there any working opportunities?
   "6. – What kind of languages must one have at command?
   "7. – Is witchcraft in practice yet in Africa?
   "8. – Where could I get a map of Africa?
   "9. – How much is the fare from New York?
   "10. – Which is the best way to go from New York?
   "11. – What are the methods and materials of Summer and Winter subsistence?

"12. – What is the best remedy for poison-snake bites?

"13. – Could outfits be bought in Africa?" – William F. Feser, Brooklyn, New York.

Answer, by Mr. Beadle: –

1. – Every chance for adventure with animals and man, crocodiles and flies.

2. – I take it you mean white man's customs. Practically only Belgian officials in the country (who are composed of nearly every nationality in Europe). You carry your own chow, canned goods; live on them, chickens and eggs (when you can) and game (when you can). There are no stores in Upper Congo as all trading is governmental.

3. – One of the finest elephant countries in Africa; also large game of all descriptions. But all game is preserved. You have to get a special license for elephant. As far as I recollect the license is about the same as on the British side: two hundred and fifty dollars for two male elephants, which carries with it about two of every species of buck.

4. – See Answer 13.

5. – Practically none. Both jobs on the Kilo mines and all others are given (or were) from Brussels.

6. – French absolutely necessary; if staying in country have to learn Kiswahili, otherwise you will always be at the mercy of a highly paid interpreter.

7. – Yes. Not to the extent that it was in districts that are under immediate white supervision; but there are vast tracts that are not.

8. – New York Public Library; to buy one go to Brentano's and ask for section maps of Upper Congo. The French are the best.

9. – Impossible to say as all steamship prices are altered now. But remember that after reaching the mouth of the Congo you have half a thousand miles by river-boat to Stanleyville or some other jumping-off place and then another half a thousand

through the forests. To get to the Upper Congo that way I should say roughly would swallow most of the small change out of five hundred dollars. If you went round to the east coast, up the Uganda Railway and across Uganda the trip would be easier but not less expensive.

10. – Again impossible to say in present conditions. If possible go to the Canaries and get a Holt or Elder-Dempster boat down the coast. Rest of the trip answered in 9.

11. – There is no Winter or Summer in tropics as we know them here. Two rainy seasons, but temperature much alike all the year 'round. Rest answered in 2.

12. – I don't know of any sure remedy. Sometimes alcohol will pull a man through; chief endeavor is to keep him awake at all costs.

13 (and 4). – Rot-proof tent, camp-bed and bar, medicine-chest, helmet or Tirai hat, usual tropic whites and khaki hunting-clothes, battery of light and heavy rifle, revolver are the chief points. On east, north, and south coasts you can buy outfits, and I suppose on the west, although I cannot say for sure as I have never been there. Ask Mr. Miller, Section 22 of "Ask Adventure" if you intend to go.

Hope this is useful to you although I'm afraid that it isn't very encouraging.

Commentary in *Adventure*'s "Camp-Fire" column, 18 January 1919

WHEN we first read Charles Beadle's novelette that appears in this issue [*Rabbit: Philosopher*] Hayes seemed such an exaggerated type of American that we wrote Mr. Beadle asking whether Hayes' extreme line of talk hadn't better be toned down a bit. He replied that Hayes really happened, that he was drawn from life. And yet, to many Americans, he will seem as exaggerated as he did to us in the office, so we're just playing safe by stating the fact that Mr. Beadle, an Englishman living in this country, didn't think he was drawing a typical American but knew he was drawing a particular and actual one. It's the old business of truth being stranger than fiction. Many a story is rejected because, though really true, to the average reader it would seem more incredible than the wildest fiction.

From "Ask *Adventure*," 18 March 1919

"The Rhodesian Mounted Police"

HERE'S a good service for those who've had a taste of war, and like it, as so many of the fellows do:

Question: – "I should like to get some information concerning the Rhodesian Mounted Police, especially concerning the work they do. I should also like to obtain the titles of any books written about them. If this letter is published in *Adventure* please withhold my name." –, 33rd Inf., Gatun, C.Z.

Answer, by Mr. Beadle: – The Rhodesian Mounted Police are the British South African Police with headquarters at Bulawayo and Salisbury, South Rhodesia. They are military police; mounted but usually on foot by reason of the horse sickness. Mostly stationed at posts on the *veld*, where they patrol among the natives and assist in collecting hut tax, etc.; arrest cattle thieves, odd murderers, etc. Those in towns do patrol through town and reservations (forestry, farms, etc.). Some stations are fairly healthy; others rotten with malaria. Pay: troopers, five shillings per diem. Commissions through ranks; except for O.C.'s, usually seconded for service from the regulars. At one time used regularly to be provided with rebellions; but this practice has become unfashionable of late years.

I am speaking of the police in my day – about 1900. Since the Boer War they have probably – I have not heard so – been incorporated with the South African Constabulary (Transvaal and Orange Free State – that is, Orange River Colony now). Baden–Powell wrote a book on them in the early days, but have no means of looking up title here. For information apply to Secretary, the British South African Chartered Company, London Wall, London, G.B.

Hope this is of service. If other details are required, write me. But I have no up-to-date information.

From "Ask *Adventure*," 18 August 1919

"Juba Land, British East Africa"

BEFORE going into the tropics, it's the wise man who learns what manner of folks and things, pleasant or otherwise, he must prepare to face:

Question: – "I am shortly going out as a radio operator to a station in East Africa Protectorate. The station is at Kismayu, Juba Land, and I shall probably be at other stations in Juba Land as well. I should like you to tell me something of the district, especially of the living conditions, and the characteristics of the natives.

I should be interested to hear of the superstitions and witchcraft of the latter. I should like to know of any out of the ordinary dangers and special precautions, and also what style of a small, handy revolver you would recommend." – L. A. WOODHEAD, Bradford, England.

Answer, by Mr. Beadle: – I am unable to give you any precise details of the particular district of Juba Land as I have never actually been there. But it is *Iknow-Kismayu* – on the coast – and therefore general climatic conditions apply. It is fairly hot and humid and probably mosquito-ridden, which means malaria.

There is no certain preventive against malaria that I am aware of. Various people, various theories. Some take five grains of quinine every day; others, on Koch's principle that the parasite takes twelve (about) days to develop, take ten grains every week on the obvious idea of soaking the possible agent before he gets busy. Again, others never touch quinine except when they actually are down with malaria.

Living conditions will probably be in a Government bungalow, with native servants or a mess; probable canned goods mostly, unless you happen to have a township nearby to get occasionally beef or goat. Eggs and chickens galore will probably be your chief article of fresh diet.

Neither clothes nor outfit would I advise you to bother about in England. You will most likely land at Mombasa where are stores from which you can get anything you want in tropical outfit for living or hunting.

General health hints are: take exercise, keep the bowels always open; that's the principal thing; don't drink; I mean excessively, as most are inclined to do in the monotony of up-country life. Drink has killed far more than malaria ever did; avoid being bitten by mosquitoes as much as possible; and never drink unboiled water.

Any make of revolver or automatic would do; but there is little possibility that you will ever need one. A shotgun would be more useful for sport and self-protection. Also, a rifle, say a sporting Mauser or .303, as you may get good shooting in the neighborhood.

Regarding witchcraft and superstitions: good Lord! that would mean a book or two. If ever, when you are out there in the years to come, when you have some of the dialects and you should come across any unusual beliefs or practices among the natives, I should be very glad to hear of them from you. Care of the Authors' League of America, New York, will always find me.

Letter to *Romance* magazine, January 1920

CHARLES BEADLE, who wrote "The Inner Hero" for our November issue, also writes this greeting from Paris:

ALLAH yahdik O Romance! as the Arabs would say. However, that's another side of my life than the milieu of "The Inner Hero." Personally I have a theory that a writer should only use material which he has more or less actually lived. Anyway, I work on that principle. I was born at sea somewhere in mid-Atlantic and my people have been seafaring on both sides for some generations back; two grandfathers were North Sea Whalers – which doesn't in the least prove that I know anything about it you will probably say! Well, the tang of the sea seems good to me and I will defy any storm on any ship on any sea to make me seasick. The most exhilarating spectacle in the Universe to me is a storm at sea – preferably in mid-Atlantic – my native heath! Naturally I met with sailors and firemen of all sorts in my kidhood, but the principal material for this story was gained during an abortive attempt to become a marine engineer; about twelve months in the "shops" which persuaded me, incorrectly enough, that there was no romance in greasy pistons, valves and what not and set me wandering in Africa for a decade. I'm afraid that this confession won't convince anyone that I really lived that life; that I have done more than walk through a portion of it as it were. But then the whole point depends on what one can see in that walk, the possession of the "seeing eye" as Conrad has it. After all, baldly speaking, that is all writing is (to me); a mania to tell other folk what I see in my walks abroad. As Arnold Bennett, I think, pointed out once, the primitive novelist is the man who insists upon telling all his pals, often, to boredom, about the astonishing dog fight he has seen in the street.

Charles Beadle.

Commentary in *Adventure*'s "Camp-Fire" column, 18 January 1920

HERE is some more about the walled cities of Zululand, from Charles Beadle of our writers' brigade who, as you will note, has wandered from the States to Paris:

Paris, France.

Dear Camp-Fire:

W. E. Keever's article on the walled cities of Zululand is particularly interesting to me as I happen to have been in the Niekerk Zimbabwe district – (Inyanga – The Spell: Motokos – The White Frog) and he gives me much information which I did not know. The currently accepted theory there – among whites of course – is that it is the work of the Phoenician or else of Arabic origin built or taught by Arab slave raiders from the north.

AS I have seen them and camped among 'em, they covered several acres at a time as if they were the ruins of a small town: triangles and squares of *stone* walls usually about a foot or two high – said conformation suggesting that some crazy giant had been teaching Euclid and illustrating the propositions for the benefit of his pupils. On the tops, too, of kopjes – usually granite and boulder-strewn – were what had been decidedly fortifications: walls remaining breast high with vents for arrows – equally useful for rifles. Upon the side of hills were terraces built up by stone suggesting the terraced vine hills of Greece. On the back of the Inyanga station on a rough kopje was quite an extensive old fortification which we adapted and rebuilt as a fort. "Old workings" of gold mines are all over Rhodesia from Tuli (Big Zimbabwe) in the south to the Ruania River in the North and, as the Britannica says, are now operated with profit.

PERSONALLY I cannot swallow the idea that ever the Bantu progressed as far as building these structures or mining as illustrated there. I have almost a conviction that Solomon or some of the Pharaohs sent their people right down through Uganda, etc., to Rhodesia by *land* and not fleets by sea. Certainly in comparatively modern times Arabs from as far north as the White Nile came down through or round Abyssinia as far south as this, slave raiding as they did upon the other side of Africa, Dongola and Barotseland. I think it is quite conceivable that, say, Solomon's parties would establish distant camps as the Romans did where they would teach their native slaves to build houses as they knew them; for certainly they would remain there some time after such a trip, say, from Egypt.

NOW there is no trace that I have ever heard of the Bantu constructing anything like such permanent dwellings. The Baganda were renowned upon discovery – first I think by Burton although I am not sure. Or was it Baker Pasha? – for the fact that they, a Bantu race, made more or less real roads, broad, and with bridges across swamps etc. If such an advanced race of the Bantu existed, where has it disappeared to? And why? Africa is fairly well explored now. There cannot remain a sufficiently large area unknown as to provide a safe hiding-place for this super-Bantu tribe – and report of such doings and things would spread for many hundreds of miles. I cannot even imagine a plausible theory to account for their having been wiped out. The men who made those ancient dwellings must have been equally advanced in the arts of war.

Another point: the setting of the sites surrounded with fortified kopjes gives quite the sense of men living in an occupied territory. The baptismal records of the Dominicans mentioned by Mr. Keever do not, I think, dispose of the theory of a ruling or a different race for the "powerful king" might well have been a titular king – the Sultan of Morocco at the present moment is Mulai Ali Mohammed (I *think*, for they change so darned quick out there!) but the French are the rulers all the same.

However I wonder whether someone else can put forward a more plausible theory.

– Chas. Beadle.

Beadle's contribution to the forum "Contemporary Writers and Their Work," *The Editor: The Journal of Information for Literary Workers* **(NJ: Ridgewood), 25 February 1920**

To recall the conception of the idea of "The Inner Hero" (*Romance* for November)* is difficult. It is one of a series of sailor and fireman stories conceived some years ago, and with the exception of two others abandoned. I think that I may express myself better if I speak generally rather than particularly, for as I have said, I can scarcely recall the genesis and parturition of this story, although it was born actually in New York. Usually I decide upon what class of mankind and in what environment I am going to ponder in search of an idea – too often, I regret to say, influenced by what I imagine will stand a sporting chance of selling: sometimes they sell; sometimes they don't; there are other gorgeous moments when intoxicated by a check – and rarer ones when I don't give a damn whether the heavens fall or the price of coal goes up – that I defy the gods by writing what I damn well please; they do not sell … except, in justice I must admit, with a few exceptions. Well, to continue; having decided upon a character or characters, usually based upon some person I have bumped against – maybe for for merely ten minutes – I seek a natural environment and his probable circumstances, male and female, I set them, as it were upon a stage in my mind. Then when they have become "real" I obtain an illusion that they are and merely sit down and record what they "insist" upon doing. I say "insist" because frequently when I, playing god, choose a nice comfortable and orthodox end for them they refuse to obey me, and as I have sunk into merely the position of reporter, the result is usually lamentable as far as editors and my bank account are concerned.

This account of writing "The Inner Hero" may not be accounted of much use to would-be writers (there is no inference in the phrase for I am merely a would-be writer; I merely mention the fact because association brings to my mind cheap sneers which have been perpetrated), but if you will permit me to say, said account may teach more than a dozen "How to write short stories" instructions. That is to say that one can write or one cannot write and no amount of instructions will teach a man or woman. Again, that is to say that I do not mean anything about divine afflatus. To me as I see it – if you will again permit me to lapse into the "ideal world" – there is a métier for everyone. One man can make chairs perfectly or nearly so; another design bridges and engines; another make money – the least of all! The trouble is that there are so many chair makers trying to write short stories and many story writers trying to make chairs. Am I a chair maker or a story writer? Damned if I know! I'm trying to find out. Personally, as I am vain, I think that I could make chairs; but I don't think that the third chair would interest me much.

Well, experiences as a writer: I began when I was 28 or 29. I was stuck in the center of Morocco, isolated, and finding a library abandoned by – well, no names, no pack drill! – I read to pass the time, novels, and became so bored with them that I swore that if I could not write a better yarn than those in particular I would eat my hat and other clothes! Since then I have been trying to avoid eating my hat, etc. Personally, I don't think that I am called upon to do so. I began a novel there and finished it in London when I returned – broke; and being broke took it into my head that I would be a writer or bust! Every publisher in London turned it down; Public won't stand for it, etc. A friendly critic said to me, "Stick your tongue in your cheek, old man, and write something to please 'em!" I did. First publisher to whom it was offered gave special terms. My hoary aunt, I actually made money! Not much, but real money! That book is selling in cheap edition. I sat down again to write "something that would please 'em!" Then occurred the process to which I have already referred. My "creations" would not obey their god (how very human). They would insist upon making a tragedy of it. After the fourteenth publisher I took to sending it round in couples. Two publishers, young, made an offer simultaneously. I accepted the better offer. My publisher on the day of publication eloped to Morocco with his typist and incidentally the firm's funds – and a few months afterwards the other fellow was in gaol for embezzlement. Fate "got me going and coming," as they say!

On further reflection, recalling the process of story making seems more difficult than ever. What I have already said is fundamentally true. I may add that the character, the atmosphere or the "meaning" of the story attracts me. The great thing that I am incapable of understanding is "plot." Personally, plot does not interest me in the least. It is merely the hobby horse on which to hang the clothes, but I do not feel that I need a hobby horse.

That's all there is to it. A cinema has need of a plot. Writing has not (I didn't say literature; I don't like the word and I am not a literateur. I am a writer. What's the matter with the word anyway?). The cinema – as it is now – cannot utilize the cadence of words, the nuances, the motivating psychology – except in very primitive form. (Uproar! Good!)†

As one editor was kind enough to say to me: We don't care a damn about atmosphere writing, psychology; we want a plot!

Bien!

A publisher who played the young girl with the petals, He loves me! He loves me not! business remarked upon the "faulty construction" of a manuscript. "What," said I, "do you mean by construction?" After vague explanations I saw a great light. "A-ah!" I cried, "plot you mean! "Oh, well," said he, "that's what the lowbrows call it!"

Well, the snow is here and no coal is nigh, but life's rather ridiculous, isn't it?

---

* Beadle's story, "The Inner Hero," published in *Romance* magazine, November 1919.

† Beadle is referring to the placards or "subtitles" used in silent films from the mid-1890s to the late 1920s.

Commentary in *Adventure*'s "Camp-Fire," 3 October 1920

SOMETHING from Charles Beadle about the facts back of his novelette ["The McIntosh"] in this issue:

Paris, France.

This yarn was suggested by a real episode perpetrated by a bunch of the British South African Police who came down to Beira on leave, got in a mix-up and actually put the police in their own jail and then played Old Harry with the town. The torturing stunt is not in the least exaggerated, nor the possibilities on the Beira railway. It's great, that rail. Coming down from Beira, our train pulled up in the open veldt. Got out to see what was up. A Scotch engineer and the Irish conductor had worked up a dispute *en route* and, with the passengers forming a ring, fought it out. Then we continued peaceably. Another time someone spotted a lion. We stopped the train and everybody joined in the hunt – for some hours, for we didn't get him after all. – Charles Beadle.

Commentary in *Adventure*'s "Camp-Fire," 18 January 1921

A WORD from Charles Beadle about his novelette in this issue ["The City of Baal"]. Also something of interest in connection with one of his former stories in our magazine:

Paris, France.

The source of the story is obvious to anyone who happens to recollect the short Camp-Fire discussion about Phoenician ruins in Rhodesia. I had had the nucleus of the idea in my head for some while but that kind of stirred it up, fertilized it as it were.

By the way, came across an item today that weirdly enough corroborates the possibility of the Alabaster Goddess and the Bowl of Alabaster. It is a report of an expedition which has just been completed through the very corner near the Gamballagalla or Ruenzori range of mountains. I quote:

"From Kigezi the expedition set out for Banyoro ... but instead of retracing its steps struck out a new route moving westward ... turned northward and followed the line of these lakes and Albert Lake. Some of the scenery in this little known country ... was found to be beautiful beyond description, comprising crater lakes surrounded by tropical vegetation of wonderful luxuriance. *The people, cut off from the world live happily in ignorance of their fellows a few miles distant.* In this African Arcadia ... met the Bakunta, the descendants of a few Baganda who many years ago killed a prince in battle and fled their country to escape the avengers of blood." – *Man.* June, 1920, The Mackie Ethnological Expedition to Central Africa.

– Charles Beadle.

Commentary in *Adventure*'s "Camp-Fire," 3 May 1921

HERE is an amusing and interesting thing. Several of you wrote in saying that Charles Beadle's novelette, "The Bowl of Alabaster," showed strong signs of having borrowed much of its material and setting from another story. Though no one could remember just what the other story was, one or two mentioned some of Haggard's tales. While we here in the office could not detect any plagiarism and had never had any reason to suspect Mr. Beadle of plagiarism, we of course forwarded the letters to him.

Mr. Beadle promptly explained the "mystery." He had "plagiarized" all right, in a way of speaking, but quite legitimately and from his own work. The setting and material of the story were naturally somewhat the same as in his earlier story, for "The Bowl of Alabaster" was a sequel to "The Alabaster Goddess." Also, the sequel was written at my suggestion, which makes me all the more to blame for not having made plain in the magazine beyond any possible misunderstanding that the second story was a sequel to one published quite a number of issues earlier.

WE DID get badly caught by a plagiarist last year and some fifty of you called our attention to it. And I thank every one of the fifty for doing so. Every magazine gets victimized in this way and naturally, while it isn't pleasant news to receive, finding out about it is the necessary first step toward doing anything about it.

That is, I thank all but two or three of the fifty. These two or three at once wrote me down as a cold-blooded crook and, without waiting to give me a hearing or any chance at self-defense, proceeded to call me all the names in the calendar. A man like that is not only a .22 caliber rim-fire short but, well, he's shy on common-sense. Even if I were as much a crook as they said, I am not idiot enough to do a thing like that. Nor is any other editor of any other magazine of any standing. There is nothing to be gained for a magazine by plagiarism, and a great deal to be lost by it.

Also, this magazine has been demonstrating for more than ten years that it is entirely able to get all the original stories it needs. But these two or three half-cocked little toy pistols exploded without stopping to think of any of these things.

I don't mind saying that I had personally read the story plagiarized by ours, but that was twenty or twenty-five years ago. I've read many, many thousands of stories since then and it is not surprising that I didn't recognize the plot when transferred to another country and another age.

I DO not give the plagiarist's name. He seemed to me foolish and careless rather than a crook. He has made every possible atonement, feels the disgrace bitterly, and I'm willing to bet will never offend again. To brand him by name publicly will ruin his life as a man, and he has good standing in his community and can be useful there. Ordinarily I have no use or mercy for a plagiarist, but in this case I don't feel I am all-wise enough to be justified in ruining his life by exposure. Maybe I'm doing wrong, but when a man who has fallen in the mire is trying to get up I can't believe in kicking him in the face. Most of us get into the mire at some time or other and what we need is a hand, not a foot. He will not appear in our pages again, nor I think, in the pages of any other magazine. That ought to be enough.

When the matter was brought to our attention we at once took the matter up with the victimized author's publishers. Naturally we apologize to you our readers and regret the occurrence sincerely. If it is necessary to say in so many words that we, were entirely innocent in the matter, I say so now.

BUT to return to Mr. Beadle's case, here is his letter and, following it, a sample letter from one of the men who brought up the question of plagiarism against him. I'd like to say that these men were men. No one branded anybody a crook without waiting for facts or giving the other fellow a chance. They merely raised the question (and we are always grateful to our readers for that kind of watchful service) and, when Mr. Beadle made his reply, investigated the case anew and promptly and manfully owned up to their quite natural mistake.

Paris, France.

Dear Sir: The editor of Adventure has been kind enough to forward me your letter of the 5 October.

Yes, the story in question was sold as new and original and not as a reprint.

The source or inspiration for the yarn was a passage or several in the "Golden Bough" (Frazer) in which he speaks of a certain valley – I think – somewhere in Asia Minor where bodies of beasts, birds, and humans, are preserved by the action of calcium; in another passage he refreshed my mind regarding the earthquake god in Uganda; the rest was evolved from my knowledge of the country in which the story is placed, a dozen facts, the possibility – and existence of – Phoenician gold bangles, the ancient presence of said Phoenicians or Egyptians, the conformation of the volcanic country, the existence of a vast district – as described – then unexplored – which has since been. I wrote to Camp-Fire pointing out the coincidence – explored and a tribe allied to the Waganda and carrying many of the traits which I attributed to them.

Your accusation apparently carries considerable likeness in the structure, of "The Bowl of Alabaster." Now I wonder whether you have not read in some few issues previously "The Alabaster Goddess" to which this story was the sequel?

After all, you know it's rather a serious charge – in effect that I have stolen so many hundred dollars from the Ridgway Company. Wouldn't you be sore if some one accused you of theft in such a manner? Let's have a square deal and try to hunt up that magazine in which you found the story. Will you? –

Chas. Beadle.

———

Chicago, Illinois.

Some two or three weeks ago I received your letter, and the other day the one enclosed arrived from Paris from the author of "The Alabaster Goddess" and "The Bowl of Alabaster."

I must apologize for my error, for it is such. I had read the first story and, when reading the second one, did not notice that the latter was a sequel to the former. When the enclosed letter arrived I went to the Chicago Public Library, looked up the first story and came back and am writing this letter of apology. The error is altogether mine and I accused the author of stealing the settings from himself.

From "Ask *Adventure*," 10 May 1922

"Hour of the Monkey"

IN WHICH Charles Beadle, author, shakes hands with an "Ask Adventure" expert named Charles [Whitehouse]:

Question: – "A while back I came across a couple of phrases in your story 'Buried Gods,' and I would like to ask a few questions about them.

In places in your story you refer to a 'closed district.' What is meant by that?

Then in another part it says this party was up at the 'hour of the monkey.' Just what time is this?

What religion is practiced mostly in this territory?" – Charles Russell Whitehouse, Cambridge, Mass.

Answer, by Mr. Beadle – "Always glad to clear up any vagueness. 'Closed district' means a district closed to whites by the government as being unsafe on account of the natives.

'Hour of the monkey' is the equivalent in English of cock-Crow or the crack of dawn, etc.; i.e., when the monkeys begin to awake and chatter.

Usual religion is represented in such districts by a primitive form of animism – rivers, trees, etc., having spirits which are malignant. The white, being an unknown phenomenon, at first was looked upon as supernatural – a god, and therefore to be kept in the tribe, as his presence in itself was looked upon as being of very powerful magic. Yet obviously if he were loose he might be difficult to control. Therefore logically the best thing to do with your god was to keep him in a nice safe place. But the whole subject is very complicated.

On the enclosed list I have marked a few books which apply to the subject."

Commentary in *Adventure*'s "Camp-Fire," 20 June 1922

SOMETHING from Charles Beadle concerning the facts back of his complete novelette ["Gifts of Diamonds"] in this issue:

Île de Lerne, France.

The mechanism of this yarn – not the story – was suggested by Poe's "MS Found in a Bottle." I wanted to develop that and work out other methods of getting over a communication from a man or men tied up in a hopeless knot which was bound to lead to the final dive.

THE inner yarns on which the plot, if you like, is founded are historical, the strangulation of the priests by the Monomatapa, a chief who did reign over an empire as told in the story. The center of his kingdom was in ancient times in the Mazoc valley, Southern Rhodesia, and his lineal descendant is now called Mudojumbo and he lives on the Urania. I've met him in Police days and he it was who was responsible for nearly all the Mashona Rebellions.

The dogs Kopman and Oompie I had on an exploring trip with me. When passing the Zambezi I had to leave one behind because of the fly and regulations, and when I returned, I found the beast madder than ever, stuck on an island in the middle of the river because the Boer with whom I had left him was scared to death of him. Also the *Wheeler* in this story is drawn from the life of a man once on safari with me, the incident of Oompie following Kopman outside and the threat to shoot me and afterward the fantastic challenge to a duel at a hundred yards with elephant guns! Yet that chap was one of the best – in civilization. Afterward, off safari, we were great pals, but never again as a partner on the trail, thanks! –

Charles Beadle.

Appendix B:

The Letters of Charles and Isabel Beadle

When I first received Neil Pearson's partial transcript of Charles Beadle's correspondence I was convinced that, although it remained very fragmented and incomplete, any further attempt at unraveling Beadle's chicken scrawl was hopeless. But after many long hours of staring blankly at the scrunched, convoluted, hopelessly muddled hieroglyphs, suddenly a few of the words began to dance before my mind's eye, unentangled. By some inexplicable process that I still don't understand, as the days went by I was able to significantly build upon Neil's initial efforts.

The archive of letters inherited by Beadle's great-niece Patricia is composed of fourteen dossiers, labeled "letter 1" to "letter 14," as well as a fifteenth labeled "Bits and Pieces." The latter is composed of several undated sheets, most of which are "orphaned" or incomplete, making them especially difficult to date properly.

There's only one letter from Isabel to her uncle; the remainder are from Charles. Neil and Patricia numbered them according to what they guessed was their actual order, which I cited when referring to the letters in my annotated edition of Beadle's *Dark Refuge*. But thanks to this vastly expanded, almost complete transcript, by now it's apparent that this was by no means the correct order. However, although what follows represents a more logical reshuffling, a completely accurate chronology will forever elude us.

In this edition of *A Passionate Pilgrimage* I refer to the letters by using a new, alphabetical designation. The missive formerly designated as letter "9," for example, is now referred to as letter "A," as it's clearly the earliest surviving communication. Letter "7" follows next; therefore, it's letter "B."

Annotations that appear in double brackets [[like so]] represent my own commentary. Passages that remain indecipherable are represented by three ellipses enclosed in brackets; e.g., […]. A bracketed word followed by a question mark indicates that there remains doubt about whether it's been accurately transcribed; e.g., "He [wasted?] his money."

A special note of thanks goes to my friend and colleague John Locke, who came in at the bottom of the seventh as a relief pitcher and gave the entire manuscript a final read, making additional corrections and valuable suggestions. And he somehow managed to unravel a few more of Beadle's previously indecipherable phrases.

***

Although the letters tell an idiosyncratic tale, they also epitomize the roller-coaster ride that constitutes many a writer's life, especially one lingering on the margins of broader success – but not quite breaking through to a level he deserves to inhabit. While the Roaring Twenties delivered previously unheard of, roaring paychecks to many who mined the print media, the Great Depression reversed those gains overnight and ushered in a particularly difficult time for writers. Beadle's letters portray the shocking penury that dogged him in the 1930s – unable to afford even a postage stamp, turning to the Salvation Army for shelter, being kicked out of his lodgings and having his precious diary and manuscripts seized in the process – and serve as a testament to his resolve to pursue his craft no matter what. But they also serve as an example of the struggle that was occurring in the lives of so many other authors all around the world.

Even in the decade before the Depression, however, Beadle was wrestling with another demon that was well known to creative pioneers, especially during this period. Although he benefitted financially from the publication of genre fiction and enjoyed a particularly good run at *Adventure*, he was constantly at odds with himself; for the type of writing he really wanted to pursue was considered to be either too censorable or too difficult to market commercially. (It wasn't until 1938 that he cast aside all caution and delivered that uncensored masterpiece known as *Dark Refuge*.) As John Locke remarked in one of our recent discussions about the letters: "There's a consistent theme through the writers' laments, not just common to him. He can sell things he doesn't believe in, but the works close to his heart don't score with the reading public. Gets back to his two writing souls."

The latter remark refers to a brilliant passage in Locke's Postscript to *A Passionate Pilgrimage* in which he delves deeper into this conundrum. Beadle, Locke says, possessed "two writing souls. The adventure writer used his African experiences to make money, of which there is never enough; and the Bohemian poured his literary ambitions into his novels while living a marginal existence. Both souls are well worth reading today." Indeed.

Lastly, one cannot help but to be amused by the ever-shifting tone that Beadle employs to intellectually seduce his niece Isabel. She acts as a sort of literary foil through which he can display his wit, his charm, his cantankerousness, and his stubborn determination to upend any last surviving allegiance she may harbor for the fading principles of the Victorian era. Although Beadle is obviously her senior, he incarnates a New Generation that devotes itself to Dionysius (particularly in the avant-garde artistic center of Montparnasse) and thumbs its nose at everything personified by the more Apollonian Queen Victoria. But by the end, they're both comrades sailing in the same leaking ship, trying to survive the economic hardships of the times.

There's a touching poignancy here when we read of how Isabel tries to help her uncle by offering suggestions about magazine publications, or when we learn that both Isabel and her sister Barbara are now on the "dole." In difficult times, friends bond together to offer a glimmer of hope, to commiserate and share tales of woe, to express sympathy and condolence. But during the Depression this was not always so: particularly in America, neighbors were often too ashamed to acknowledge to each other that they were, in fact, starving. But in Beadle's case, the reverse was true. He even attempts to make a comedy out of this destitution – as if, through laughter, his spirit will continue to be buoyed.

As a writer gifted with an acute sense of tragicomedy, he knew that humor is the last vital possession of a man who has been stripped of everything else. And he was well aware that humor is a medium through which one may be reborn.

[[Letter "A," originally designated as letter 9. Here, Beadle replies to Isabel in what is clearly the earliest extant note of their correspondence. Four months earlier, *The Blue Rib: A Romance of the Riviera* was published in London. It's possible that Isabel contacted Beadle's publisher in an attempt to track down her peripatetic uncle, who was clearly the black sheep of the family. (Note how Beadle remarks: "I can't send you a Blue Rib as I am at the moment undergoing one of my periodical eclipses ...") Isabel may also have had an ulterior motive; from his response, it's clear that she inquired about the possibility of designing Beadle's book covers. When he asks, "How old are you two now?" he's also referring to Isabel's younger sister, Barbara (the mother of Beadle's great-niece Patricia). In the very last paragraph he turns the tables on his own thorny, porcupine cantankerousness and invites this new generation to his lair. By saying "I won't recognize you as relatives" he's paying them a high compliment – even conveying belated respect. And he concludes by extending a rare invitation to enter into his dark refuge: "Send me your sketches," he says, "and tell me all about yourselves."]]

c/o Barclays Bank Ltd.
Promenade des Anglais, Nice

? [[sic]] August 1927

My Dear Girls,

You don't seem to realize that I'm very, very old, and in consequence nothing surprises me. Your blots and smudges are a delight but the little uncle is not. Don't like relatives. Never did. Haven't seen or heard of any for 20 years.[171] And now you bob up! Well, don't. I'll accept you as human animals – perhaps intelligent, perhaps not. Anyway [in your farm?] for [them?] a sense of humor. Which like charity – altho' I don't believe it – covers a multitude of sins. (I don't believe in sins either.)

I can't send you a Blue Rib as I am at the moment undergoing one of my periodical eclipses – the sun hasn't a monopoly, nor is the moon the sole reason. But I'll send you one from here (books not moons) in the autumn.

What's all this snobbery about crests? I know a perfectly good coal merchant who has a few million whose sole ambition is to sell trucks of coal, who also is Charles Beadle and comes from Barking.[172]

About your sketches – send me some. <u>But</u> Balham[173] doesn't sound good. Reminiscent of esses and an accent. Hope neither of you have the latter? Re: book covers, nothing doing (that's for your sweet benefit). That's all my publishers' job. I'll give you an introduction perhaps, but that'll be about as much use as a match in hell. (Are you permitted to say hell? This is important.)

How old are you two now?[174] I can't add up – not even a bill, much less pay it. Are you the new generation? Tell me. Why go in for art or teaching? Why not some other form of slavery? Marriage for instance. I hear Lady Astor wants to pension wives at 60. Rotten. Go to the States. Then you can divorce your husband after 6 months and have a pension for the rest of your life. Oh boy I wish I were a gal.

As for news as I told you I don't know any relatives respected (none have any money as far as I know) or otherwise … I'm a

---

[171] Possibly a reference to his father's death in Buenos Aires, on 19 March 1906.

[172] Beadle's paternal grandfather, William Beadle, was born in Barking, England in 1812.

[173] Balham: an area in southwest London.

[174] Barbara turned twenty that summer; Isabel, twenty-three.

savage. Savages may not look at their mother-in-laws and the Esquimaux[175] bury alive their old people when they become a nuisance. Excellent. That's why I won't recognize you as relatives. Send me your sketches and tell me all about yourselves.

CB

---

[175] Although he's referring literally to Eskimos, the remark takes on added resonance since his novel, *The Esquimau of Montparnasse*, would be published in London in 1928. As discussed earlier, the main protagonist, "Esquimau," is loosely based upon Beadle and his acquaintances in Montparnasse.

[[Letter "B"; originally designated as letter 7. The last couple of pages are composed on the back of a typed manuscript. The final sheet contains a typed page number ("163") and a typed word ("Chapter"), followed by a typed line of dialogue: "Thou hast slain …"]]

Chateau Esquimau.
Cagnes-sur-Mer

Very nice of you to think of me, dear girl, when plunged in the profundity of philosophy, for as friend Rabelais says, the contemplation of death is philosophy.[176] Unfortunately I am unable to give you a sure cure for the black beetle except alcohol, or better, love! I've been suffering somewhat myself for quite a while – in fits and starts. Doesn't last long with me for fortunately I usually break the icy circle by laughing – at myself or everybody or Henry Hardy. I didn't reply before – expect nothing and ye shall receive! – because one franc and fifty centimes buys enormous quantities – relatively as everything else – of food, tobacco ~~and~~ or even a whole drink! However they say that nothing except space and time lasts forever. Well, I'm beginning to think I've got lost [and belong] in space and time!

One clause I must [insist upon?] sternly. Esquimaux have no relations, avuncular or otherwise. There are those who so pretend and who despite warnings approach and form suitable objects from which to raise the wind – even the slightest breeze is welcome to the parched traveler in the scorched desert – There is a voice which comes out of the void giving indications of being a female, young, and – apparently – of a certain

---

[176] In book three of *Gargantua and Pantagruel*, Rabelais has the physician Rondibilis counsel Panurge: "Socrates did not speak improperly when he said that philosophy was nothing else but a meditation upon death."

intelligence and tendency towards humor. Such is rare, my masters! The gods give and the gods take away – but not if I can snatch it! I am the Esquimau – but I'm not adding any bunk about worshiping other Esquimau, because unlike ~~Jahweh~~ Jehovah I have no cheap jealousy in me! In as much as this twaddle is understood you can if you wish be a great service to the cult of the Esquimau but on the understanding that the family shall not be initiated.[177] Perhaps the Barbara – to whom a chat was forestalled by certain learned dissertations upon the politics of some local mumbo-jumbo and the life and memories of an inhabitant of – oh, hell, wherever it is.

I kiss your hair, fair girl of the void!

The Esquimau.

As for the first time for 20 years or a hundred I've had to have a photo taken for [various?] purposes am sending you one – as a piece of sugar for a good girl.

---

[177] Beadle is still establishing the rules here, so one may assume this is an early letter in the correspondence.

[[Letter "C"; originally designated as letter 4.]]

Barclay's Bank
Nice

[[Circa 1928 / 1929]]

No excuses for delay in replying. I have been and am enjoying a nightly battle with a terrible monster in comparison to which mythological or Chinese dragons are harmless Pekingese[[,]] and the name of this savage beast is Economic Pressure. St George may have been a great guy in his way, but there is no record that he ever got this note of [being?] [...] roped and hogtied.

Both portraits sound interesting. Personally I like 'em handsome.

I know about Michael Arlen.[178] Never heard [of] other gent. But don't [...] what I know something about.

Yes, you are to be more than sorry about the cinema people and the book; in fact you will weep seven days and seven nights consistently and without ceasing. Much [...] [falls?] into [the?] pocket of Mr Cosmo Hamilton instead of mine which is a vile deplorable thing. However it seems I am [offering?] revenge – to play in his 3 Passions.[179] I hope I ruin his beastly play. Haven't

---

[178] Michael Arlen (1895 – 1956): Armenian writer raised in England and author of the best-selling novel, *The Green Hat* (1924). As John Locke points out, *The Green Hat* "was filmed in 1928 as the Garbo movie *A Woman of Affairs*. Perhaps this is what the subsequent reference to cinema and to the book is about. It's a 1924 novel, so why else would it have come up?" Beadle's reference to "Economic Pressure" may be related to the crash of 1929.

[179] Cosmo Hamilton (né Henry Charles Hamilton Gibbs; 1870 – 1942): prolific English playwright and novelist, whose musicals were produced on Broadway. A cinematic version of his novel, *The Three Passions* (New York: G. P. Putnam's Sons, 1928), was directed by Rex Ingram in 1928. Money,

read it yet so I'm quite safe in saying it's beastly without prejudice and anyway if it isn't mine it must be beastly. Q.E.D.

The sticky part: have been thoroughly assured by countless respectable people one may live with anyone, but [not?] with his past.

Yes, you can easily go to [...] via Nice although possibly purse will suffer damages. Inquire Cooks. Despite my best erudition I can't know everything.

Study Indian and Chinese and I should have said rather Egyptian as they are the basis of all art. We moderns haven't any sculptors or painters comparable to these ancients. You appear to be half-witted generally speaking but at end of your letter you have apparently had an attack of the D.T.s. Hope you're better?

Cheer up. Art is long and credit is short.

Out of love at the moment so many ashes to you both.

CB

---

religion, and love are "the three great passions that have swayed mankind since the hour of their discovery." My dating of Beadle's letter as "circa 1928 / 1929" is a merely speculation based upon the publication date of *The Three Passions* and the release of the Garbo film noted above.

[[Letter "D"; originally designated as letter 12.]]

[[Circa 1928 – 1929]]

Thanks sweet lass for a great disappointment! I was rejoicing after my fashion as Dowson might say[180] at being considered an imposter posing as the great writer Charles Beadle! Have had a copy of C-of-S [[*City of Shadows*]] weeks ago from a friend in London, but cinema people won't bite.[181] I have been and am exceedingly busy, trying to do several things at once. So I have little or no head for writing letters. Excellently sweet of you to 'admire' C-of-S, but personally I think it's just rotten. I've never yet written anything worth a damn that has brought me six-pence.[182] The best things are seldom if ever published. Commerce and art! No, Sirrah, to quote the great bore Dr. Johnson. One of these days when I'm rich I'll publish or at any rate have printed some M.S.S.[183] which amuse me and promise to send you a copy, but when that great day for the human race will be "lies in the womb of eternity" as Marie Corelli[184] or

---

[180] Ernest Christopher Dowson (1867 – 1900), English poet associated with the Decadent movement, principally remembered for three lines culled from his poems: "I have been faithful … in my fashion," "Gone with the wind" (both from "Non Sum Qualis eram Bonae Sub Regno Cynarae"), and "Days of wine and roses" (from "Vitae Summa Brevis").

[181] This is the first time that Beadle remarks upon his attempts at either marketing film rights or composing screenplays.

[182] Beadle must be referring to book-length publications, since he earned thousands of dollars selling stories to *Adventure*. In his letter to Isabel from early 1934, he mentions "a call from American Adventure to whom I have sold thousands of dollars of stuff." (See below.)

[183] M.S.S.: manuscripts.

[184] Marie Corelli (née Mary Mackay; 1855 –1924): best-selling English novelist who explored New Age themes such as mysticism and reincarnation and whose work was widely ridiculed by the more serious literary establishment.

Michael Arlen might have written – an extremely awkward condition as among many other professions I am no midwife.

Be sweet and gracious and write me expecting no reward and send me your photos.

Love, if I may make so bold as the pirate said, to both of you.

CB.

[[Letter "E"; originally designated as letter 14.]]

Maison Jaune[185]
Chemin St. Claude, Antibes

[[Circa 1929?]][186]

My dear child. Am back from […] and just discovered your letter among riffraff of MSS. So glad you're growing a consciousness. When I have lots of money I shall mine [[sic]] cut out – ~~but~~ it's a true, useless appendix to life.

I'm really glad [job?] is done. […] you […] – letter is [torn?] and my memory gone on strike. I'm back at my writing again. It's one of these incurable diseases.

I really don't know what I'm talking about. You see it's such a long way back to Aldebaran[187] and who knows whether I shall ever get there? Now let's see[[,]] if you like[[,]] what you are now to [[sic]] what you were 2 years ago – [all of them?]!

I'm sending you a rather large Provencal […] and I hope it bites you at night when you're thinking of me!

Tell me lots of your secrets and I will reply I promise – <u>if</u> they're interesting.

Yours as you like it – not by Shakespeare.

---

[185] Oddly enough, on the death certificate of Beadle's detested mother-in-law, Teresa Isabel Ashwell, the place of death is registered as "Maison Jaune, Chemin de St. Claude, Antibes." (Source: "England and Wales, National Probate Calendar, Index of Wills and Administrations," Ancestry.com.) Beadle also uses this as a return address on another letter to Isabel, letter "P," dated circa early 1934.

[186] See Beadle's remark in the third paragraph, comparing Isabel "now to what you were 2 years ago." Since the correspondence began in 1927, we may hazard a guess that this letter dates from 1929.

[187] Aldebaran: the fourteenth brightest star in the night sky, which plays a significant role in various cultural mythologies.

[[Letter "F"; originally designated as letter 11. Composed on stationary from the glamorous Palais de la Méditerranée, a famous Art Deco hotel-casino built in 1929 on the waterfront in Nice, which once hosted international art exhibits.]]

Chère inconnue[188] I find your second letter to greet me on my return[189] from a small Christopher Columbus adventure – to [Corte?] – Corsica, a voyage that was a cross between a dream and a nightmare. One of my few friends – mad of course – flew in from Vienna having decided in a moment of drunken intelligence that Esquimau should be disinterred and given air. He's supposed to be doing an article – he's merely a vulgar journalist – on the capitals of Europe and North Africa – he should be doing some on the guns and gods. By heroic efforts I kept him sober – myself ditto – until Calvi[190] [became?] me, or rather he was undid so to speak by the voices of imagination. After [this?] I wisely if […] went to bed. He went out and as far as I can make out he went straight for his evening lockup. I was rather impressed when [a?] gendarme – see portrait of bandits – gaily awoke me at 6 a.m. demanding family history and whether T. was really my friend and so forth. Not a cent left. So sober as Pepys[191] wd. have said. [Wanted?] his […] money. Then on to […]. […] the [clear?]! Corsican wine! He persisted in drinking aperitifs. For the last couple of years I've had an idea instilled into my benighted head that, unfortunately, eating is necessary [so?] I left him. Next morning T. discovered in his bed in hotel very sick.

Myself: who the hell might we house?

---

[188] "My dear stranger."

[189] The "second letter" remark suggests that Beadle received two missives from Isabel while he was away.

[190] A reference to the wine produced in Corsica's Calvi region.

[191] Samuel Pepys (1633 – 1703), best known for *The Diary of Samuel Pepys*, first published in 1825.

T: Lighthouse, the sun, lighthouse!

Said lighthouse was an English resident six foot eight! Who had found T. at 3 in the morning caroling his Irish songs.

Myself also had adventures. Seeking a small restaurant in [darkest?] Corsica I arrived in a kind of cave and noticing a [medallion?] of Napoleon walked up to examine it. Quite unconscious of stage effects I became a gent – I saluted [them?]. Well [heavens?]! They fell on my [walk?] literally and metaphorically! The patronne was young and Job-like. Dark smoldering Corsican eyes. The [patronne?] long had dreams of going to Hollywood and asked my advice. I played metteur en scène. Myself: Imagine I'm a beautiful young girl and you're wildly in love with me.

Candidate for [dollar?] fame looks like a bewildered Corsican sheep.

Myself: Imagine that I'm the [...] your wife.

Corsican black sheep[[:]] [...] mournful gaze.

Spectator: Show us how it [...].

My wife: I am very much in love with your wife.

Close-up regarding said lady. Wild applause. More drinks. Oh dear oh dear!

Good God! said the British lighthouse when he'd barely escaped suffocation. You'll get killed in Corsica if you go on like that!

Still we got out alive and returned to my vast estates here. Y'day said wild Irishman blew in again just fresh from gaol in Cannes. Wants her to go to Brittany with him to collaborate on a book on said country [tho the?] son, a man of very venerable [...] prefers a more or less billowy bed to prison planks. We ought to join the police to save time and get paid for it. Besides I've had no experience playing keeper in an insane asylum.

{Corsican?] history is much overrated and the [Corsican?] – [the?] celebrated maquis[192] – [w/ their?] most dismal, depressing […] [who?] desires to […] his part of a giddy bandit.

So glad that you've discovered that life is thrilling. As a matter of fact very few people seem to have done the [Columbus?] act. Personally I can't forget it which is very annoying sometimes. Some [screen?] people have inferred that a man of my advanced age should settle down. A horrible operation apparently, masochistic in nature, of burying myself to the waist in damp earth sending out invitations to the worms until the feast is about to begin. My only […] is that price of […] have settled [here?] very much down for the […] if the Esquimau doesn't go well in U.S.A. Next month I guess I'd better finish the job. Still this joyous Rabelaisian life of a bandit for a week has done me some good. More anon.

Anon. Friend T. utterly disappeared for two days. Suppose he's in goal somewhere.

Merci pour les […], ma belle! Je t'embrasse. The Esquimaux like when […] offer to house on British Culture.

Congrats! You've made a delicious sentence. Put all this down to the relative softening of – (turn over page) <u>desires</u>. Great! But opposite page is No[[.]] 2 and needs merely – brains. Much cd. be made of the relative softening of desires for an article. Would desire [wane?]; life might be less […] but [then?] bittersweet. [It] would fade too no doubt. How mad and bad and sad it was, but then, how it was sweet! as Browning said.[193]

---

[192] Maquis: Corsica's "bandits of honor" (*maquisards*) and its resistance fighters during WWII take their name from a thick evergreen underbrush that covers much of the Corsican highland. The abundant scrubby maquis made the area unmappable, thus it was an ideal hiding place.

[193] Referring to "Confessions" by Robert Browning (1812 – 1889), a poem that begins with the stanza "What is he buzzing in my ears? / 'Now that I come to die, /Do I view the world as a vale of tears?' / Ah, reverend sir, not

Now I'll await your [artist?] view of yourself by yourself.[194] In the meantime give me in tabloid form as <u>cruelly</u> as you can impression of myself on family. I always want and need to see myself as much as possible as others see me, a vision which aids one to divine somewhat the interiors of others by their confusion. Get me [love?]? I want all the unpleasant sides: none of the pomade.

I'm [settling] near my fire. This is the coldest place [except?] the pole in south – trying to crawl back into myself. And pull the hole in after me.

Esquimau.

I!" and ends with "… Alas, / We loved, sir – used to meet: / How sad and bad and mad it was – / But then, how it was sweet!"
[194] Most likely, a reference to a self-portrait painted by Isabel.

[[An undated and uncatalogued orphaned letter, now labeled "F-1," as the creases of the sheets resemble those of letter "F," above.]]

[…] make piles of money, have little or no talent – just a flashy trick – and [boasting?] did the rest. But […] to have the temperament to do that – […], put up with fools, to make love to a horror or be made love to, etc. The more talent you have the more they'll detest you, the others: mediocre you're safe. Get me? Sorry to be solemn [this time?]. I shouldn't usually give advice even when asked and what I say is merely banal, but still it shd. not be forgotten. Maybe you'll think I'm sore because The Blue Rib hasn't sold. The British have only an infantile sense of humor. That is why I warn you solemnly against your flippancy. Rib was flippant[195] and that is the sin against the Holy Ghost. I've often asked priests what this mysterious and therefore attractive sin was. Told I know![196] Quaint, this idea of sin. I'm just crazy about sin. Whenever I hear of a new sin I just make one dive for it. But alas they are <u>so</u> rare! Have you read […] story of The New Pleasure? Modern man discusses with

---

[195] A revised version of *The Esquimau of Montparnasse* (1928) was published in New York under the title *Expatriates at Large* (1930), and book reviews of the latter began to appear in March 1930. In one written by Pearl Thibos and featured in Indiana's *South Bend Tribune*, Thibos castigates the novel as being "flippant" (among other unpleasant things). At the culmination of her pejorative appraisal, she adds: "There are some love affairs that float lightly over a thin surface, never getting down to the level of really human emotions, and the whole effect of the work is as of someone glazing over a most commonplace list of occurrences, with flippant remarks and a constant lighting of cigarettes, the whole submerged most of the time in unlimited numbers of drinks." Perhaps as a result, this stinging adjective became lodged in Beadle's brain. See Sunday morning edition of the *South Bend Tribune*, 27 April 1930, p. 5, "The Reading Lamp" feature column.

[196] Possibly a reference to the "sin" of masturbation.

resurrected mummy sin – pleasures of the world and they discover only new one since Egypt is the cigarette. And most disheartening I call it [old?] when […] old things.

CB.

[[Letter "G"; originally designated as letter 5. Composed on stationary from the "International School, 1, Avenue St-Hilaire, Grasse, France," located on the Côte d'Azur.

[[Circa 1930]]

Aldebaran dear, I am old and gray and my eyesight's all shot to hell![197] If you can't use ink to say your say don't write – and be damned as well![198] Here endeth the first lesson, dearly beloved. I received him most politely and offered him – a chair, old soul. (Erratum: read for 'a chair' 'the chair.') Biographies, auto or otherwise – <u>real</u> ones – are forbidden by the police regulations. Personally I haven't the slightest object [[sic]] to stripping before anyone – but I have to parading in my underclothes which act I find indecent.

Am at this moment on the beach at St. Malo as nude as said regulations will permit. Have been in sea up to my knees but couldn't face any more of North Pole conditions. For the first time since arriving there is a candle flame in the sky which [local?] inhabitant assures me is the sun. Fortunately I am a credulous person. My lush idiot friend got drunk last night – they woke me at 1:30 to make him come home – and was still drunk this morning. Burst into my room this morning and declared that someone had stolen his bedclothes. I ~~said~~ looked [...] Haven't they stolen your clothes as well? He was fully [naked?] and ~~lying on~~ [...] had been lying on bed. State of mind – if any [inferred?]. Since then he's disappeared. Thank Bacchus! And I'm alone all day on the beach with my candle flame.

No definite news of Esquimau adventures in the U.S.A. except to my disappointment, they didn't get mad. Only one

---

[197] During the summer of 1930 Beadle was forty-eight years old

[198] Perhaps she was using a lightly toned pencil to compose her notes.

from South Bend[199] – wherever and whatever that is – suggested that I ought to be persecuted for libel[200] – if they only would. I think that it's a dud as far as selling goes.

Haven't got your letter, but deciphered something about Freud and a higher life. Query: if Professor Freud had married Mrs. Eddy[201] would his offspring have benefited humanity? Suggest this to John London's[202] or to some other high bough monkey magazine. I think Freud must have suffered from a sexual frustration at the age of two and then recovered from it: otherwise there's lots of basic truth in his theories – yes, quite lots. As for higher life stuff yes of course. But recollect there's no reason to condemn the others. Life is like a pendulum – the higher the swing one side the higher the other. Most great men if not all were great lovers. Now don't dig up Carlyle.[203] It's obvious and I'm sorry for his wife. Probably if he hadn't been impotent he wd. never have had enough force – libido if you like – left to write at all.

You mention having read only two books of mine. Esquimau and City of Shadows? Latter isn't a book it's drivel – or

---

[199] If Beadle is citing the *South Bend Tribune* review, this letter would probably date from the spring or summer of 1930.

[200] As there's no mention of libel in the review, he may be confusing it with another review.

[201] Mary Baker Eddy (1821 – 1910): American religious leader who created The Church of Christ, Scientist, and founded the *Christian Science Monitor.*

[202] Once considered Britain's premier literary magazine, *John O'London's Weekly* was published from 1919 to 1954, by George Newnes Ltd. Regular contributors included Winston Churchill, Rebecca West, Max Beerbohm, and W. Somerset Maugham. Newnes also published *The Wide World Magazine* and *The Captain*, both of which (between 1907 and 1912) featured Beadle's nonfiction chronicles of travel and adventure in Africa. George Newnes (1851 – 1910), the original publisher of these periodicals, is regarded as one of the founders of popular journalism.

[203] Thomas Carlyle (1795 – 1881): Scottish philosopher and historian who Emerson dubbed the Victorian era's "undoubted head of English letters."

journalism which is prostitution. Didn't you get the Blue Rib? I gave one to The Family. It's amusing I think – but back of it is an idea – intended at any rate. Best stuff has of course never been published and probably never will be. If you've been good I'll loan – damn the Americans! – I mean lend you a copy of Witch-Doctors at so many kisses per day, but you'll have to pay and return this book as I only have 2 copies left and – of course it's out of print.

By the way will you buy me a pair of bathing trunks – the <u>triangular kind</u> which are unobtainable in prudish France. I shall be back in [London?] sometime in July probably the beginning if not sometime before. Doesn't look as if I can stick this maniac much longer. He hasn't any brains and when he's drunk or after he's impossible. So address to chateau.

It's near six and the candle is beginning to flicker so I'll have to cover myself into a sack and a couple of tubes of cloth. The beach is literally crawling with children. Heavens, think of the sordid happenings to produce this swarm! Romance, I suppose Miss Dell[204] et al would term them. Still what matter. Nature doesn't care as long as she accomplishes her apparently silly ends. ~~Still~~ But she might have been more of an aesthete in her selection methods. The contemplation […] ~~revolts~~ makes one revolt at the very idea of physical love which shd. be beautiful – yet one [eats?]. Old Esquimau is right after all – it's the attitude of mind and the fashion of the act that matters as in painting or anything else.[205]

I'm going back to try to write a short story wherein as usual I may not say the things I think.

Esquimau.[206]

---

[204] Ethel M. Dell: a popular English romance and adventure novelist.

[205] The protagonist of *The Esquimau of Montparnasse* declares: "Bohemian isn't a manner of living, it's an attitude of mind."

[206] On page 110 of *The Esquimau of Montparnasse*, when the character "Frank" accuses Esquimau (Beadle) of being "cold-blooded" and of having

[[Letter "H"; originally designated as letter 10.]]

San Malo.

[[Circa 1930]]

Letter got mislaid in this rush. Wild Irish been off to Cannes on a bust, rushed in and insisted on catching first train for Brittany. [...] have [been?] on delay. Last time I left him to get shaved, when I came back he'd gone – on a three day absentee with lamentable results. That's a week ago or 10 days and I've kept him sober, but God knows when he'll fall again. He is naturally that way, but more since he lost his wife last year. He fell off a bridge – you can guess why! – and she trying to rescue him fell and broke her neck. Now he's a bit loony and very difficult to handle. I may be collaborate [[sic]] with him on a Guide on Brittany but I doubt if ever he'll keep up. [...]: Guide to Britt: off. publishers backed out.

Queer: find myself writing as if in my diary to myself. Advantage possibly if writing to the [confessor?] – where they say lies truth! ~~Britt.~~ Breton sleet and wind today. Not unpleasant after years of sub-tropics, but triste as is all Brittany, whence arises their nostalgic songs and character. Destiny monkeying around with my personal affairs as usual. Don't know what's going to happen next. But that's my life ever since I can remember. Always waiting for something to turn up, as says

---

"no feelings," Esquimau replies: "You're wrong. I've got feelings all right, but I reflect first before I give 'em their heads." Perhaps this is one reason that he's referred to as "Esquimau," although the moniker may also reflect Beadle's inability to pay the coal merchant on far too many freezing winter nights.

Mr. Micawber[207] although usually it just don't. God knows why I'm writing to you like this, but then God's a humorist such as the Jews never suspected. Impossible to get any information for your […] tobacco friend here. Will try to remember later. Shall try to get to Paris if I can first to see whether it's still on the same spot or whether the Yanks have carted it all over to Kalamazoo, Ohio.

Alarums and excursions. God's getting busy on some joke.

Au revoir, fascination of the ballroom!

Esquimau

Write chateau

---

[207] A character from Charles Dickens' *David Copperfield*. Despite such dire financial straits, Beadle always remained optimistic that, eventually, "Something will turn up."

[[Letter "I"; a fragment composed on a single page, originally included in "Bits and Pieces" (Bits 2, p. 2).]]

[…] interesting, but as I can't bang machine for lack of ribbon and paper and have nothing to read. It's about 3 – my watch of course is broken and I can't pay to get it! – and I'm waiting to see whether my partner who is a poet and sells verses in cafés, is going to return with something to eat! We also make lampshades, but they are hard to sell and moreover no material left!

Funny too, because I'm not a bit romantic and particularly detest a Bohemian life – and how! I prefer good and beautiful things and a bath. This is comparative lux as I have hot and cold water and central heating. Even the tiniest and cheapest hotels have that in Paris. London is still in the 19th cent. except for the rich. I haven't a hankering to turn on the gas (plus, that's money too!) but the way things are going![208] I've wrangled a 2nd packet of gaspers[209] on credit so I am in Paradise!

[[A marginal note scrawled along the vertical edge of the sheet reads:]] Just y'day morning couldn't get matches so have to keep gas burning in order to have a light!

---

[208] A sardonic reference to suicide.
[209] Gaspers (British slang): a cheap, low-quality (and often high-nicotine) cigarette.

[[Letter "J"; originally included in "Bits and Pieces" (Bits 4, pp. 1-2.). Composed on the back of a handwritten manuscript.]]

My [Dear?], I don't know when you'll get this letter – depends on when I get some pennies! Anyway yours by air arrived Wednesday – just as said[[,]] ordinarily should be by boat. Don't bother about Blue Rib publication. I'll write when I can. But I don't suppose they have any. They always remainder those left: sell them as [custom?] made paper! […] no news or no encouragement – killer to write or to hire!

As said [before?] I knew this […] may [take?] years. They wd. have led me on the briar path to this [weak figure?] who […] [published] […] first article […] [Zambezi?] with [photos?]. These latter they invariably respect but have no use for fiction form: it's fiction of course but […] as […] but may be […] all the same.

The coast here is very dull – from a mundane point of view. Some misguided English stood me drinks at Juan les Pins[210] the other day and it was like a deserted village. [Cannes?] they say and […]. However that doesn't keep me awake at night although other things do.

Many thanks for Statesman [etc.?]. Provided an evenings decent reading. No pennies so I can't send this or anything else off. Got hold of a Strand[211] which I see has made changes. I don't think Pearson's and Newnes have combined. Unfortunately, English mags pay so little and cannot sell to American after

---

[210] Picasso frequently spent his extensive summer holidays in the South of France, especially at Juan-Les-Pins. While vacationing there during this same period, on August 18, 1931 he painted the vividly rendered *Villa Chêne-Roc at Juan-Les-Pins*. (Currently housed at the Almine and Bernard Ruiz-Picasso Foundation for Art, Madrid.) Beadle moved in many of the same circles as Picasso in both Montmartre and Montparnasse, and he includes some of his reflections on Picasso and Cubism in *Artist Quarter*.

[211] *The Strand*: a monthly magazine created by George Newnes.

publication [however?] you can sell U.S.A. stuff to England. Anyway American [matter?] although not brilliant isn't on such an altar type level as the English. Am hoping to make some much needed [...] on old Adventure stuff. As long as I can get up [enough?] 'action' as they call it, even beating each other up, or animals rushing about with evil intent there's a market. But I just can't – I never cd. do [their?] sentimental [slop mags?] for 'love' stories. I'm between [...] rewriting In Love with Love which I hope to have ready by autumn if [...] to buy paper for my [...] typist. Well, now I'm going on with my baboon story. Hoping for an American mail.

[[Letter "K"; originally included in "Bits and Pieces" (Bits 3, p. 1).]]

[…] seen another occasionally which was more entertaining British weekly I think? Do you know it? There's a more interesting mag still but I can't ~~think~~ recall its name. It's a comedy issue in typescript giving supposedly real news which newspapers won't or don't print. If I can dig up the news I'll tell you. I remember it gave a lot of information in advance of the Brownshirt[212] menace of Germany. Of course nothing is of any real importance[[,]] even keeping alive. [[A missing sentence follows, cropped from the photo reproduction of this letter.]] […] certainly in lots of people I've met. Yet life is a beautiful performance if one wasn't bothered by eating[[,]] shelter and other absurd necessities. I'm not in a [better?] writing mood as no doubt you can [feel?]. Later I'll give you a day in my hectic existence! – most of it [flat monotony?] or […] since ['peau'?] as the French say is […] my dear.
 [T'embrasse?] sur la main.

Esquimau

P.S. No, Blue Rib hasn't turned up yet. If sent let me know about [insurance?]. They are rather careless here sometimes – [frantic?] – especially as I've changed address to Nice.

---

[212] A reference to Hitler's *Sturmabteilung* or "Storm Troopers," aka Brownshirts because of the khaki-brown color of their uniforms. They formed the paramilitary wing of the Nazi Party from 5 October 1921 to 8 May 1945.

[[Letter "L"; originally included in "Bits and Pieces" (Bits 1, pp. 1-2 and Bits 2, p. 1.). According to Neal Pearson, who examined the original, it's composed on the reverse of a typed manuscript, which appears to be a short story written for a boys magazine.]]

[…] I was wrong about music. Tonight – I go to bed about 7:30 or 8 more comfortable to write – and have a special performance on. A nightingale is the prima donna accompanied by a cri-cri, chorus of frogs, distant motor traffic in the high road and a queer fellow who says hoo! hoo! – an owl I expect although I'm not sure. Anyway it's really great.

You were talking about a gentleman [and that is very?] presumably for a lady friend in a sketching […]. Splendid idea – although the poor dear must be very ugly or unenterprising if he has money. Thanks for the compliment, cherie, although you know what Esquimaux are! I'd love to! Maybe we will. Maybe not. That's up to the god of the Esquimaux maybe.

Given her need of money and my dire need too[[,]] for if I cannot get to U.S.A. I have no chance of ever selling my commercial stuff there under the new Rooseveltian[213] policy, we have decided to raise a loan here. Unfortunately she is still a minor and so under French law a *Conseil de Famille*[214] is necessary[[:]] a long and costly affair. There are no members of either family here except for that old woman – the

---

[213] Franklin Delano Roosevelt (1882 – 1945), governor of New York from 1929 to 1932, and U.S. president from 4 March 1933 until his death on 12 April 1945. Since the letter is undated it's not clear if Beadle is referring to a state or federal policy of Rooseveltian origin.

[214] *Conseil de Famille*: a family council, formed to look after the interests of a minor. During this period a minor was allowed to marry with parental consent at the age of fifteen (and sometimes even earlier), which, in Jane's case, would have been on 8 July 1930. Both girls and boys were considered to be minors until the age of twenty-one. Jane reached her "age of majority" on 8 July 1936.

grandmother.[215] And myself. To comply with this law I have to get letters from blood relations in England or elsewhere requesting them to come here which of course is absurd. Otherwise they must refuse to have anything to do with it and then local 'friends' – dummies! – are appointed. I have the [others?] and want one more if you will write me a letter in the following lines that will serve legal purposes.

You must forgive me telling [[sic]] you more details [now?]. I will later. [Solely?] I will say that my daughter resembles me in features and writes – poetry up to the present – wherefore she is hated by that family and her grandmother!

If and when we do get this loan though we shall be in London, I, on my way to New York.

Forgive my being in hurry. I kiss your hand.

CB

---

[215] His notorious mother-in-law, Teresa Isabel Ashwell (1866 – 1940), whom he pilloried in *Dark Refuge*, would have been sixty-four years old. Beadle was staunchly opposed to the principles of the tightly buttoned-up, heavily corseted Victorian era, so the fact that Teresa applied for a patent for the *Perfectionnements aux corsets et ceintures* (Improvements for corsets and belts) on 29 November 1920 – at the very inception of the Roaring (and uncorseted) Twenties – takes on a delightfully ironic symbolism. Her patent was registered in France and published on 13 May 1922. (Source: "International Patents, 1890-2020," Ancestry.com.)

[[Letter "M"; originally designated as letter 1. Isabel's handwriting bears an uncanny resemblance to that of her uncle's. Circa late 1930 / early 1931.]]

Dear Uncle,

I must say I was very much surprised ~~at~~ to get your news, for as you know I was not aware that I had a cousin in France! Someday I hope to meet her but, although I send all my wishes for her happy marriage I can neither come over to France to act as a member of ~~the~~ le conseil de famille nor do I feel competent to act in that capacity in any way, knowing nothing whatever of the circumstances nor parties concerned.
I feel anyway that you, and you only as her father, can judge ~~about the~~ about will [[sic]] bring her happiness.

Your affect. niece,
Isabel Beadle

[[Letter "N"; originally designated as letter 6. Composed on stationery from Le Normandy Café-Bar in Nice. After referring to "le juge de paix" (the justice of the peace), Beadle complains about wasting his time "waiting on these half-witted idiots." He also says he "gave the damned property" to his daughter, which might explain why Jane remained in Nice for most of her adult life. And he adds: "My kid is crazy to meet you." Thanks to this missive, we know that he maintained some sort of relationship with Jane.]]

Le Normandy Café-Bar
1, Place Grimaldi, Nice
19 February 1931[216]

Many thanks for letter […], my dear. However it wasn't needed. All lawyers, French, English, Esquimeaux are born idiots. The […] is one has to pay – if one has it – for their imbecilities! I told him according to the – specially imbecile – Code Napoleon that if in a case of the Conseil de famille there are no blood relations within 10 kilometers, that local friends had to be appointed. No, Monsieur le Juge de Paix thought otherwise. Finally they found that I was right. Now more trouble because I can't offer any stocks, land or whatnot as security to my own daughter to whom I gave the damn property. They have a legal mania – doubtless founded on experience of peasants – that father and daughter are deadly enemies. Internecine warfare and all that. So now I don't know whether we'll get the money or not. I wish I felt old and feeble and fed up with life, but unfortunately I don't. I got overhauled by a doctor the other day – one tick[217] naturally – vaguely hoping for a nice hospital case where everybody (?) would be sorry for me and watch me die nicely.

---

[216] At this date, Jane would have been fifteen years, seven months old.

[217] Tick: for just a moment; a brief duration; a quick visit.

Nothing doing. Silly fool couldn't find anything wrong and assured me I'd make a fine insurance 'life'. Hell of a bit of use that is! My kid is crazy to meet you. (I'm here writing an American story!) Oh, I'm just so mad and irritated as I want to write and instead have to fool time away[218] waiting on these half-witted idiots.

I can't dream.

I can't think.

I feel like a chewed star spat out by God's yellow teeth on the tattered carpet of the infinite![219]

Zut, allure!

Oh, yes, thanks again for a copy of 'Rib' duly recd. y'day.

Yours

---

[218] Fool away: To waste (time or money) foolishly; squander.

[219] In a passage in *Dark Refuge* the autobiographical narrator declaims (quoting from his own verse): "I cannot think, / I cannot dream! / I can neither enter Heaven nor Hell, / but lie like a chewed star / spat out from God's yellow teeth / on the dusty carpet of the Infinite!" And in a letter to Isabel, circa 1933, he writes: "New Year '32 having nothing else to do I broke my ankle and when able to crawl sufficiently for a boat went to sea as a cabin boy on a yacht having taken an oath that I would neither write for myself, editors, men, women, or gods: nor think nor dream." (See below.)

[[Letter "O"; originally designated as letter 3.]]

c/o Barclays Bank,
Promenade des Anglais,
Nice, October ? 1934

Very glad to see your [mature?] writing again, my dear.
Certainly more legible than mine. Yes, I guessed [birthdays?]
had something to do with your silence.[220] I'm bound for
America if soon I can persuade a friendly whale to swallow me
and vomit me forth in due course on Staten Island beach –
otherwise ordinary human ways are pretty slender. I have been
officially notified that they won't buy commercial stuff from any
authors not living in the States. Rooseveltian propaganda – each
nation to take in its own washing and gradually die in their
repulsive muck holes. These [bloody?] scenario people have
again put off producing until 1935 – if ever! Still flapping along
somehow. Sometimes a stamp to spare – mostly not! The few
friends I have are as broke almost as I am. Others don't know
me; the rich ones I mean. One thing am getting a usual stipend.
I'm translating a book on ɡ – now I nearly wrote gods, but I
mean dogs – much the same in the end: amusing but for the
French national. For Anglo Saxon readers I'm afraid. This [came
about as] [...] since I think that dogs shd. live for man but he
insists that man shd. live for his bow-wows! Takes all kinds to
make a world they say – although personally I think we all
could do without a lot of kinds. Don't bother about the States –
now. I do find it rather lacks a sense of humor in the [grand?]
style! I've [...]at C[aspers?] who [...] around with me and went
off when he got money without as much as a handshake turned

---

[220] Most likely a reference to the recent birthdays of Isabel and Barbara.
Isabel (age 30) was born in Ormskirk, Lancashire, on 2 July 1904; Barbara
(age 27) in Tickencote, Rutland, on 22 August 1907.

up and in a fit of contriteness is [stopping affair or end't it?]. If he thinks I'll make money to pay him ever he's more fantastic than I! America's my only chance of financial salvation – then that means goodbye to literature and wallowing in melodrama as ~~far~~ deep as I may.[221] Don't know the Conn.[222] bloke. Tell me about him.

---

[221] Here Beadle draws a distinction between literary authorship and commercial screenwriting, with the implication being that he'll have to focus on the latter in order to achieve success in America.

[222] Presumably a "Connecticut" bloke.

[[Letter "P"; originally designated as letter 2.]]

Maison Jaune,
Chemin St. Claude
Antibes, A.M. [[Alpes Maritime]]

[[Circa early 1934]]

Well, well, and I'd been thinking that you'd got married or something and gone off to Aldebaran or the Island of the Blest for a honeymoon!

Somehow we all seem to be in the same [mud?] hole, although you all are evidently pampered children of the dole!

I was never paid for that cursed scenario and in consequence was locked out in the street by my hotel who seized every thing I owned, manuscripts, books, machine.

After most exhilarating experiences of the streets of Paris and the overwhelming generosity of fellow men – particularly those I had helped in a distant past – I, after getting as far down as a Salvation Army Shelter, dodged the Seine[223] by scrambling down here once more.

Thanks for your sweet thoughts for me. But I've nothing for the hotel mag for reasons: 1 Don't write French. 2 Have neither means to travel nor clothes to interview [snobs?]. (Monsieur le Marie or the concierge of a big hotel wld. probably send for the police!) 3 I am about as much use selling things or getting orders as a monkey on the wireless. (I know this from experience.)[224]

---

[223] Jumping into the Seine or throwing oneself in front of a speeding metro were the two most popular forms of self-immolation in Paris. The remark represents Beadle's second jocular reference to suicide.

[224] Possibly referring to his experience as a door-to-door jewelry salesman, which is humorously portrayed in *A Passionate Pilgrimage*.

Thanks [amiably?] all the same. But your mention of an apparently new mag (to me) Adventure pubd. by Newnes[225] may prove a new market. The only English Adventure I know is one for small boys not yet grown up (in contradistinction to small boys who wear trousers and smoke). The only bit of luck which I may have had – I'm not sure yet – is a call from American Adventure to whom I have sold thousands of dollars of stuff. After the old editor left about 8 years ago[226] I haven't sold [even?] a single story. New author-editor who knows me has become editor of Adventure, so I may yet be able to climb back to a semblance of prosperity. At any rate as soon as I can get my [M.S.S.?] back and the fare I'm off for New York. Allah only knows when that will be. Some day you'll hear of me entering New York Harbor with a nonchalant Australian crawl on my ninetieth birthday!

I'll find out about the Newnes mag as soon as I can raise [postage?] which [will?] be also the date of the departure of this letter!

By all means write when the […] [bank?] to coincide […]. But that doesn't worry me at present as I haven't any livres

---

[225] Again referring to the publishing conglomerate George Newnes Ltd.

[226] Beadle published twenty-six stories in *Adventure* between 18 May 1918 and 20 April 1925, all under the editorship of Arthur Hoffman, who worked there from 1912 to 1927. Hoffman's departure from the magazine "about 8 years ago" would suggest the letter was composed circa 1934 / 1935. Thanks to his meticulous research, John Locke has further narrowed down the time frame: "William Corcoran is most likely the author-editor Beadle is referring to," he says, since Corcoran stepped in to edit *Adventure* on 2 January 1934 and continued through June of '34. (After which he resigned, to devote himself to writing.) Locke adds that "Corcoran appears to have been associated with the magazine, probably as an assistant editor, during the time that Beadle was selling to them, in the early Twenties." Corcoran was succeeded by Howard Bloomfield, who edited *Adventure*'s special 25th Anniversary issue, published in November 1935.

sterling,[227] or anything else. A roof to sleep under and food of sorts for the present.

Well, cheerio and I hope I'll send good news for you soon.

Yours ever
CB

&3. Instead of a check for 162 livres just got news about the magazine in question. Here's your answer. My usual luck. What I'm going to do now Allah only knows. I certainly don't.

[[A typed note on the facing page appears next (see below). It's not clear if this was written at the same time as the rest of the letter or if it was composed earlier (and never sent), and thus the sheet is being re-used. The latter is a possibility, as in the typed section he asks for a copy of *The Blue Rib*, but in an earlier letter he acknowledges receipt of the book from Isabel.]]

May I [[referring here to the first day of May]]. I've been waiting all this time for a stamp to arrive. I MAY have some tomorrow! Life is real! Life is earnest! If ever you find out who wrote that, slay and spare not!

You are able to do me a great service! A Paris firm wants to see THE BLUE RIB for possible publication in Cintinental [[sic: *Continental*]] edition. I believe you or some of the family have a copy. If you can procure and send me I shall be most grateful. As all my books and MSS. as well are still locked up in the Paris hotel.

---

[227] "Livre": French currency used before the adoption of the franc in 1795, although the term "livre" continued to be used until the mid-1800s, especially when referring to large transactions involving property or real estate. "Livres sterling": a French term for British pounds sterling (normally referred to as "pounds" or "sterling" in English).

The scenario people are not paying as they can't or won't turn [[sic: return?]] till next year and they offer five hundred francs – perhaps – for the option for another year – hence perhaps the stamp.

[[Handwritten on reverse, forming the final page of this composition:]] I will bet at the moment neither do. I'm [slugging?] out a 30,000 word story as requested, but I'm a bit dizzy swinging like a pendulum from an introvert to an extrovert and back ad nauseam.

What went wrong? I [fed?] him – at first. But your [...] job was good for his life of democracy anyway! How's painting getting on? Paris has that point of view as well as others [less?] painful. How are things really in England? Some say breaking up. And [...] I hear, is cheaper to live than here. As a matter of fact with exchange as it is, life _is_ expensive [here.]

[[Letter "Q"; originally designated as letter 13.]]

Palais-Royal Press
9, rue de Beaujolais
Paris

[[Circa early 1933]]

Well, I suppose that from the angle of Aldebaran I merit this sinister silence? However, even a woman has an excuse for not being a gossip. New Year '32 having nothing else to do I broke my ankle and when able to crawl sufficiently for a boat went to sea as a cabin boy on a yacht having taken an oath that I would neither write for myself, editors, men, women, or gods: nor think nor dream.[228] This year after much to do and a typewriter I am as you may infer at Paris – living a story entitled The Mystery of the Resurrection of a Corpse Interred in the Côte d'Azur. Which is guaranteed to defy all medical or any other investigation.

For particulars apply to above address.

---

[228] See Beadle's letter from 19 February 1931, in which he writes: "I can't dream / I can't think / I feel like a chewed star spat out by God's yellow teeth on the tattered carpet of the infinite. Zut alors!"

[[Letter "R"; originally designated as letter 8. Composed on stationery from Café de la Rotonde, a legendary artistic hub located just a few blocks away from Hôtel des Capucines.]]

Hôtel des Capucines,
13, rue des Feuillantines,
Paris V

[[Circa spring 1933]]

On reading your epistle, my dear lady of Aldebaran, my first thought was J'ai envie de te bien fesser![229] Why? Because I was annoyed with myself for having been so stupid as to imagine that something might have happened to you – something dreadful such as death – or marriage. Painting portraiture! You reply Bien! Nai le nai! When vanity stops death to nigh.

To appease your flattering curiosity I traveled from my blue coffin[230] with seven [indis...] parfumés! Paris seems to be in the same place as when last I saw it – about 18 months ago,[231] slightly sadder but no wiser. Much guttural lingue and Semitic profile is heard of Jews, particularly around this quarter – which I detest. I'm living in my favorite [haunt?] Quartier Latin, by the rue St Jacques, beloved of Villon of pious memory.[232] The

---

[229] "J'ai envie de te bien fesser!": "I want to give you a good spanking!"

[230] I.e., the coastal waters of the French Riviera, which Beadle envisions as a blue rib.

[231] This would suggest Beadle was in Paris around October 1931.

[232] Francis Carco, a fellow Montparno author whom Beadle frequently quotes in *Artist Quarter*, had recently published *Le Roman de François Villon* (1926): a "fictionalized" biography of the great French poet. Beadle's remarks about Jews reflect a common prejudice of the time, especially among long-term residents of Montmartre, who bemoaned the growing "foreign influence." See for example Carco's 1924 Parisian memoir, in which he writes: "Alas! with time, how many illusions have I left behind! When I think of them, and when I see Montmartre, not as it was then, but as it is

street has nearly disappeared now even from what it was when first I knew it. Still there remain parts where one has to flatten oneself to allow a snorting, stinking bus pass. Wonder what cher François wd. have thought of it now? Rather like to write a story of François's return to the Val de Grace! Sounds like poaching in George Moore's[233] grounds.

Well, now behold me, dearly beloved, in the guise of a cineaste – I think that's the word. My cinema vocab: has got to be improved! Someone dug up one of the first stories I ever wrote – (and very badly) and proposed for scenario; then said then done and – eventually – then sold – altho' I don't get any cash until the sausage machine starts to go round. What they – the metteur en scène – will do with it, Allah, master of all secrets only knows – and I hope I shall never. Probably I shouldn't recognize it. Anyway has dawned upon my medieval intelligence the brilliant fact that perhaps we may make money out of the cinema – they're the only people who seem to have any anyhow. Thus, dear cherished child, I have made my debut in this land of weird infantile complexes. I have indeed to goodness, to strip myself before you, continued to write more scenarios. They wanted a nice thuggy murder – amusing how most humans want to murder and [duke?] it out in the dream palace – fiction. Well that being so I hunted up somebody I'd really like to strangle and thus became inspired for a nice Frankenstein story. Detective stories bore me. There's always a corpse, any old corpse. As soon as I've gathered who the person is, my interest flops except possibly to find the murderer and

---

now, with its high buildings and its *guinguettes* full of foreigners, I feel as if I had lived a dream, and I don't know where I am." Francis Carco, *From Montmartre to the Latin Quarter. Edited with Annotations and an Introduction by Rob Couteau* (New York: Dominantstar, 2024), p. 173.

[233] George Moore (1852 – 1933): Irish novelist, memoirist, and art critic, who regarded François Villon as a major literary influence.

give him the V.C. or something of that sort.[234] Now, thought I – being stuck with one of my brilliant ideas that ever come to naught – if we're going to have murder let's <u>wallow</u>. So I have my nice <u>prolonged</u> murder right on the stage-screen [...]. The idea is that you <u>see</u> it, and wallow in it – imagine that person <u>you</u> want to murder or enjoy by proxy (it's so much cheaper – a couple of shillings or so instead of expensive K.C's,[235] and in these days of scarcity –). I wanted to flash on the screen just as the murder begins. <u>Let us wallow!</u> – but – ! then you see the villain – best looking actor in the company for getting away with it and the hero a village idiot of course, heading straight for a sticky and worst of all official death. The end – ah! ah! millions will shudder and tremble, and have epileptic seizures and [cheer?] [...] and – well, the faithful wife of the hero – <u>all</u> village idiots have faithful wives, have you noticed? The specific for this ownership of faithful wives is as yet unpatented! – oh yes, the F.W. [[faithful wife]] of the St. James the aforesaid V.I. [[village idiot]] by seducing (small cries, giggles) the naughty but very good looking villain (who's quite a brilliant person, but oh! Girls[[,]] such a bad man!) up to the point when he's getting into bed with her (bedroom scenes always go) when she repulses him virtuously and denounces him as the real murderer! (Ooo-er!) Then ~~in rush the witness [...] from the bath~~ he falls back on his favorite indoor amusement – strangling (Hah!) Enter the [...] witness from bathroom and virtue is once more, if boringly, triumphant! I finished the job this morning and – well, now I'm going to write an article on The Defense of Prostitution. I think they ought to be better paid. I think it ought to be rather good as obviously I'm so very much interested in

---

[234] "V.C.": presumably a satirical reference to the Victoria Cross, Britain's most prestigious military decoration.

[235] K.C.s: possibly shorthand for "King's Crowns," a colloquial term for British five-shilling coins.

the earnings of prostitutes. If I am paid well I'll come over to London, get some decent clothes and – really, positively – invite you to dinner – if you wd. accept of course the hospitality of a prostitute?

Oh by the way I've had another novel [out?] published in Paris.[236] Of course it doesn't sell but plan sending [[sic]] you a copy. Paris is rather nice for a change. Today she's put on a silver gray dress which rather suits her.

Well, dearly beloved, here endeth the first lesson – in prostitution. (There won't be any more unless they pay!)

Je t'embrasse,[237] sweet lady of Aldebaran.

CB

---

[236] In May 1933, Palais-Royal Press released *The White Gambit*. Beadle's only other Paris-based book was *Dark Refuge* (June 1938), but since he's still attempting to write screenplays it's more likely that this letter dates from early '33, rather than '38. Also note that the previous letter, which complains about Isabel's silence (which has now been broken), uses the Palais-Royal Press as a return address.

Harriet Thurgood, Isabel's mother, died in Stamford, Lincolnshire on 25 May 1933, a few weeks short of her fifty-third birthday. Harriet was survived by her husband, William Beadle (1876 – 1952; who, like his brother Charles, was born at sea). According to the "National Probate Calendar, Index of Wills and Administrations," "Isabel Hettie Beadle spinster and Barbara Katherine Colson married woman" inherited William's estate, with "effects" worth £1317. If this letter was composed that same year, the upbeat tone suggests that it was posted before Beadle received news of Harriet's death.

[237] I kiss you.

ALSO BY ROB COUTEAU

Fiction:

Doctor Pluss
Afterword by Jim Feast

Essays and Interviews:

Collected Couteau

More Collected Couteau
Introduction by James Dempsey

*Portraits from the Revolution: Interviews with the
Protestors from Occupy Wall Street*

Biography:

*A Blind Man Crazy for Color. A Tribute to Leon Angély: Illustrated
by Picasso's Model and Muse, Sylvette David*

Poetry:

The Sleeping Mermaid
Introduction by Christopher Sawyer-Lauçanno

Selected Poems
Introduction by Ed Foster

Memoir:

Intimate Souvenirs
Introduction by Robert Roper

"Here we have a new, possibly classic memoir of New York. It begins in Gravesend, Brooklyn, and moves outward, to Manhattan and Paris ... That there still exists a path to a writer's life that is not a dutiful march through creative writing academies, with perhaps the apotheosis of becoming a teacher of yet more academy-shaped writers, is heartening to learn. Couteau does not make fun of that approach nor of any other, but he does model something much different, and to see him continuing to write books like this one, which well deserves a place on his already considerable shelf of valued books, is excellent news." – Robert Roper, author of *Nabokov in America: On the Road to Lolita* and *Now the Drum of War*.

"*Intimate Souvenirs* is a memoir with a message that embraces a coming-of-age story with a background in!1970s Brooklyn. This influenced Rob Couteau's progressive work as an adult with the homeless and impoverished, from America to Venezuela ... Couteau brings to vivid life his impressions of the world from an early age, and his evolving place in it ... As Couteau moves through different worlds (including France), encountering literary, artistic, and social figures, he finds a new sense of home, place, and purpose which translates to social and philosophical revelations about life, religion, and the world. Ultimately, his very method of engaging with other worlds is what links readers to his life and the exuberant march of its encounters and revelations.

Five hundred pages go by in the blink of an eye as readers absorb an intriguing memoir that deserves a place in any library strong in memoirs that embrace literary, artistic, and social transformation The book features an Introduction by acclaimed novelist Robert Roper and an Afterword by literary biographer Christopher Sawyer-Lauçanno." – Diane Donovan, Senior editor, *Midwest Book Review*.

A Blind Man Crazy for Color. A Tribute to Leon Angély: Illustrated by Picasso's Model and Muse, Sylvette David

"In the lanes and alleys of Paris, at the turn of the!9th century, a nearly sightless art collector wandered on the arm of a young girl. The collector, aided by his guide, amassed a treasure trove of work by the greatest artists of the day: Modigliani, Picasso, Utrillo, and more. Yet he died poor, forced to sell the work for a fraction of its value during the dark days of World War I. Little is known about the life – or the fate – of the girl who led the blind collector through the City of Light. This is the story of Léon Angély, the myopic lover of art, and Joséphine, the 'eyes' of Angély, the girl who enabled him to visit artists and 'see' their art. The story is told with a rare grace by author Rob Couteau in his new book, *A Blind Man Crazy for Color*. Couteau has mined the literature for gems, and displays them with abandon, through the generous quotations and anecdotes set within his own lustrous prose. The fine text is accompanied by enchanting illustrations by Sylvette David. In David, the book finds both painter and participant in the milieu Angély so loved: in!954, David began modeling for Picasso, becoming the 'girl with the ponytail' in hundreds of works, including the artist's monumental sculpture, *Sylvette*, in Rotterdam ... We found the friendship of Léon and Joséphine a balm for our souls, so bruised in these difficult days of violence and disease. We hope the story is healing for you, too."
– *Witty Partition*

"In his strange, fascinating new book, writer-painter Rob Couteau assembles and unearths what little can be known about the mysterious collector Léon Angély ... Adding another layer of resonance to Couteau's slim volume are the charming illustrations by Lydia Corbett, also known as Sylvette David, the ponytailed model and muse who inspired Picasso's 'Sylvette' period."
– Scott Sublett, *New Art Examiner*.

"Sylvette David's sketches accent this colorful portrait of Léon's life, motivations, involvement in the art world, and the pieces he collected. Previously unpublished information about the blind man's passion and his influence on the art world enhances a survey that should be required reading and acquisition for any serious art history student and the libraries catering to them ... Readers also receive revealing inspections of the process of interviewing artists and capturing their historical impact, adding to *A Blind Man Crazy for Color*'s importance as a survey that goes beyond a singular biography of an art enthusiast to delve into the world of artists, art appreciation, and muses ... Serious art libraries should consider this extraordinary recreation of artistic ambitions against all odds a mainstay that stands out in many different ways." – Diane Donovan, *Midwest Book Review*.

SELECTED POEMS

"There is a deep tenderness in these words, mingled with the sadness of age. If one goes back to the early poems addressed to Edda Maria Sangrígoli, one can find the tenderness there, too, as it is in his work as a case manager for the poor and homeless. There is much to admire in Couteau's oeuvre, but this tenderness stands out among so many things that make reading his work clearly an important experience."
– Ed Foster, founder of Talisman House Publishers, and editor
of *Talisman: A Journal of Contemporary Poetry and Poetics*.

"*Selected Poems* features 101 poems, 40 of which have been printed in numerous print and online journals since 1985. The rest are new to this collection and represent a satisfying blend of old and new works designed to appeal to newcomers and prior fans alike. Rob Couteau's works are diverse. They follow no set poetic structure, even defying some of them when the muse strikes and special needs indicate that the subject is more important than poetic form ... His inspections of artistic, literary, and social issues are astute and compelling. Don't anticipate set structures, uniform poetic approaches, or singular subjects. *Selected Poems* offers a freewheeling approach to poems and life alike and is a thought provoking, evocative gathering of works recommended for literary readers not bound by convention or rules."
– Diane Donovan, *Midwest Book Review*.

is that readers needn't have prior familiarity with the writers' works. Couteau provides that familiarity by the structure of his interview questions, which probe the foundation beliefs of each figure … From the possibility that Nabokov suffered unconscious doubts about his own value that led him to insist that the world acknowledge him as a genius to the underlying patriotism of counterculture icons who were commonly seen as rebels ('Ginsberg continually affirmed that, essentially, Jack had always been a sort of patriotic American,' says Sawyer-Lauçanno. 'This had never not been part of who he was. It was patriotic to get into an automobile made in Detroit and drive across the country'), both essays and interviews are designed to make readers think about underlying psychology, social perceptions, and cultural change.

Readers seeking not just a literary presentation but a lively analysis of selected wordsmiths and their lives and influences must add *More Collected Couteau* to their reading lists. It's a powerful presentation that offers much insight … and which should find its way into many a college classroom as well." – Diane Donovan, *Midwest Book Review*.

"Good luck trying to pin down Rob Couteau. Name the genre, and Couteau has almost certainly been there and done that. Poet, novelist, essayist, critic, journalist, memoirist, and travel writer, Couteau is not one to be hampered by constraints. He passes easily from one form of literature to another as if the borders between them did not exist for him. Perhaps they don't.

Couteau has been called a 'literary enthusiast,' and although he certainly is enthusiastic about literature (and indeed all art), the phrase carries the smack of the amateur about it, and Couteau is anything but. He is, in fact, an undeniably consummate professional. He is an independent scholar in every meaning of the word – unaligned with any institution except for the literary and artistic canon he so loves, and a thinker who comes to his own conclusions …

This collection gives the reader a good sampling of Couteau's literary and scholarly talents, not the least of which are his interviews with writers he admires. Having spent many years as a journalist, I believe I have some ability to recognize and admire an artful interviewer, and Couteau is a master. His preparation is comprehensive, meticulous, and profound. His understanding of the process of writing in so many genres allows him insights into the particular problems faced by the writers he interviews. His style is conversational and relaxed, but deceptively so; he is always in control of the interview. This said, however, when a sudden fact or insight takes the interview down unexpected pathways, Couteau has the aesthetic nimbleness to recognize the opening and to follow it.

The collection features interviews with biographers, memoirists, historians, an inner-city antiviolence activist, and the creator of LSD. You'll also find herein Couteau's writings on literature, which I hesitate to call criticism since they lack the worst features of much literary criticism, which can be clogged with so much pretentiousness, cant, and philosophical obfuscation that it would take a plunger of Brobdingnagian proportions to restore a healthy flow. Couteau's essays are often rhapsodic appreciations and evocations of the work under study, and are stuffed with both insights and joy.
– James Dempsey, author of *The Tortured Life of Scofield Thayer*.

THE SLEEPING MERMAID

"Novelist and literary enthusiast Rob Couteau brings readers part of his love with *The Sleeping Mermaid*, a book of flowing poetry and thought that asks plenty of questions and offers plenty of answers. *The Sleeping Mermaid* is a poetry collection well-worth considering."
– Willis M. Buhle, *Midwest Book Review*.

"In Couteau's work there is no phoniness, no artifice for the sake of artifice – though in the great French tradition this poet knows so well, there is some art for the sake of art. Couteau does not venture into realms of obscurity where meaning is confined to the interior of a Klein bottle; his poems all have direct force, subjects, even verbs. He is intent on having his readers share in his observations, whether it be his artful retelling and reinterpretations of Native American story and song, or his appraisal of how a woman parades across the avenue. He does not ever sacrifice ordinary sense for an extra-ordinary significance. Instead, he speaks with fervor, with something to say, with something he wants us to hang onto and, in the process, come to an understanding of why it matters not just to him but should matter to us.

I think it was William Carlos Williams who said that poetry is belief. Couteau believes in belief, believes that poetic worth is measured in faithfulness to what is, what has been, and what could be. These are his talismans; these are the points where he begins and ends. His poetic excursions take us to many places: to the Paris of Rimbaud and Picasso, to the Native North Americans, to mythology and history and how the woman he is encountering is seducing him as he seduces her (and us), and finally, how alone, the cosmos plays itself out at 3 a.m. when the only lap dog is memory."
– Christopher Sawyer-Lauçanno.

PORTRAITS FROM THE REVOLUTION: INTERVIEWS WITH THE PROTESTORS FROM OCCUPY WALL STREET

"Most American readers will harbor a prior, casual familiarity with the Occupy Wall Street movement of 2011 based on newspaper headlines and events of the times; but for a more in-depth survey of the philosophies, approaches, and concerns of the protests, *Portraits from the* Revolution is the item of choice, offering unprecedented depth and detail on the history and lasting impact of the Occupy Wall Street movement.

Chapters explore not just each individual's actions but their backgrounds, reasons for participating in Occupy Wall Street, and their experiences. And it offers criticism of media reporting of the movement's history, intentions, and approaches.

From how participants decided to react to violent antagonism against the Occupy movement to the social and political ramifications of not just Occupy but the elements it opposed, these interviews capture participants from all walks of life, from teens to full-time workers, and turn the newspaper reports into a series of personal vignettes about Occupy's deeper meaning.
– Diane Donovan, *Midwest Book Review*

"Intellectual freshness, richness, and potency ... Couteau is an impressively creative writer, whom Barney Rosset urged me to review." – Jim Feast, *Evergreen Review*.

"Rob Couteau describes *Doctor Pluss* as 'fiction based on actual dialogues with schizophrenic patients, diabolically "sane" psychotherapists, and well-meaning yet unerringly destructive social workers. It chronicles the descent of an eccentric, sardonic, and witty psychiatrist into what appears to be a state of complete madness.'

His intention to metaphorically and realistically portray and contrast the madness of psychiatric process as well as its patients is powerfully wrought in a story about patients 'surviving this holocaust of forgetfulness.' During this process, their identities and personalities are lost in the institutional morass of a center purported to excel in rehabilitation, but which actually contains many ethical and personal challenges to the new psychiatric resident at the Walt Whitman Asylum for Adults, Dr. Pluss.

It's a place of rage and despair, of ambiguity where hope and horror run close together, and daily gives Dr. Pluss pause for thought about his patients and his role in their lives: 'In her own unwitting way,' Pluss mused, Evelyn personified the dual aspects of the godhead: horror and joy; awe and fascination.'

Novellas typically are hard-hitting but often artificially succinct in their brevity. Often, one is left wanting for more. The best of them (of which *Doctor Pluss* is one) excels in taking this succinctness to its most logical conclusion, creating slices of life which are narrow enough to receive full-bodied flavor as the plot and characters develop.

One does not wish for more in *Doctor Pluss*. It's complete unto itself, exceptionally well developed, and emotionally compelling, connecting metaphorical traditional roles of doctor and patient, linking them in unexpected ways.

Couteau is not afraid to push the literary boundaries of convention in pursuit of a different form of descriptive truth, bringing readers along in a rollicking ride through schizophrenic experience that ultimately questions the foundations of reality and perception from both sides of the therapist's couch. His interpretations and descriptions of the schizophrenic experience are particularly astute, astonishing, and evocatively described …

Readers who choose *Doctor Pluss* are in for a treat. It's like *One Flew Over the Cuckoo's Nest* on steroids: a thought-provoking examination of sanity, insanity, and the crossover process that leaves readers thinking long after this therapeutic slice of life is consumed.

– Diane Donovan, *Midwest Book Review*